VANISHED!

The ancient ring bore a strange inscription. And now it was gone, hidden by the man who had murdered to possess it.

Who had taken the ring? Was it the eminently respectable Sir Tristram, the fiancé Eustacie had left? Or was it—as the world supposed—the man into whose arms she had fled, the handsome adventurer who had claimed her wild, young heart? Eustacie had to know . . .

THE TALISMAN RING

A novel of love and danger in the dazzling, romantic world of 18th-century England.

GEORGETTE HEYER
THE TALISMAN RING

BANTAM BOOKS
TORONTO · NEW YORK · LONDON

THE TALISMAN RING

*A Bantam Book / published by arrangement with
E. P. Dutton & Company, Inc.*

PRINTING HISTORY
Dutton edition published August 1967
Bantam edition published April 1969
2nd printing

*Bantam Books are published by Bantam Books, Inc., a subsidiary
of Grosset & Dunlap, Inc. Its trade-mark, consisting of the words
"Bantam Books" and the portrayal of a bantam, is registered in the
United States Patent Office and in other countries. Marca Registrada.
Bantam Books, Inc., 271 Madison Avenue, New York, N.Y. 10016.*

PRINTED IN THE UNITED STATES OF AMERICA

The
Talisman
Ring

Chapter I

SIR TRISTRAM SHIELD, arriving at Lavenham Court in the wintry dusk, was informed at the door that his great-uncle was very weak, not expected to live many more days out. He received these tidings without comment, but as the butler helped him to take off his heavy-caped driving-coat, he inquired in an unemotional voice: "Is Mr. Lavenham here?"

"At the Dower House, sir," replied the butler, handing the coat and the high-crowned beaver hat to a footman. He nodded austere dismissal to this underling, and added with a slight cough: "His lordship has been a little difficult, sir. So far his lordship has not received Mr. Lavenham."

He paused, waiting for Sir Tristram to inquire after Mademoiselle de Vauban. Sir Tristram, however, merely asked to be conducted to his bedchamber, that he might change his dress before being admitted to his great-uncle's presence.

The butler, as well aware as everyone else at the Court of the reason of Sir Tristram's sudden arrival, was disappointed at this lack of interest, but reflected that Sir Tristram, after all, had never been one to show what he was thinking. He led the way in person across the hall to the oak stairway and went with Sir Tristram up to the Long Gallery. Here, on one side, portraits of dead Lavenhams hung, and, on the other, tall, square-headed mullioned windows looked south over a well-timbered park to the Downs. The silence of the house was disturbed by the rustle of a skirt and the hasty closing of a door at one end of the Gallery. The butler had a shrewd suspicion that Mademoiselle de Vauban, more curious than Sir Tristram, had been waiting in the Gallery to obtain a glimpse of him. As he opened the door into one of the bedchambers he cast a glance at Shield, and said: "His lordship has seen no one but the doctor, sir—once, and Mamzelle Eustacie, of course."

That dark, harsh face told him nothing. "Yes?" said Shield. It occurred to the butler that perhaps Sir Tristram might

1

not know why he had been summoned into Sussex. If that were so there was no saying how he might take it. He was not an easy man to drive, as his great-uncle had found more than once in the past. Ten to one there might be trouble.

Sir Tristram's voice interrupted these reflections. "Send my man up to me, Porson, and inform his lordship of my arrival," he said.

The butler bowed and withdrew. Sir Tristram walked over to the window, and stood looking out over the formal gardens to the woods beyond, still dimly visible through the gathering twilight. There was a sombre frown in his eyes, and his mouth was compressed in a way that made it appear more grim than usual. He did not turn when the door opened to admit his valet, accompanied by one footman carrying his cloak-bag, and another bearing two gilded candelabra, which he set down on the dressing-table. The sudden candlelight darkened the prospect outside. After a moment Shield came away from the window to the fireplace and stood leaning his arm along the high mantelshelf, and looking down at the smouldering logs. The footman drew the curtains across the windows and went softly away. Jupp, the valet, began to unpack the contents of the cloak-bag, and to lay out upon the bed an evening coat and breeches of mulberry velvet, and a Florentine waistcoat. Sir Tristram stirred the logs in the grate with one top-booted foot. Jupp glanced at him sideways, wondering what was in the wind to make him look so forbidding. "You'll wear powder, sir?" he suggested, setting the pounce-box and the pomatum down on the dressing-table.

"No."

Jupp sighed. He had already learned of Mr. Lavenham's presence at the Dower House. It seemed probable that the Beau might come up to the Court to visit his cousin, and Jupp, knowing how skilled was Mr. Lavenham's gentleman in the arrangement of his master's locks, would have liked for his pride's sake to have sent his own master down to dinner properly curled and powdered. He said nothing, however, but knelt down to pull off Sir Tristram's boots.

Half an hour later Shield, summoned by Lord Lavenham's valet, walked down the Gallery to the Great Chamber, and went in unannounced.

The room, wainscoted with oak and hung with crimson curtains, was warmed by a leaping fire and lit by as many as fifty candles in branching candelabra. At the far end a vast

four-poster bed was set upon a slight dais. In it, banked up
with pillows, covered with a quilt of flaming brocade, wearing an exotic bedgown and the powdered wig without which
no one but his valet could ever remember to have seen him,
was old Sylvester, ninth Baron Lavenham.

Sir Tristram paused on the threshold, dazzled momentarily
by the blaze of unexpected light. The grimness of his face
was lessened by a slight sardonic smile as his eyes took in the
magnificence and the colour about him. "Your death-bed,
sir?" he inquired.

A thin chuckle came from the four-poster. "My death-
bed," corroborated Sylvester with a twinkle.

Sir Tristram walked across the floor to the dais. A wasted
hand on which a great ruby ring glowed was held out to him.
He took it, and stood holding it, looking down into his great-
uncle's parchment-coloured face, with its hawk-nose, and
bloodless lips, and its deep-sunk brilliant eyes. Sylvester was
eighty, and dying, but he still wore his wig and his patches,
and clasped in his left hand his snuff-box and laced handkerchief.

Sylvester returned his great-nephew's steady look with one
of malicious satisfaction. "I knew you'd come," he remarked.
He withdrew his hand from the light clasp about it, and
waved it towards a chair which had been set on the dais. "Sit
down." He opened his snuff-box and dipped in his finger and
thumb. "When did I see you last?" he inquired, shaking away
the residue of the snuff and holding an infinitesimal pinch to
one nostril.

Sir Tristram sat down, full in the glare of a cluster of candles on a torchère pedestal. The golden light cast his profile
into strong relief against the crimson velvet bed-curtains. "It
must have been about two years ago, I believe," he answered.

Sylvester gave another chuckle. "A loving family, ain't
we?" He shut his snuff-box and dusted his fingers with his
handkerchief. "That other great-nephew of mine is here," he
remarked abruptly.

"So I've heard."

"Seen him?"

"No."

"You will," said Sylvester. "I shan't."

"Why not?" asked Shield, looking at him under his black
brows.

"Because I don't want to," replied Sylvester frankly. "Beau

Lavenham! *I* was Beau Lavenham in my day, but d'ye suppose that I decked myself out in a green coat and yellow pantaloons?"

"Probably not," said Shield.

"Damned smooth-spoken fellow!" said Sylvester. "Never liked him. Never liked his father either. His mother used to suffer from the vapours. She suffered from them—whole series of 'em!—when she wanted me to let her have the Dower House."

"Well, she got the Dower House," said Shield dryly.

"Of course she did!" said Sylvester snappishly, and relapsed into one of the forgetful silences of old age. A log falling out on to the hearth recalled him. He opened his eyes again and said: "Did I tell you why I wanted you?"

Sir Tristram had risen and gone over to the fire to replace the smoking log. He did not answer until he had done so, and then he said in his cool, disinterested voice: "You wrote that you had arranged a marriage for me with your granddaughter."

The piercing eyes gleamed. "It don't please you much, eh?"

"Not much," admitted Shield, coming back to the dais.

"It's a good match," offered Sylvester, "I've settled most of the unentailed property on her, and she's half French, you know—understands these arrangements. You can go your own road. She's not at all like her mother."

"I never knew her mother," said Shield discouragingly.

"She was a fool!" said Sylvester. "Never think she could be a daughter of mine. She eloped with a frippery Frenchman: that shows you. What was his damned name?"

"De Vauban."

"So it was. The Vidame de Vauban. I forget when he died. Marie died three years ago, and I went over to Paris—a year later, I think, but my memory's not what it was."

"A little more than a year later, sir."

"I dare say. It was after—" He paused for a moment, and then added harshly: "—after Ludovic's affair. I thought France was growing too hot for any grandchild of mine, and by God I was right! How long is it now since they sent the King to the guillotine? Over a month, eh? Mark me, Tristram, the Queen will go the same road before the year is out. I'm happy to think I shan't be here to see it. Charming she was, charming! But you wouldn't remember. Twenty years ago we used to wear her colour. Everything was Queen's Hair: satins, ribbons, shoes. Now"—his lip curled into a sneer—"now I've a great-nephew who wears a green coat and yellow pantaloons, and a damned absurd sugar-loaf on his head!" He raised his heavy eyelids suddenly, and added: "But the boy is still my heir!"

Sir Tristram said nothing in answer to this remark, which had been flung at him almost like a challenge. Sylvester took snuff again, and when he next spoke it was once more in his faintly mocking drawl. "He'd marry Eustacie if he could, but she don't like him." He fobbed his snuff-box with a flick of his finger. "The long and the short of it is, I've a fancy to see her married to you before I die, Tristram."

"Why?" asked Shield.

"There's no one else," replied Sylvester bluntly. "My fault, of course. I should have provided for her—taken her up to London. But I'm old, and I've never pleased anyone but myself. I haven't been to London above twice in the last three years. Too late to think of that now. I'm dying, and damme, the chit's my grandchild! I'll leave her safely bestowed. Time you was thinking of marriage."

"I have thought of it."

Sylvester looked sharply at him. "Not in love, are you?"

Shield's face hardened. "No."

"If you're still letting a cursed silly calf affair rankle with you, you're a fool!" said Sylvester. "I've forgotten the rights of it, if ever I knew them, but they don't interest me. Most women will play you false, and I never met one yet that wasn't a fool at heart. I'm offering you a marriage of convenience."

"Does she understand that?" asked Shield.

"Wouldn't understand anything else," replied Sylvester. "She's a Frenchwoman."

Sir Tristram stepped down from the dais, and went over to the fireplace. Sylvester watched him in silence, and after a moment he said: "It might answer."

"You're the last of your name," Sylvester reminded him.

"I know it. I've every intention of marrying."

"No one in your eye?"

"No."

"Then you'll marry Eustacie," said Sylvester. "Pull the bell!"

Sir Tristram obeyed, but said with a look of amusement: "Your dying wish, Sylvester?"

"I shan't live the week out," replied Sylvester cheerfully. "Heart and hard living, Tristram. Don't pull a long face at my funeral! Eighty years is enough for any man, and I've had the gout for twenty of them." He saw his valet come into the room, and said: "Send Mademoiselle to me."

"You take a great deal for granted, Sylvester," remarked Sir Tristram, as the valet went out again.

Sylvester had leaned his head back against the pillows, and closed his eyes. There was a suggestion of exhaustion in his attitude, but when he opened his eyes they were very much alive, and impishly intelligent. "You would not have come here, my dear Tristram, had you not already made up your mind."

Sir Tristram smiled a little reluctantly, and transferred his attention to the fire.

It was not long before the door opened again. Sir Tristram turned as Mademoiselle de Vauban came into the room, and stood looking at her under bent brows.

His first thought was that she was unmistakably a French-woman, and not in the least the type of female he admired. She had glossy black hair, dressed in the newest fashion, and her eyes were so dark that it was hard to know whether they were brown or black. Her inches were few, but her figure was extremely good, and she bore herself with an air. She paused just inside the door, and, at once perceiving Sir Tristram, gave back his stare with one every whit as searching and a good deal more speculative.

Sylvester allowed them to weigh one another for several moments before he spoke, but presently he said: "Come here, my child. And you, Tristram."

The promptness with which his granddaughter obeyed this summons augured a docility wholly belied by the resolute, not to say wilful, set of her pretty mouth. She trod gracefully across the room, and curtseyed to Sylvester before stepping up on to the dais. Sir Tristram came more slowly to the bed-side, nor did it escape Eustacie's notice that he had appar-ently looked his fill at her. His eyes, still sombre and slightly frowning, now rested on Sylvester.

Sylvester stretched out his left hand to Eustacie. "Let me present to you, my child, your cousin Tristram."

"Your very obedient cousin," said Shield, bowing.

"It is to me a great happiness to meet my cousin," enunci-ated Eustacie with prim civility and a slight, not unpleasing French accent.

"I am a little tired," said Sylvester. "If I were not I might allow you time to become better acquainted. And yet I don't know: I dare say it's as well as it is," he added cynically. "If you want a formal offer, Eustacia, no doubt Tristram will make you one—after dinner."

"I do not want a formal offer," replied Mademoiselle de Vauban. "It is to me a matter quite immaterial, but my name is Eustacie, which is, *enfin,* a very good name, and it is *not* Eu-sta-ci-a, which I cannot at all pronounce, and which I find excessively ugly."

This speech, which was delivered in a firm and perfectly self-possessed voice, had the effect of making Sir Tristram cast another of his searching glances at the lady. He said with a faint smile: "I hope I may be permitted to call you Eustacie, cousin?"

"Certainly; it will be quite *convenable,*" replied Eustacie, bestowing a brilliant smile upon him.

"She's eighteen," said Sylvester abruptly. "How old are you?"

"Thirty-one," answered Sir Tristram uncompromisingly.

"H'm!" said Sylvester. "A very excellent age."

"For what?" asked Eustacie.

"For marriage, miss!"

Eustacie gave him a thoughtful look, but volunteered no further remark.

"You may go down to dinner now," said Sylvester. "I regret that I am unable to bear you company, but I trust that the Nuits I have instructed Porson to give you will help you to overcome any feeling of *gêne* which might conceivably attack you."

"You are all consideration, sir," said Shield. "Shall we go, cousin?"

Eustacie, who did not appear to suffer from *gêne,* assented, curtseyed again to her grandfather, and accompanied Sir Tristram downstairs to the dining-room.

The butler had set their places at opposite ends of the great table, an arrangement in which both tacitly acquiesced, though it made conversation a trifle remote. Dinner, which was served in the grand manner, was well chosen, well cooked, and very long. Sir Tristram noticed that his prospective bride enjoyed a hearty appetite, and discovered after five minutes that she possessed a flow of artless conversation, quite unlike any he had been used to listen to in London drawing-rooms. He was prepared to find her embarrassed by a situation which struck him as being fantastic, and was somewhat startled when she remarked: "It is a pity that you are so dark, because I do not like dark men in general. However, one must accustom oneself."

"Thank you," said Shield.

"If my grandpapa had left me in France it is probable that I should have married a Duke," said Eustacie. "My uncle—the present Vidame, you understand—certainly intended it."

"You would more probably have gone to the guillotine," replied Sir Tristram, depressingly matter of fact.

"Yes, that is quite true," agreed Eustacie. "We used to talk of it, my cousin Henriette and I. We made up our minds we should be entirely brave, not crying, of course, but perhaps a little pale, in a proud way. Henriette wished to go to the guillotine *en grande tenue,* but that was only because she had a court dress of yellow satin which she thought became her much better than it did really. For me, I think one should wear white to the guillotine if one is quite young, and not carry anything except perhaps a handkerchief. Do you not agree?"

"I don't think it signifies what you wear if you are on your way to the scaffold," replied Sir Tristram, quite unappreciative of the picture his cousin was dwelling on with such evident admiration.

She looked at him in surprise. "Don't you? But consider! You would be very sorry for a young girl in a tumbril, dressed all in white, pale, but *quite* unafraid, and not attending to the *canaille* at all, but——"

"I should be very sorry for anyone in a tumbril, whatever their age or sex or apparel," interrupted Sir Tristram.

"You would be more sorry for a young girl—all alone, and perhaps bound," said Eustacie positively.

"You wouldn't be all alone. There would be a great many other people in the tumbril with you," said Sir Tristram.

Eustacie eyed him with considerable displeasure. "In my tumbril there would *not* have been a great many other people," she said.

Perceiving that argument on this point would be fruitless, Sir Tristram merely looked sceptical and refrained from speech.

"A Frenchman," said Eustacie, "would understand at once."

"I am not a Frenchman," replied Sir Tristram.

"Ca se voit!" retorted Eustacie.

Sir Tristram served himself from a dish of mutton steaks and cucumber.

"The people whom I have met in England," said Eustacie after a short silence, "consider it very romantic that I was rescued from the Terror."

Her tone suggested strongly that he also ought to consider it romantic, but as he was fully aware that Sylvester had travelled to Paris some time before the start of the Terror, and had removed his granddaughter from France in the most unexciting way possible, he only replied: "I dare say."

"I know a family who escaped from Paris in a cart full of turnips," said Eustacie. "The soldiers stuck their bayonets into the turnips, too."

"I trust they did not also stick them into the family?"

"No, but they might easily have done so. You do not at all realize what it is like in Paris now. One lives in constant anxiety. It is even dangerous to step out of doors."

"It must be a great relief for you to find yourself in Sussex."

She fixed her large eyes on his face, and said: "Yes, but—do you not like exciting things, *mon cousin?*"

"I do not like revolutions, if that is what you mean."

She shook her head. "Ah no, but romance, and—and adventure!"

He smiled. "When I was eighteen I expect I did."

A depressed silence fell. "Grandpère says that you will make me a very good husband," said Eustacie presently.

Taken by surprise, Shield replied stiffly: "I shall endeavour to do so, cousin."

"And I expect," said Eustacie, despondently inspecting a dish of damson tartlets, "that he is quite right. You look to me like a good husband."

"Indeed?" said Sir Tristram, unreasonably annoyed by this remark. "I am sorry that I cannot return the compliment by telling you that you look like a good wife."

The gentle melancholy which had descended on Eustacie vanished. She dimpled delightfully, and said: "No, I don't, do I? But do you think that I am pretty?"

"Very," answered Shield in a damping tone.

"Yes, so do I," agreed Eustacie. "In London I think I might have a great success, because I do not look like an English-woman, and I have noticed that the English think that foreigners are very *épatantes.*"

"Unfortunately," said Sir Tristram, "London is becoming so full of French *émigrés* that I doubt whether you would find yourself in any way remarkable."

"I remember now," said Eustacie. "You do not like women."

Sir Tristram, uncomfortably aware of the footman behind his chair, cast a glance at his cousin's empty plate, and got up. "Let us go into the drawing-room," he said. "This is hardly the place to discuss such—er—intimate matters!"

Eustacie, who seemed to regard the servants as so many pieces of furniture, looked round in a puzzled way, but made no objection to leaving the dining-table. She accompanied Sir Tristram to the drawing-room, and said, almost before he had shut the door: "Tell me, do you mind very much that you are to marry me?"

He answered in an annoyed voice: "My dear cousin, I do not know who told you that I dislike women, but it is a gross exaggeration."

"Yes, but do you mind?"

"I should not be here if I minded."

"Truly? But everybody has to do what Grandpère tells them."

"Not quite everybody," said Shield. "Sylvester knows, however, that——"

"You should not call your great-uncle Sylvester!" interrupted Eustacie. "It is not at all respectful."

"My good child, the whole world has called him Sylvester for the past forty years!"

"Oh!" said Eustacie doubtfully. She sat down on a sofa upholstered in blue-and-gold-striped satin, folded her hands, and looked expectantly at her suitor.

He found this wide, innocent gaze a trifle disconcerting, but after a moment he said with a gleam of amusement: "There is an awkwardness in this situation, cousin, which I, alas, do not seem to be the man to overcome. You must forgive me if I appear to you to be lacking in sensibility. Sylvester has arranged a marriage of convenience for us, and allowed neither of us time to become in the least degree acquainted before we go to the altar."

"In France," replied Eustacie, "one is not acquainted with one's betrothed, because it is not permitted that one should converse with him alone until one is married."

This remark certainly seemed to bear out Sylvester's assurance that his granddaughter understood the nature of his arrangements. Sir Tristram said: "It would be absurd to pretend that either of us can feel for the other any of those passions which are ordinarily to be looked for in betrothed couples, but——"

"Oh yes, it *would!*" agreed Eustacie heartily.

"Nevertheless," pursued Sir Tristram, "I believe such marriages as ours often prosper. You have accused me of disliking females, but believe me——"

"I can see very well that you dislike females," interrupted Eustacie. "I ask myself why it is that you wish to be married."

He hesitated, and then answered bluntly: "Perhaps if I had a brother I should not wish it, but I am the last of my name, and I must not let it die with me. I shall count myself fortunate if you will consent to be my wife, and so far as it may lie in my power I will promise that you shall not have cause to regret it. May I tell Sylvester that we have agreed to join hands?"

"Qu'importe? It is his command, and naturally he knows we shall be married. Do you think we shall be happy?"

"I hope so, cousin."

"Yes, but I must tell you that you are not at all the sort of man I thought I should marry. It is very disheartening. I thought that in England one was permitted to fall in love and marry of one's own choice. Now I see that it is just the same as it is in France."

He said with a touch of compassion: "You are certainly very young to be married, but when Sylvester dies you will be alone, and your situation would be awkward indeed."

"That is quite true," nodded Eustacie. "I have considered it well. And I dare say it will not be so very bad, our marriage, if I can have a house in town, and perhaps a lover."

"Perhaps a *what?*" demanded Shield, in a voice that made her jump.

"Well, in France it is quite *comme il faut*—in fact, quite *à la mode*—to have a lover when one is married," she explained, not in the least abashed.

"In England," said Sir Tristram, "it is neither *comme il faut* nor *à la mode.*"

"Vraiment? I do not yet know what is the fashion in England, but naturally if you assure me it is not *à la mode,* I won't have any lover. Can I have a house in town?"

"I don't think you know what you are talking about," said Sir Tristram, on a note of relief. "My home is in Berkshire, and I hope you will grow to like it as I do, but I can hire a house in town for the season if your heart is set on it."

Eustacie was just about to inform him that her heart was irrevocably set on it when the butler opened the door and announced the arrival of Mr. Lavenham. Eustacie broke off in mid-sentence, and said under her breath: "Well, I would much rather be married to you than to him, at all events!"

Her expression did not lead Sir Tristram to set undue store by this handsome admission. He frowned reprovingly at her, and went forward to greet his cousin.

Beau Lavenham, who was two years younger than Shield, did not resemble him in the least. Sir Tristram was a large, lean man, very dark, harsh-featured, and with few airs or graces; the Beau was of medium height only, slim rather than lean, of a medium complexion and delicately-moulded features, and his graces were many. Nothing could have been more exquisite than the arrangement of his powdered curls, or the cut of his brown-spotted silk coat and breeches. He wore a waistcoat embroidered with gold and silver, and stockings of palest pink, a jewel in the snowy folds of his cravat, knots of ribbons at his knees, and rings on his slender white fingers. In one hand he carried his snuff-box and scented handkerchief; in the other he held up an ornate quizzing-glass that hung on a riband round his neck. Through this he surveyed his two cousins, blandly smiling and quite at his ease. "Ah, Tristram!" he said in a soft, languid voice, and, letting fall his quizzing-glass, held out his hand. "How do you do, my dear fellow?"

Sir Tristram shook hands with him. "How do you do, Basil? It's some time since we met."

The Beau made a gesture of deprecation. "But, my dear Tristram, if you *will* bury yourself in Berkshire what is one to do? Eustacie——!" He went to her, and bowed over her hand with incomparable grace. "So you have been making Tristram's acquaintance?"

"Yes," said Eustacie. "We are betrothed."

The Beau raised his brows, smiling. "Oh la, la! so soon? Did Sylvester call this tune? Well, you are, both of you, very obedient, but are you quite, quite sure that you will deal well together?"

"Oh, I hope so!" replied Sir Tristram bracingly.

"If you are determined—and I must warn you, Eustacie, that he is the most determined fellow imaginable—I must hope so too. But I do not think I expected either of you to be so *very* obedient. Sylvester is prodigious—quite prodigious!

One cannot believe that he is really dying. A world without Sylvester! Surely it must be impossible!"

"It will seem odd, indeed," Shield said calmly.

Eustacie looked disparagingly at the Beau. "And it will seem odd to me when you are Lord Lavenham—very odd!"

There was a moment's silence. The Beau glanced at Sir Tristram, and then said: "Ah yes, but, you see, I shall not be Lord Lavenham. My dear Tristram, do, I beg of you, try some of this snuff of mine, and let me have your opinion of it. I have added the veriest dash of Macouba to my old blend. Now, was I right?"

"I'm not a judge," said Shield, helping himself to a pinch. "It seems well enough."

Eustacie was frowning. "But I don't understand! Why will you not be Lord Lavenham?"

The Beau turned courteously towards her. "Well, Eustacie, I am not Sylvester's grandson, but only his great-nephew."

"But when there is no grandson it must surely be you who are the heir?"

"Precisely, but there is a grandson, dear cousin. Did you not know that?"

"Certainly I know that there was Ludovic, but he is dead after all!"

"Who told you Ludovic was dead?" asked Shield, looking at her under knit brows.

She spread out her hands. "But Grandpère, naturally! And I have often wanted to know what it was that he did that was so entirely wicked that no one must speak of him. It is a mystery, and, I think, very romantic."

"There is no mystery," said Shield, "nor is it in the least romantic. Ludovic was a wild young man who crowned a series of follies with murder, and had in consequence to fly the country."

"Murder!" exclaimed Eustacie. *"Voyons,* do you mean he killed someone in a duel?"

"No. Not in a duel."

"But, Tristram," said the Beau gently, "you must not forget that it was never proved that Ludovic was the man who shot Matthew Plunkett. For my part I did not believe it possible then, and I still do not."

"Very handsome of you, but the circumstances were too damning," replied Shield. "Remember that I myself heard the shot that must have killed Plunkett not ten minutes after I had parted from Ludovic."

"But I," said the Beau, languidly polishing his quizzing-glass, "prefer to believe Ludovic's own story, that it was an owl he shot at."

"Shot—but missed!" said Shield. "Yet I have watched Ludovic shoot the pips out of a playing-card at twenty yards."

"Oh, admitted, Tristram, admitted, but on that particular night I think Ludovic was not entirely sober, was he?"

Eustacie struck her hands together impatiently. "But tell me, one of you! What did he do, my cousin Ludovic?"

The Beau tossed back the ruffles from his hand, and dipped his finger and thumb in his snuff-box. "Well, Tristram," he said with his glinting smile. "You know more about it than I do. Are you going to tell her?"

"It is not an edifying story," Shield said. "Why do you want to hear it?"

"Because I think perhaps my cousin Ludovic is of this family the most romantic person!" replied Eustacie.

"Oh, romantic!" said Sir Tristram, turning away with a shrug of the shoulders.

The Beau fobbed his snuff-box. "Romantic?" he said meditatively. "No, I do not think Ludovic was romantic. A little rash, perhaps. He was a gamester—whence the disasters which befell him. He lost a very large sum of money one night at the Cocoa-Tree to a man who lived at Furze House, not two miles from here."

"No one lives at Furze House," interrupted Eustacie.

"Not now," agreed the Beau. "Three years ago Sir Matthew Plunkett lived there. But Sir Matthew—three years ago —was shot in the Longshaw Spinney, and his widow removed from the neighbourhood."

"Did my cousin Ludovic shoot him?"

"That, my dear Eustacie, is a matter of opinion. You will get one answer from Tristram, and another from me."

"But why?" she demanded. "Not just because he had lost money to him! That, after all, is not such a great matter—unless perhaps he was quite ruined?"

"Oh, by no means! He did lose a large sum to him, however, and Sir Matthew, being a person of—let us say indifferent breeding—was ill-mannered enough to demand a pledge in security before he would continue playing. Of course, one should never play with Cits, but poor dear Ludovic was always so headstrong. The game was piquet, and both were in their cups. Ludovic took from his finger a certain ring, and gave it to Sir Matthew as a pledge—to be redeemed, naturally. It was a talisman ring of great antiquity which had come to Ludovic through his mother, who was the last of a much older house than ours."

Eustacie stopped him. "Please, I do not know what is a talisman ring."

"Just a golden ring with figures engraved upon it. This of Ludovic's was, as I have said, very old. The characters on it were supposed to be magical. It should, according to ancient belief, have protected him from any harm. More important, it was an heirloom. I don't know its precise value. Tristram, you are a judge of such things—you must make him show you his collection, Eustacie—what was the value of the ring?"

"I don't know," answered Shield curtly. "It was very old —perhaps priceless."

"Such a rash creature, poor Ludovic!" sighed the Beau. "I believe there was no stopping him—was there, Tristram?"

"No."

Eustacie turned towards Shield. "But were you there, then?"

"Yes, I was there."

"But no one, not even Tristram, could manage Ludovic in his wilder moods," explained the Beau. "He pledged the ring, and continued to lose. Sir Matthew, with what one cannot but feel to have been a lamentable want of taste, left the Cocoa-Tree with the ring upon his finger. To redeem it Ludovic was forced to go to the Jews—ah, that means money-lenders, my dear!"

"There was nothing new in that," said Shield. "Ludovic had been in the Jews' hands since he came down from Oxford—and before."

"Like so many of us," murmured the Beau.

"And did he get the money from the Jews?" asked Eustacie.

"Oh yes," replied the Beau, "but the matter was not so easily settled. When Ludovic called upon Plunkett to redeem the ring our ingenious friend pretended that the bargain had been quite misunderstood, that he had in fact staked his guineas against the ring, and won it outright. He would not give it up, nor could anyone but Tristram be found who had been sober enough to vouch for the truth of Ludovic's version of the affair."

Eustacie's eyes flashed. "I am not at all surprised that Ludovic killed this *canaille!* He was without honour!"

The Beau played with his quizzing-glass. "People who collect objects of rarity, my dear Eustacie, will often, so I believe, go to quite unheard-of lengths to acquire the prize they covet."

"But you!" said Eustacie, looking fiercely at Sir Tristram. "You knew the truth!"

"Unfortunately," replied Sir Tristram, "Plunkett did not wait for my ruling. He retired into the country—to Furze House, in fact—and somewhat unwisely refused to see Ludovic."

"Did Grandpère know of this?" Eustacie asked.

"Dear me, no!" said the Beau. "Sylvester and Ludovic were so rarely on amicable terms. And then there was that little matter of Ludovic's indebtedness to the Jews. One can hardly blame Ludovic for not taking Sylvester into his confidence. However, Ludovic came home to this house, bringing Tristram, with the intention of confronting Plunkett with the one—er—reliable witness to the affair. But Plunkett was singularly elusive—not unnaturally, of course. When Ludovic called at Furze House he was never at home. One must admit that Ludovic was not precisely the man to accept such treatment patiently. And he was drinking rather heavily at that time, too. Discovering that Plunkett was to dine at a house in Slaugham upon the very day that he had been refused admittance to Furze House for the third time, he conceived the plan of waylaying him upon his return home, and forcing him to accept bills in exchange for the ring. Only Tristram, finding him gone from here, guessed what he would be at, and followed him."

"The boy was three parts drunk!" said Sir Tristram over his shoulder.

"I have no doubt he was in a very dangerous humour," agreed the Beau. "It has always been a source of wonderment to me how you persuaded him to relinquish his purpose and return home."

"I promised to see Plunkett in his stead," replied Shield. "Like a fool I let him take the path through the spinney."

"My dear fellow, no one could have expected you to have foreseen that Plunkett would return by that path," said the Beau gently.

"On the contrary, if he came from Slaugham it was the most natural way for him to take," retorted Shield. "And we knew he was riding, not driving."

"So what happened?" breathed Eustacie.

It was Shield who answered her. "Ludovic rode back through the Longshaw Spinney, while I went on towards Furze House. Not ten minutes after we had parted I heard a shot fired in the distance. At the time I made nothing of it: it might have been a poacher. Next morning Plunkett's body was discovered in the spinney with a shot through the heart, and a crumpled handkerchief of Ludovic's lying beside it."

"And the ring?" Eustacie said quickly.

"The ring was gone," said Shield. "There was money in Plunkett's pockets, and a diamond pin in his cravat, but of the talisman ring no sign."

"And it has never been seen since," added the Beau.

"By us, no!" said Sir Tristram.

"Yes, yes, I know that you think Ludovic has it," said the Beau, "but Ludovic swore he did not meet Plunkett that night, and I for one do not think that Ludovic was a liar. He admitted freely that he carried a pistol in his pocket, he even admitted that he had fired it—at an owl."

"Why should he not shoot this Plunkett?" demanded Eustacie. "He deserved to be shot! I am very glad that he was shot!"

"Possibly," said Sir Tristram in his driest tone, "but in England, whatever it may be in France, murder is a capital offence."

"But they did not hang him just for killing such a one as this Plunkett?" said Eustacie, shocked.

"No, because we got him out of the country before he could be arrested," Shield answered.

The Beau lifted his hand. "Sylvester and you got him out of the country," he corrected. "I had no hand in that, if you please."

"Had he stayed to face a trial nothing could have saved his neck."

"There I beg to differ from you, my dear Tristram," said the Beau calmly. "Had he been permitted to face his trial the truth might have been found out. When you—and Sylvester, of course—smuggled him out of the country you made him appear a murderer confessed."

Sir Tristram was spared the necessity of answering by the entrance of Sylvester's valet, who came to summon him to his great-uncle's presence again. He went at once, a circumstance which provoked the Beau to murmur as the door closed behind him: "It is really most gratifying to see Tristram so complaisant."

Eustacie paid no heed to this, but said: "Where is my cousin Ludovic now?"

"No one knows, my dear. He has vanished."

"And you do not do anything to help him, any of you!" she said indignantly.

"Well, dear cousin, it is a little difficult, is it not?" replied the Beau. "After that well-meaning but fatal piece of meddling, what could one do?"

"I think," said Eustacie with a darkling brow, "that Tristram did not like my cousin Ludovic."

The Beau laughed. "How clever of you, my dear!"

She looked at him. "What did you mean when you said he must show me his collection?" she asked directly.

He raised his brows in exaggerated surprise. "Why, what should I mean? Merely that he has quite a notable collection. I am not a judge, but I have sometimes felt that I should like to see that collection myself."

"Will he not let you, then?"

"Oh, but with the greatest goodwill in the world!" said the Beau, smiling. "But one has to remember that collectors do not always show one quite *all* their treasures, you know!"

Chapter II

SIR TRISTRAM, standing once more beside Sylvester's bed, was a little shocked to perceive already a change in him. Sylvester was still propped up by a number of pillows, and he still wore his wig, but he seemed suddenly to have grown frailer and more withdrawn. Only his eyes were very much alive, startlingly dark in his waxen face.

Sir Tristram said in his deep voice: "I'm sorry, sir: I believe my visit has too much exhausted you."

"Thank you, I am the best judge of what exhausts me," replied Sylvester. "I shan't last much longer, I admit, but by God, I'll last long enough to settle my affairs! Are you going to marry that chit?"

"Yes, I'll marry her," said Shield. "Will that content you?"

"I've a fancy to see the knot well tied," said Sylvester. "Fortunately, she's not a Papist. What do you make of her?"

Sir Tristram hesitated. "I hardly know. She's very young."

"All the better, as long as her husband has the moulding of her."

"You may be right, but I wish you had broached this matter earlier."

"I'm always right. What did you want to do? Come a-courting her?" jibed Sylvester. "Poor girl!"

"You are forcing her to a marriage she may easily regret. She is romantic."

"Fiddlededee!" said Sylvester. "Most women are, but they get the better of it in time. Is that damned mincing puppy-dog downstairs?"

"Yes," said Shield.

"He'll put you in the shade if he can," said Sylvester warningly.

Sir Tristram looked contemptuous. "Well, if you expect me to vie with his graces you'll be disappointed, sir."

"I expect nothing but folly from any of my family!" snapped Sylvester.

Sir Tristram picked up a vinaigrette from the table by the bed and held it under his great-uncle's nose. "You're tiring yourself, sir."

"Damn you!" said Sylvester faintly. He lifted his hand with a perceptible effort and took the bottle, and lay in silence for a time, breathing its aromatic fumes. After a minute or two his lips twitched in a wry smile, and he murmured: "I would give much to have been able to see the three of you together. What did you talk of?"

"Ludovic," replied Shield with a certain cool deliberation.

Sylvester's hand clenched suddenly; the smile left his face. He said scarcely above a whisper: "I thought you knew his name is never to be mentioned in this house! Do you count me dead already that you should dare?"

"You're not a greater object of awe to me on your death-bed, Sylvester, than you have ever been," said Shield.

Sylvester's eyes flashed momentarily, but his sudden wrath vanished in a chuckle. "You're an impudent dog, Tristram. Did you ever care for what I said?"

"Very rarely," said Shield.

"Quite right," approved Sylvester. "Damme, I always liked you for it! What have you been saying about the boy?"

"Eustacie wanted to hear the story. Apparently you told her he was dead."

"He is dead to me," said Sylvester harshly. "Of what use to let her make a hero of him? You may depend upon it she would. Did you tell her?"

"Basil told her."

"You should have stopped him." Sylvester lay frowning, his fingers plucking a little at the gorgeous coverlet. "Basil believed the boy's story," he said abruptly.

"I have never known why, sir."

Sylvester flashed a glance at him. "You didn't believe it, did you?"

"Did any of us, save only Basil?"

"He said we should have let him stand his trial. I wonder. I wonder."

"He was wrong. We did what we could for Ludovic when we shipped him to France. Why tease yourself now?"

"You never liked him, did you?"

"You have only to add that I am something of a collector of antique jewellery, Sylvester, and you will have said very much what Basil has been saying, far more delicately, below stairs."

"Don't be a fool!" said Sylvester irritably. "I told you he'd do what he could to spoil your chances. Send him about his business!"

"You will have to excuse me, sir. This is not my house."

"No, by God, and nor is it his!" said Sylvester, shaken by a gust of anger. "The estate will be in ward when I die, and I have not made him a trustee!"

"Then you are doing him an injustice, sir. Who are your trustees?"

"My lawyer, Pickering, and yourself," answered Sylvester.

"Good God, what induced you to name me?" said Shield. "I have not the smallest desire to manage your affairs!"

"I trust you, and I don't trust him," said Sylvester. "Moreover," he added with a spark of malice, "I've a fancy to make you run in my harness even if I can only do it by dying. Pour me out a little of that cordial."

Sir Tristram obeyed his behest, and held the glass to Sylvester's lips. Perversely, Sylvester chose to hold it himself, but it was apparent that even this slight effort was almost too great a tax on his strength.

"Weak as a cat!" he complained, letting Shield take the glass again. "You'd better go downstairs before that fellow has time to poison Eustacie's mind. I'll have you married in this very room just as soon as I can get the parson here. Send Jarvis to me; I'm tired."

When Sir Tristram reached the drawing-room again the tea-table had been brought in. Beau Lavenham inquired after his great-uncle, and upon Sir Tristram's saying that he found him very much weaker, shrugged slightly, and said: "I shall believe Sylvester is dead when I see him in his coffin. I hope you did not forget to tell him that I am dutifully in attendance?"

"He knows you are here," said Shield, taking a cup and saucer from Eustacie, "but I doubt whether he has strength enough to see any more visitors to-night."

"My dear Tristram, are you trying to be tactful?" inquired the Beau, amused. "I am quite sure Sylvester said that he would be damned if he would see that frippery fellow Basil."

Shield smiled. "Something of the sort. You should not wear a sugar-loaf hat."

"No, no; it cannot be my taste in dress which makes him dislike me so much, for that is almost impeccable," said the Beau, lovingly smoothing a wrinkle from his satin sleeve. "I can only think that it is because I stand next in the succession to poor Ludovic, and that is really no fault of mine."

"For all we know you may be further removed than that," said Tristram. "Ludovic may be married by now."

"Very true," agreed the Beau, sipping his tea. "And in some ways a son of Ludovic's might best solve the vexed question of who is to reign in Sylvester's stead."

"The estate is left in trust."

"From your gloomy expression, Tristram, I infer that you are one of the trustees," remarked the Beau. "Am I right?"

"Oh yes, you're right. Pickering is joined with me. I told Sylvester he should have named you."

"You are too modest, my dear fellow. He could not have made a better choice."

"I am not modest," replied Shield. "I don't want the charge of another man's estate; that is all."

The Beau laughed, and setting down his tea-cup turned to Eustacie. "It has occurred to me that I am here merely in the rôle of chaperon to a betrothed couple," he said. "I do not feel that I am cut out for such a rôle, so I shall go away now. Dear cousin!——" He raised her hand to his lips. "Tristram, my felicitations. If we do not meet before we shall certainly meet at Sylvester's funeral."

There was a short silence after he had gone. Sir Tristram snuffed a candle which was guttering, and glanced down at Eustacie, sitting still and apparently pensive by the fire. As though aware of his look, she raised her eyes and gazed at him in the intent, considering way which was so peculiarly her own.

"Sylvester wants to see us married before he dies," Shield said.

"Basil does not think he will die."

"I believe he is nearer to it than we know. What did the doctor say?"

"He said he was very irreligious, and altogether insupportable," replied Eustacie literally.

Sir Tristram laughed, surprising his cousin, who had not imagined that his countenance could lighten so suddenly. "I dare say he might, but was that all he said?"

"No, he said also that it was useless for him to come any more to see Grandpère, because when he said he should have gruel Grandpère at once sent for a green goose and a bottle of burgundy. The doctor said that it would kill him, and *du vrai*, I think he is piqued because it did not kill Grandpère at all. So perhaps Grandpère will not die, but on the contrary get quite well again."

"I am afraid it is only his will which keeps him alive." Shield moved towards the fire and said, looking curiously down at Eustacie: "Are you fond of him? Will it make you unhappy if he dies?"

"No," she replied frankly. "I am a little fond of him, but not very much, because he is not fond of anybody, he. It is not his wish that one should be fond of him."

"He brought you out of France," Shield reminded her.

"Yes, but I did not want to be brought out of France," said Eustacie bitterly.

"Perhaps you did not then, but you are surely glad to be in England now?"

"I am not at all glad, but, on the contrary, very sorry," said Eustacie. "If he had left me with my uncle I should have gone to Vienna, which would have been not only very gay, but also romantic, because my uncle fled from France with all his family, in a berline, just like the King and Queen."

"Not quite like the King and Queen if he succeeded in crossing the frontier," said Shield.

"I will tell you something," said Eustacie, incensed. "Whenever I recount to you an interesting story you make me an answer which is like—which is like those snuffers—*enfin!*"

"I'm sorry," said Shield, rather startled.

"Well, I am sorry too," said Eustacie, getting up from the sofa, "because it makes it very difficult to converse. I shall wish you good night, *mon cousin.*"

If she expected him to try to detain her she was disappointed. He merely bowed formally and opened the door for her to pass out of the room.

Five minutes later her maid, hurrying to her bedchamber in answer to a somewhat vehement tug at the bell-rope, found her seated before her mirror, stormily regarding her own reflection.

"I will undress, and I will go to bed," announced Eustacie.

"Yes, miss."

"And I wish, moreover, that I had gone to Madame Guillotine *in* a tumbril, *alone!*"

Country-bred Lucy, a far more appreciative audience than Sir Tristram, gave a shudder, and said: "Oh, miss, don't speak of such a thing! To think of you having your head cut off, and you so young and beautiful!"

Eustacie stepped out of her muslin gown, and pushed her

arms into the wrapper Lucy was holding. "And I should have worn a white dress, and even the *sans-culottes* would have been sorry to have seen me in a tumbril!"

Lucy had no very clear idea who the *sans-culottes* might be, but she assented readily, and added, in all sincerity, that her mistress would have looked lovely.

"Well, I think I should have looked nice," said Eustacie candidly. "Only it is no use thinking of that, because instead I am going to be married."

Lucy paused in her task of taking the pins out of her mistress's hair to clasp her hands, and breathe ecstatically: "Yes, miss, and if I may make so bold as I do wish you so happy!"

"When one is forced into a marriage infinitely distasteful one does not hope for happiness," said Eustacie in a hollow voice.

"Good gracious, miss, his lordship surely isn't a-going to force you?" gasped Lucy. "I never heard such a thing!"

"Oh!" said Eustacie. "Then it *is* true what I have heard in France, that English ladies are permitted to choose for themselves whom they will marry!" She added despondently: "But I have not seen anyone whom I should like to have for my husband, so it does not signify in the least."

"No, miss, but—don't you like Sir Tristram, miss? I'm sure he's a very nice gentleman, and would make anyone a good husband."

"I do not want a good husband who is thirty-one years old and who has no conversation!" said Eustacie, her lip trembling.

Lucy put down the hair-brush. "There, miss, you're feeling vapourish, and no wonder, with everything come upon you sudden, like it has! No one can't force you to marry against your true wishes—not in England, they can't, whatever they may do in France, which everyone knows is a nasty murdering place!"

Eustacie dried her eyes and said: "No, but if I do not marry my cousin I shall have to live with a horrid chaperon when my grandpapa dies, and that would be much, much worse. One must resign oneself."

Downstairs Sir Tristram had just reached the same conclusion. Since, sooner or later, he would have to marry someone, and since he had determined never again to commit the folly of falling in love, his bride might as well be Eustacie as another. She seemed to be tiresomely volatile, but no sillier than any other young woman of his acquaintance. She was of

good birth (though he thought her French blood to be de-
plored), and in spite of the fact that if he had a preference it
was for fair women, he was bound to admit that she was very
pretty. He could have wished she were older, but it was possible that Sylvester, whose experience was undoubtedly wide,
knew what he was talking about when he said that her ex-
treme youth was in her favour. In fact, one must resign oneself.

Upon the following morning the betrothed couple met at
the breakfast-table and took fresh stock of each other. Sir
Tristram, whose mulberry evening-dress had not met with
Eustacie's approval, had had the unwitting tact to put on a
riding-suit, in which severe garb he looked his best and Eustacie, who had decided that, if she must marry her cousin, it
was only proper that he should be stimulated to admiration
of her charms, had arrayed herself in a *bergère* gown of
charming colour and design. Each at first glance felt moder-
ately pleased with the other, a complacent mood which lasted
for perhaps ten minutes, at the end of which time Sir Tristram was contemplating with grim misgiving the prospect of
encountering vivacity at the breakfast-table for the rest of his
life, and Eustacie was wondering whether her betrothed was
capable of uttering anything but the most damping of mono-
syllables.

During the course of the morning, Sir Tristram was sent
for to Sylvester's bedroom. He found his great-uncle propped
up very high in bed, and alarmingly brisk, and learned from
him that his nuptials would be celebrated upon the following
day. When he reminded Sylvester that marriages could not be
performed thus out of hand, Sylvester flourished a special li-
cence before his eyes, and said that he was not so moribund
that he could not still manage his affairs. Sir Tristram, who
liked being driven as little as most men, found this instance
of his great-uncle's forethought so annoying that he left him
somewhat abruptly, and went away to cool his temper with a
gallop over the Downs. When he returned it was some time
later, and he found the doctor's horse being walked up and
down before the Court, and the household in a state of
hushed expectancy. Sylvester, having managed his affairs to
his own satisfaction, drunk two glasses of Madeira, and
thrown his snuff-box at his valet for daring to remonstrate
with him, had seemed suddenly to collapse. He had sunk into
a deep swoon from which he had been with difficulty brought
round, and the doctor, summoned post-haste, had announced

that the end could not now be distant more than a few hours.

Regaining consciousness, Sylvester had, in a painful but determined whisper, declined the offices of a clergyman, recommended the doctor to go to hell, forbidden the servants to open his doors to his nephew Basil, announced his intention of dying without a pack of women weeping over him, and demanding the instant attendance of his nephew Tristram.

Sir Tristram, hearing these details from the butler, stayed only to cast his hat and coat on a chair, and went quickly up the stairs to the Great Chamber.

Both the valet and the doctor were in the room, the valet looking genuinely grieved and the doctor very sour. Sylvester was lying flat in the huge bed with his eyes shut, but when Tristram stepped softly on to the dais, he opened them at once, and whispered: "Damn you, you have kept me waiting!"

"I beg your pardon, sir."

"I did not mean to die until to-morrow," said Sylvester, labouring for breath. "Damme, I've a mind to make a push to last the night if only to spite that snivelling leech! . . . Tristram!"

"Sir?"

Sylvester grasped his wrist with thin, enfeebled fingers. "You'll marry that child?"

"I will, Sylvester: don't tease yourself!"

"Always meant Ludovic to have her . . . damned young scoundrel! Often wondered. Do you think he was telling the truth—after all?"

Shield was silent. Sylvester's pale lips twisted. "Oh, you don't, eh? Well, you can give him my ring if ever you see him again—and tell him not to pledge it! Take it: I've done with it." He slid the great ruby from his finger as he spoke, and dropped it into Shield's hand. "That Madeira was a mistake. I ought to have kept to the Burgundy. You can go now. Don't let there be any mawkish sentiment over my death!"

"Very well, sir," said Shield. He bent, kissed Sylvester's hand, and without more ado turned and went out of the room.

Sylvester died an hour later. The doctor who brought the news to Shield, and to Beau Lavenham, both waiting in the library, said that he had only spoken once more before the end.

"Indeed, and what did he say?" inquired the Beau.

"He made a remark, sir—I may say, a gross remark!—derogatory to my calling!" said the doctor. "I shall not repeat it!"

Both cousins burst out laughing. The doctor cast a look of shocked dislike at them and went away, disgusted but not surprised by their behaviour. A wild, godless family, he thought. They were not even profitable patients, these Lavenhams: he was glad to be rid of them.

"I suppose we shall never know what it was that he said," remarked the Beau. "I am afraid it may have been a trifle lewd."

"I should think probably very lewd," agreed Shield.

"But how right, how fitting that Sylvester should die with a lewd jest on his lips!" said the Beau. He patted his ruffles. "Do you still mean to be married to-morrow?"

"No, that must be postponed," Shield answered.

"I expect you are wise. Yet one cannot help suspecting that Sylvester would enjoy the slightly macabre flavour of a bridal presided over by his mortal remains."

"Possibly, but I never shared Sylvester's tastes," said Shield.

The Beau laughed gently, and bent to pick up his hat and cane from the chair on which he had laid them. "Well, I do not think I envy you the next few days, Tristram," he said. "If I can be of assistance to you, do by all means call upon me! I shall remain at the Dower House for some little time yet."

"Thank you, but I don't anticipate the need. I rely on Pickering. The charge of the estate would be better borne by him than by me. God knows what is to be done, with the succession in this accursed muddle!"

"There is one thing which ought to be done," said the Beau. "Some effort should be made to find Ludovic."

"A good deal easier said than done!" replied Sir Tristram. "He could not set foot in England if he were found, either. If he stayed in France he may have lost his head for all we know. It would be extremely like him to embroil himself in a revolution which was no concern of his."

"Well," said the Beau softly, "I do not want to appear unfeeling, but if Lodovic has lost his head, it would be of some slight interest to me to hear of it."

"Naturally. Your position is most uncertain."

"Oh, I am not repining," smiled the Beau. "But I still think you ought—as trustee—to find Ludovic."

During the next few days, however, Sir Tristram had

enough to occupy him without adding a search for the heir to his duties. Upon the arrival of the lawyer, Sylvester's will was read, a document complicated enough to try the temper of a more patient man than Shield. A thousand and one things had to be done, and in addition to the duties attendant upon the death of Sylvester there was the problem of Eustacie to worry her betrothed.

She accepted both her bereavement and the postponement of her wedding-day with perfect fortitude, but when Sir Tristram asked her to name some lady living in the neighbourhood in whose charge she could for the present remain, she declared herself quite unable to do so. She had no acquaintance in Sussex, Sylvester having quarrelled with one half of the county and ignored the other half. "Besides," she said, "I do not wish to be put in charge of a chaperon. I shall stay here."

Sir Tristram, feeling that Sylvester had in his time created enough scandal in Sussex, was strongly averse from giving the gossips anything further to wag their tongues over. Betrothed or not, his and Eustacie's sojourn under the same roof was an irregularity which every virtuous dame who thought the Lavenhams a godless family would be swift to pounce upon. He said: "Well, it is confoundedly awkward, but I don't see what I can do about it. I suppose I shall have to let you stay."

"I shall stay because I wish to," said Eustacie, bristling. "I do not have to do what you say yet!"

"Don't be silly!" said Sir Tristram, harassed, and therefore irritable.

"I am not silly. It is you who have a habit which I find much more silly of telling me what I must do and what I must not do. I am quite tired of being *bien élevée,* and I think I will now arrange my own affairs."

"You are a great deal too young to manage your own affairs, I am afraid."

"That we shall see."

"We shall, indeed. Have you thought to order your mourning clothes? That must be done, you know."

"I do not know it," said Eustacie. "Grandpère said I was not to mourn for him, and I shall not."

"That may be, but this is a censorious world, my child, and it will be thought very odd if you don't accord Sylvester's memory that mark of respect."

"Well, I shan't," said Eustacie simply.

Sir Tristram looked her over in frowning silence.

"You look very cross," said Eustacie.

"I am not cross," said Sir Tristram in a somewhat brittle voice, "but I think you should know that while I am prepared to allow you all the freedom possible, I shall expect my wife to pay some slight heed to my wishes."

Eustacie considered this dispassionately. "Well, I do not think I shall," she said. "You seem to me to have very stupid wishes—quite absurd, in fact."

"This argument is singularly pointless," said Sir Tristram, quelling a strong desire to box her ears. "Perhaps my mother will know better how to persuade you."

Eustacie pricked up her ears at that. "I did not know you had a mother! Where is she?"

"She is in Bath. When the funeral is over I am going to take you to her, and put you in her care until we can be married."

"As to that, it is not yet decided. Describe to me your mother! Is she like you?"

"No, not at all."

"*Tant mieux!* What, then, is she like?"

"Well," said Sir Tristram lamely, "I don't think I know how to describe her. She will be very kind to you, I know."

"But what does she do?" demanded Eustacie. "Does she amuse herself at Bath? Is she gay?"

"Hardly. She does not enjoy good health, you see."

"Oh!" Eustacie digested this. "No parties?"

"I believe she enjoys card-parties."

Eustacie grimaced expressively. "Me, I know those card-parties. I think she plays Whist, and perhaps Commerce."

"I dare say she does. I know of no reason why she should not," said Shield rather stiffly.

"There is not any reason, but I do not play Whist or Commerce, and I find such parties quite abominable."

"That need not concern you, for whatever Sylvester's views may have been, I feel sure that my mother will agree that it would be improper for you to go out in public immediately after his death."

"But if I am not to go to any parties, what then am I to do in Bath?"

"Well, I suppose you will have to reconcile yourself to a period of quiet."

"Quiet?" gasped Eustacie. "*More* quiet? No, and no, and no!"

He could not help laughing, but said: "Is it so terrible?"

"Yes, it is!" said Eustacie. "First I have to live in Sussex, and now I am to go to Bath—to play backgammon! And after that you will take me to Berkshire, where I expect I shall die."

"I hope not!" said Shield.

"Yes, but I think I shall," said Eustacie, propping her chin in her hands and gazing mournfully into the fire. "After all, I have had a very unhappy life without any adventures, and it would not be wonderful if I went into a decline. Only nothing that is interesting ever happens to me," she added bitterly, "so I dare say I shall just die in child-bed, which is a thing anyone can do."

Sir Tristram flushed uncomfortably. "Really, Eustacie!" he protested.

Eustacie was too much absorbed in the contemplation of her dark destiny to pay any heed to him. "I shall present to you an heir," she said, "and then I shall die." The picture suddenly appealed to her; she continued in a more cheerful tone: "Everyone will say that I was very young to die, and they will fetch you from the gaming-hell where you——"

"Fetch me from where?" interrupted Sir Tristram, momentarily led away by this flight of imagination.

"From a gaming-hell," repeated Eustacie impatiently. "Or perhaps the Cock-Pit. It does not signify; it is quite unimportant! But I think you will feel great remorse when it is told to you that I am dying, and you will spring up and fling yourself on your horse, and ride *ventre à terre* to come to my death-bed. And *then* I shall forgive you, and——"

"What in heaven's name are you talking about?" demanded Sir Tristram. "Why should you forgive me? Why should—What *is* this nonsense?"

Eustacie, thus rudely awakened from her pleasant dream, sighed and abandoned it. "It is just what I thought might happen," she explained.

Sir Tristram said severely: "It seems to me that you indulge your fancy a deal too freely. Let me assure you that I don't frequent gaming-hells or cock-pits! Nor," he added, with a flicker of humour, "am I very much in the habit of flinging myself upon my horses."

"No, and you do not ride *ventre à terre*. It does not need that you should tell me so. *I* know!"

"Well, only on the hunting-field," said Sir Tristram.

"Do you think you might if I were on my death-bed?" said Eustacie hopefully.

"Certainly not. If you were on your death-bed it is hardly likely that I should be from home. I wish you would put this notion of dying out of your head. Why should you die?"

"But I have told you!" said Eustacie, brightening at this sign of interest. "I shall——"

"Yes, I know," said Sir Tristram hastily. "You need not tell me again. There will be time enough to discuss such matters when we are married."

"But I thought it was because you must have an heir that you want to marry me?" said Eustacie practically. "Grandpère explained it to me, and you yourself said——"

"Eustacie," interposed Sir Tristram, "if you must talk in this extremely frank vein, I'll listen, but I do beg of you not to say such things to anyone but me! It will give people a very odd idea of you."

"Grandpère," said Eustacie, with the air of one quoting a major prophet, "told me not to mind what I said, but on no account to be a simpering little *innocente*."

"It sounds to me exactly the kind of advice Sylvester would give you," said Shield.

"And you sound to me exactly the kind of person I do not at all wish to have for my husband!" retorted Eustacie. "It will be better, I think, if we do not marry!"

"Possibly!" said Sir Tristram, nettled. "But I gave my word to Sylvester that I would marry you, and marry you I will!"

"You will not, because I shall instantly run away!"

"Don't be a little fool!" said Sir Tristram unwisely, and walked out of the room, leaving her simmering with indignation.

Her wrath did not last long, for by the time she had taken a vow to put her threat into execution, all the adventurous possibilities of such a resolve struck her so forcibly that Sir Tristram's iniquities were quite ousted from her mind. She spent a pleasurable hour in thinking out a number of plans for her future. These were varied, but all of them impracticable, a circumstance which her common sense regretfully acknowledged. She was forced in the end to take her handmaiden into her confidence, having abandoned such attractive schemes as masquerading in male attire, or taking London by storm by enacting an unspecified tragic rôle at Drury Lane. It was a pity, but if one had the misfortune to be a person of

Quality one could not become an actress; and although the notion of masquerading as a man appealed strongly to her, she was quite unable to carry her imagination farther than the first chapter of this exciting story. One would naturally leap into the saddle and ride off somewhere, but she could not decide where, or what to do.

Lucy, at first scandalized by the idea of a young lady setting out into the world alone, was not a difficult person to inspire. The portrait drawn for her edification of a shrinking damsel condemned to espouse a tyrant of callous instincts and brutal manners profoundly affected her mind, and by the time Eustacie had graphically described her almost inevitable demise in child-bed, she was ready to lend her support to any plan her mistress might see fit to adopt. Her own brain, though appreciative, was not fertile, but upon being adjured to think of some means whereby a lady could evade a distasteful marriage and arrange her own life, she had the happy notion of suggesting a perusal of the advertisements in the *Morning Post*.

Together mistress and maid pored over the columns of this useful periodical. It was not, at first glance, very helpful, for most of its advertisements appeared to be of Well-matched Carriage Horses, or Superb Residences to be Hired for a Short Term. Further study, however, enlarged the horizon. A lady domiciled in Brook Street required a Governess with a knowledge of Astronomy, Botany, Water-Colour Painting, and the French Tongue to instruct her daughters. Dismissing the first three requirements as irrelevancies, Eustacie triumphantly pointed to the last, and said that here was the very thing.

That a governess's career was unlikely to prove adventurous was a consideration that did not weigh with her for more than two minutes, for it did not take her longer than this to realize that her young charges would possess a handsome brother, who would naturally fall in love with his sisters' governess. Persecution from his Mama was to be expected, but after various vicissitudes it would be discovered that the humble governess was an aristocrat and an heiress, and all would end happily. Lucy, in spite of never having read any of the romances which formed her mistress's chief study, saw nothing improbable in this picture, but doubted whether Sir Tristram would permit his betrothed to leave the Court.

"He will know nothing of it," said Eustacie, "because I shall escape very late at night when he thinks I am in bed, and ride to Hand Cross to catch the mail-coach to London."

"Oh, miss, you couldn't do that, not all by yourself!" said Lucy. "It wouldn't be seemly!"

Paying no need to this poor-spirited criticism, Eustacie clasped her hands round her knees, and began to ponder the details of her flight. The scheme itself might be fantastical, but there was a streak of French rationality in her nature which could be trusted to cope with the intricacies of the wildest escapade. She said: "We shall need the stable keys."

"*We,* miss?" faltered Lucy.

Eustacie nodded. "But yes, because I have never saddled a horse, and though I think it would be a better adventure if I did everything quite by myself, one must be practical, after all. Can you saddle a horse?"

"Oh yes, miss!" replied Lucy, a farmer's daughter, "but——"

"Very well, then, that is arranged. And it is you, moreover, who must steal the stable keys. That will not be a great matter. And you will pack for me two bandboxes, but not any more, because I cannot carry much on horseback. And when I reach Hand Cross I shall let Rufus go, and it is certain that he will find his way home, and that will put my cousin Tristram in a terrible fright when he sees my horse quite riderless. I dare say he will think I am dead."

"Miss, you don't really mean it?" said Lucy, who had been listening open-mouthed.

"But of course I mean it," replied Eustacie calmly. "When does the night mail reach Hand Cross?"

"Just before midnight, miss, but they do say we shall be having snow, and that would make the mail late as like as not. But, miss, it's all of five miles to Hand Cross, and the road that lonely, and running through the Forest—oh, I'd be afeard!"

"I am not afraid of anything," said Eustacie loftily.

Lucy sank her voice impressively. "Perhaps you haven't ever heard tell of the Headless Horseman, miss?"

"No!" Eustacie's eyes sparkled. "Tell me at once all about him!"

"They say he rides the Forest, miss, but never on a horse of his own," said Lucy throbbingly. "You'll find him up behind you on the crupper with his arms round your waist."

Even in the comfortable daylight this story was hideous enough to daunt the most fearless. Eustacie shuddered, but said stoutly: "I do not believe it. It is just a tale!"

"Ask anyone, miss, if it's not true!" said Lucy.

Eustacie, thinking this advice good, asked Sir Tristram at the first opportunity.

"The Headless Horseman?" he said. "Yes, I believe there is some such legend."

"But is it true?" asked Eustacie breathlessly.

"Why, no, of course not!"

"You would not then be afraid to ride through the Forest at night?"

"Not in the least. I've often done so, and never encountered a headless horseman, I assure you!"

"Thank you," said Eustacie. "Thank you very much!"

He looked a little surprised, but as she said nothing more very soon forgot the episode.

"My cousin Tristram," Eustacie told Lucy, "says that it is nothing but a legend. I shall not regard it."

Chapter III

HAD Sir Tristram been less preoccupied he might have found something to wonder at in his cousin's sudden docility. As it was, he was much too busy unravelling the intricacies of Sylvester's affairs with Mr. Pickering to pay any heed to Eustacie's change of front. If he thought about it at all he supposed merely that she had recovered from a fit of tantrums, and was heartily glad of it. He had half expected her to raise objections to his plan to convey her to Bath on the day after her grandfather's burial, but when he broached the matter to her she listened to him with folded hands and downcast eyes, and answered never a word. A man more learned in female wiles might have found this circumstance suspicious; Sir Tristram was only grateful. He himself would be returning to Lavenham Court, but he told Eustacie that he did not expect to be obliged to remain for more than a week or two, after which time he would join the household in Bath, and set forward the marriage arrangements. Eustacie curtseyed politely.

She did not attend Sylvester's funeral, which took place on the third day after his death, but busied herself instead with choosing from her wardrobe the garments she considered most suited to her new calling, and directing Lucy how to bestow them in the two bandboxes. Lucy, too devoted to her glamorous young mistress to think of betraying her, but very much alarmed at the idea of all the dangers she might encounter on her solitary journey, sniffed dolefully as she folded caracos and fichus and said that she would almost prefer to accompany Miss, braving the terror of the Headless Horseman, than be left behind to face Sir Tristram's wrath. Eustacie, feeling that to take her maid with her would be to destroy at a blow all the romance of the adventure, told her to pretend the most complete ignorance of the affair, and promised that she would send for her to London at the first opportunity.

The forlorn sight of snowflakes drifting down from a

leaden sky affected Lucy with a sense of even deeper fore-boding, but only inspired her mistress to say she would wear her fur-lined cloak after all, and the beaver hat with the crimson plume.

Her actual escape from the Court was accomplished without the least difficulty, the servants having gone to bed, and Sir Tristram being shut up in the library with Beau Lavenham, who had come over from the Dower House to dine with his cousins. Eustacie had excused herself from their company soon after dinner, and gone up to her bedchamber. At eleven o'clock, looking quite enchanting in her riding-dress and crimson cloak and wide-brimmed beaver, with its red feather curling over to mingle with her dark, silky curls, she tiptoed down the back stairs, holding up her skirts in one hand and in the other grasping her whip and gloves. Behind her tottered the shrinking Lucy, carrying the two bandboxes and a lantern.

Half-way down the stairs Eustacie stopped. "I ought to have a pistol!"

"Good gracious sakes alive, miss!" whispered Lucy. "Whatever would you do with one of them nasty, dangerous things?"

"But, of course, I must have a pistol!" said Eustacie. "And I know where there is a pistol, too!" She turned, ignoring her abigail's tearful protests, and ran lightly up the stairs again, and disappeared in the direction of the Long Gallery.

When she returned she was flushed and rather out of breath and carried in her right hand a peculiarly deadly-look-ing duelling pistol with a ten-inch barrel and silver sights. Lucy nearly dropped the bandboxes when she saw it, and im-plored her mistress in an agitated whisper to put it down.

"It is my cousin Ludovic's," said Eustacie triumphantly. "There were two of them in a case in the bedchamber that was his. How fortunate that I should have remembered! I saw them—oh, a long time ago!—when they put the new cur-tains in that room. Do you think it is loaded?"

"Oh, mercy, miss, I hope not!"

"I must be careful," decided Eustacie, handling the weapon somewhat gingerly. "I think it has a hair-trigger, but I do not properly understand guns. Hurry, now!"

The snow had stopped falling some time before, but a light covering of it lay upon the ground, and there was a sharp, frosty nip in the air. The two females, one of them in high fettle and the other shivering with mingled cold and fright, trod softly down the drive that led from the house to the stables. No light showed in the coachman's cottage, nor in the grooms' quarters, and no one appeared to offer the least hindrance to Eustacie's escape. She unlocked the door of the harness-room, pulled Lucy in after her, and setting the lantern down on the table, selected a bridle from the wall, and pointed out her saddle to the abigail. The next thing was to unlock the stable door, and to saddle and bridle Rufus, who seemed sleepy but not displeased to see his mistress. Lucy, dreading the consequences of this exploit, had begun to weep softly, but was told in a fierce whisper to saddle Rufus and to stop being a fool. She was an obedient girl, so she gulped down her tears, and heaved the saddle up on to Rufus's back. The girths having been pulled tight, the headstall removed and the bridle put on, it only remained to attach the two bandboxes to the saddle. This called for a further search in the harness-room for a pair of suitable straps, and by the time these had been found and the bandboxes suspended from them, Eustacie had decided that the only possible way to carry a pistol was in a holster. A lady's saddle not being equipped with this necessary adjunct, one had to be removed from a saddle of Sylvester's, and buckled rather precariously on to the strap that held one of the bandboxes. It seemed to be far too large a holster for the slender pistol that was pushed into it, but that could not be helped. Eustacie remarked that it was fortunate there was snow upon the ground, since it would muffle the sound of Rufus's hooves on the cobble-stones, and led him out to the mounting-block. Once safely in the saddle, she reminded Lucy to lock all the doors again and to replace the keys, gave her her hand to kiss, and set off, not by way of the avenue leading to the closed lodge gates, but across the park to a farm-track with an unguarded gate at the end of it which could be opened without dismounting.

This feat presently accomplished, Eustacie urged Rufus to a trot, and set off down the lane towards the rough road that ran north through Warninglid to join the turnpike road from London to Brighton at Hand Cross.

She knew the way well, but to one wholly unaccustomed to be abroad after nightfall, the countryside looked oddly unfamiliar in the moonlight. Everything was very silent, and the trees, grown suddenly to preposterous heights, cast black, distorted shadows that might, to those of nervous disposition, seem almost to hold a menace. Eustacie was glad to think that she was a de Vauban, and therefore afraid of nothing, and wondered why a stillness unbroken by so much as the crackle of a twig should, instead of convincing her that she was alone, have the quite opposite effect of making her imagine hidden dangers behind every bush or thicket. She was enjoying herself hugely, of course—that went without saying—but perhaps she would not be entirely sorry to reach Hand Cross and the protection of the mail-coach. Moreover, the bandboxes bobbed up and down in a tiresome way, and one of them showed signs of working loose from its strap. She tried to rectify this, but only succeeded in making things worse.

The lane presently met the road to Hand Cross, and here the country began to be more thickly wooded, and consequently darker, for there were a good many pines and hollies which had not shed their foliage and so obscured the moonlight. It was very cold, and the carpet of snow made it sometimes difficult to keep to the road. Once Rufus stumbled almost into the ditch, and once some creature (only a fox, Eustacie assured herself) slipped across the road ahead of her. It began to seem a very long way to Hand Cross. A thorn-bush beside the road cast a shadow that was unpleasantly like that of a misshapen man. Eustacie's heart gave a sickening bump, and all at once she remembered the Headless Horseman, and for one dreadful moment felt positive that he was close behind her. Every horrid story she had heard of St. Leonard's Forest now came unbidden to her mind, and she discovered that she could even recall with painful accuracy the details of *A Discourse relating a strange and monstrous Serpent (or Dragon) lately discovered and yet living,* which she had found in a musty old volume in Sylvester's library.

Past Warninglid the country grew more open, but although it was a relief to get away from the trees Eustacie knew, because Sylvester had told her, that the Forest had once covered all this tract of ground, and she was therefore unable to place any reliance on the Headless Horseman keeping to the existing bounds. She began to imagine moving forms in the hedges, and when, about a mile beyond the Slaugham turning, her horse suddenly put forward his ears at a flutter of white seen fleetingly in the gloom of a thicket and shied violently across the road, she gave a sob of pure fright, and was nearly unseated. She pulled Rufus up, but his plunge had done all that was necessary to set the troublesome bandbox free. It slipped from the strap and went rolling away over the snow, and came to rest finally quite close to the thicket at the side of the road.

Eustacie, patting Rufus's neck with a hand which, though meant to convey reassurance, was actually trembling more than he was, looked after her property with dismay. She did not feel that she could abandon it (which she would have liked to have done), for in spite of being afraid of nothing, she was extremely loth to dismount and pick it up. She sat still for a few minutes, intently staring at the thicket. Rufus stared, too, with his head up and his ears forward. Nothing seemed to be stirring, however, and Eustacie, telling herself that the Headless Horseman was only a legend, and that the monstrous Serpent (or Dragon) had flourished nearly two hundred years ago and must surely be dead by now, gritted her teeth, and dismounted. She was disgusted to find that her knees were shaking, so to give herself more courage she pulled the duelling pistol out of the holster and grasped it firmly in her right hand.

Rufus, though suspicious of the thicket, allowed her to lead him up to the bandbox. She had just stooped to pick it up when the shrill neigh of a pony not five yards distant startled her almost out of her wits. She gave a scream of terror, saw something move in the shadow, and the next minute was struggling dementedly in the hold of a man who had seemed to pounce upon her from nowhere. She could not scream again because a hand was clamped over her mouth, and when she pulled the trigger of her pistol nothing happened. A sinewy arm was round her; she was half lifted, half dragged into the cover of the thicket; and heard a rough voice behind her growl: "Hit her over the head, blast the wench!"

Her terrified eyes, piercing the gloom, saw the dim outline of a face above her. Her captor said: "I'll be damned if I do!" in the unmistakable accents of a gentleman, and bent over her, and added softly: "I'm sorry, but you mustn't screech. If I take my hand away, will you be quiet—quite quiet?"

She nodded. At the first sound of his voice, which was oddly attractive, a large measure of her fright had left her. Now, as her eyes grew accustomed to the darkness, she saw that he was quite a young man, and, judging from the outline of his profile against the moonlit sky, a very personable young man.

The voice of the man behind her spoke again. "Adone do! She'll be the ruin o' we! Let me shut her mouth for her!"

Eustacie made a strangled sound in her throat and tried to bring her hands up to clutch at the young man's arm. The barrel of her pistol, which she was still clutching, gleamed in the moonlight, and caught the attention of her captor, who said under his breath: "If you let that pistol off I'll murder you! Ned, take the gun away from her!"

A heavy hand wrenched it out of her grasp; the rough voice said: "It ain't loaded. If you won't do more, tie her up with a gag in her mouth!"

"No, no, she's much too pretty," said the young man, taking the pistol and slipping it into the pocket of his frieze coat. "You won't squeak, will you, darling?"

As well as she could Eustacie shook her head. The hand left her mouth and patted her cheek. "Good girl! Don't be frightened: I swear I won't hurt you!"

Eustacie, who had been almost suffocated, gasped thankfully: "I thought you were the Headless Horseman!"

"You thought I was what?"

"The Headless Horseman."

He laughed. "Well, I'm not."

"No, I can see you are not. But why did you seize me like that? What are you doing here?"

"If it comes to that, what are *you* doing here?"

"I am going to London," replied Eustacie.

"Oh!" said the young man, rather doubtfully. "It's no concern of mine, of course, but it's a plaguey queer time to be going to London, isn't it?"

"No, because I am going to catch the night mail at Hand Cross. You must instantly let me go or I shall be too late."

The other man, who had been listening in scowling silence, muttered: "She'll have the pack of them down on us!"

"Be damned to you, don't croak so!" said the young man. "Tether that nag of hers!"

"If you let her go——"

"I'm not going to let her go. You keep a look-out for Abel, and stop spoiling sport!"

"But certainly you are going to let me go!" interposed Eustacie in an urgent undertone. "I must go!"

The young man said apologetically: "The devil's in it that I can't let you go. I would if I could, but to tell you the truth——"

"There's no call to do that!" growled his companion. "Dang me, master, if I don't think you're unaccountable crazed!"

Eustacie, who had had time by now to take stock of her surroundings, discovered that the darker shadows a little way off were not shadows at all, but ponies. There seemed to be about a dozen of them, and as she peered at them she was gradually able to descry what they were carrying. She had been living in Sussex for two years, and she was perfectly familiar with the appearance of a keg of brandy. She exclaimed: "You are smugglers, then!"

"Free-traders, my dear, free-traders!" replied the young man cheerfully. "At least, I am. Ned here is only what we call a land smuggler. You need not heed him."

Eustacie was so intrigued that for the moment she forgot all about the mail-coach. She had heard a great deal about smugglers, but although she knew that they were in general a desperate, cut-throat set of outlaws, she was so accustomed to her grandfather and most of his neighbours having dealings with them that she did not think their illicit trade in the least shocking. She said: "Well, you need not be afraid of me, I assure you. I do not at all mind that you are smug—free-traders."

"Are you French?" asked the young man.

"Yes. But tell me, why are you hiding here?"

"Excisemen," he replied. "They're on the watch. You know, the more I think of it the more it seems a very odd thing to me that you should be riding about by yourself in the middle of the night."

"I have told you: I am going to London."

"Well, it still seems very odd to me."

"Yes, but, you see, I am running away," explained Eustacie. "That is why I have to catch the night mail. I am going to London to be a governess."

She had the impression that he was laughing, but he said quite gravely: "You'll never do for a governess. You don't look like one. Besides, you're not old enough."

"Yes, I am, and I shall look just like a governess."

"You can't know anything about governesses if that's what you think."

"Well, I don't, but I thought it would be a very good thing to become."

"I dare say you know best, but to my mind you're making a mistake. From all I've heard, they have a devilish poor time of it."

"I wish I could be a smuggler," said Eustacie wistfully. "I think I should like that."

"You wouldn't do for a smuggler," he replied, shaking his head. "We don't encourage females in the trade. It's too dangerous."

"Well, I do not think it is fair that just because one is a female one should never be allowed to have any adventures!"

"You seem to me to be having a deal of adventure," he pointed out. "I might easily have choked the life out of you —in fact, I may still if you don't behave yourself. You're in a mighty tight corner."

"Yes, I know I am having an adventure now," agreed Eustacie, "and, of course, I am enjoying it, but I should like to continue having adventures, which is a thing not at all easy to arrange."

"No, I suppose it's not," said the free-trader thoughtfully.

"You see, if I were a man I could be a highwayman, or a smuggler like you. I expect you have had many, many adventures."

"I have," said the young man rather ruefully. "So many that I'm devilish tired of 'em."

"But I have had only this one small adventure and I am not yet tired. That is why I am going to London."

"If you take my advice," said the young man, "you'll give up this notion of being a governess. Try something else!"

"Well, perhaps I will be a milliner," said Eustacie. "When I get to London I shall consider carefully what is best for me to do."

"Yes, but you aren't going to London to-night," he said.

"I am going to-night! You do not understand! If I do not go to-night I shall be found, and then I shall have to go to Bath to play backgammon, and be married to a person without sensibility!"

He seemed to be much struck by this, and said seriously: "No, that would be too bad. We must think of something. You'll have to stay with me, at least till Abel reports all clear, of course, but there's bound to be a London coach through Hand Cross in the morning."

"And I tell you that in the morning it will be too late!" said Eustacie crossly. "I find that you are quite abominable! You spoil everything, and, what is more, I think you are excessively impertinent, because you have taken my horse away and stolen my pistol!"

"No, I haven't," he replied. "I've only had your horse tethered so that he can't stray. As for your pistol, you can have that back now if you wish," he added, diving his hand into his pocket and pulling out the weapon. "Though what in the world you want with an unloaded duelling pistol——" He stopped suddenly, feeling the balance of the gun, and stepped into the moonlight to examine it more closely. Eustacie saw that he was very tall and fair, dressed in a common frieze coat and breeches, with a coloured handkerchief round his neck, and his pale gold hair loosely tied back from his face. He looked up from the pistol in his hand, and said sharply: "How did you come by this?"

"Well, it is not precisely my own," said Eustacie. "It——"

"I know that. Who gave it to you?"

"Nobody gave it to me!"

"Do you mean you stole it?"

"Of course I did not steal it! I have just borrowed it because I thought it would be a good thing to take a pistol with me. *Du vrai,* it belongs to my cousin Ludovic, but I feel very certain that he would not mind lending it to me, because he is of all my family the most romantic."

The free-trader came back to her side in two quick strides. "Who the devil are you?" he demanded.

"I do not see what concern it is——"

He put his hands on her shoulders and shook her. "Never mind that! Who are you?"

"I am Eustacie de Vauban," she answered, with dignity.

"Eustacie de Vauban. . . . Oh yes, I have it! But how do you come to be in England?"

"Well, my grandpapa thought that they would send me to the guillotine if I stayed in France, so he fetched me away. But if I had known that he would make me marry my cousin Tristram, who is not amusing, I should have preferred infinitely to have gone to the guillotine."

"I don't blame you," he said. "Is he at the Court? If you're running away from him I'll do what I can to help you!"

"Do you know him, then?" asked Eustacie, surprised.

"Do I know him! I'm your romantic cousin Ludovic!"

She gave a small shriek, which had the effect of making him clap his hand over her mouth again. "Fiend seize you, don't make that noise! Do you want to bring the Excisemen down on me?"

She pulled his hand down and stood clasping it between both her own. "No, no, I promise I will be entirely quiet! I am so enchanted to meet you! I thought I never should, because Tristram said you could not set foot in England any more."

"I dare say he did," replied Ludovic. "But here I am for all that. You've only to breathe one word and I shall have Bow Street Runners as well as Excisemen on my trail."

She said fiercely: "I shall not breathe any word at all, and I think you are quite insulting to say that!"

He put his other hand over hers. "Did they tell you why I can't set foot in England?"

"Yes, but I do not care. Did you kill that person whose name I have forgotten?"

"No, I did not."

"*Bon!* Then we must at once discover who did do it," said Eustacie briskly. "I see now that this is a much better adventure than I thought."

"Do you believe me, then?" he asked.

"But certainly I believe you!"

He laughed, and pulling her to him, kissed her cheek. "Well, save for Basil, you're the only person who does."

"Yes," said Eustacie. "But me, I do not like Basil."

He was about to answer her when Ned Bundy loomed up through the darkness and twitched his sleeve. "Abel," he said laconically.

Eustacie heard the crunch of a pony's hooves on the snow and the next moment saw the pony, with a short, thick-set man sitting astride the pack-saddle. Ludovic took her hand and led her up to the newcomer. "Well?" he said.

"There's a dunnamany Excisemen out. We'll have to make back to Cowfold—if we can," said Mr. Bundy, dismounting. He became aware of Eustacie, and favoured her with a long, dispassionate look. "Where did that dentical wench come from?" he inquired.

"She's my cousin. Can't we win through to Hand Cross?"

Mr. Bundy accepted Eustacie's identity without comment and apparently without interest. "We'm not likely to win to Cowfold," he replied. "They're on to us."

At this gloomy pronouncement his brother Ned, pulling him a little apart, broke into urgent, low-voiced speech. Ludovic strode over to join in the discussion, and returned in a few minutes to Eustacie's side, saying briskly: "Well, I'm sorry for it, but I can't let you go to London to-night. You'll have to come with us."

"Oh, I would much rather come with you," Eustacie assured him. "Where are we going?"

"South," he replied briefly. "Those damned riding officers

must have got wind of this convoy. There may be some rough work done before the night's out, I warn you. Come along!"

He seized her by the wrist again and strode off with her to where her horse had been tethered, and without ceremony tossed her up into the saddle. Eustacie, seeing the two Bundys busy with the laden ponies, said emulatively: "Can I help to lead them, please?"

"No. Keep quiet."

"But what *can* I do?"

"Nothing."

Ned Bundy said something under his breath.

"I dare say, but I'm not going to have a cousin of mine hit over the head," said Ludovic. "Ready, Abel?"

A grunt answered him; the train began to move southward, Abel at its head. Ludovic mounted a rough pony and brought up the rear, still holding Eustacie's bridle. She took instant exception to this, and after a short but pungent argument he let her go free, much against the advice of Ned Bundy, who was ranging alongside the convoy, whipping up the stragglers.

Eustacie interrupted Mr. Bundy's muttered suggestions for the disposal of her person by announcing calmly that she was quite tired of him, a remark which surprised that ferocious gentleman so much that he could think of nothing to say, and retired towards the head of the train. "Why does he want to hit me on the head?" asked Eustacie, looking critically after him. "He seems to me entirely stupid."

"Well, he don't hold with women being mixed up in these affairs," explained Ludovic. "You're devilish in the way, you know."

"But you do not mind having me with you, do you?" asked Eustacie anxiously.

"Lord, no, I like it!" replied Ludovic light-heartedly. "Only you won't care for it if there's any shooting done."

"Yes, I shall," said Eustacie. "In fact, I wish very much that you will load my pistol for me and give it back to me, because if there is to be shooting I should like to shoot, too."

"It's not your pistol," retorted Ludovic. "It's mine, and let me tell you that I don't lend my duelling-pistols to anyone. Where is the other?"

"I left it in the case. I think you should be glad to lend it to me."

"Well, I'm not. Where did you get this notion I was romantic?"

"But you have had a very romantic life; of course, I knew you were romantic!"

"I've had a damned uncomfortable life. Tell me more about this marriage of yours. Why must you marry Tristram if you don't want to? Is it Sylvester's doing?"

"Yes, he made for me a *mariage de convenance*, but he is dead now, and I am going to arrange my own affairs."

"What! Is Sylvester dead?" exclaimed Ludovic.

"Yes, since three days. So now it is you who are Lord Lavenham."

"Much good will that do me!" said Ludovic. "Where's Basil?"

"He is at the Dower House, of course, and Tristram is at the Court."

"I must try to see Basil. Something will have to be done about the succession. *I* can't wear Sylvester's shoes."

"Well, I do not want him to wear them, and I think it would be better if you did not see him," said Eustacie.

"Oh, there's no harm in the Beau!" He broke off suddenly as the convoy halted, and grasped Rufus's bridle above the bit, pulling him to a standstill. "Quiet, now!" He sat still, intently listening. Eustacie, straining her ears, caught faintly the sound of horses' hooves in the distance. "Stay where you are!" ordered Ludovic, and went forward to the head of the train.

Eustacie, though she would have liked to have taken part in the council which was being held between the three men, thought it as well to obey. Her cousin Ludovic seemed to be of an autocratic disposition, reminding her strongly of his grandfather.

He came back to her side after a short colloquy with the Bundys and said in his quick, authoritative way: "We shall have to try and lead these damned Excisemen off the trail. I don't know what the devil to do with you, so you'd better come with me. After all, you wanted an adventure, and I can't let you jaunt about the countryside alone at this hour of night."

That a solitary journey to London might conceivably be attended by fewer dangers than a night spent hand-in-glove with a party of smugglers apparently did not occur to him. He dismounted from his pony, adding: "Besides, I want your horse."

"Am I to ride the pony, then?" asked Eustacie, willing but dubious.

"No, I'm going to take you up before me," he replied. "I

can look after you better that way. Moreover, the pony
couldn't keep up." He gave the animal to the elder Bundy's
care as he spoke, and said: "Good luck to you, Abel. Don't
trouble your head on my account!"

"You'd best be careful," said Mr. Bundy gloomily. "You
never had no sense and never will have."

Ludovic had got up behind Eustacie by this time, and settled her in the crook of his arm. "It beats me how you can
ride with a saddle like this," he remarked, wheeling Rufus
about. "And what in thunder is this thing?"

"It is a bandbox, of course!"

"Well, it's devilishly in the way," said Ludovic. "Do you
mind if I cut it loose?"

"No, certainly I do not mind. I, too, am quite tired of it,"
replied Eustacie blithely. "Besides, I have already lost the
other one."

The bandbox was soon got rid of. Eustacie watched it
bounce to the ground, and remarked with a giggle that if Tristram found it he would be sure to think she had been murdered.

Ludovic had urged Rufus to a canter. He seemed to Eustacie to be heading straight in the direction of the pursuing Excisemen. She pointed this out to him, and he replied: "Of
course I am. I told you I was going to lead them off the trail.
If I can get them to chase me Abel will have time to reach a
hiding-place he knows of. We'll lead them into the Forest."

"And when we have done that what shall we do?"

"Oh, give 'em the slip!" said Ludovic carelessly. "I shall
have to think what's to be done with you after that, but
there's no time to waste on that now." He reined in as he
spoke, and Eustacie saw that they had retraced their steps almost to the thicket where she had first encountered the train.
She could hear movement somewhere near at hand, and
the faint sound of voices. Ludovic rode softly forward, off
the road into the shelter of the trees. "I thought as much," he
said. "They're searching the thicket. Mustn't give 'em time to
find the pony-tracks. Now keep quiet, and hold on to that
pommel."

His gyrations after that were bewildering, but apparently
purposeful. It seemed to Eustacie, dutifully grasping the pommel, that they were circling round the thicket to the north.
She could now hear plainly the sound of trampling hooves
and snapping twigs.

"We must give the poor devils something to think about," said Ludovic in her ear. "Don't screech now!"

It was as well that he uttered this warning, for the immediate explosion of his pistol made Eustacie jump nearly out of her skin. She managed by the exercise of heroic self-control not to scream, but when a shot almost at once answered Ludovic's she could not forbear a gasp of fright.

"I thought that would tickle them up," said Ludovic. "Now for it!"

He wheeled the snorting, trembling Rufus, and let him have his head. Rufus plunged forward, crashing through the undergrowth with the maximum amount of noise and alarm; a shot sounded somewhere in the rear; another shot was fired; and Eustacie had the satisfaction of knowing that she was now fairly embroiled with His Majesty's Excise Office. She removed one hand from the pommel and took a firm grasp of Ludovic's coat, which seemed to her to afford a safer hold. He glanced down at her, smiling. "Frightened?"

"No!"

"Well, we're going to have a trifle of a gallop now, so cling tight!"

They came out from the cover of the trees as he spoke on to a tract of more open ground. The moon was momentarily obscured by a drifting cloud, but there was light enough for the flying horse to be seen by its pursuers. Two shots cracked almost simultaneously, and Eustacie felt the arm that cradled her give a queer jerk, and her cousin catch his breath sharply. "Winged, by Gad!" he said. "Now, who'd have thought an Exciseman could shoot as straight as that?"

"Are you hurt?" Eustacie cried.

"Devil a bit!" was the cheerful response. He looked fleetingly back over his shoulder. "Four of 'em, I think. Riding hard, too. You can always trust an Exciseman to follow his nose. . . . That's better."

They were under cover again, and he let Rufus slacken his pace to a trot, bending him easily this way and that through the outskirts of the Forest. Eustacie, after a very little of this erratic progress, began to feel quite lost, but it was evident that her cousin knew the Forest like the palm of his hand, for they steadily penetrated further into its darkness. Behind them the pursuit sounded as though it were in difficulties, but they had not yet outstripped it, and once Ludovic reined in altogether to give it time to come nearer, and, since it showed signs of abandoning the chase, fired his second pistol invitingly. This had the required effect; the Forest reverberated with shots, and they moved forward again, heading northward.

It was fully half an hour later before they finally lost the Excisemen, and Ludovic was swaying in the saddle.

"You *are* hurt!" Eustacie said, alarmed.

"Oh no, only a scratch!" he murmured. "Anyway, we've led them in such circles they'll be hunting one another till daylight."

Eustacie put her hands over his, and pulled Rufus up. "Where are you hurt?" she demanded.

"Left shoulder. I think we'd better take the risk and make Hand Cross."

"Yes, but first I will bind up your shoulder. Are you bleeding very much?"

"Like a pig," said Ludovic.

She slid to the ground, stiff and somewhat bruised, and said imperatively: "Get down! If you bleed like a pig you will die, and I do not at all want you to die."

He laughed, but dismounted, and found himself steadied by two small but capable hands. He reeled and sank on his knees, saying: "Damme, I must be worse hit than I knew! You'd best take the horse and leave me."

"I shall not leave you," replied Eustacie, busily ripping the flounce off her petticoat. "I shall take you to Hand Cross."

Receiving no answer, she looked closely at him and found to her dismay that he had fainted. For a moment she was at a loss to know what to do, but when she touched him and brought her hand away wet with blood, she decided that the most urgent need was to bind up his wound, and promptly set about the task of extricating him from his coat. It was by no means easy, but she accomplished it at last, and managed as well as she could for the lack of light to twist the strips of her petticoat round his shoulder. He regained consciousness while she was straining her bandage as tight as possible, and lay for a moment blinking at her.

"What in—oh, I remember!" he said faintly. "Give me some brandy. Flask in my coat."

She tied a firm knot, found the brandy, and, raising his head, held the flask to his lips. He recovered sufficiently to struggle up and to put on his coat again. "You know, you'd be wasted on Tristram," he told her. "Help me into the saddle, and we'll make Hand Cross yet."

"Yes, but this time it is I who will take the reins," said Eustacie.

"Just as you say, my dear," he replied meekly.

"And you will put your arms round me and not fall off."

"Don't worry, I shan't fall off."

Eustacie, finding a conveniently fallen tree-trunk, led her weary horse to it, and by using it as a mounting-block contrived to get into the saddle. She then rode back to Ludovic, and adjured him to mount behind her. He managed to do this, but the effort very nearly brought on another swooning fit. He had recourse to the brandy again, which cleared his head sufficiently to enable him to say: "Follow this track; it'll bring us out on to the pike-road, north of Hand Cross. If you can wake old Nye at the Red Lion he'll take me in."

"What shall I do if I see an Exciseman?" inquired Eustacie.

"Say your prayers," he replied irrepressibly.

No Exciseman, however, was encountered on the track that led through the Forest, and by the time they came out on to the turnpike road, a mile from Hand Cross, Eustacie was far too anxious about her cousin to have much thought to spare for a questing Excise-officer. Ludovic seemed to stay in the saddle more by instinct than by any conscious effort. Eustacie dared not urge Rufus even to a trot. She had drawn Ludovic's sound arm round her waist, and held it there, clasping his slack hand. It seemed an interminable way to Hand Cross, but at last the lonely inn came into sight, a dark huddle against the sky. It was by now long after midnight, and no light shone behind the shuttered windows. Eustacie pulled Rufus up before the door and let go of Ludovic's hand. It fell nervelessly to his side; she realized that he must have swooned again; he was certainly sagging against her very heavily; she hoped he would not fall out of the saddle when she dismounted. She slid down, and was relieved to find that he only fell forward across Rufus's neck. The next moment she had grasped the bell-pull and sent an agitated peal ringing through the silent inn.

It was answered so speedily that Eustacie, who had heard rumours that Joseph Nye, of the Red Lion, knew more about the free-traders than he would admit, instantly suspected that he had been waiting up for the very convoy she had met. He opened the door in person, fully dressed, and holding a lantern, and looking a good deal startled. When he saw Eustacie he stared as though he could not believe his eyes, and gasped: "Miss! Why, *miss!*"

Eustacie grasped his arm urgently. "Please help me at once! I have brought my cousin Ludovic, and he said you would take him in but he is wounded, and I think dying!" With which, because she had been through a great deal of excitement and was quite worn out by it, she burst into tears.

Chapter IV

THE landlord took an involuntary step backwards. "Miss, have you gone mad?"

"No!" sobbed Eustacie.

He looked incredulously out into the moonlight, but when he saw the sagging figure on Rufus's back he gave an exclamation of horror, thrust his lantern into Eustacie's hand, and strode out. He was a big man, with mighty muscles, and he lifted Ludovic down from the saddle with surprising ease, and carried him into the inn, and lowered him on to a wooden settle by the fireplace. "My God, what's come to him? What's he doing here?" he demanded under his breath.

"An Exciseman shot him. Oh, do you think he will die?"

"Die! No! But if he's found here——!" He broke off. "I must get that horse stabled and out of sight. Stay you here, miss, and don't touch him! Lordy, lordy, this is a pretty kettle of fish!" He took a taper from the high mantelpiece, kindled it at the lantern's flame, and gave it to Eustacie. "Do you light them candles, miss, and keep as quiet as you can! I've people putting up in the house." He took up the lantern as he spoke and went out of the inn, softly closing the door behind him.

A branch of half-burned candles was standing on the table. Eustacie lit them, and turned to look fearfully down at her cousin.

He was lying with one arm hanging over the edge of the settle, and his face alarmingly pale. Not knowing what to do for him, she sank down on her knees beside him and lifted his dangling hand, and held it between her own. For the first time she was able to see him clearly; she thought that had she met him in daylight she must have known him for a Lavenham, for here was Sylvester's hawk-nose and humorous mouth, softened indeed by youth but unmistakable. He was lean and long-limbed, taller than Sylvester had been, but with the same slender hands and arched feet, and the same cleft in his wilful chin.

He seemed to Eustacie scarcely to breathe; she laid his arm across his chest and loosened the handkerchief about his neck. "Oh, please, Cousin Ludovic, don't die!" she begged.

She heard a slight movement on the stairs behind her, and, turning her head, beheld a tall woman in a dressing-gown standing on the top step with a candle in her hand, looking down at her. She sprang up and stood as though defending the unconscious Ludovic, staring up at the new-comer in a challenging way.

The lady with the candle said with a twinkle in her grey eyes: "Don't be alarmed! I'm no ghost, I assure you. You woke me with your ring at the bell, and because I'm of a prying disposition, I got up to see what in the world was going forward." She came down the stairs as she spoke, and saw Ludovic. Her eyebrows went up, but she said placidly: "I see I've thrust myself into an adventure. Is he badly hurt?"

"I think he's dying," answered Eustacie tragically. "He has bled, and bled, and bled!"

The lady put down her candle and came to the settle. "That sounds very bad, certainly, but perhaps it is not desperate after all," she said. "Shall we see where he is hurt?"

"Nye said I was not to touch him," replied Eustacie doubtfully.

"Oh, he's a friend of Nye's, is he?" said the lady.

"No—at least, yes, in a way he is. He is my cousin, but you must not ask me anything about him, and you must not tell anyone that you have ever seen him!"

"Very well, I won't," said the lady imperturbably.

At that moment the landlord came into the coffee-room from the back of the house, followed by a little man with a wizened, leathery face and thin legs. When he saw the tall woman, Nye looked very much discomfited, and said in his deep, rough voice: "I beg your pardon, ma'am: you've been disturbed. It's nothing—naught but a lad I know who's been getting into trouble through a bit of poaching."

"Of course, he would be poaching in the middle of February," agreed the lady. "You had better get him to bed and take a look at his hurt."

"It's what I'm going to do, ma'am," returned Nye in a grim voice. "Take his legs, Clem!"

Eustacie watched the two men carefully lift her cousin from the settle and begin to carry him upstairs, and turned her attention to the tall woman, who was rewarding her with a kind of amused interest. "I dare say it seems very odd to you," she said austerely, "but you should not have come downstairs."

"I know," apologized the lady, "but pray don't tell me to go to bed again, for I couldn't sleep a wink with an adventure going on under my very nose! Let me present myself to you: I'm one Sarah Thane, a creature of no importance at all, travelling to London with my brother, whom you may hear snoring upstairs."

"Oh!" said Eustacie. "Of course, if you quite understand that this is a very secret affair——"

"Oh, I do!" said Miss Thane earnestly.

"But I must warn you that there is a great deal of danger."

"Nothing could be better!" declared Miss Thane. "You must know that I have hitherto led the most humdrum existence."

"Do you, too, like adventure?" asked Eustacie, looking her over with a more lenient eye.

"My dear ma'am, I have been looking for adventure all my life!"

"Well," said Eustacie darkly, "this is an adventure of the most romantic, and it is certain that my cousin Tris—— that people will come to search for me. You must promise not to betray me, and in particular not my cousin Ludovic, who is not permitted to set foot in England, you understand."

"No power on earth shall ring a syllable from me," Miss Thane assured her.

"Then perhaps I will let you help me to conceal my cousin Ludovic," said Eustacie handsomely. "Only I think it will be better if I do not tell you anything at all until I have spoken with him, because I do not know him very well, and perhaps he would prefer that you should know nothing."

"Oh no, don't tell me anything!" said Miss Thane. "I feel it would almost spoil it for me if you explained it. You're not eloping with your cousin, by any chance?"

"But, of course, I am not eloping with him! *Voyons,* how could I elope with him when I have only just met him? It would be quite absurd!"

"Oh, if you have only just met him, I suppose it would," agreed Miss Thane regretfully. "It is a pity, for I have often thought that I should like to assist an elopement. However, one can't have everything. You know, I feel very strongly that we ought to see what can be done for that wound of his. Not that I wish to interfere, of course."

"You are entirely right," said Eustacie. "I shall immediately go up to him. You may come with me if you like."

"Thank you," said Miss Thane meekly.

Joseph Nye had carried Ludovic to a little bedchamber at the back of the house and laid him upon his side on the chintz-hung bed. The tapster was kindling a fire in the grate, and Nye had just taken off Ludovic's coat and laid bare his shoulder when the two women came into the room.

Eustacie shuddered at the sight of the ugly wound, still sluggishly bleeding, but Miss Thane went up to the bed and watched what Nye was about. In spite of their size, his hands were deft enough. Miss Thane nodded, as though satisfied, and said: "Can you get the bullet out, do you think?"

"Ay, but I'll want water and bandages. Clem! leave that and fetch me a bowl and all the linen you can find!"

"You had better bring some brandy as well," added Miss Thane, taking the bellows out of the tapster's hands and beginning to ply them.

Eustacie, standing at the foot of the bed, watched Nye draw from his pocket a clasp-knife and open it, and somewhat hastily quitted her post. "I think," she said in a rather faint voice, "that it will be better if it is I who attend to the fire, mademoiselle, and you who assist Nye. It is not that I do not like blood," she explained, "but I find that I do not wish to watch him dig bullets out of my cousin Ludovic."

Miss Thane at once surrendered the bellows into her charge, saying that such scruples were readily understandable. Clem came back in a few minutes with a bowl and a quantity of old linen, and for quite some time Eustacie kept her attention strictly confined to the fire.

Miss Thane, finding that the landlord knew what he was about, silently did what he told her, offering no criticism. Only when he had extracted the bullet and was bathing the wound did she venture to inquire in a low voice whether he thought any vital spot had been touched. Nye shook his head.

"I'll get some Basilicum Powder," said Miss Thane, and went softly away to her own room.

By the time the powder had been applied and the shoulder bandaged, Ludovic was showing signs of recovering consciousness. Miss Thane's hartshorn held under his nose made his eyelids flutter, and a little neat brandy administered by Nye brought him fully to his senses. He opened a pair of dazed blue eyes, and blinked uncomprehendingly at the landlord.

"Eh, Mr. Ludovic, that's better!" Nye said.

Ludovic's gaze wandered past him to Miss Thane, dwelt on her for a frowning moment, and returned to the contemplation of Nye's square countenance. A look of recognition dawned. "Joe?" said Ludovic in a faint, puzzled voice.

"Ay, it's Joe, sir. Do you take it easy, now!"

Remembrance came back to Ludovic. He struggled up on his sound elbow. "Damn that Exciseman! The child—a cousin of mine—where is she?"

Eustacie at the first sound of his voice had dropped the bellows and flown to the bedside. "I'm here, *mon cousin!*" she said, dropping on her knees beside him.

He put out his sound hand and took her chin in it, turning her face up that he might scrutinize it. "I've been wanting to look at you, my little cousin," he said. A smile hovered round his mouth. "I thought as much! You're as pretty as any picture." He saw a tear sparkling on her cheek, and said at once: "What are you crying for? Don't you like your romantic cousin Ludovic?"

"Oh yes, but I thought you were going to die!"

"Lord, no!" he said cheerfully. He let Nye put him back on to the pillows, and drew Eustacie's hand to his lips, and kissed it. "You must promise me you'll not go further with this trip of yours to London. It won't do."

"Oh no, of course I shall not! I shall stay with you."

"Egad, I wish you could!" he said.

"But certainly I can. Why should I not?"

"*Les convenances,*" murmured Ludovic.

"Ah bah, I do not regard them! When one is engaged upon an adventure it is not the time to be thinking of such things. Besides, if I do not stay with you, I shall have to marry Tristram, because I have lost both my bandboxes, which makes it impossible that I should any longer go to London."

"Oh well, you can't marry Tristram, that's certain!" said Ludovic, apparently impressed by this reasoning.

Nye interposed at this point. "Mr. Ludovic, what be you doing here?" he demanded. "Have you gone crazy to come into the Weald? Who shot you?"

"Some damned Exciseman. We landed a cargo of brandy and rum two nights ago, and I'd a fancy to learn what's been going forward here. I came up with Abel."

Nye laid a quick hand across his lips and glanced warningly in Miss Thane's direction.

"You needn't regard me," she said encouragingly. "I am pledged to secrecy."

Ludovic turned his head to look at her. "I beg pardon, but who in thunder are you?" he said.

"It's Miss Thane, sir, who's putting up in the house."

"Yes," interrupted Eustacie, "and I think she is truly very sensible, *mon cousin*, and she would like infinitely to help us."

"But we don't want any help!"

"Certainly we want help, because Tristram will search for me, and perhaps the Exciseman for you, and you must be hidden."

"And that's true, too," muttered Nye. "You'll stay where you are to-night, sir, but it ain't safe for longer. I'll have you where you can slip into the cellar if the alarm's raised."

"I'll be damned if I'll be put in any cellar!" said Ludovic. "I'll be off as soon as I can stand on my feet."

"No, you will not," said Eustacie. "I have quite decided that you must stop being a free-trader and become instead Lord Lavenham."

"That seems to me a most excellent idea," remarked Miss Thane. "I suppose it will be quite easy?"

"If Sylvester's dead, I am Lord Lavenham, but it don't help me. I can't stay in England."

"But we are going to discover who it was who killed that man whose name I cannot remember," explained Eustacie.

"Oh, are we?" said Ludovic. "I'm agreeable, but how are we going to set about it?"

"Well, I do not know yet, but we shall arrange a plan, and I think perhaps Miss Thane might be very useful, because she seems to me to be a person of large ideas, and when it is shown to her that she holds your life in her hands, she will be interested, and wish to assist us."

"Do I really hold his life in my hands?" inquired Miss Thane. "If that's so, of course I'm much interested. I will certainly assist you. In fact, I wouldn't be left out of this for the world."

Ludovic moved on his pillows, and said with a grimace of pain: "You seem to know so much, ma'am, that you may as well know also that I am wanted by the Law for murder!"

"Are you?" said Miss Thane, gently removing one of the pillows. "How shocking! Do you think you could get a little sleep if we left you?"

He looked up into her face and gave a weak laugh. "Ma'am, take care of my cousin for me till morning, and I shall be very much in your debt."

"Why, certainly!" said Miss Thane in her placid way.

Ten minutes later Eustacie was ensconced in a chair by the fire in Miss Thane's bedchamber, gratefully sipping a cup of hot milk. Miss Thane sat down beside her, and said with her friendly smile: "I hope you mean to tell me all about it, for I'm dying of curiosity, and I don't even know your name."

Eustacie considered her for a moment. "Well, I think I will tell you," she decided. "I am Eustacie de Vauban, and my cousin Ludovic is Lord Lavenham of Lavenham Court. He is the tenth Baron."

Miss Thane shook her head. "It just shows how easily one may be mistaken," she said. "I thought he was a smuggler."

"He prefers," said Eustacie, with dignity, "that one should call him a free-trader."

"I'm sorry," apologized Miss Thane. "Of course, it is a much better title. I should have known. What made him take to s—— free trading? It seems a trifle unusual."

"I see that I must explain to you the talisman ring," said Eustacie, and drew a deep breath.

Miss Thane, a sympathetic listener, followed the story of the talisman ring with keen interest, only interpolating a question when the tale became too involved to be intelligible. She accepted Ludovic's innocence without the smallest hesitation, and said at the 'end of the recital that nothing would give her greater pleasure than to assist in unmasking the real culprit.

"Yes," said Eustacie, "and me, I think that it was perhaps my cousin Tristram, for he has a collection of jewellery, and, besides, he is a person who might murder people—except that he is not at all romantic," she added.

"He sounds very disagreeable," said Miss Thane.

"He is—very! And, do you know, I have suddenly thought that perhaps I had better marry him, because then he would have to show me his collection, and if I found the talisman ring it would make everything right for Ludovic."

Miss Thane bent down to poke the fire. She said with a slight tremor in her voice: "But then if you did not find the ring it would be tiresome to have married him all to no purpose. And one has to consider that he might not wish to marry you."

"Oh, but he does!" said Eustacie. "In fact, we are betrothed. That is why I have run away. He has no conversation. Moreover, he said that if I went to London, I should not find myself in any way remarkable."

"He was wrong," said Miss Thane with conviction.

"Yes, I think he was wrong, but you see he is not *sympathique,* and he does not like women."

Miss Thane blinked at her. "Are you sure?" she said. "I mean, if he wants to marry you——"

"But he does not *want* to marry me! It is just that he must have an heir, and because Grandpère made for us a *mariage de convenance.* Only Grandpère is dead now, and I am not going to marry a person who says that he would not care if I went to the guillotine in a tumbril!"

"Did he really say that?" inquired Miss Thane. "He must be a positive Monster!"

"Well, no, he did not say exactly that," admitted Eustacie. "But when I asked him if he would not be sorry to see me, a *jeune fille,* in a tumbril, and dressed all in white, he said he would be sorry for anyone in a tumbril, 'whatever their age or sex—or apparel'!"

"You need say no more; I can see that he is a person of no sensibility," said Miss Thane. "I am not surprised that you ran away from him to join your cousin Ludovic."

"Oh, I didn't!" replied Eustacie. "I mean, I never knew I was going to meet Ludovic. I ran away to become a governess."

"Forgive me," said Miss Thane, "but have you then just met your cousin Ludovic by chance, and for the first time?"

"But yes, I have told you! And he said I should not do for a governess." She sighed. "I wish I could think of something to be which is exciting! If only I were a man!"

"Yes," agreed Miss Thane. "I feel very strongly that you should have been a man and gone smuggling with your cousin."

Eustacie threw her a glowing look. "That is just what I should have liked! But Ludovic says they never take females with them."

"How wretchedly selfish!" said Miss Thane in accents of disgust.

"Yes, but I think it is not perhaps entirely Ludovic's fault, for he said he liked to have me with him. But the others did not like it at all, in particular Ned, who wanted to hit me on the head."

"Is Ned a s—— free-trader too?"

"Yes, and Abel. But they are not precisely free-traders, but only land-smugglers, which is, I think, a thing inferior."

"It sounds quite inferior," said Miss Thane. "Did you meet your cousin Ludovic, and Ned, and Abel on your way here?"

"Yes, and when he seized me of course I thought Ludovic was the Headless Horseman!"

Miss Thane was regarding her as one entranced. "Of course!" she echoed. "I suppose you were expecting to meet a headless horseman?"

"Well," replied Eustacie judicially, "my maid told me that he rides the Forest, and that one finds him upon the crupper behind one, but my cousin Tristram said that it was only a legend."

"The more I hear about your cousin Tristram," said Miss Thane, "the more I am convinced he is not at all the husband for you."

"No, and what is more he is thirty-one years old, and he does not frequent gaming-hells or cock-pits, and when I asked him if he would ride *ventre à terre* to come to my deathbed, he said 'Certainly not'!"

"This is more shocking than all the rest!" declared Miss Thane. "He must be quite heartless!"

"Yes," said Eustacie bitterly. "He says I am not in the least likely to die."

"A man like that," pronounced Miss Thane, "would be bound to say the Headless Horseman was only a legend."

"That is what I thought, but my cousin Ludovic was not after all the Headless Horseman, and I must admit that I have not yet seen him—or the Dragon which was once in the Forest."

"Really, you have had a very dull ride when one comes to think of it."

"Yes, until I met my cousin Ludovic, and after that it was not dull, because when he discovered who I was Ludovic said I must go with him, and I helped to lead the Excisemen into the Forest. He mounted behind me on Rufus, you see. That was when I lost the other bandbox."

"Oh, you had a bandbox?"

"But yes, I had two, for one must be practical, you understand. But one I dropped just before I met Ludovic, and I forgot about that one. We threw the other away."

Miss Thane bent over the fire again rather hastily. "I expect it was the right thing to do," she said in an unsteady voice.

"Well, it was in the way," explained Eustacie. "But I must say it now becomes awkward a little because all my things were in it."

"Don't let a miserable circumstance like that worry you!" said Miss Thane. "I will lend you a nightdress, and to-morrow we will decide whether to go and look for the bandboxes (though I feel that would be a spiritless thing to do) or whether to break into your home at dead of night and steal some more clothes for you."

This suggestion appealed instantly to Eustacie. While she got ready for bed she discussed with Miss Thane the various ways in which it might be possible to break into the Court. Miss Thane entered into every plan with an enthusiasm which made Eustacie say as she blew out the candle: "I am *very* glad I have met you. I shall tell my cousin Ludovic that he must permit you to share the adventure."

The excitements of the night had quite worn her out, and it was not long before she fell asleep, curled up beside Miss Thane in the big four-poster.

Sarah Thane lay awake for some little time. It seemed to her that she had undertaken a responsibility that would keep her well occupied during the immediate future. What would be the outcome of it all she had not the smallest idea, but she was fully determined, being entered into the adventure, to remain in it to the finish.

She was twenty-eight years old, an orphan, and for the past ten years had been living with her brother, an easy-going baronet some six or seven years her senior. Having been left in his ward, she considered, upon leaving school, that her proper place was at his side. Sir Hugh had not the least objection, so in defiance of several female relatives who one and all expressed the most complete disapproval she assumed control of the old manor-house in Gloucestershire, and when Sir Hugh took it into his head to travel (which was often) packed her trunks and went with him. For the first few years she had consented to take an elderly cousin with her as chaperon; the elderly cousin was indeed still nominally her chaperon, but she had long since ceased to accompany Sir Hugh and his sister upon their erratic journeys. For no one could deny that Sarah Thane was very well able to take care of herself, and the elderly cousin had not in the least enjoyed wandering about Europe in the wake of Sir Hugh's vague fancy. Sarah, on the other hand, enjoyed it so much that she had never yet been tempted to exchange the companionship of a brother for that of a husband.

She and Sir Hugh were, at the moment, on their way to town, having been visiting friends in the neighbourhood of Brighton. They had spent a dull fortnight, and were now intending to spend two or three months in London. Their presence at the Red Lion was attributable to two causes, the first being an incipient cold in Sir Hugh's head, and the second the excellence of Mr. Nye's brandy. Their original intention had been to stop only for a change of horses, but by the time they had arrived at Hand Cross it had begun to snow, and Sir Hugh had sneezed twice. While the horses were being taken out of the shafts, Sir Hugh, regarding the weather with a jaundiced eye, had let down the chaise-window to call for some brandy. It had been brought to him; he had taken one sip, and announced his intention of putting up at the Red Lion for the night.

"Just as you wish," had said Miss Thane, most admirable of sisters. "But I don't fancy the snow will amount to much."

"Snow?" said Sir Hugh. "Oh, the *snow!* I believe I'm going to have a demmed bad cold, Sally."

"Then we had better push on to London," said Miss Thane.

"This brandy," said Sir Hugh earnestly, "is some of the best I've tasted."

"Oh!" said Miss Thane, instantly comprehending the situation, "I see!"

That the excellence of the brandy was not a matter of interest to her was an objection she did not dream of putting forward. She was far too well used to Sir Hugh's vagaries not to accept them with equanimity, and she had followed him into the inn, resigning herself to a spell of inaction.

From this she seemed to have been miraculously saved. Sir Hugh might not know it, but there was now small chance of his journey being resumed upon the morrow. His sister had stumbled upon an adventure which appealed forcibly to her ever-lively sense of humour, and she had no intention of abandoning it.

In the morning she awoke before Eustacie, and got up out of bed without disturbing her. As soon as she was dressed she went along the passage to her brother's room, and found him sitting up in bed, with his night-cap still on, being waited on by the tapster, who seemed to combine his calling with the duties of a general factotum. A tray piled high with dishes was placed on a table by the bed: Sir Hugh was breakfasting.

He gave his sister a sleepy smile as she entered the room, and, of habit rather than of necessity, picked up his quizzing-glass, and through it inspected a plate of grilled ham and eggs from which Clem had lifted the cover. He nodded, and Clem heaved a sigh of relief.

Miss Thane, taking in at a glance the proportions of this breakfast, shook her head, and said: "My dear, you must be very unwell indeed! Only one plate of ham, and those few wretched slices of beef to follow! How paltry!"

Sir Hugh, accustomed like so many large men to being a butt, received this sally with unruffled placidity, and waved Clem away. The tapster went out, and Miss Thane thoughtfully handed her brother the mustard. "What are your engagements in town, Hugo?"

Sir Hugh reflected while masticating a mouthful of ham. "Have I any?" he asked after a pause.

"I don't know. Should you mind remaining here for a time?"

"Not while the Chambertin lasts," replied Sir Hugh simply. He consumed another mouthful, and added: "It's my belief the liquor in this place never paid duty at any port."

"No, I think it was probably all smuggled," agreed Miss Thane. "I met a smuggler last night, when you had gone to bed."

"Oh, did you?" Sir Hugh washed down the ham with a draught of ale, and emerged from the tankard to say, as a thought occurred to him: "You ought to be more careful. Where did you meet him?"

"He arrived at the inn, very late, and wounded. He's here now."

A faint interest gleamed in Sir Hugh's eye. He lowered his fork. "Did he bring anything with him?"

"Yes, a lady," said Miss Thane.

"No sense in that," said Sir Hugh, his interest fading. He went on eating, but added in a moment: "Couldn't have been a smuggler."

"He is a smuggler, a nobleman, and one of the most handsome young men I have ever clapped eyes on," said Miss Thane. "Tell me now, did you ever hear of one Ludovic Lavenham?"

"No," said Sir Hugh, exchanging his empty plate for one covered with slices of cold beef.

"Are you sure, Hugo? He was used to play cards at the Cocoa-Tree—rather a wild youth, I apprehend."

"They fuzz the cards at the Cocoa-Tree," said Sir Hugh. "It's full of Greeks. Foulest play in town."

"This boy lost a valuable ring at play there, and was afterwards accused of having shot the man he played against," persisted Miss Thane.

"I was very nearly done-up myself there once," said Sir Hugh reminiscently. "Found a regular Captain Sharp at the table, thought the dice ran devilish queerly——"

"Yes, dear, but do you remember?"

"Of course I remember. Sent for a hammer, split the dice, and found they were up-hills, just as I'd expected."

"No, not that," said Miss Thane patiently. "Do you recall this other affair?"

"What other affair?"

Miss Thane sighed, and began painstakingly to recount all that Eustacie had told her. Sir Hugh listened to her with an expression of considerable bewilderment, and at the end shook his head. "It sounds a demmed silly story to me," he said. "You shouldn't talk to strangers."

When it was conveyed to him that his sister had pledged herself to assist these strangers in whatever perilous course they might decide to adopt he at first protested as forcibly as a man of his natural indolence could be expected to, and finally begged her not to embroil him in any crazy adventure.

"I won't," promised Miss Thane. "But you must swear an oath of secrecy, Hugh!"

Sir Hugh laid down his knife and fork. "Sally, what the deuce is all this about?" he demanded.

She laughed. "My dear, I've scarcely any more notion than you have. But I am quite sure of my clear duty, which is to chaperon the little heroine. Moreover, I admit to a slight feeling of curiosity to see the wicked cousin. I am at present at a loss to decide whether Sir Tristram Shield is the villain of the piece or merely a plain man goaded to madness."

"Shield?" repeated Sir Hugh. "Member of Brooks's?"

"I don't know. Do you?"

"If he's the man I'm thinking of he hunts with the Quorn. Bruising rider to hounds. Good man in a turn-up, too."

"This sounds very promising," said Miss Thane.

"Spars with Mendoza," pursued Sir Hugh. "If he's the man, I've met him at Mendoza's place. But I dare say I'm thinking of someone else."

"What is he like?" inquired Miss Thane.

"I've told you," said Sir Hugh, buttering a slice of bread. "He's got a right," he added helpfully.

Miss Thane gave it up, and went back to her own bed-chamber to see how her protégée did.

Eustacie, not a whit the worse for her adventure, was trying to arrange her hair before the mirror. As she had never attempted anything of the kind before the result was not entirely successful. Miss Thane laughed at her, and took the brush and the pins out of her hand. "Let me do it for you," she said. "How do you feel this morning?"

Eustacie announced buoyantly that she had never felt better. Her first and most pressing desire was to see how her cousin did, so as soon as Miss Thane had finished dressing her hair they went off to the little back bedchamber.

Nye was with Ludovic, apparently trying to induce him to descend into the cellar. Ludovic, whose eyes were a trifle too bright and whose cheeks were rather flushed, was sitting up in bed with a bowl of thin gruel. As the two ladies came into the room he was saying carelessly: "Don't croak so, Joe! I tell you I have it all fixed." He looked up and greeted his visitors with a smile of pure mischief. "Good morning, my cousin! Ma'am, your very obedient! Have you seen any Excisemen below-stairs yet?"

"Mr. Ludovic, I tell you your tracks lead right to my door, and there's blood on the snow!"

"You've told me that twice already," said Ludovic, quite unmoved. "Why don't you send Clem to clear the snow away?"

"I have sent him to clear it away, sir, but don't you realize they'll be able to trace you all the way from the Forest?"

"Of course I realize it! Haven't I made my plans? Eustacie, my sweet cousin, will you have me for your groom?"

"But yes, I will have you for anything you wish!" said Eustacie instantly.

His eyes danced. "Will you so? Begad, if I can settle my affairs creditably I'll remind you of that!"

"Sir, will you listen to reason?" implored Nye.

An imperious finger admonished him. "Quiet you! I'll thank you to remember I'm in the saddle now, Joe."

"Are you indeed, Mr. Ludovic? Well, I'll do no pillion-riding behind you, for well I know what will come of it!"

"Take away this gruel!" commanded Ludovic. "And get it into your head that I'm not Mr. Ludovic! I'm mademoiselle's groom, whom the wicked smugglers fired at." He cocked his head, considering. "I think I'll be called Jem," he decided. "Jem Brown."

"No!" said Eustacie, revolted. "It is a name of the most undistinguished."

"Well, grooms aren't distinguished. I think it's a good name."

"It is not. It will be better if you are Humphrey."

"No, I'll be damned if I'll be called Humphrey! If there's one name I dislike that's it."

Miss Thane interposed placably. "Don't argue with him, Eustacie. It's my belief he's in a high fever."

He grinned at her. "I am," he agreed. "But my head's remarkably clear for all that."

"Well, if it's clear enough to grapple with the details of this story of yours, tell us what became of the groom's horse," said Miss Thane.

"The smugglers killed it," offered Eustacie.

Ludovic shook his head. "No, that won't do. No corpse. Damn the horse, it's a nuisance! Oh, I have it! When I was shot the brute threw me, and made off home."

"Maddened by fright," nodded Miss Thane. "Well, I'm glad to have that point settled. I feel I can now face any number of Excisemen."

"Mon cousin," interrupted Eustacie suddenly, "do you think it is Tristram who has your ring?"

The laugh vanished from Ludovic's eyes. "I'd give something to know!"

"Well, but I must tell you that I thought of a very good plan last night," said Eustacie. "I will marry Tristram, and then I can search in his collection for the ring."

"You'll do no such thing!" snapped Ludovic.

Nye said roughly: "For shame, Mr. Ludovic! What's this unaccountable nonsense? Sir Tristram's no enemy of yours!"

"Is he not?" retorted Ludovic. "Will you tell me who, besides myself, was in the Longshaw Spinney that accursed night?"

Nye's face darkened. "Are you saying it was Sir Tristram as did a foul murder all for the sake of a trumpery ring, my lord? Eh, you're crazed!"

"I'm saying it was he who met me in the spinney, he who would have given his whole collection for that same trumpery ring! Didn't he always dislike me? Can you say he did not?"

"What I wish to say," interrupted Miss Thane in a calm voice, "is that I want my breakfast."

Ludovic sank back on to his pillows with a short laugh. Nye, reminded of his duty, at once led both ladies down to the parlour, apologizing as he went for there being no one but himself and Clem to wait upon them. "I've only my sister besides, who does the cooking," he told them, "and a couple of ostlers, of course. We don't get folk stopping here in the winter in the general way. Maybe it's as well, seeing who's under my roof, but I doubt it's not what you're accustomed to, ma'am."

Miss Thane reassured him. He set a coffee-pot down on the table before her, and said gloomily: "It's in my mind that no one in his senses would take Mr. Ludovic for a groom, ma'am. If you could get him only to see reason——! But there, he never did, and I doubt he never will! As to this notion he's taken into his head that 'tis Sir Tristram who has his ring, I never heard the like of it! It was Sir Tristram as got him out of England—ay, and in the very nick!"

"Yes, and my cousin Basil says that it was to make him a murderer confessed!" said Eustacie.

Nye looked at her from under his rugged brows. "Ay, does he so? Well, I've not had the gloves on with Mr. Lavenham, miss, but I've sparred with Sir Tristram a-many times, and I say he's a clean-hitting gentleman! With your leave, ma'am, I'll go back to Mr. Ludovic now."

He went out, and Miss Thane, pouring out two cups of coffee, said cheerfully: "At all events there seems to be some doubt about Sir Tristram's guilt. I think, if I were you, I would not marry him until we can be positive he is the murderer."

Upon reflection Eustacie agreed to the wisdom of this course. She ate a hearty breakfast, and returned to Ludovic's room, leaving Miss Thane in sole possession of the parlour. Miss Thane finished her meal in a leisurely fashion, and had gone out into the coffee-room, on her way to the stairs, when the sound of an arrival made her pause. An authoritative, not to say peremptory voice outside called the landlord by name, and the next moment the door was flung open and a tall gentleman in riding-dress strode in, carrying a somewhat battered bandbox in either hand. He checked at sight of Miss Thane, favouring her with a hard stare, and putting down the bandboxes, took off his hat, and bowed slightly. "I beg your pardon: do you know where I may find the landlord?" he asked.

Miss Thane, one hand on the banisters, one foot on the bottom stair, looked at him keenly. A pair of stern, rather frowning grey eyes met hers with an expression of the most complete indifference. Miss Thane let go of the banisters, and came forward. "Do tell me!" she said invitingly. "Are you 'my cousin Tristram'?"

Chapter V

SIR TRISTRAM'S worried frown lightened. He stared at Miss Thane with an arrested look in his eyes, and his stern mouth relaxed a little. "Oh!" he said slowly, and seemed for the first time to take stock of Sarah Thane. He saw before him a tall, graceful woman, with a quantity of light, curling brown hair, a generous mouth, and a pair of steady grey eyes which held a distinct twinkle. He noticed that she was dressed fashionably but without furbelows in a caraco jacket over a plain blue gown, a habit as nearly resembling a man's riding-dress as was seemly. She looked to be a sensible woman, and she was obviously gently born. Sir Tristram was thankful to think that his betrothed had (apparently) fallen into such unexceptionable hands, and said with a slight smile: "Yes, I am Tristram Shield, ma'am. I am afraid you have the advantage of me?"

Miss Thane saw her duty clear before her, and answered at once: "Let me beg of you to come into the parlour, Sir Tristram, and I will explain to you who I am."

He looked rather surprised. "Thank you, but as you have no doubt guessed, I am come in search of my cousin, Mademoiselle de Vauban."

"Of course," agreed Miss Thane, "and if you will step into the parlour——"

"Is my cousin in the house?" interrupted Sir Tristram.

"Well, yes," admitted Miss Thane, "but I am not at all sure that you can see her. Come into the parlour, and I will see what can be done."

Sir Tristram cast a glance up the stairs, and said in a voice edged with annoyance: "Very well, ma'am, but why there should be any doubt about my seeing my cousin I am at a loss to understand."

"I can tell you that too," said Miss Thane, leading the way to the private parlour. She shut the door, and said cheerfully:

"One cannot after all be surprised. You have behaved with a shocking lack of sensibility, have you not?"

"I was not aware of it, ma'am. Nor do I know why my cousin should leave her home at dead of night and undertake a solitary journey to London."

"She was wishful to become a governess," explained Sarah.

He stared at her in the blankest surprise. "Wishful to become a governess? Nonsense! Why should she wish anything of the kind?"

"Just for the sake of adventure," said Miss Thane.

"I have yet to learn that a governess's life is adventurous!" he said. "I should be grateful to you if you would tell me the truth!"

"Come, come, sir!" said Miss Thane pityingly, "it must surely be within your knowledge that the eldest son of the house always falls in love with the governess, and elopes with her in the teeth of all opposition?"

Sir Tristram drew a breath. *"Does* he?" he said.

"Yes, but not, of course, until he has rescued her from an oubliette, and a band of masked ruffians set on to her by his mother," said Miss Thane matter-of-factly. "She has to suffer a good deal of persecution before she elopes."

"I am of the opinion," said Sir Tristram with asperity, "that a little persecution would do my cousin a world of good! Her thirst for romance is likely to lead her into trouble. In fact, I was very much afraid that she had already run into trouble when I found her bandboxes upon the road. Perhaps, since she appears to have told you so much, she has also told you how she came to lose them?"

Miss Thane, perceiving that this question would lead her on to dangerous ground, mendaciously denied all knowledge of the bandboxes. She then made the discovery that Sir Tristram Shield's eyes were uncomfortably penetrating. She met their sceptical gaze with all the blandness she could summon to her aid.

"Indeed!" he said, politely incredulous. "But perhaps you can tell me why, if she was bound for London by the night-mail, as her maid informed me, she is still in this inn?"

"Certainly!" said Sarah, rising to the occasion. "She arrived too late for the mail, and was forced to put up for the night."

"What did she do for night-gear?" inquired Shield.

"Oh, I lent her what she needed!"

"I suppose she did not think the loss of her baggage of sufficient interest to call for explanation?"

"To tell you the truth——" began Sarah confidingly.

"Thank you! I *should* like to hear the truth."

"To tell you the truth," repeated Sarah coldly, "she had a fright, and the bandboxes broke loose."

"What frightened her?"

"A Headless Horseman," said Sarah.

He was frowning again. "Headless Horsemen? Fiddlesticks!"

"Very well," said Sarah, as one making a concession, "then it was a dragon."

"I think," said Sir Tristram in a very level voice, "that it will be better if I see my cousin and hear her story from her own lips."

"Not if you are going to approach it in this deplorable spirit," replied Miss Thane. "I dare say you would tell her there are no such things as dragons or headless horsemen!"

"Well?"

Miss Thane cast down her eyes to hide the laughter in them, and replied in a saddened tone: "When she told me the whole I thought it impossible that anyone could be so devoid of all sensibility, but now that I have seen you I realize that she spoke no less than the melancholy truth. A man who could remain unaffected by the thought of a young girl, dressed in white, all alone, and in a tumbril——"

His brow cleared; he gave a short laugh. "Does that rankle? But really I am past the age of being impressed by such absurdities."

Miss Thane sighed. "Perhaps *that* might be forgiven, but your heartlessness in refusing to ride *ventre à terre* to her death-bed——"

"Good God, surely she cannot have fled the house for such a ridiculous reason?" exclaimed Shield, considerably exasperated. "Why she should continually be harping on the notion of her own death passes my comprehension! She seems to me a perfectly healthy young woman."

Miss Thane looked at him in horror. "You did not tell her *that*, I trust?"

"I don't know what I told her. I might very easily."

"If I were you," said Miss Thane, "I would give up this idea you have of marrying your cousin. You would not suit."

"I'm fast coming to that conclusion myself," he said. "Moreover, Miss—— What *is* your name?"

"Thane," replied Sarah.

"Thane?" he repeated. "I fancy I have met someone of that name, but I do not immediately recall——"

"At Mendoza's Saloon," interpolated Sarah helpfully.

He looked a little amused. "Yes, possibly. But do you——"

"Or even at Brooks's."

"*I* am certainly a member."

"My brother," said Sarah. "He is at present in bed, nursing a severe cold, but I dare say he will like to receive you."

"It is extremely obliging of him, but my sole desire is to see my cousin, Miss Thane."

Sarah, whose attention had been caught by the sound of an arrival, paid no heed to this hint, but peeped over the short window-blind. What she saw made her feel uneasy; she turned her head and requested Sir Tristram to come at once. "Tell me," she commanded, "who are these two men in uniform?"

He came to the window. "Only a couple of Excisemen," he answered, after a casual glance.

"Oh, is *that* all?" said Miss Thane in rather a hollow voice. "I expect they have come to see what Nye keeps in his cellars. My brother fancies it is all smuggled liquor."

He looked at her in some perplexity. "They won't find anything. May I remind you, ma'am, that I wish to see my cousin?"

Miss Thane, having watched one of the Excisemen dismount and go into the inn, was straining her ears to catch what was being said in the coffee-room. She heard the landlord's deep voice, and wondered whether he had succeeded in persuading Ludovic to descend into the cellar. She looked at Sir Tristram, reflecting that he could not have chosen a more inopportune moment for his arrival. She ought to get rid of him, she supposed, but he did not seem to be the sort of man to be easily fobbed off. She said confidentially: "Do you know, I think it would be wisest if you were to leave your cousin with me for the present?"

"You are extremely good, ma'am, but I mean to carry her to my mother in Bath."

"Backgammon?" said Miss Thane knowledgeably. "She won't go. In fact, I hardly think it's worth your while to remain here, for she is set against seeing you."

"Miss Thane," said Sir Tristram dangerously, "it is quite evident to me that you are trying to prevent my seeing my cousin. I have not the smallest notion why she does not wish to see me. But I am going to see her. I trust I have made myself quite plain?"

"Yes, quite," said Miss Thane, catching an echo of Eustacie's voice joined with Nye's in the coffee-room.

It seemed as though Shield had heard it too, for he turned his head towards the door, listening. Then he looked back at Sarah and said: "You had better tell me at once, ma'am: what scrape is she in?"

"Oh, none at all!" Miss Thane assured him, and added sharply: "Where are you going?"

"To find out for myself!" said Shield, opening the door, and striding off to the coffee-room.

Miss Thane, feeling that as an accomplice she had not been a success, followed him helplessly.

In the coffee-room were gathered the landlord, Mademoiselle de Vauban, an Excise officer, and the tapster. The Excise officer was looking suspiciously from Eustacie to Nye, and Eustacie was talking volubly and with a great deal of gesticulation. When she saw her cousin on the threshold she broke off, and stared at him in consternation. The landlord shot a look at Sir Tristram under his jutting brows, but said nothing.

"I'm sorry," said Miss Thane, in answer to a reproachful glance from Eustacie. "I could not stop him."

"You should have stopped him!" said Eustacie. "Now what are we to do?"

Miss Thane turned to Sir Tristram. "The truth is, my dear sir, that your cousin fell in with a band of smugglers last night upon the road here, and had a sad fright."

"Smugglers?" repeated Shield.

"Yes," averred Eustacie. "And I am just telling this stupid person that it was I who came here last night, and not a smuggler."

"Begging your pardon, sir," said the riding-officer, "but the young lady's telling me that she rid here last night to catch the mail-coach." His tone inferred that he found the story incredible, as well he might.

"I'll have you know," growled Nye, "that the Red Lion's a respectable house! You'll find no smugglers here."

"And it's my belief I'd find a deal you'd like to hide if I knew just where those cellars of yours are, Mr. Nye!" retorted the Exciseman. "It's a fine tale you've hatched, and Miss knowing no better than to back you up in it, but you don't gammon me so easily! Ay, you've been careful to sweep the snow from your doorstep, but I've followed the trail down the road, and seen the blood on it!"

"Certainly you have seen the blood," said Eustacie. "There was a great deal of blood."

"Miss, do you ask me to believe that you went gallivanting about on horseback in the middle of the night? Come now, that won't do!"

"Yes, but you do not understand. I was making my escape," said Eustacie.

"Making your *escape*, miss?"

"Yes, and my cousin here will tell you that what I say is true. I am Mademoiselle de Vauban, and I am the grand-daughter of Lord Lavenham, and he is Sir Tristram Shield."

The Exciseman seemed to be a little impressed by this. He touched his hat to Sir Tristram, but still looked unconvinced. "Well, miss, and supposing you are, what call have you to go riding off in the night? I never heard of the Quality doing such!"

"I was running away from Sir Tristram," said Eustacie.

"Oh!" said the Exciseman, looking more dubious than ever.

Sir Tristram stood like a rock. Miss Thane, taking one look at his outraged profile, was shaken by inward laughter, and said unsteadily: "This is a—a matter of no little delicacy, you understand?"

"I'm bound to say I don't, ma'am," said the Exciseman bluntly. "What for would the young lady want to run away from her cousin?"

"Because he would have forced me to marry him!" said Eustacie recklessly.

The Exciseman cast a glance of considerable respect at Sir Tristram, and said: "Well, but surely to goodness, miss——"

"My grandfather is dead, and I am quite in my cousin's power," announced Eustacie. "And when I was on my way here I met the smugglers. And I was naturally very much afraid, and they were too, because they fired at my groom, and wounded him, and he fell off his horse with *both* my bandboxes."

Sir Tristram continued to preserve a grim silence, but at mention of the groom a slight frown knit his brows, and he looked intently at Eustacie.

"Indeed, miss?" said the Exciseman. "Then it queers me

how there come to be only the tracks of one horse down the road!"

"The other horse bolted, of course," said Eustacie. "It went back to its stable."

"Maddened by fright," murmured Miss Thane, and encountered a glance from Shield which spoke volumes.

"And may I inquire, miss, how you come to know that the horse went back to its stable?"

Miss Thane held Sir Tristram's eyes with her own. "Why, Sir Tristram here has just been telling us!" she said with calm audacity. "When the riderless horse arrived at the Court he at once feared some mishap had overtaken his cousin, and set out to ride—*ventre à terre*—to the rescue. Is that not so, dear sir?"

Aware of one compelling pair of humorous grey eyes upon him, and one imploring pair of black ones, Sir Tristram said: "Just so, ma'am."

The look he received from his cousin should have rewarded him. Eustacie said: "And then I must tell you that I took my poor groom up behind me on my own horse, but I did not know the way very well, and he was too faint to direct me, and so I was lost a long time in the Forest."

The Exciseman scratched his chin. "I'll take a look at this groom of yours, miss, if it's all the same to you. I'm not saying I don't believe your story, but what I do say is that ladies take queer notions into their heads when it comes to wounded men, and the late lord—begging your pardon, sir, and miss—was never one to help us officers against them pesky smugglers, any more than what most of the gentry hereabouts are!"

"Help a smuggler?" said Miss Thane in shocked accents. "My good man, do you know that you are addressing the sister of a Justice of the Peace? Let me tell you that my brother, who is in the house at this moment, holds the strongest views on smugglers and smuggled goods!" This, after all, she reflected, was quite true, and ought to impress the Exciseman—provided, of course, that Sir Hugh did not take it into his head to appear suddenly and explain the nature of his views.

The Exciseman certainly seemed rather shaken. He looked uncertainly from Miss Thane to Eustacie, and said in a sulky voice that his orders were to search the house.

"Oh, they are, are they?" said Nye. "P'raps you'd like to go and tell Sir Hugh Thane yourself that you're wishful to search his bedchamber? And him a Justice, like miss has told you! You get out of this before I lose my temper, that's my advice to you!"

"You lay a hand on me and you'll suffer for it, Mr. Nye!" said the Exciseman, keeping a wary eye on the landlord's massive form.

"Just a moment!" said Sir Tristram. "There is no need for all this to-do. If you suspect my cousin's groom of being a smuggler——"

"Well, sir, we fired on one last night, and I'm ready to swear we hit him. And it can't be denied that females is notably soft-hearted when it comes to a wounded man!"

"Possibly," said Shield, "but I am not soft-hearted, nor am I in the habit of assisting smugglers, or any other kind of law-breaker."

"No, sir," said the Exciseman, abashed by Sir Tristram's blighting tone. "I'm sure I didn't mean——"

"If the wounded man is indeed a groom from the Court I shall recognize him," continued Shield. "The affair can quite easily be settled by taking me to his room."

There was one moment's frozen silence. Sir Tristram was looking not at the Exciseman, but at Eustacie, who had turned as white as her fichu, and was staring at him in patent horror.

Nye's voice broke the silence. "And that's a mighty sound notion, sir!" he said deliberately. "I'll lay your honour knows the lad as well as I do myself."

Sir Tristram's eyes narrowed. "Do I?" he said.

Eustacie said breathlessly: "You cannot see him! He is in a fever!"

"Never you fret, miss," said Nye. "Sir Tristram's not one to go blaming the lad for doing what you ordered him to, nor he won't do anything to upset him. If you'll come upstairs, sir, I'll take you to him right away."

"Begging your pardon, but I'd as lief come too," said the Exciseman firmly.

"That's it, Nosy, you come!" replied Nye. "No one ain't stopping you."

Eustacie moved swiftly to the foot of the stairs, as though she would bar the way, but before she could speak Miss Thane was at her side, and had swept her forward, up the stairs, with an arm round her waist. "Yes, my love, by all means let us go too, in case the lad should be alarmed at having to face Sir Tristram."

"He must not see him! He must not!" whispered Eustacie, anguished.

"In my back bedchamber, sir," said Nye loudly. "I always house smugglers there to be handy for the riding-officers."

This withering piece of sarcasm made the Exciseman say, defensively, that he was only trying to do his duty. Nye ignored him, and threw open the door of the back bedchamber, saying: "Step in, Sir Tristram: I know I needn't warn you not to go for to startle a sick lad."

A small, insistent hand grasped Sir Tristram's coat-sleeve. He glanced down into Eustacie's white face, saw in it entreaty and alarm, and shaking off her hand strode into the room.

Ludovic had raised himself on his elbow. Across the room his strained blue eyes met Shield's hard grey ones. Shield checked for an instant on the threshold, while Miss Thane gave Eustacie's hand a reassuring squeeze, and the Exciseman said hopefully: "Do you know him, sir?"

"Very well indeed," replied Shield coolly. He went forward to the bed, and laid a hand on Ludovic's shoulder. "Well, my lad, you have got yourself into trouble through this piece of folly. Lie down now: I'll talk to you later." He turned, addressing the Exciseman: "I can vouch for this fellow. He does not look very like a smuggler, do you think?"

"No, sir, I'm bound to say he don't," said the Exciseman slowly, staring at Ludovic. "I'd say he looked uncommon like the old lord—from what I remember. It's the nose. It ain't a nose one forgets, somehow."

"It is a nose often seen in these parts," said Sir Tristram with dry significance.

The Exciseman blinked at him for a moment, and then, as light broke in on him, said hurriedly: "Oh, that's the way it is! I beg pardon, I'm sure! No offence meant! If you can vouch for the young fellow of course I ain't got no more to say, sir."

"Then if you ain't got no more to say you can take yourself off!" said Nye, thrusting him out of the room. "It don't do the house any good having your kind in it. Next you'll be telling me I've got smuggled liquor in my cellar!"

"And so you have!" rejoined the Exciseman immediately.

The door closed behind them; those in the little chamber

could hear the altercation gradually growing fainter as Nye shepherded his unwelcome guest down the stairs.

No one moved or spoke until the voices had died away. Then Eustacie caught Sir Tristram's hand, and pressed it to her cheek, saying simply: "I will do anything you wish. I will even marry you!"

"Oh no, you will not!" exploded Ludovic, struggling to sit up. "If this last don't beat all! What the devil did you mean by telling that long-nosed tidesman that I'm one of Sylvester's by-blows?"

"But no, Ludovic, no! I find that was very clever of him!" protested Eustacie. "Did you not think so, Sarah?"

Miss Thane said gravely: "I'm lost in admiration of so quick a wit. You never told me he was such an excellent conspirator."

"Well, truly I did not think that he would be," confessed Eustacie.

Sir Tristram, ignoring this interchange, said: "In God's name, Ludovic, what are you doing here?"

"Free-trading," replied Ludovic, with complete sang-froid.

Shield's face darkened. "Are you jesting?"

"No, no, he really is a smuggler, Cousin Tristram!" said Eustacie earnestly. "It is very romantic, I think. Do not you?"

"No, I do not!" said Shield. "Hasn't your name been smirched enough, you young fool? Smuggling! And you can lie there and blandly tell me of it!"

"You see!" Eustacie made a disgusted face at Miss Thane.

"Yes, he seems to have no feeling for romance at all," agreed Sarah.

Ludovic said savagely: "You may be thankful I can do nothing but lie here! Do you think I care whether I'm hanged for a free-trader or a murderer? I'm ruined, aren't I? Then, damn it, I'll go to the devil my own way!"

"I don't want to interrupt you," said Miss Thane, "but you'll find yourself with the devil sooner than you think if that wound of yours starts bleeding again."

"Ah, let be!" Ludovic said, his right hand clenching on the coverlet.

Sir Tristram was looking at that hand. He bent, and grasped Ludovic's wrist, and lifted it, staring at the bare fingers. "Show me your other hand!" he said harshly.

Ludovic's lips twisted into a bitter smile. He wrenched his

wrist out of Shield's hold, and put back the bedclothes to
show his left arm in a sling. The fingers were as bare as those
of his right hand.

Sir Tristram raised his eyes to that haggard young face. "If
you had it it would never leave your finger!" he said. "Ludovic, where is the ring?"

"Famous!" mocked Ludovic. "Brazen it out, Tristram!
Where is the ring indeed? *You* do not know, of course!"

"What the devil do you mean by that?" demanded Shield,
in a voice that made Eustacie jump.

Ludovic flung off Miss Thane's restraining hand, and sat
up as though moved by a spring. "You know what I mean!"
he said, quick and panting. "You laid your plans very skil-
fully, my clever cousin, and you took care to ship me out of
England before I'd time to think who, besides myself, could
want the ring more than anything on earth! Does it grace
your collection now? Tell me, does it give you satisfaction
when you look at it?"

"If you were not a wounded man I'd give you the thrash-
ing of your life, Ludovic!" said Shield, very white about the
mouth. "I have stood veiled hints from Basil, but not even he
dare say to my face what you have said!"

"Basil—Basil believed in me!" Ludovic gasped. "It was you
—you!"

Miss Thane caught him as he fell back, and lowered him
on to his pillows. "Now see what you have done!" she said
severely. "Hartshorn, Eustacie!"

"I would like very much to kill you!" Eustacie told her
cousin fiercely, and bent over the bed, holding the hartshorn
under Ludovic's nose.

He came round in a minute or two, and opened his eyes.
"Tristram!" he muttered. "My ring, Tristram!"

Shield brought a glass of water to the bed, and, raising Ludovic, held it to his lips. "Drink this, and don't be a fool!"

"Damn you, take your hands off me!" Ludovic whispered.

Sir Tristram paid no heed to this, but obliged him to drink
some of the water. He laid him down again, and handed the
glass to Miss Thane. "Listen to me!" he said, standing over
Ludovic. "I never had your ring in my hands in my life.
Until this moment I would have sworn it was in your possession."

Ludovic had averted his face, but he turned his head at
that. "If you have not got it who has?" he said wearily.

"I don't know, but I'll do my best to find out," replied Shield.

Eustacie drew a deep breath. "I see that I have misjudged you, Cousin Tristram," she said handsomely. "One must make reparation, *enfin*. I will marry you."

"Thank you," said Sir Tristram, "but the matter does not call for such a sacrifice as that, I assure you." He saw a certain raptness steal into her eyes, and added: "Don't waste time picturing yourself in the rôle of a martyred bride, I beg of you! I haven't the smallest desire to marry you."

Eustacie frowned. "But you must have an——"

"Yes, we won't go into that again," he said hastily.

"And I think," continued Eustacie, visibly attracted by the vision of herself as a martyred bride, "that perhaps it is my duty to marry you."

Ludovic raised his head from the pillows. "Well, you can't marry him. I'm the head of the family now, and I forbid it."

"Oh, very well!" submitted Eustacie. "I dare say I should not like always to be a sacrifice, after all."

"Am I to understand," inquired Miss Thane, "that Sir Tristram is to become one of us? If you are satisfied he is not the villain it is not for me to raise objections, of course, but I must say I am disappointed. We shall have to remake all our plans."

"Yes, we shall," agreed Eustacie. "And that reminds me that if Tristram truly did not steal Ludovic's ring, there is not any need for me to marry him. I had forgotten."

Sir Tristram looked rather startled, observing which, Miss Thane said kindly: "You must know that we had it all fixed that Eustacie was to marry you so as to be able to search in your collection for the missing ring."

"What a splendid notion, to be sure!" said Sir Tristram sardonically.

"Yes, it was, wasn't it?" said Eustacie. "But now we do not know who is the villain, so it is of no use."

Ludovic was watching Shield intently. "Tristram, you know something!"

Shield glanced down at him. "No. But Plunkett was shot by someone who wanted the talisman ring and only that. If you were not the man I know of only one other who could have done it."

Ludovic raised himself slightly, staring at his cousin with knit brows. "My God, but he believed me! He was the only one who believed me!"

"So implicitly," said Shield, "that he advised you to face your trial—with evidence enough against you to hang you twice over! Have *you* never wondered why he did that?"

Ludovic made a gesture as though brushing it aside. "Oh, I guessed he would be glad to step into my shoes, but damme, he would not run the risk of committing murder—he of all men!"

Eustacie gave a joyful shriek. "Basil!" she exclaimed, clapping her hands together. "Yes, yes, of a certainty it was he! Why did I not think of that before? Miss Thane, it is my cousin Basil who is the villain, and although you do not know him I assure you it is much, much, better, because he wears a silly hat, and I do not at all like him!"

"Oh well, in that case I am perfectly willing to have him for the villain in Sir Tristram's place," said Sarah. "I did not like to seem to criticize your choice, but to tell you the truth, Sir Tristram is not sinister enough for my taste."

Sir Tristram looked a little amused. Ludovic said: "Wait, Eustacie, wait! This is not certain! Let me think!"

"But there is not any need to think, *mon cousin*. It is clear to me that Basil is the man, because he wants very much to be Lord Lavenham, and besides, there is no one else."

"I can't believe he'd put his neck in such jeopardy!" Ludovic said. "When did the Beau ever court a risk?"

"Whoever did it, Ludovic, was able to obtain a handkerchief of yours to leave beside the body," Shield reminded him. "He must also have known that Plunkett was dining at Slaugham that evening, and guessed at least that he would return by the path through the Longshaw Spinney."

"Yes, but to plan a cold-blooded murder just to dispose of me, and then pretend belief in my story—— No, surely he could not do it!"

"Hush!" said Miss Thane impressively. "The whole affair is becoming as clear as daylight to me. He did not plan it; I dare say he never went beyond wishing that some accident would befall Ludovic—oh, I beg your pardon! befall Lord Lavenham——"

" 'Ludovic' will do," interposed his lordship, grinning up at her. "I count you as quite one of the family."

"I wish you may, for I assure you I regard myself as irrevocably bound to this adventure. Do not interrupt me! Let us say that he thought quite idly how fortunate it would be if Ludovic met with an accident. He would not dare to contrive one, for being the next in succession suspicion might fall on him. Well then, Ludovic lost his talisman ring, and Basil saw —— No, I am wrong! At first he saw nothing. But Ludovic began to play into his hands—really, Ludovic, I believe it was all your fault: you tempted Basil beyond what he could resist."

"I did not!" said Ludovic indignantly.

"You know nothing of the matter, my dear boy. You and Chance between you showed Basil how he could be rid of you. You became enraged with the man whose name Eustacie cannot remember (or I, for that matter), and I dare say you were drinking heavily, and——"

"He was," said Sir Tristram.

"Of course. He was in a mood for violence. I've no doubt he talked very wildly, and swore he would be avenged. Now you must think, Ludovic, if you please! Did not Basil know that you meant to waylay that man upon—upon the fatal night?"

"I don't know. I think I made no secret of it. Basil knew the whole story."

"I am quite sure he did," said Miss Thane. "Now you see, do you not, how easy it was for him? It needed no planning at all. He had only to lie in wait for that man in the spinney, to leave a handkerchief of yours beside the body, and to steal the ring. Afterwards he had nothing to do but enact the rôle of champion. I perceive that he must have a very subtle brain." She closed her eyes, and said in a seer-like voice: "He is, I am sure, a sinister person."

"The Beau?" said Ludovic. "No, he isn't!"

Miss Thane frowned. "Nonsense, he must be!"

"Yes," said Eustacie regretfully, "but truly he is not."

Miss Thane opened her eyes again. "You put me out. What then is he like?"

"He is very civil," said Eustacie. "He has manners of the most polished."

Miss Thane readjusted her ideas. "I will allow him to be smooth-spoken. I think he smiles."

"Yes, he does," admitted Eustacie.

Miss Thane gave a shudder. "His smile hides a wolfish soul!" she announced.

Ludovic burst out laughing. "Devil a bit! There's nothing wolfish about him. He's a mighty pleasant fellow, and I'd have sworn not one to wish anybody harm."

"Alas, it is true!" said Eustacie sadly. "He is just nothing."

Sir Tristram's eyebrows went up a shade. Miss Thane pointed a triumphant finger at him, and said: "Sir Tristram knows better! A wolf, sir?"

He shook his head. "No, I don't think I should put it quite like that, Miss Thane. He is pleasant enough—a little too pleasant. He purrs like a cat."

"He does," agreed Ludovic. "But do you know any ill of him? I don't."

"One thing," replied Shield. "I know that Sylvester mistrusted him."

"Sylvester!" said Ludovic scornfully.

"Oh, Sylvester was no fool," answered Shield.

"Good God, he mistrusted scores of people, me amongst them!"

"So little did he mistrust you," said Shield, putting his hand into his waistcoat-pocket, "that he bade me give you that if ever I should see you again, and tell you not to pledge it."

Ludovic stared at the great ruby. "Thunder and Turf, did he leave me *that?*"

"As you see. He asked me just before he died whether I thought your story had been true after all."

"I dare swear you told him No," remarked Ludovic, slipping the ring on to his finger.

"I did," said Shield calmly. "You must remember that I heard that shot not ten minutes after I had parted from you, and I knew what sort of a humour you were in."

Ludovic shot him a fiery glance. "You thought me capable of murder, in fact!"

"I thought you three-parts drunk," said Shield. "I also thought you a rash young fool. I still think that. What possessed you to turn smuggler? Have you been sailing off the coast of Sussex all this time?"

" 'Hovering' is the word," said Ludovic, with a gleam of mischief. "Free-trading seemed to me an occupation eminently suited to an outlaw. Besides, I always liked the sea."

Sir Tristram said scathingly: "I suppose that was reason enough."

"Why not? I knew some of the Gentlemen, too, from old days. But I was never off these shores till now. Don't like 'em: there's too much creeping done, and the tidesmen are too cursed sharp. I've been helping to run cargoes of brandy and rum—under Bergen papers, you know—into Lincolnshire. That's the place, I can tell you. I've been dodging revenue cruisers for the past fifteen months. It's not a bad life, but the fact of the matter is I wasn't reared to it. I only came into Sussex to glean what news there might be from Nye."

"But you will stay, *mon cousin*, won't you?" asked Eustacie anxiously.

"He can't stay," Shield said. "It was madness to come at all."

Ludovic lifted his head, and regarded Sylvester's ring through half-closed eyes. "I shall stay," he said nonchalantly, "and I shall find out who holds the talisman ring."

"Ludovic, you may trust me to do all I can to discover it, but you must not be found here!"

"I'm not going to be found here," replied Ludovic. "You don't know Joe's cellars. I do."

"Go over to Holland, and wait there," Shield said. "You can do no good here."

"Oh yes, I can!" said Ludovic, turning his hand so that the jewel caught the light. "Moreover, I'll be damned if I'll be elbowed out of my own business!"

"What can you hope to do in hiding that I cannot do openly?" asked Shield. "Why add to your folly by running the risk of being arrested?"

"Because," said Ludovic, at last raising his eyes from the ruby, "if the Beau has the ring I know where to look for it."

Chapter VI

THIS announcement produced all the effect upon the ladies which Ludovic could have desired. They gazed at him in surprise and admiration, breathlessly waiting for him to tell them more. Shield, not so easily impressed, said: "If you really know where to look for it you had better tell me, and I'll do it for you."

"That's just the trouble," replied Ludovic shamelessly. "I'm not at all sure of the place." He saw Eustacie's face fall, and added: "Oh, I should know it again if I saw it! The thing is that I'd be mighty hard put to it to direct anyone how to find it. I shall have to go myself."

"Go where?" demanded Sir Tristram.

"Oh, to the Dower House!" replied Ludovic airily. "There's a secret panel. You wouldn't know it."

"A secret panel?" repeated Miss Thane in an awed voice. "You mean actually a secret panel?"

Ludovic regarded her in some slight concern. "Yes, why not?"

"I thought it too good to be true," said Miss Thane. "If there is one thing above all others I have wanted all my life to do it is to search for a secret panel! I suppose," she added hopefully, "it would be too much to expect to find an underground passage leading from the secret panel?"

Eustacie clasped her hands ecstatically. "But yes, of course! An underground passage——"

"With bats and dead men's bones," shuddered Miss Thane.

French common sense asserted itself. Eustacie frowned. "Not bats, no. That is not reasonable. But certainly some bones, chained to the wall."

"And damp—it must be damp!"

"Not damp; cobwebs," put in Ludovic. "Huge ones, which cling to you like——"

"Ghostly fingers!" supplied Miss Thane.

"Oh, Ludovic, there is a passage?" breathed Eustacie.

85

He laughed. "Lord, no! It's just a priest's hole, that's all."

"How wretched!" said Miss Thane, quite disgusted. "It makes me lose all heart."

"If there is not a passage we must do without one," decreed Eustacie stoutly. "One must be practical. *Tout même,* it is a pity there is not a passage. I thought it would lead from the Court to the Dower House. It would have been *magnifique!* We might have found treasure!"

"That is precisely what I was thinking," agreed Miss Thane. "An old iron chest, full of jewels."

Sir Tristram broke in on these fancies with a somewhat withering comment. "Since we are not searching for treasure, and no passage exists save in your imaginations, this discussion is singularly unprofitable," he said. "Where is the panel, Ludovic?"

"There you have the matter in a nutshell," confessed Ludovic. "I know my uncle used to use it as a strong-room, and I remember Sylvester showing it to me when I was a lad, but what I can't for the life of me recall is which room it's in."

"That," said Tristram, "is, to say the least of it, unfortunate, since the Dower House is panelled almost throughout."

"I think it's either in the library or the dining-room," said Ludovic. "There are two tiers of pillars with a lot of fluted pilasters and carvings. I dare say I shall recognize it when I see it. You twist one of the bosses on the frieze between the tiers, and one of the square panels below slides back."

"How do you propose to see it?" asked Shield. "The Beau is at the Dower House now, and means to stay there."

"Well, I shall have to break in at night," replied Ludovic.

"A very proper resolve," approved Miss Thane, before Sir Tristram could condemn it. "But something a trifle disturbing has occurred to me: are you sure that your cousin would have kept the ring?"

"Yes, for he would not dare to sell it," replied Ludovic at once.

"He would not perhaps have thrown it away?"

Ludovic shook his head. "Not he. He knows its worth," he answered simply.

"Oh well, in that case, all we have to do is to find the panel!" said Miss Thane.

Sir Tristram looked at her across Ludovic's bed. "We?" he said.

"Certainly," replied Sarah. "Eustacie told me I might share the adventure."

"You are surely not proposing to remain here!"

"Sir," said Miss Thane. "I shall remain here until we have cleared Ludovic's fair name."

"But, of course!" said Eustacie, opening her eyes very wide. "What else?"

Sir Tristram told her in a few brief words. When it was made plain to him that both ladies meant to play important parts in Ludovic's affair, and that neither of them would so much as listen to the notion of retiring, the one to London, the other to Bath, he said roundly that he would have nothing to do with so crazy an escapade. Eustacie at once replied with the utmost cordiality that he might retire from it with her good-will, but Ludovic objected that since his left arm would be useless for some little time, he would need Tristram to help him with his housebreaking.

"Do you imagine that I am going to break into Basil's house?" demanded Sir Tristram.

"Why not?" said Ludovic.

"Not only that," said Miss Thane thoughtfully, "but we might need you if there is to be any fighting. My brother tells me you have a Right."

"If," said Sir Tristram forcibly, "you would all of you rid yourselves of the notion that you are living within the pages of one of Mrs. Radcliffe's romances, I should be grateful! Do you realize that tongues are already wagging up at the Court over Eustacie's ill-judged, unnecessary, and foolish flight? I dare swear the news of it has even now reached Basil's ears. If she remains here, what am I to tell him?"

"Let me think," said Miss Thane.

"Don't put yourself to that trouble!" said Sir Tristram, with asperity. "Eustacie must go to my mother in Bath."

"I have it!" said Miss Thane, paying no heed to him. "I knew Eustacie in Paris some years ago. Finding myself in the vicinity of her home, I sent to inform her of my arrival, whereupon the dear creature, misliking the Bath scheme, formed the idea of putting herself under my protection. Unfortunately, you, Sir Tristram, knowing nothing of me, and being possessed of a tyrannical disposition—I beg your pardon?"

"I did not speak," replied Sir Tristram, eyeing her frostily.

Miss Thane met his look with one of limpid innocence. "Oh, I quite thought you did!"

"I choked," explained Sir Tristram. "Pray continue! You had reached my tyrannical disposition."

"Precisely," nodded Sarah. "You refused to accede to Eustacie's request, thus leaving her no alternative to instant flight. But now that you have seen me, you realize that I am a respectable female, altogether a proper person to have the charge of a young lady, and you relent."

The corners of his mouth twitched slightly. "Do I?" he said.

"Certainly. We arrange that Eustacie shall stay with me in London on a visit. All is in train for our departure when my brother, finding his cold to be no better, declares himself to be unable to risk the dangers of travel in this inclement weather. Which reminds me," she added, rising from her chair, "that I had better go and inform Hugh that his cold is worse."

A little while later, coming down from Sir Hugh's bedchamber, she found Sir Tristram waiting in the coffee-room. He looked up as she rounded the bend in the stairs, and said sardonically: "I trust you were able to convince your brother, ma'am?"

"It was unnecessary," she returned. "Nye has taken him up a bottle of Old Constantia. He thinks it would be fool-hardy to brave the journey to London until he is perfectly recovered."

"I thought he held strong views of the subject of smuggled liquor?" remarked Sir Tristram.

"He does," replied Miss Thane, not in the least abashed. "Very strong views." She went to the fire and seated herself on one of the high-backed settles placed on either side of it. A gesture invited Sir Tristram to occupy the other. "I think those two children will make a match of it, do not you?"

"Ludovic cannot ask any woman to be his wife as matters now stand," he responded, frowning into the fire.

"Then we must certainly establish his innocence," said Miss Thane.

He glanced up. "Believe me, I should be glad to do anything in my power to help the boy, but this coming into Sussex is madness!"

"Well," said Miss Thane reasonably, "he cannot be moved until his wound is in some sort healed, so we must make the best of it. Tell me, do you think his cousin Basil is indeed the real culprit?"

He was silent for a moment. At last he said: "I may be prejudiced against him. It sounds fantastic, but I would not for the world have him know of Ludovic's whereabouts now." He looked at her searchingly. "What is your part in this, Miss Thane?"

She laughed. "My dear sir, my part is that of Eustacie's chaperon, of course. To tell you the truth, I have taken a liking to your romantic cousins, and I mean to see this adventure to a close."

"You are very good, ma'am, but——"

"But you would do very much better without any females," nodded Miss Thane.

"Yes," said Sir Tristram bluntly. "I should!"

"I expect you would," said Miss Thane, quite without rancour. "But if you imagine you can induce Eustacie to leave this place now that she has found her cousin Ludovic, you have a remarkably sanguine nature. And if you are bound to have Eustacie, you may just as well have me as well."

"Certainly," said Shield, "but do you—does your brother realize that this is an adventure that is likely to lead us all to Newgate?"

"I do," she replied placidly. "I doubt whether my brother realizes anything beyond the facts of a cold in the head and a well-stocked cellar. If we do reach Newgate, perhaps you will be able to get us out again."

"You are very intrepid!" he said, with a look of amusement.

"Sir," said Miss Thane, "during the course of the past twelve hours my life seems to have become so full of smuglers, Excisemen, and wicked cousins that I now feel I can face anything. What in the world possessed the boy to take to smuggling, by-the-by?"

"God knows! You might as well ask what possessed Eustacie to leave the Court at midnight to become a governess. They should deal extremely together if ever they can be married." He rose. "I must go back and do what I can to avert suspicion. Somehow or other we must find this panel Ludovic speaks of before he can thrust his head into a noose."

Miss Thane gave a discreet cough. "Do you—er—place much dependence on the panel, Sir Tristram?"

"No, very little, but I place every dependence upon Ludovic's breaking into the Dower House in search of it," he replied frankly. "For the moment we have him tied by the heels, but that won't be for long, if I know him. They are tough stock, the Lavenhams." He walked to the table and picked up his hat and riding-whip. "I'll take my leave now. I fancy we have fobbed off the riding-officer, but there may be others. If you should want me, send Clem over to the Court with a message, and I'll come."

She nodded. "Meanwhile, is Ludovic in danger, do you think?"

"Not at Nye's hands, but if information were lodged against him at Bow Street by anyone suspecting his presence here, yes, in great danger."

"And at his cousin's hands?"

He met her questioning look thoughtfully, and after a moment said: "I may be wrong, but I believe so. There is a great deal at stake." He tapped his riding-whip against his top-boot. "It all turns on the talisman ring," he said seriously. "Whoever has that is the man who shot Plunkett. I must cultivate a more intimate acquaintance with the Beau."

He took his leave of her and went out, calling for his horse to be brought round. Miss Thane saw him ride away, and went slowly back to her patient.

Had it been possible to have sent for a surgeon to attend Ludovic, cupping would certainly have been prescribed. Miss Thane was little anxious lest serious fever should set in, but both Shield and the landlord maintained that Ludovic had a strong enough constitution to weather worse things than a mere wound in his shoulder, and after a couple of days she was bound to acknowledge that they were right. The wound began to heal just as it should, and the patient announced his intention of leaving his sick-bed. This perilous resolve was frustrated by Shield, who, though he visited the Red Lion every day, omitted to bring with him the raiment he had promised to procure from Ludovic's abandoned wardrobe at the Court.

While Ludovic lay in the back bedchamber, either playing piquet with his cousin or evolving plans for the recovery of his ring, Sir Hugh Thane continued to occupy one of the front rooms. His cold really had been a great deal worse on the morning of Shield's first visit, and once having gained a hold on the unfortunate baronet, it ran the whole gamut of sore throat, thick head, watering eyes, loss of taste, and ended up with a cough on the chest which Sarah, with unwonted solicitude, declared to be bad enough to lead (if great care were not taken) to an inflammation of the lungs.

It was not, therefore, in the least difficult to persuade Sir Hugh to keep his room. His only complaint was that he was without his valet, this indispensable person having gone to London in advance of his master with the major part of the baggage and Sarah's abigail. It took all Sarah's ingenuity to think out enough plausible reasons for not summoning Satchell to his master's sick-bed. Satchell had been in Sir Hugh's employment for some years, but Miss Thane did not feel that he could be trusted with the secret of Ludovic's presence at the Red Lion. Luckily Clem proved himself a deft attendant, and beyond remarking two or three times a day that he wished he had Satchell with him, Sir Hugh made no complaint. He accepted Sarah's story of the heiress fleeing from a distasteful marriage. It was doubtful whether the original tale of Ludovic's misfortunes occupied any place in his erratic memory, but he did once ask his sister whether she had not mentioned having met a smuggler. She admitted it, but said that he had left the inn.

"Oh!" said Sir Hugh. "A pity. If you should see him again, you might let me know."

What Sir Tristram Shield told Beau Lavenham the ladies did not know, but it brought him over to Hand Cross within two days. He came in his elegant chaise, a graceful affair slung on swan-neck perches, and upholstered with squabs of pale blue. He was ushered into the parlour, where Miss Thane and Eustacie were sitting, early one afternoon, and was greeted by his cousin with a baleful stare.

He had discarded his fur-lined cloak in the coffee-room, so that all the glory of his primrose pantaloons and lilac-striped coat burst upon Miss Thane without warning. He wore the fashionable short boot, and bunches of ribbons at the ends of his pantaloons; his cravat was monstrous, his coat collar very high at the back, and he carried a tall sugar-loaf hat in his hand. He paused in the doorway and lifted his ornate quizzing-glass, smiling. "So here we have the little runaway!" he said. "My dear cousin, all my felicitations! Poor, poor Tristram!"

"I do not know why you have come here," responded Eustacie, "but I do not at all wish to see you. It is my cousin, Sarah. This is my friend, Miss Thane, Basil."

He bowed, a hand on his heart. "Ah yes, the—er—acquaintance of Paris days, I believe. What a singularly happy chance it was that brought you to this unlikely spot, ma'am!"

"Yes, was it not?" agreed Miss Thane cordially. "Though until my brother was took ill, I had really no notion of remaining here. But the opportunity of seeing my dear Eustacie again quite reconciled me to the necessity of putting up at this inn. Pray, will you not be seated?"

He thanked her, and took the chair she indicated, carefully setting his hat down upon the table. Looking at Eustacie with an amused glint in his eyes, he said: "So you have decided not to marry Tristram after all! I liked the notion of your spirited flight to the arms of your friend. But how dark you kept her, my dear cousin! Now if only you had confided with me, I would have conveyed you to her in my carriage, and you would have been spared a singularly uncomfortable ride through the night."

"I preferred to go myself," said Eustacie. "It was an adventure."

He said: "It is a pity you dislike me so much, and trust me so little, for I am very much your servant."

To Miss Thane's surprise Eustacie smiled quite graciously, and answered: "I do not dislike you: that is quite absurd. It is merely that I think you wear a silly hat, and, besides, I wanted to have an adventure all by myself."

He gave his soft laugh. "I wish you did not dislike my hat, but that can be remedied. Shall I wear an old-fashioned tricorne like Tristram, or do you favour the *chapeau-bras?*"

"You would look very odd in a *chapeau-bras*," she commented.

"Yes, I am afraid you are right. Tell me, what do you mean to do with your life, Eustacie, now that you have given Tristram his *congé?*"

"I am going to stay in town with Miss Thane."

He looked thoughtfully at Miss Thane. "Yes? Have I Miss Thane's permission to call upon her in London?"

"Oh, but certainly! She will be delighted," said Eustacie. *"Du vrai*, she would like very much to call upon you at the Dower House, because it is such a very old house, and that is with her a veritable passion. But I said, No, it would not be *convenable."*

Miss Thane cast her a look of considerable respect, and tried to assume the expression of an eager archæologist.

The Beau said politely: "I should be honoured by a visit from Miss Thane, but surely the Court would be better worth her study?"

"Yes, but you must know that I will not go to the Court with her," said Eustacie glibly. "Tristram is very angry, and I do not wish that there should be any awkwardness."

The Beau raised his brows. "Is Tristram importuning you to marry him?" he inquired.

Not having any exact knowledge of what Tristram had told

him, Eustacie thought it prudent to return an evasive answer. She spread out her hands, and said darkly: "It is that he gave his word to Grandpère, you know. I do not understand him."

"Ah!" sighed the Beau, running his hand gently up and down the riband of his quizzing-glass. "You are, of course, an heiress." He let that shaft sink in, and continued smoothly: "I have never been able to feel that you and Tristram were quite made for each other, but I confess your sudden flight took me by surprise. They tell me that your ride was fraught with adventure, too. Some tale of smugglers— but I dare say much exaggerated."

"I suppose," said Miss Thane opportunely, "that there is a great deal of smuggling done in these parts?"

"I believe so," he responded. "I have always understood that my great-uncle encouraged the Trade."

"Basil," interrupted Eustacie, "is it permitted that I bring Miss Thane to the Dower House one morning, perhaps? I thought that you would be like Tristram, and try to make me go to Bath, but now I see that you are truly *sympathique*, and I do not at all mind coming with Sarah to call on you."

He looked at her for a moment. "But, pray do!" he said. "Have I not said that I shall count myself honoured?"

Miss Thane, summoning up every recollection of historical houses she had visited during the course of her travels, at once engaged him in conversation. Luckily she had her foreign journeys to draw upon. This she did with great enthusiasm, and no lack of imagination. The Beau was diverted from the topic of smugglers, and although his knowledge of antiques was slight and his interest in them almost non-existent, he was too well-bred to attempt to change the subject. Miss Thane kept his attention engaged for the remaining twenty minutes of his visit, and when he got up to go, thanked him profusely for his permission to visit the Dower House, and promised herself the treat of exploring his premises on the first fine day that offered. Eustacie thoughtfully reminded her that she would like to bring her sketching-book, to which she assented, as one in honour bound.

The Beau bowed himself out, was shepherded to his chaise by the mistrustful Nye, and drove off, watched from behind the parlour blinds by his gleeful cousin.

Miss Thane sank into a chair, and said: "Eustacie, you are a wretch!"

"But no, but no!" Eustacie cried, dancing in triumph. "You did it so very well!"

"I am not at all sure that I convinced him. My dear, I know nothing of pictures, or wood-panelling! If he had not taken his leave of us when he did, my tongue must have run dry. I am convinced he thought me a chattering fool."

"It does not matter in the least. We shall go to the Dower House, and while I talk to Basil you will find the secret panel and steal the ring!"

"Oh," said Miss Thane blinking. "Just—just find the panel and steal the ring. Yes, I see. I dare say it will be quite easy."

"Certainly it will be easy, because I have thought of a very good plan, which is to pretend to Basil that I do not at all know what to do. I shall say to him that I have no one to advise me, and I am afraid of Tristram, and you will go away to draw a picture and you will see that he will be very glad to let you. Come, we must immediately tell Ludovic what we have done!"

Ludovic, when the scheme was breathlessly divulged to him, at first objected to it on the score that he had thought of a better plan. Once the coast was clear, he said, Abel Bundy would be bound to work his way up to the Red Lion to deliver his kegs of brandy, and to try to get news of him. If Tristram misliked the notion of breaking into the Dower House Abel, not so nice, would make a very good substitute.

"Yes, but it is altogether dangerous for you, and for us not at all," Eustacie pointed out. "Besides, I do *not* see that it is fair that you should keep the whole adventure to yourself."

"Damme, it's my adventure, isn't it?"

"It is not your adventure. It is mine too, and also it is Sarah's, and she will not help us any more if you do not share it with her."

"Oh, very well!" said Ludovic. "Not that I believe in this precious scheme of yours, mind you! Ten to one the Beau will suspect something. You can't hunt for the catch to the panel under his very nose."

"*Entendu,* but I have provided. I shall desire to speak with Basil alone, and he will like that, and permit it."

Ludovic eyed her somewhat narrowly. "He will, will he?"

"Yes, because he has said that he would like to marry me."

Ludovic sat up. "I won't have you going up to the Dower House to let that fellow make love to you, so don't think it!"

"Not that, stupid! I shall ask for his advice, and he will not make love to me, because Sarah will be there.

"She won't. She'll be hunting for the panel."

"But I could scream if he tried to make love to me!"

"Ay, so you could. You've a mighty shrill scream, what's more. All the same, it's my belief the scheme will fail. It's a pity I can't recall which room the curst panel is in."

"Yes, I have been feeling that, too," agreed Miss Thane. "I mean—it would be easier, wouldn't it?"

"In an adventure," said Eustacie severely, "it is not proper to have everything quite easy."

Miss Thane was about to beg pardon when the sound of a quick, firm footstep on the stairs made them all look towards the door. It opened, but it was only Sir Tristram who came in, so that both ladies were able to relax their suddenly strained attitudes.

"Oh, it's you, is it?" said Ludovic, withdrawing his hand from under his pillows, where it had been grasping the butt of a serviceable pistol. "Come in, and shut the door. Eustacie has thought of a plan. I don't say it's a good one, but it might answer."

"Has the Beau been here?" Sir Tristram demanded.

"Yes, that's what put this scheme of hers into Eustacie's head. I wish I might have seen him. She tells me he has taken to wearing a lilac-striped coat."

"I thought I could not be mistaken in his chaise. Why did he come?"

"He came to see me, and you must at once listen to me, *mon cousin,* because I have made a plot. I am going to take Sarah to the Dower House, because she has an *envie* to see it. I have told Basil that she likes old houses, and he was very content that she should see his. And when we are there I shall pretend that I wish to consult Basil, and while I am explaining to him how it is that I do not wish to marry you, Sarah will ask leave to make a drawing of the woodwork in the library. In that way she will be able to search for the secret panel, and when she has found it, she must steal the ring, and make just one little drawing to show Basil. Is it not a very good plot?"

"Yes," said Shield, somewhat to her surprise, "it is a good plot, but if you do find the ring you must on no account remove it, Miss Thane. Make a sketch of that particular portion of the frieze so that we may easily find it again, and leave the rest to me."

"Certainly," said Miss Thane. "But there is just one thing——"

"Where's the sense in leaving it there?" interrupted Ludovic. "I want my ring. I haven't had a day's good luck since I lost it."

"There is just one thing," began Miss Thane again, "which perhaps I ought to——"

"Of course, he must have the ring at once!" declared Eustacie. "Why should she leave it?"

"Because we must be able to prove that the ring is in the Beau's possession. Steal it, and it is merely a matter of your word against his. Once we can prove that the Beau has it, Ludovic is cleared. Until then Ludovic is the last person in the world to hold the ring. If Miss Thane can find the panel, and sketch the frieze for us——"

"Yes," said Miss Thane. "But I have been trying to tell you for quite some time now that there is a—a trifling hitch. I cannot draw."

They stared at her in incredulity. "Can't *draw?*" repeated Ludovic. "Nonsense, of course you can! All females can draw!"

"I can't."

"I thought," said Sir Tristram, with a touch of scorn, "that drawing and water-colour painting were taught in every young ladies' seminary?"

"They may be," retorted Sarah, "but I still cannot draw."

"Well, why the devil can't you, if you were taught?" demanded Ludovic reasonably.

"I had no aptitude," explained Sarah.

"But consider, Sarah!" said Eustacie. "It is most important that you should be able to make just a *little* drawing!"

"I know," said Sarah. "I am very sorry, and I quite see that a person who is unable to draw is unfit to take part in any adventure."

"It seems to me," said Ludovic, "that girls merely waste their time at school."

"Yes, and what is worse, I have told Basil that she will bring her sketching-book," added Eustacie. "Now it appears that she has not got one, and we are quite undone."

"If she can't draw, she can't," said Sir Tristram. "I shall have to join your party."

Eustacie shook her head. "No, because I have told Basil that I do not care to see you, and he would think it very odd if you were to be of my party."

Sir Tristram gave a resigned sigh. "You had better let me

know at once just what lie it is you have told the Beau. What am I now held to have done?"

Eustacie's eyes twinkled wickedly. "Well, you see, I had to make up a reason why I could not take Sarah to the Court, so I said that you were very angry with me."

"Oh, is that all?" Sir Tristram sounded relieved.

Miss Thane, feeling that she had something to avenge, said meditatively: "Yes, it was the Beau himself who suggested the rest. No one could really blame Eustacie."

"The rest?"

"Oh, it was nothing to signify!" said Sarah, with an airy gesture. "Mr. Lavenham just asked if you were still importuning Eustacie to marry you."

"Why should I be doing anything of the sort?"

"On account of her being an heiress," explained Sarah.

Sir Tristram said dryly: "Of course. I should have thought of that. I trust neither of you will hesitate to vilify my character whenever it seems expedient to you to do so."

"No, of course we shall not," Miss Thane assured him.

"But you do not mind, *mon cousin*, do you?"

"On the contrary, I am becoming quite accustomed to it. But I am afraid even your imagination must fail soon. I have been in swift succession a tyrant, a thief and a murderer, and now a fortune-hunter. There is really nothing left."

"Oh!" said Ludovic gaily, "we have acquitted you of theft and murder, you know."

"True," Shield retorted. "But as your acquittals are invariably accompanied by fresh and more outrageous slanders, I almost dread the moment when you acquit me of fortune-hunting."

Eustacie looked a little distressed. "But, Tristram, you do not understand! We do not really think you are a fortune-hunter!"

Ludovic gave a delighted crack of laughter, and caught her hand to his lips. "I lied, I lied! I have had one day's good luck at least, when I met my cousin Eustacie!"

"Yes, but——"

Sir Tristram said gravely: "Of course, if you do not really think it——"

"No, I do not. In fact, I am beginning quite to like you," Eustacie assured him.

"Thank you," said Sir Tristram, much moved.

"But I thought it would be a very good thing to pretend to

Basil that you still wished to marry me, and so, you see, you cannot come to his house with us. I perceive now that it is a pity that I said it, perhaps, but one cannot always look far enough ahead."

"On the whole," said Shield, "I am inclined to think that you did right. I must, after all, have some excuse for visiting this inn so often. I will join your party at the Dower House, and you may counterfeit all the disgust you please."

Miss Thane nodded approvingly. "*I* see! You will arrive upon some pretext, just in time to rescue Mr. Lavenham from my importunities. Eustacie having signified her desire to hold private speech with him, he will hail your arrival with joy. I shall have to be a very stupid sort of a woman, and ask a great many questions. Tell me something to say about his house."

"Comment enthusiastically upon the silver-figured oak wainscoting in the dining-room," said Sir Tristram.

"Also the strap-and-jewel work overmantel in the drawing-room," struck in Ludovic. "Sylvester used to say it was devilish fine; that I *do* remember."

"Strap-and-jewel work," repeated Miss Thane, committing it to memory.

"Dutch influence," said Sir Tristram. "Detect the school of Torrigiano in the library."

"Is it there?" inquired Ludovic, vaguely interested.

"Heaven knows. Basil won't, at any rate. Say that it is a pity the muntins are not covered by pilasters. Talk of cartouches, and caryatids, and scratch-mouldings. Ask for the history of every picture, and discover that the staircase reminds you of one you have seen somewhere else, though you cannot immediately recall where."

"Say no more! I see it all!" declared Miss Thane. "Heaven send he does not fob me off on to the housekeeper!"

Fortunately for the success of her plot the Beau's manners were far too polished to permit of his resorting to this expedient. According to a carefully-laid plan, the two ladies set out upon the following morning in Sir Hugh's chaise, and drove at a sedate pace to the Dower House, which was situated on the northern side of Lavenham Court, about five miles from Hand Cross. It was a sixteenth-century house of respectable size, approached by a short carriage-sweep. Its gardens, which were separated from the Park by a kind of ha-ha, were laid out with great propriety of taste, and some very fine clipped yews, flanking the oaken front door, at once met with Miss Thane's approbation.

They were admitted into the house by a town-bred and somewhat supercilious butler, and led through the hall to the drawing-room. This was an elegant apartment, furnished in the first style of fashion, but Miss Thane had no time to waste in admiring what were obviously quite up-to-date chairs and tables. Her attention was fixed anxiously upon the overmantel.

The Beau joined his guests in a very few minutes. If he felt any surprise at a somewhat vague engagement having been kept with such promptness, no trace of it appeared in his countenance. He greeted both ladies with his usual grace, feared they must have been chilled during their drive in such hard weather, and begged them to draw near the fire. Eustacie, whose cheeks were rosy where a nipping east wind had caught them, promptly complied with the suggestion, but Miss Thane was unable to tear herself from the contemplation of the overmantel. She stood well back from it, assuming a devout expression, and breathed: "Such exquisite strap-and-jewel work! You did not tell me you had anything so fine, Mr. Lavenham! I declare, I do not know how to take my eyes from it!"

"I believe it is considered to be a very good example, ma'am," the Beau acknowledged. "The late Lord Lavenham was used to say it was finer than the one up at the Court, but I am afraid I am not a judge of such things."

But this Miss Thane would not allow to be true. No protestations that he could make succeeded in shaking her belief that it was his modesty which spoke. She launched forth into a sea of talk, in which Dutch influence, the style of the Renaissance, the inferiority of Flemish craftsmanship, and the singular beauty of the Gothic jostled one another like rudderless boats adrift in a whirlpool. From the overmantel she passed with scarcely a check to the pictures on the walls. She detected a De Hooge with unerring judgment, and was at once reminded of a few weeks spent in the Netherlands some years go. Her reminiscences, recounted with a vivacious artlessness which made Eustacie stare at her in rapt admiration, were only put an end to by the Beau's seizing the opportunity afforded by her pausing to take breath to propose that they should step into the dining-parlour for some refreshment.

The Beau opened the door for the ladies to pass out into

the hall. Miss Thane went first, still chattering, leaving Eustacie to hang back for a moment, and to say in an urgent undertone to her cousin: "We came to-day because I have suddenly thought that perhaps you, who are very much of the world, could advise me. Only, you understand, I do not like to say anything before Sarah, because although she is extremely amiable, she is not, after all, of my family."

He bowed. "I am always at your service, my dear cousin, even though I may be—surprised."

"Surprised?" said Eustacie, with a look of child-like innocence.

"Well," said the Beau softly, "you have not been precisely in the habit of seeking either my company or my advice, have you, *ma chère?*"

"Oh!" said Eustacie, brushing that aside with a flutter of her expressive little hands, *"quant à ça,* when Grandpapa was alive I did not wish for anyone's advice but his. But I find myself now in a situation of the most awkward."

He looked at her with narrowed eyes, as though appraising her. "Yes, your situation is awkward," he said. "I could show you how to end that."

Miss Thane's voice, requesting him to tell her whether the staircase was original, put an end to all private conversation. He followed Eustacie out into the hall, saying that he believed it was quite original.

Wine and sandwiches had been set out on the table in the dining-parlour. While she ate, and sipped her glass of ratafie, Miss Thane took the opportunity of scrutinizing the wainscoting as closely as she dared. It was in two tiers, as Ludovic had described, the upper being composed of circular cartouches, carved with heads and devices, and separated from the lower by a broad frieze. The lower tier was divided vertically at every third panel by fluted pilasters with carved capitals. The whole was extremely beautiful, but the predominant thought in Miss Thane's mind was that to find one particular boss, or carved fruit, amongst the wealth on the wall would be an arduous labour.

Her meaningless prattle flowed on; she could not help being diverted by her own idiocies; nor, though she did not like him, could she fail to give the Beau credit for unwearied civility. By the time she had exhibited her commonplace book (in which Sir Tristram had had the forethought to sketch a few rough pictures of totally imaginary houses), and hoped that her host would grant her the indulgence of draw-

ing just a tiny corner of his lovely panelled dining-parlour,
her tongue was beginning to cleave to the roof of her mouth,
and she heard with feelings of profound relief the ringing of
a bell. It was at this moment that the Beau proposed escorting her to the library, in which room the wainscoting, though
similar to that in the dining-parlour, was generally held, he
believed, to be superior. They passed out into the hall, just as
the butler opened the front door to admit Sir Tristram. The
first sound that met his ears as he stepped over the threshold
was Miss Thane's voice extolling the style of Torrigiano. A
quiver of emotion for an instant disturbed the severity of his
expression, but he controlled it immediately, and taking a
hasty step forward, addressed Eustacie in outraged tones. "I
have been to the Red Lion, and was told I should find you
here! I do not understand what your purpose can have been
in coming, for I particularly requested the favour of an interview with you this morning!"

Eustacie drew back with a gesture conveying both alarm
and repugnance. "I told you I would not have any interview
with you. I do not see why you must follow me, for it is not
at all your affair that I choose to bring mademoiselle on a
visit to my own cousin!"

"It is very much my affair, since I am held responsible for
you!" he retorted.

The Beau intervened in his sweetest voice. "My dear Tristram, do pray come in! You are the very man of all others
we need. I believe you are acquainted with Miss Thane?"

Sir Tristram bowed stiffly. "Miss Thane and I have met,
but——"

"Nothing could be better!" declared the Beau. "Miss Thane
has done me the honour of coming to see my house, and,
alas, you know how lamentably ignorant I am on questions
of antiquity! But you, my dear fellow, know so much——"

"Oh!" exclaimed Miss Thane, clasping her hands together.
"If it would not be troubling Sir Tristram——!"

Sir Tristram assumed the expression of a man forced
against his will to be complaisant, and said somewhat ungra-
ciously that he would, of course, be pleased to tell Miss
Thane anything in his power. The Beau at once reminded
him that the wainscoting in the library was held to be worthy
of close study, and begged him to take Miss Thane there. He
added that if she cared to make a sketch of the room, he was
sure his cousin's taste and knowledge would be of assistance
to her.

"Eustacie and I will wait for you in the drawing-room," he said.

It seemed as though Sir Tristram would have demurred, but Miss Thane frustrated this by breaking into profuse expressions of gratitude. He made the best of it, and the instant the library door was closed on them, said: "Have you been talking like that all the time?"

Miss Thane sank into a chair in an exhausted attitude. "But without pause!" she said faintly. "My dear sir, I have been inspired! The mantle of my own cousin fell upon my shoulders, and I spoke like her, tittered like her, even thought like her! She is the silliest woman I know. It worked like a charm! He was itching to be rid of me!"

"I should imagine he might well!" said Sir Tristram. "The wonder is that he did not strangle you."

She chuckled. "He is too well-bred. Did I sound really feather-headed? I tried to."

"Yes," he said. He looked at her with a hint of a smile. "You are an extremely accomplished woman, Miss Thane."

"I have a natural talent for acting," she replied modestly. "But your own efforts were by no means contemptible, I assure you." She got up. "We have no time to waste if we are to find this panel. Do you take this side of the room and I will take that."

"Oh—the panel!" said Sir Tristram. "Yes, of course."

Chapter VII

HAVING got rid of his cousin and of Miss Thane, the Beau turned to Eustacie, and murmured: "Could anything be better? Shall we go into the drawing-room?"

Eustacie assented, wondering how long she would be able to hold him in conversation. She did not feel that she possessed quite Miss Thane's talent for discursive chatter, and she was far too ingenuous to realize that her enchanting little face was enough to keep the Beau by her side until she herself should be pleased to declare the interview at an end. It did not occur to her that he was looking at her with an expression of unusual warmth in his eyes, but beyond deciding that she did not like it, she paid very little heed to it. She sat down by the fire, her soft, dove-coloured skirts billowing about her, and remarked that if her dearest Sarah had a fault it was that she was a trifle too talkative.

"Just a trifle," agreed the Beau. "Do you really propose to accompany her to town?"

"Oh yes, certainly!" she replied. "But I cannot remain with her for ever, and it is that which makes everything very awkward. I meant to become a governess, but Sarah does not advise it. What do you think I should do?"

"Well," said the Beau slowly, "you could, of course, engage a lady of birth and propriety to live with you and be your chaperon. Sylvester had left you well provided for, you know."

"But I do not want a chaperon!" said Eustacie.

"No? There is an alternative."

"Tell me, then!"

"Marriage," he said.

She shook her head. "I will *not* marry Tristram. He is not amusing, and, besides, I do not like him."

"I am aware," said the Beau, "but Tristram is not the only man in the world, my little cousin."

Foreseeing what was coming, Eustacie at once agreed with

103

this pronouncement, and launched out into a eulogy of the Duke she would have married had her grandfather not brought her to England. The fact that she had never laid eyes on this gentleman did not deter her from describing him in detail, and it was fully fifteen minutes before her invention gave out and her cousin was able to interpolate a remark. He observed that since the Duke had gone to the guillotine, her fate, had she married him, would have been a melancholy one.

In this opinion, however, Eustacie could not concur. To have become a widow at the age of eighteen would, she held, have been *épatant*, and of all things the most romantic. "Moreover," she added, "it was a very good match. I should have been a duchess, and although Grandpapa says—said—that it is vulgar to care for such things, I do think that I should have liked to have been a duchess."

"Oh, I agree with you, *ma chère!*" he said cordially. "You would have made a charming duchess. But in these revolutionary times one must moderate one's ideas, you know. Consider, instead, the advantages of becoming a baroness."

"A baroness?" she faltered, fixing her eyes on his face with an expression of painful intensity. "What do you mean?"

He met her eyes with slightly raised brows, and for a moment stood looking down at her as though he were trying to read her thoughts. "My dear cousin, what in the world have I said to alarm you?" he asked.

Recollecting herself, she answered quickly: "I am not at all alarmed, but I do not understand what you mean. Why should I think about being a baroness?"

He pulled up a chair and sat down on it, rather nearer to her than she liked, and stretching out his hand laid it on one of hers. "I might make you one," he said.

She sat as straight and as stiff as a wooden puppet, but her cheeks glowed with the indignation that welled up in her. The glance she bent on him was a very fiery one, and she said bluntly: "You are not a baron, you!"

"We don't know that," he replied, "but we might find out. In fact, I have already recommended Tristram to do so."

"You mean that you would like very much to know that Ludovic is dead?"

He smiled. "Let us say rather than I should like very much to know *whether* he is dead, my dear."

She repressed the impulse to throw off his hand, and said

in a thoughtful voice: "Yes, I suppose you want to be Lord Lavenham. It is very natural."

He shrugged. "I do not set great store by it, but I should be glad of the title if it could win me the one thing I want."

This was too much for Eustacie, and she did pull her hand away, exclaiming: *"Voyons,* do you think I marry just for a title, me?"

"Oh no, no, no!" he said, smiling. "You would undoubtedly marry for love were it possible, but you have said yourself that your situation is awkward, and, alas, I know that you are not in love with me. I am offering a marriage of expediency, and when one is debarred from a love-match, dear cousin, it is time to give weight to material considerations."

"True, very true!" she said. "And you have given weight to them, *n'est-ce pas?* I am an heiress, as you reminded me yesterday."

"You are also enchanting," he said, with unwonted feeling.

"Merci du compliment! I regret infinitely that I do not find you enchanting, too."

"Ah, you are in love with romance!" he replied. "You imagine to yourself some hero of adventure, but it is a sad truth that in these humdrum days such people no longer exist."

"You know nothing of the matter: they do exist!" said Eustacie hotly.

"They would make undesirable husbands," he remarked. "Take poor Ludovic, for instance, whose story has, I believe, a little caught your fancy. You think him a very figure of romance, but you would be disappointed in him if ever you met him, I dare say."

She blushed, and turned her face away. "I do not wish to talk of Ludovic. I do not think of him at all."

He looked amused. "My dear, is it as bad as that? I should not—I really should not waste a moment's thought on him. One is sorry for him, one even liked him, but he was nothing but a rather stupid young man, after all."

She compressed her lips tightly, as though afraid some unguarded words might escape her. He watched her for a moment, and presently said: "Do you know, you look quite cross, cousin? Now, why?"

She replied, keeping her gaze fixed on a blazing log of wood in the grate: "It does not please me that you should suppose I am in love with someone I have never seen. It is a *bêtise.*"

"It would be," he agreed. "Let us by all means banish Ludovic from our minds, and talk, instead, of ourselves. You want certain things, Eustacie, which I could give you."

"I do not think it."

"It is nevertheless true. You would like a house in town, and to lead precisely the life I lead. You could not support the thought of becoming Tristram's wife, because he would expect you to be happy in Berkshire, rearing his children. Now, I should not expect anything so dull of you. Indeed, I should deprecate it. I do not think the domestic virtues are very strong in me. I should require only of my wife that her taste in dress should do me justice."

"You propose to me a *mariage de convenance*," said Eustacie, "and I have made up my mind that that is just what I do not want."

"I proposed to you what I thought might be acceptable. Forget it! I love you."

She got up quickly, a vague idea of flight in her mind. He, too, rose, and before she could stop him, put his arms round her. "Eustacie!" he said. "From the moment of first laying eyes on you I have loved you!"

An uncontrollable shudder ran through her. She wrenched herself out of his embrace, and cast him such a glance of repulsion that he stepped back, the smile wiped suddenly from his face.

He looked at her with narrowed eyes, but after a slight pause the ugly gleam vanished, and he was smiling again. He moved away to the other side of the fireplace, and drawled: "It seems that you do not find me so sympathetic as you would have had me believe, cousin. Now, I wonder why you wanted to come here to-day?"

"I thought you would advise me. I did not suppose that you would try to make love to me. That is quite another thing!"

He lifted an eyebrow at her. "Is it? But I think—yes, I think I have once or twice before informed you of my very earnest desire to marry you."

"Yes, but I have said already that I will not. It is finished."

"Perfectly," he bowed. "Let us talk of something else. There *was* something I had in mind to ask you, as I remember. What can it have been? Something that intrigued me." He half closed his eyes, as though in an effort of memory. "Something to do with your flight from the Court . . . ah yes, I have it! The mysterious groom! Who was the mysterious groom, Eustacie?"

The question came as a shock to her; her heart seemed to leap in her chest. To gain time she repeated: "The mysterious groom?"

"Yes," he smiled. "The groom who did not exist. Do tell me!"

"Oh!" she said, with a rather artificial laugh, "that is my very own adventure, and quite a romantic history! I assure you. How did you know of it?"

"In the simplest way imaginable, my dear cousin. My man Gregg fell in with a certain riding-officer at Cowfold yesterday, and from him gleaned this most interesting tale. I am consumed by curiosity. A groom whom you vouched for, and whom Tristram vouched for and who yet did not exist."

"Well, truly, I think it was wrong of me to save him from the riding-officer," confessed Eustacie, with a great air of candour, "but you must understand that I was under an obligation to him. One pays one's debts, after all!"

"Such a sentiment does you credit," said the Beau affably. "What was the debt?"

"Oh, the most exciting thing!" she replied. "I did not tell you the whole yesterday, because Sarah's brother is a Justice of the Peace, and one must be careful, but I was captured by smugglers that night, and but for the man I saved I should have been killed. Murdered, you know. Conceive of it!"

"How very, very alarming for you!" said the Beau.

"Yes, it was. There were a great many of them, and they were afraid I should betray them, and they said I must at once be killed. Only this one—the one I said was my groom —took my part, and he would not permit that I should be killed. I think he was the leader, because they listened to him."

"I never till now heard that chivalry existed amongst smugglers," remarked the Beau.

"No, but he was not a *preux chevalier,* you know. He was quite rough, and not at all civil, but he had compassion upon me, and that led to a great quarrel between him and the other men. Then the riding-officers came, and my smuggler threw me up on to my horse and mounted behind me, because he said that the Excisemen must not find me, which, I see, was quite reasonable. Only the Excisemen fired at him, and he was wounded, and Rufus bolted into the Forest. And

I did not know what to do, so I went to the Red Lion and asked Nye to help the smuggler, because it seemed to me that I could not give him up after he had saved me from being killed."

The Beau was listening with his usual air of courteous interest. He said: "What strange, what incredible things do happen, to be sure! Now if I had heard this tale at second-hand, or perhaps read it in a romance, I should have said it was far too improbable to bear the least resemblance to the truth. It shows how easily one may be mistaken. I, for instance, on what I conceived to be my knowledge of Nye's character, can even now scarcely credit him with so much noble disregard for his own good name. You must possess great influence over him, dear cousin."

Eustacie felt a little uneasy, but replied carelessly: "Yes, perhaps I have some influence, but I am bound to confess he did not at all like it, and he would not by any means keep the smuggler in his house."

"Oh, the smuggler has departed, has he?"

"But yes, the very next day! What else?"

"I am sure I do not know. I expect I am very stupid," he added apologetically, "but there do seem to me to be one or two unexplained points to this adventure. I find myself quite at a loss to understand Tristram's part in it. How were you able to persuade so stern a pattern of rectitude to support your story, my dear?"

Eustacie began to wish very much that Tristram and Sarah would finish their search and come to her rescue. "Oh, but, you see, when it was explained to him Tristram was grateful to my smuggler for saving me!"

"Oh!" said the Beau, blinking. "Tristram was grateful. Yes, I see. How little one knows of people, after all! It must have gone sadly against the grain with him, I feel. He has not breathed a word of it to me."

"No, and I think it is very foolish of him," returned Eustacie. "Tristram does not wish anyone to know of my adventure, because he says I have behaved with impropriety, and it had better immediately be forgotten."

"Ah, that is much better!" said the Beau approvingly. "I feel that he may well have said that."

This rejoinder, which seemed to convey a disturbing disbelief in the rest of her story, left Eustacie without a word to say. The Beau, seeing her discomfiture, smiled more broadly, and said: "You know, you have quite forgotten to tell me that your smuggler was one of Sylvester's bastards."

Eustacie felt the colour rise in her cheeks, and at once turned it to account, exclaiming in shocked tones: "Cousin!"

"I beg your pardon!" he said, with exaggerated concern. "I should have said love-children."

She threw him a reproachful, outraged look, and replied: "Certainly I have not forgotten, but I do not speak of indelicate things, and I am very much *émue* to think that you could mention it to me."

He apologized profusely, but with an ironical air which made her feel rather uncomfortable. Luckily an interruption occurred before he could ask any more awkward questions. Miss Thane and Sir Tristram came into the room. Sir Tristram wore an expression of long-suffering, but in Miss Thane's eyes there peeped an irrepressible twinkle.

The quick, anguished glance thrown at him by Eustacie was enough to warn Shield that all was not well. He gave no sign of having noticed it, however, but waited for Miss Thane to come to the end of her eulogies and thanks. The Beau received these with smiling civility, and when they ceased, turned to his cousin, and said in a languid voice that he had been hearing more of her adventure from Eustacie. Sir Tristram quite unwittingly bore out the character bestowed on him by Eustacie by saying curtly that the sooner the adventure was forgotten the better it would be.

"You are too harsh, my dear Tristram," said the Beau. "But we know how kind-hearted you are under your—er severity."

"Indeed!" said Shield, looking most forbidding.

"Yes, yes, I have heard all about Eustacie's smuggler, and how you helped to protect him from the riding-officers. I have been much moved. A—a connection of Sylvester, I believe?"

Sir Tristram replied coolly: "Just so. I thought there would be less noise made over the affair if he were allowed to escape."

"I expect you were right, my dear fellow. How quick of you to recognize one of Sylvester's—ah, I must not offend Eustacie's sensibilities again!—one of Sylvester's relations."

Sir Tristram was not in the least put out by this. He said: "Oh, I knew him at once! So would you have done. You remember Jem Sunning, don't you?"

"Jem Sunning!" There was just the faintest suggestion of chagrin in the Beau's voice. "Is that who it was? I thought he went to America."

"So did I. Apparently he found free-trading more to his taste, however. Eustacie, if you are ready to return to Hand Cross, I shall do myself the honour of escorting your carriage."

Bearing in mind her avowed dislike of him, Eustacie thought it proper to demur at this suggestion, and some time was wasted in argument. Miss Thane enacted the rôle of peacemaker, and finally the whole party took their leave of the Beau, and set off for Hand Cross.

When he had handed the ladies into their chaise, and seen it drive off with Sir Tristram riding beside it, the Beau walked slowly back to the house, and made his way to the library. His face wore an expression of pensive abstraction, and he did not immediately occupy himself in any way. He wandered instead to the window and looked out over the neat beds of his formal garden. His gaze seemed to question the clipped hedges; his eyebrows were a little raised; his hand went as though unconsciously to his quizzing-glass, and began to play with it, sliding it up and down the silk ribbon that was knotted through the chased ring at the end of the shaft. At this idle employment he was found a few minutes later by his valet, a discreet, colourless person of self-effacing manners and unequalled skill in all details concerning a gentleman's toilet. He came into the room with his usual hushed tread, and laid a folded journal on the table with a finicking care that seemed to indicate the handling of some precious and brittle object.

The Beau, recognizing these stealthy sounds, spoke without turning his head. "Ah, Gregg! That riding-officer."

The valet folded his hands meekly and stood with slightly bowed head. "Yes, sir?"

"He described mademoiselle's groom to you, I think?"

"Imperfectly, sir. He was struck by a resemblance to the late lord, but I could not discover that this lay in anything but the nose." He coughed, and added apologetically: "That may be seen in Sussex—occasionally, sir."

The Beau made no response. Gregg waited, his eyes lowered. After a short interval the Beau said slowly: "A young man, I think?"

"I was informed so, sir."

The Beau bit the rim of his quizzing-glass meditatively.

"How old by your reckoning would Jem Sunning be at this present?"

The valet's eyes lifted, and for a moment stared in surprise at the back of his master's powdered head. He replied after a moment's reflection: "I regret, sir, I am unable to answer with any degree of certainty. I should suppose him to be somewhere in the region of one- or two-and-thirty."

"My memory is very imperfect," sighed the Beau, "but I think he was always used to be dark, was he not?"

"Yes, sir." The valet gave another of his deprecating coughs. "It is generally said amongst the country people, sir, that my lord gave his own colouring to his descendants."

"Yes," agreed the Beau. "Yes, I have heard that. In fact, I think I can call only one exception to mind." He turned, and came away from the window to stand in front of the fire. "I cannot but feel that it would be interesting to know whether mademoiselle's groom conformed to the rule—or not."

"The riding-officer, sir," said Gregg, in an expressionless voice, "spoke of a fair young man."

"Ah!" said the Beau gently. "A fair young man! Well, that is very odd, to be sure."

"Yes, sir. A trifle unusual, I believe."

The Beau's gaze dwelled thoughtfully upon a portrait hanging on the opposite wall. "I think, Gregg, that we sometimes purchase our brandy from Joseph Nye?"

"We have very often done so, sir."

"We will purchase some more," said the Beau, polishing his eye-glass on his sleeve. "Attend to it, Gregg."

"Yes, sir."

"That is all," said the Beau.

The valet bowed and walked towards the door. As he reached it the Beau said softly: "I should not like you to display any vulgar curiosity at the Red Lion, Gregg."

"No, sir. You may rely on me."

"Oh, I do, Gregg, I do!" said the Beau, and picking up the journal from the table, sat down with it in a winged armchair by the fire.

The valet lingered for a moment. "If I may venture to say something, sir?" he suggested meekly.

"By all means, Gregg."

"The lady who accompanied Sir Tristram into this room, sir. I understand she was desirous of inspecting the panelling?"

The Beau raised his eyes from the journal. "Well?"

"Just so, sir. It would, of course, explain conduct which seemed to Thomson and myself a trifle odd. I beg pardon, I'm sure."

"In what way odd?"

"Well, sir, it appeared to Thomson and myself that Sir Tristram and the lady were inspecting the woodwork very closely," said the valet. "The lady went so far as to stand upon a chair to inspect the frieze, and Sir Tristram, when I entered the room, seemed to me (but I might be mistaken) to be sounding the lower panels."

The Beau lowered the journal. "Did he?" he said slowly. "Did he, indeed? Well, well!"

Gregg bowed himself out. It was a few minutes before the Beau picked up his journal again. His eyes stared across the room at a certain portion of the wainscoting; and there was for once no trace of a smile upon his thin lips.

Meanwhile Miss Thane, seated beside Eustacie in the chaise, had nothing to report but failure. She said that her fingers were sore from pulling and pressing wooden bosses, and that her nervous system was shattered for ever. No fewer than three interruptions had occurred during the short time she and Sir Tristram had had at their disposal. First had come the housekeeper with a bowl of flowers to set upon the table, and a tongue only too ready to wag. She had hardly been got rid of when the door opened again, this time to admit the butler, who had come in to make up the fire. "And what he must have thought, I dare not imagine!" said Miss Thane. "I was standing upon a chair at that precise moment, trying to move a wooden pear well above my reach."

Eustacie gave a giggle. "What did you do?"

"Most unfortunately," said Miss Thane, "my back was turned to the door, and I had not heard it open. I am bound to confess, however, that your cousin Tristram showed great presence of mind, for he immediately told me to look closely at the carving, and to observe most particularly the top chamfer of the cross-rail."

"One must admit that Tristram is not stupid," said Eustacie fair-mindedly.

"No," agreed Miss Thane, casting a glance out of the window at the straight figure riding beside the chaise, "not stupid, but (I am sorry to say) both autocratic and dictatorial. His remarks to me once the butler had left the room were quite unappreciative and not a little unfeeling, while his way of handing me down from the chair left much to be desired."

"He does not like females," explained Eustacie.

Miss Thane's eyes returned to the contemplation of Sir Tristram's stern profile. "Ah!" she said. "That would account for it, of course. Well, we did what we could to make my standing upon a chair seem a natural proceeding—but I doubt the butler thinks us a pair of lunatics—and being once more alone, and Sir Tristram having spoken his mind to me on the subject of female folly, we returned to our search. It affords me some satisfaction to reflect that it was Sir Tristram, and not I, who was engaged in sounding the panels when a most odiously soft-footed individual stole in to place a snuff-jar upon the desk. At least, it afforded me the opportunity to show that I, too, have some presence of mind. I begged your cousin to admire the spear-head finish."

"I think that you are very clever!" said Eustacie approvingly. "I should not have known that there was a—a spear-head finish."

"There wasn't," said Miss Thane. "In fact, the mere mention of a spear-head finish in connection with those panels was a solecism which caused a spasm to cross Sir Tristram's features. When the snuff-bearer had taken himself off he was obliging enough to inform me that before he accompanied me on another such search he would give me a few simple lessons in what to look for in wood-panelling of that particular kind. By that time I had undergone so many frights that my spirit was quite in abeyance, and I not only thanked him meekly, but I even acquiesced in his decision to abandon the quest. Yes, I know it was wretchedly weak of me," she added, in answer to a look of reproach from Eustacie, "but to tell you the truth, I think the task is well-nigh hopeless. Ludovic must remember more precisely where the panel is."

"But you know very well that he cannot!"

"Then he must go and look for it himself," said Miss Thane firmly.

Eustacie was inclined to be indignant but the chaise had by this time drawn up outside the Red Lion, and she was forced to postpone her recriminations until a more convenient occasion. Shield, dismounting lightly from his horse, himself opened the door and let down the steps for the ladies to descend. Having handed them out of the chaise, he gave his horse into the charge of one of the ostlers and followed them into the inn. Here they were met by Nye, who informed them in the voice of one who had done his best to avert disaster but failed that they should find Ludovic in Sir Hugh Thane's room.

"In my brother's room?" exclaimed Miss Thane. "What in the world is he doing there?"

"He's playing cards, ma'am," replied Nye grimly.

"But how came he to go into my brother's room at all?" demanded Miss Thane. "We left him in bed!"

"You did, ma'am, but you hadn't been gone above five minutes before his lordship started ringing the bell for Clem. Nothing else would do for him but to get up and dress, and me not being by Clem helped him. That's how it always was: what Mr. Ludovic took it into his head to do, Clem would help him to, no matter what."

Eustacie turned to her cousin. "You should not have brought his clothes!"

"Nonsense!" said Shield. "Ludovic must leave his bed sooner or later. He'll take no hurt."

"That is all very well," said Miss Thane, "but even though he might get up, I can see no reason for him to go into Hugh's room. I have a great value for Hugh, but I cannot feel that he is the man to keep a momentous secret. Nye, you should have intervened."

Nye smiled somewhat wryly. "It's plain you don't know his lordship, ma'am. No sooner was he dressed than what must he do but walk out of his room just to see how his legs would carry him. While he was showing Clem how well he could manage, Sir Hugh (who'd been pulling his bell fit to break it, according to what he told me) put his head out of his room to shout for Clem. By what I can make out from Clem, Sir Hugh and Mr. Ludovic got into conversation right away, Sir Hugh not seeming to be surprised at finding another gentleman in the house, and Mr. Ludovic, of course, as friendly as you please. 'Oh, are you Sir Hugh Thane?' he says. 'My name's Lavenham——' oh yes, ma'am, he came out with that quite brazen! That's Mr. Ludovic all over. 'Well,' says Sir Hugh, 'I can't say I call your face to mind at the moment, but if you know me I'm devilish glad of it, for I've had more than enough of my own company. Do you play piquet?' Well, that was quite sufficient for Mr. Ludovic, and before Clem rightly knew what was happening, he'd been sent off downstairs to fetch up a couple of packs of cards and a bottle of wine. By the time I was back in the house there was no doing anything, ma'am, for they was both in Sir Hugh's room, as thick as thieves, as the saying is."

The ladies looked at one another in consternation. "I had better go upstairs and see what is happening," said Miss Thane resignedly.

It was, however, just as Nye had described. Lord Lavenham and Sir Hugh Thane, both attired in dressing-gowns, were seated on opposite sides of a small table drawn close to the fire in Sir Hugh's bed-chamber playing piquet. A glass of wine was at each gentleman's elbow, and so absorbed were they in the game that neither paid the least heed to the opening of the door, or, in fact, became aware of Miss Thane's presence until she stepped right up to the table. Sir Hugh glanced up then, and said in an abstracted voice: "Oh, there you are, Sally!" and turned his attention to the cards again.

Miss Thane laid her hand on Ludovic's shoulder to prevent his rising but remarked significantly: "What if I had been the Beau, or an Exciseman?"

"Oh, I'm well prepared!" Ludovic assured her, and in the twinkling of an eye had whisked a small, silver-mounted pistol from his pocket.

"Good God, I hope you don't mean to fire on sight!" said Miss Thane.

Sir Hugh put up his glass to look at the pistol. "That's a nice little gun," he observed.

Ludovic handed it to him. "Yes, it's one of Manton's. I've a pair of his duelling-pistols, too—beautiful pieces of work!"

Sir Hugh subjected the pistol to a careful inspection. "Myself I don't care for silver sights. Apt to dazzle the eye." He sighted along the pistol. "Nice balance, but too short in the barrel. No accuracy over twelve yards."

Ludovic's eye gleamed. "Do you think so? I'll engage to culp a wafer at twenty!"

"With this gun?" said Sir Hugh incredulously.

"With that gun."

"I'll lay you a pony you don't."

"Done!" said Ludovic promptly.

"And where," inquired Miss Thane, "do you propose to hold this contest?"

"Oh, in the yard!" said Ludovic, receiving the pistol back from Sir Hugh.

"That, of course, will be very nice," said Miss Thane politely. "The ostlers will thus be able to see you. I forbid you to encourage him, Hugh. Let us admit that he is a crack shot, and be done with it."

"Well, I am a crack shot," said Ludovic, smiling most disarmingly up at her.

"Talking of crack shots," said Sir Hugh, "what was the name of the fellow who put out all the candles in the big chandelier at Mrs. Archer's once? There were fifteen of them, and he never missed one!"

"Fifteen?" said Ludovic. "Sixteen!"

"Fifteen was what I was told. He did it for a wager."

"That's true enough, but I tell you there were sixteen candles!"

Sir Hugh shook his head. "You've got that wrong. Fifteen."

"Damn it, I ought to know!" said Ludovic. "I did it!"

"You did it?" Sir Hugh regarded him with renewed interest. "You mean to tell me you are the man who shot the wicks off fifteen candles at Mrs. Archer's?"

"I shot the wicks off *sixteen* candles!" said Ludovic.

"Well, all I can say is that it was devilish fine shooting," said Sir Hugh. "But are you sure you have the figure right? I rather fancy fifteen was the number."

"Where's Tristram?" demanded Ludovic of Miss Thane. "He was there! Sixteen candles I shot. I used my Mantons, and Jerry Matthews loaded for me."

"I don't know him," remarked Sir Hugh. "Would he be a son of old Frederick Matthews?"

Miss Thane at this point withdrew to summon Sir Tristram. When she returned with him she found that the question of Mr. Jerry Matthews's parentage had led inexplicably to an argument on the precise nature of a certain bet entered in the book at White's three years before. The argument was broken off as soon as Sir Tristram entered the room, for Ludovic at once commanded him to say whether he had put out fifteen or sixteen candles at Mrs. Archer's house.

"I don't remember," replied Sir Tristram. "All I remember is that you shattered a big mirror to smithereens and brought the Watch in on us."

Sir Hugh, who was looking fixedly at Sir Tristram, said suddenly, and with a pleased air: "Shield! That's who you are! I recognized you at once. What's more, I know where I saw you last."

Sir Tristram shook hands with him. "At Mendoza's fight

with Warr last year," he said, without hesitation. "I recall that you were on the roof of the coach next to my curricle."

"That's it!" said Thane. "A grand turn-up! Did you see Dan's last fight with Humphries? A couple of years ago that would be, or maybe three."

"I saw him beat Humphries twice, and I was at the Fitzgerald turn-up in '91."

"You were? Then tell me this—Was Fitzgerald shy, or was he not?"

"Not shy, no. Rather glaringly abroad once or twice, I thought."

"He was, was he? I'm glad to know that, because——"

"If you are going to talk about prize-fights, I'll leave you," interposed Miss Thane.

"No, don't do that," said Ludovic. "I'm not interested in prize-fights. By-the-by, did you find that panel?"

This casual reference to her morning's labour made Miss Thane reply tartly: "No, Ludovic, we did *not* find that panel."

"I didn't think you would," he said.

Miss Thane appeared to struggle with emotions. Her brother, showing a faint interest in what he had caught of the conversation, said sympathetically: "Lost something?"

"No, dear," replied Sarah, with awful calm. "It is Lord Lavenham who has lost a talisman ring. I told you all about it three days ago. He lost it at play one night at the Cocoa-Tree."

"I do remember you telling me some rigmarole or another," admitted Thane. "If you want my advice, Lavenham, you won't play at the Cocoa-Tree. I met a Captain Sharp there myself once. Hazard it was, and the dice kept running devilish high. I'd my suspicions of them from the start, and sure enough they were up-hills."

"Oh, the play was fair enough," said Ludovic indifferently.

"What I'm telling you is that it wasn't," said Sir Hugh, patient but obstinate. "I split the dice myself and found 'em loaded."

"I wasn't talking about that. *My* game was piquet. Never played hazard at the Cocoa-Tree in my life. I used to play at Almack's, and Brooks's, of course."

"Very high-going at Brooks's," said Thane, with a reflective shake of the head.

Sarah, seeing that a discussion of the play at the various

gaming clubs in London was in a fair way to being begun, intervened before Ludovic could say anything more. She reminded him severely that they had more important things to discuss than gaming, and added with a good deal of feeling that her efforts on his behalf had not only been fruitless, but quite possibly disastrous as well. "Your cousin," she said, "has heard about Eustacie's groom, and there is no doubt that he feels suspicious. Luckily, Sir Tristram had the presence of mind to tell him that the groom was——whom did you say he was, Sir Tristram?"

"Jem Sunning," replied Shield. "You remember him, Ludovic?"

"Yes, but I thought he went to America."

"He did," said Shield. "That was why I chose him. But I'm not sure that the Beau believed me. It is more imperative than ever that you should get to some place of safety. If you won't go to Holland——"

"Well, I won't," said Ludovic flatly.

Sir Hugh came unexpectedly to his support. "Holland?" he said. "I shouldn't go to Holland if I were you. I didn't like it at all. Rome, now! That's the place—though they have a demmed sight too many pictures there, too," he added gloomily.

"I am going to stay here," said Ludovic. "If the worst comes to the worst, there's always the cellar."

"Just what I was thinking myself!" said Thane approvingly "I've a strong notion there's more in that cellar than we've discovered. Why, I didn't get hold of this Canary till yesterday!"

No one paid the slightest heed to this interruption. Sir Tristram said: "Very well, if you are determined, Ludovic, I don't propose to waste time in trying to persuade you. Are you serious in thinking that the ring may be behind that panel?"

"Of course I'm serious! It's the very place for it. Where else would he be likely to put it?"

"If I help you to get into the house, can you find the panel?"

"I can try," said Ludovic hopefully.

"Yes, no doubt," returned Shield, "but I have assisted in one aimless search for it, and I've no desire to repeat the experience."

"Once I'm in the house you can leave it to me," said Ludovic. "I'm bound to recognize the panelling when I see it."

"I hope you may," replied Shield. "The Beau spoke of going to town one day this week, and that should be our opportunity."

Miss Thane coughed. "And how—the question just occurs to me, you know—shall you get into the Dower House, sir?"

"We can break in through a window," answered Ludovic. "There's no difficulty about that."

She cast a demure glance up at Shield. "I am afraid you will never get Sir Tristram to agree to do anything so rash," she said.

He returned her glance with one of his measuring looks. "I must seem to you a very spiritless creature, Miss Thane."

She smiled, and shook her head, but would not answer. Her brother, who had been following the conversation with a puzzled frown, suddenly observed that it all sounded very odd to him. "You can't break into someone's house!" he objected.

"Yes, I can," returned Ludovic. "I'm not such a cripple as that!"

"But it's a criminal offence!" Sir Hugh pointed out.

"If it comes to that it's a criminal offence to smuggle liquor into the country," replied Ludovic. "I can tell you, I'm in so deep that it don't much signify what I do now."

Sir Hugh sat up. "You're never the smuggler my sister spoke to me about?"

"I'm a free-trader," said Ludovic, grinning.

"Then just tell me this!" said Thane, his interest in housebreaking vanishing before a more important topic. "Can you get me a pipe of the same Chambertin Nye has in his cellar?"

Chapter VIII

It was agreed finally that Ludovic should attempt nothing in the way of housebreaking until his cousin had discovered which day the Beau proposed to go to London. Ludovic, incurably optimistic, considered his ring as good as found already, but Shield, taking a more sober view of the situation, saw pitfalls ahead. If the Beau, like his father before him, were indeed in the habit of using the priest's hole as a hiding-place for his strong-box, nothing was more likely than his keeping the ring there as well. Almost the only point on which Shield found himself at one with his volatile young cousin was the belief, firmly held by Ludovic, that the Beau, if he ever had the ring, would neither have sold it nor have thrown it away. To sell it would be too dangerous a procedure; to throw away an antique of great value would require more resolution than Sir Tristram believed the Beau possessed. But Sir Tristram could not share Ludovic's easy-going contempt of the Beau. Ludovic persisted in laughing at his affectations, and thinking him a mere fop of no particular courage or enterprise. Sir Tristram, though he had no opinion of the Beau's courage, profoundly mistrusted his suavity, and considered him to be a great deal more astute than he seemed.

The circumstance of the Beau's butler and valet having seen part at least of the search for the secret panel Sir Tristram found disturbing. That the Beau was already suspicious of Eustacie's supposed groom was apparent; Sir Tristram believed that if he got wind of his cousins' odd behaviour in his library he would be quite capable of putting two and two together and not only connecting Ludovic with the episode but realizing that he himself had at last fallen under suspicion. And if the Beau suspected that Ludovic, who knew the position of the priest's hole, had come into Sussex to find his ring he would surely be very unlikely to leave it where it would certainly be looked for.

Some part of these forebodings Shield confided to Miss Thane, enjoining her to do all that lay in her power to keep Ludovic hidden from all eyes but their own.

"Well, I will do my best," replied Sarah, "but it is not an easy task, Sir Tristram."

"I know it is not an easy task," he said impatiently, "but it is the only way in which you can assist us—which I understand you to be desirous of doing."

She could not forbear giving him a look of reproach. "You must be forgetting what assistance I rendered you at the Dower House," she said.

"No," replied Sir Tristram, at his dryest. "I was not forgetting that."

Miss Thane rested her chin in her hand, pensively surveying him. "Will you tell me something, Sir Tristram?"

"Perhaps. What is it?"

"What induced you ever to contemplate marriage with your cousin?"

He looked startled, and not too well pleased. "I can hardly suppose, ma'am, that my private affairs can be of interest to you," he said.

"Some people," remarked Miss Thane wisely, "would take that for a set-down."

Their eyes met; Sir Tristram smiled reluctantly. "You do not seem to be of the number, ma'am."

"I am very thick-skinned," explained Sarah. "You see, I have not had the benefit of a correct upbringing."

"Have you always lived with your brother?" he inquired.

"Since I left school, sir."

"I suppose that accounts for it," he said, half to himself.

"Accounts for what?" asked Miss Thane suspiciously.

"Your—unusual quality, ma'am."

"I hope that is a compliment," said Miss Thane, not without misgiving.

"I am not very apt at compliments!" he retorted.

Her eyes twinkled appreciatively. "Yes, I deserved that. Very well, Sir Tristram, but you have not answered my question. Why did you take it into your head to marry your cousin?"

"You have been misinformed, ma'am. The idea was taken into my great-uncle's head, not mine."

She raised her brows. "Had you no voice in the matter then? Now, from what I have seen of you, I find that very hard to believe."

"Do you imagine that I wanted to marry Eustacie for the sake of her money?" he demanded.

"No," replied Miss Thane calmly. "I do not imagine anything of the kind."

His momentary flash of anger died down; he said, less harshly: "Being the last of my name, ma'am, I conceive it to be my duty to marry. The alliance proposed to me by my great-uncle was one of convenience, and as such agreeable to me. Owing to the precarious circumstances to which the upheaval in France has reduced her paternal relatives, her grandfather's death leaves Eustacie alone in the world, a contingency he sought to provide against by this match. I promised Sylvester upon his death-bed that I would marry Eustacie. That is all the story."

"How do you propose to salve your conscience?" asked Miss Thane.

"My conscience is not likely to trouble me in this instance," he answered. "Eustacie does not wish to marry me, and it would take more than a promise made to Sylvester to make me pursue a suit which she has declared to be distasteful to her. Moreover, had events turned out otherwise, Sylvester would have given her to Ludovic, not to me."

"Oh, that is famous!" said Miss Thane. "We can now promote her betrothal to him with clear consciences. But it is vexing for you to be obliged to look about you for another lady eligible for the post you require her to fill. Are you set on marrying a young female?"

"I am not set on marrying anyone, and I beg that you——"

"Well, that should make it easier," said Miss Thane. "Very young ladies are apt to be romantic, and that would never do."

"I certainly do not look for romance in marriage, but pray do not let my affairs——"

"It must be someone past the age of being hopeful of getting a husband," pursued Miss Thane, sinking her chin in her hand again.

"Thank you!" said Sir Tristram.

"Not handsome—I do not think we can expect her to be more than passable," decided Miss Thane. "Good birth would of course be an essential?"

"Really, Miss Thane, this conversation——"

"Luckily," she said, "there are any number of plain females of good birth but small fortune to be found in town.

You may meet a few at the subscription balls at Almack's, but I dare say I could find you a dozen to choose from whose Mamas have long since ceased to take them to the 'Marriage Market.' After a certain number of seasons they have to yield place to younger sisters, you know."

"You are too kind, ma'am!"

"Not at all; I shall be delighted to help you," Miss Thane assured him. "I have just the sort of female that would suit you in my mind's eye. A good, affectionate girl, with no pretensions to beauty, and a grateful disposition. She must be past the age of wanting to go to parties, and she must not expect you to make pretty speeches to her. I wonder—— Would you object to her having a slight—a *very* slight squint in one eye?"

"Yes, I should," said Sir Tristram. "Nor have I the smallest desire to——"

Miss Thane sighed. "Well, that is a pity. I had thought of the very person for you."

"Let me beg you not to waste your time thinking of another! The matter is not urgent."

She shook her head. "I cannot agree with you. After all, when one approaches middle age——"

"Middle—— Has anyone ever boxed your ears, Miss Thane?"

"No, never," said Miss Thane, looking blandly up at him.

"You have been undeservedly fortunate," said Sir Tristram grimly. "We will, if you please, leave the subject of my marriage. I do not anticipate an immediate entry into wedlock."

"Do you know," said Miss Thane, with an air of candour, "I believe you are wise. You are not cut out for matrimony. Your faith in females was shattered by an unfortunate affair in your youth; your eyes were opened to the defects of the female character; you are——"

Sir Tristram looked thunderous. "Who told you this?" he snapped.

"Why, you did!"

"*I?*" he repeated.

"Most certainly."

"You are mistaken. I am ready to allow that there may be many excellent women in the world. I do not know by what sign you knew that there had been an affair in my past about which I do not care to think. I can assure you that it has not prejudiced me against your sex."

Miss Thane listened to this with her usual placidity, and,

far from showing discomfiture, merely said: "It seems to me very inexplicable that you can have met your cousin with so open a mind and yet failed to fall instantly in love with her."

He gave a short laugh. "There is no fear of my falling in love, ma'am. I learned my lesson early in life, but believe me, I have not forgotten it!"

"How melancholy it is to reflect that so few people have the good sense to profit by their experience as you have done!" said Miss Thane soulfully. "I wonder if we should warn your cousins of the disillusionment in store for them?"

"I do not think it will be necessary, Miss Thane. Moreover, there is no immediate likelihood of their being married. Ludovic's affairs seem to me to be in as bad a way as they well might be."

She became serious at once. "Do you think them hopeless?"

"No, not hopeless," he replied. "But we have no certainty of the talisman ring being in Basil Lavenham's possession, and to be frank with you, I don't place much dependence upon its being in the priest's hole, even if he has got it. Assuming that he has, I think he would remove it from a hiding-place known to Ludovic the instant he suspected his presence in the neighborhood."

"But does he suspect his presence?"

"There is no saying what the Beau suspects, Miss Thane. Don't allow Ludovic to convince you that we have to deal with a fool! He is no such thing, I assure you."

"You need not tell me that: I have met him. Will you think me fanciful if I say that I have a strong feeling that he is truly at the bottom of all Ludovic's troubles?"

"No, I think it myself. The difficulty will be to prove it."

"If you cannot find the ring what is to be done?"

She saw his mouth harden. He had evidently considered this question, for he replied at once: "If the worst come to the worst, the truth will have to be got out of him by other methods."

Miss Thane, looking at Sir Tristram's powerful frame, and observing the grimness in his face, could not help feeling sorry for the Beau if the worst should come to the worst. She replied lightly: "Would—er—other methods answer, do you suppose?"

"Probably," said Sir Tristram. "He has very little physical courage. But until we have more to go upon than conjecture, we need not consider that."

She sat thinking for a few moments, and presently said: "In one way it might not be so bad a thing if he did suspect Ludovic's presence here. If he suspected it he must, I imagine, realize that you have been convinced of Ludovic's innocence. I have frequently observed that when people are a little alarmed they are apt to behave with less than common sense. Your cousin has been so secure until now that it has been easy to act with coolness and presence of mind."

"Very true," he conceded. "I have thought of that, but the risks outweigh the advantages. If it were not for one circumstance I should seriously consider removing Ludovic from this country."

"He seems very determined. I don't think that he would consent to go," said Miss Thane.

"I shouldn't ask his consent," replied Shield.

"Dear me, you seem to be in a very ruthless mood!" she remarked. "What makes you hesitate to kidnap poor Ludovic?"

"His marksmanship," he answered. "A man would have to be in desperate straits before he engaged in a shooting-match with Ludovic. The Beau won't risk it."

"Well," said Miss Thane, getting up from her chair, "I am far from wishing you to ship Ludovic out of the country (besides, it's my belief he would come back), but I've a notion we are going to see some stirring adventures before we leave this place."

"It's very possible," he agreed. "Are you afraid?"

She raised her eyes to his face. There was a hint of amusement in them. "My dear sir, can you not see that I am positively trembling with fright?" she said.

He smiled. "I beg your pardon. But to have a finger in a pie of Ludovic's making is enough to cause the bravest to quail! What I chiefly dread is his taking it into his head to break into the Dower House without waiting for word from me. Do you think you can prevent him?"

"I don't know," said Sarah candidly. "But I can at least get word to you if he becomes unmanageable."

For the time being, however, even Ludovic himself was forced to admit that his strength was not sufficiently recovered to permit of his riding five miles to the Dower House. He had lost a good deal of blood, and had been feverish for long enough to make him tiresomely weak upon first getting up out of his sick bed. He was not one to submit patiently to being an invalid, nor did it seem to be possible to impress him with a sense of the dangerous nature of his situation. Once he was possessed of his clothes, nothing short of turning the key on him could keep him in his room. He strolled about the inn in the most careless way imaginable, his left arm disposed in a sling and Sylvester's great ruby on his finger. When begged to conceal this too well-known ring somewhere about his person, or to give it back to Tristram for safe-keeping, he said No, he had a fancy to wear Sylvester's ruby. Twice he nearly walked into the arms of local visitors to the Red Lion, who had come in for a tankard of ale and a chat over the coffee-room fire, and only Miss Thane's timely intervention prevented him sallying forth into the yard with Sir Hugh to win his bet with a little marksmanship. Miss Thane, accustomed to handling the male, did not attempt to dissuade him from shooting. She merely suggested that if he wished to fire a noisy pistol the cellar would be the best place for such a pastime. Ludovic was just about to argue the point when Sir Hugh providentially pooh-poohed his sister's suggestion, on the score that no one could be expected to culp a wafer in the wretched light afforded by a branch of candles. This was quite enough to make Ludovic instantly engage to win his wager under these or any other conditions, and down they both went, with Clem in attendance. There being no wafers available, a playing-card had to suffice. When Ludovic tossed the ace of hearts to Clem, and said carelessly: "Hold it for me, Clem!" Sir Hugh was shocked almost out of his sleepy placidity, and indeed went so far as to adjure the tapster not to be fool enough to obey. Clem, who, besides possessing boundless faith in Ludovic, would never have dreamed of disobeying his orders, merely grinned at this piece of advice, and held up the card by one corner. Ludovic, lounging on a barrel, inspected the priming of his pistol, requested Thane to move the candles a little to one side, levelled the pistol, and fired. The card fluttered to the ground. Clem, grinning more than ever, picked it up and showed it to Sir Hugh with the pip blown clean out of it.

This feat seemed to call for celebration, and Miss Thane, descending into the cellar in search of them some time later, found that they had broached a keg of Nantes brandy, and had no immediate intention of returning to upper ground. Invigorated by the brandy, Sir Hugh was seized by a desire to emulate Ludovic's skill—but without Clem's assistance. His efforts, unattended by success, brought Nye down to put a stop to a sport which was not only riddling the walls of the cellar, but creating enough noise to lead anyone above-stairs to suppose that the inn was being besieged.

Since he was not allowed to step outside the Red Lion, and dissuaded from wandering about at large in it, it was a fortunate circumstance that Eustacie was staying under the same roof with Ludovic. Her presence beguiled the most tedious hour, and her vehement way of saying: "But no, Ludovic, you shall not!" had the power of restraining him where Miss Thane's reasoned arguments might have failed. He taught Eustacie how to throw dice and how to play piquet; he told her hair-raising and entirely apocryphal tales of adventures to be met with at sea; he teased her, and laughed at her, and ended inevitably by catching her in his sound arm and kissing her.

No sooner had he done it than he recollected the impropriety of such conduct. He released her at once, and said, rather pale, and with the laugh quite vanished from his eyes: "I'm sorry! Forgive me!"

Eustacie said earnestly: "Oh, I did not mind at all! Besides, you kissed me before, do you not remember?"

"Oh, that!" he said. "That was a mere cousinly kiss!"

"And this one, not?" she said simply. "I am glad."

He ran his hand through his fair locks. "I'm a villain to have kissed you at all! Forget that I did! I had no right—I ought to be shot for doing such a thing!"

Eustacie stared at him in the blankest surprise. *"Voyons,* I find that you are excessively rude! I thought you wanted to kiss me!"

"Of course I wanted to! Oh, devil take it, this won't do! Eustacie, if everything were different: if I were not a smuggler and an exile I should beg you to marry me. But I am these things, and——"

"I do not mind about that," she interrupted. "It is not at all *convenable* that you should kiss me and then refuse to marry me. I am quite mortified."

"I wish to God I could ask you to marry me!"

"It doesn't signify," said Eustacie, handsomely waiving this formality. "If it is against your honour you need not make me an offer. We will just be betrothed without it."

"No, we won't. Not until I have cleared my name."

"Yes, but if you cannot clear your name, what then are we to do?" she demanded.

"Forget we ever met!" said Ludovic with a groan.

This Spartan resolve did not commend itself to Eustacie at all. Two large tears sparkled on the ends of her eyelashes, and she said in a forlorn voice: "But me, I have a memory of the very longest!"

Ludovic, seeing the tears, could not help putting his arm round her again. "Sweetheart, don't cry! I can't possibly let you marry me if I'm to remain an exile all my life."

Eustacie stood on tiptoe, and kissed his chin. "Yes, you can. It is quite my own affair. If I want to marry an exile I shall."

"You won't."

"But yes, I have thought of a very good plan. We will go and live in Austria, where my uncle the Vidame is."

"Nothing would induce me to live in Austria!"

"*Bien,* then we will live in Italy, at Rome."

"Not Rome," objected Ludovic. "Too many English there."

"Oh! Then you will choose for us some place where there are not any English people, and Tristram who is a—is a trustee will arrange that you can have some money there."

"Tristram is more likely to send you to Bath and kick me out of the country," said Ludovic. "What's more, I don't blame him."

But Sir Tristram, when the news of the betrothal was broken to him, did not evince any desire to resort to such violent methods. He did not even show much surprise, and when Ludovic, half defiant, half contrite, said: "I ought never to have done it, I know," he merely replied: "I don't suppose you did do it."

Eustacie, taking this as a compliment, said cordially: "You are quite right, *mon cousin;* it was I who did it, which was not perhaps *comme il faut,* but entirely necessary, on account of Ludovic's honour. And if we do not find that ring we shall go away to Italy, and you will arrange for Ludovic to have his money there, will you not?"

"I expect so," said Shield. "But if you are determined to marry Ludovic I think we had better find the ring."

Miss Thane, who had come into the parlour in the middle of this speech, thought it proper to assume an expression of astonishment and to say incredulously: "Do I understand, Sir Tristram, that this betrothal has your blessing?"

He turned. "Oh, you are there, are you? No, it has *not* my blessing, though I have no doubt it has yours?"

"Of course it has," said Miss Thane. "I think it is delightful. Have you discovered when the Beau means to go to London?"

But this he had been unable to do, the Beau having apparently decided to postpone the date. Shield had come to inform Ludovic of it, and to warn him that this change of plan might well mean that the Beau's suspicions had been aroused. When he heard from Nye that Gregg had visited the inn on the previous day for the ostensible purpose of purchasing a keg of brandy for his master, he felt more uneasy than ever, and said that if only Ludovic had not entered upon an ill-timed engagement he would have had no hesitation in forcibly removing him to Holland.

Miss Thane, to whom, in the coffee-room, this remark was addressed, said that the betrothal, though perhaps a complication, had been inevitable from the start.

"Quite so, ma'am. But if you had not encouraged Eustacie to remain here it need not have been inevitable."

"I might have known you would lay it at my door!" said Miss Thane in a voice of pious resignation.

"I imagine you might, since you are very well aware of having fostered the engagement!" retorted Shield. "I had thought you a woman of too much sense to encourage such an insane affair."

"Oh!" said Miss Thane idiotically, "but I think it is so romantic!"

"Don't be so foolish!" said Sir Tristram, refusing to smile at this sally.

"How cross you are!" marvelled Miss Thane. "I suppose when one reaches middle age it is difficult to sympathize with the follies of youth."

Sir Tristram had walked over to the other side of the room to pick up his coat and hat, but this was too much for him, and he turned and said with undue emphasis: "It may interest you to know, ma'am, that I am one-and-thirty years old, and not yet in my dotage!"

"Why, of course not!" said Miss Thane soothingly. "You have only entered upon what one may call the sober time of life. Let me help you to put on your coat!"

"Thank you," said Sir Tristram. "Perhaps you would also like to give me the support of your arm as far as to the door?"

She laughed. "Can I not persuade you to remain a little while? This has been a very fleeting visit. Do you not find it dull alone at the Court?"

"Very, but I am not going to the Court. I am on my way to Brighton, to talk to the Beau's late butler."

She said approvingly: "You may be shockingly cross, but you are certainly not idle. Tell me about this butler!"

"There is nothing to tell as yet. He was in the Beau's employment at the time of Plunkett's murder, and it occurred to me some days ago that it might be interesting to trace him, and discover what he can remember of the Beau's movements upon that night."

This scheme, though it would not have appealed to Eustacie, who preferred her plans to be attended by excitement, seemed eminently practical to Miss Thane. She parted from Sir Tristram very cordially, and went back into the parlour to tell Ludovic that although he might still be unable to do anything towards his reinstatement, his cousin had the matter well in hand.

As she had expected, Eustacie did not regard Sir Tristram's errand with much favour. She said that it was very well for Tristram, but for herself she preferred that there should be adventure.

But upon the following morning, when Miss Thane had gone out with her brother for a sedate walk, adventure took Eustacie unawares and in a guise that frightened her a good deal more than she liked.

She was seated in the parlour, waiting for Ludovic, who was dressing, to come downstairs, when the mail-coach from London arrived. She heard it draw up outside the inn, but paid no attention to it, for it was a daily occurrence, and the coach only stopped at the Red Lion to change horses. But a minute or two later Clem put his head into the room, and said, his face as white as his shirt: "It's the Runners, miss!"

Eustacie's embroidery-frame slipped out of her hands. She gazed at Clem in horror, and stammered: "The B-Bow Street Runners?"

"Yes, miss, I'm telling you! And there's Mr. Ludovic trapped upstairs, and Mr. Nye not in!" said Clem, wringing his hands.

Eustacie pulled herself together. "He must instantly go into the cellar. I will talk to the Runners while you take him there."

"It's too late, miss! Whoever it was sent them knew about the cellars, for there's one of them standing over the back-stairs at this very moment! I never knew they was even on the coach till they come walking into the place, as bold as brass!"

"They may be searching the house now!" exclaimed Eustacie in sudden alarm. "You should not have left them! Oh dear, do you think my cousin will shoot them? If he does we must bury them quickly, before anyone knows!"

"No, no, miss, it ain't as bad as that yet! What they wants is to see Mr. Nye. They daresn't go searching the place afore ever they tell him what they're here for. They think I've gone to look for him, but what I've got to do is to hide the young master, and lordy, lordy, how can I get upstairs without them knowing when one of 'em's lounging round the backstairs, and t'other sitting in the coffee-room?"

"Go immediately, and find Nye!" ordered Eustacie. "He must think of a way. I will talk to these Runners, and if I can I will coax the one in the coffee-room to come into the parlour."

With this praiseworthy resolve in mind, and an uncomfortable feeling of panic in her breast, she sallied forth from the parlour and made her way to the coffee-room. Here, at a table in the middle of the room which commanded a view of the staircase and the front door, was seated a stockily-built individual in a blue coat and a wide-brimmed hat, casually glancing over the contents of a folded journal, which he had extricated from one capacious pocket. Eustacie, surveying him from the open doorway, noticed that his figure was on the portly side, a circumstance which afforded her a certain amount of satisfaction, since it seemed improbable that a stout, middle-aged man would have much hope of catching Ludovic if that young gentleman were forced to take to his heels.

Summoning up a smile, and a look of inquiry, Eustacie said, as though startled: "Oh! Why, who are you?"

The Bow Street officer looked up, and finding that he was being addressed by a young and enchantingly pretty female, laid the journal down upon the table and rose to his feet. He touched his hat, and said that he was wishful to see the landlord.

"But yes, of course!" said Eustacie. "You have come on the mail-couch, *sans doute,* and you want a drink! I understand!"

By this time the Runner had assimilated the fact that she was not English. He did not care for foreigners, but her instant grasp of his most pressing need inclined him to regard her with less disapproval than he might otherwise have done. He did not precisely admit that he wanted a drink, but he said that it was a very cold, raw day to be sure, and waited hopefully to see what she would do about it.

"Yes," she said, "and it is, moreover, very draughty in a coach. I think you ought to have some cognac."

The Runner thought so too. He had not wanted to come down to Sussex on what would probably turn out to be a wild-goose chase. He felt gloomily that he would not have been chosen for the task if the authorities over him had set much store by the information lodged with them, for he was not at the moment in very good odour at Bow Street. Such epithets as Blockhead and Blunderer had been used in connection with his last case, since when he had not been employed upon any very important business. In his more optimistic moments he dreamed rosily of the glory attaching to the capture of so desperate a character as Ludovic Lavenham, but when his throat was dry and his fingers chilled he did not feel optimistic.

"When Nye comes he must at once give you some cognac," announced Eustacie. "But I do not understand what you are doing here and you have not told me who you are."

The Runner was not much acquainted with the Quality, but it did occur to him that it was a little unusual for young ladies to address strange men in public coffee-rooms. He bent a penetrating and severe eye upon her, and replied, awe-inspiringly, that he was an Officer of the Law.

Eustacie at once clasped her hands together, and cried: "I *thought* you were! Are you perhaps a Bow Street Runner?"

The Runner was accustomed to having his identity discovered with fear, even loathing, but he had not till now encountered anyone who became ecstatic upon learning his dread profession. He admitted that he was a Runner, but looked so suspiciously at Eustacie that she made haste to explain that in France they had no such people, which was the reason why she was so particularly anxious to meet one.

When she mentioned France the Runner's brow cleared. The French, what with their guillotines and one thing and another, were the worst kinds of foreigners, and it was no use being surprised at them behaving queerly. They were born that way; there wasn't any sense in them; and the silly habit they had of holding that everyone was equal accounted for this young lady speaking so friendly to a mere Bow Street Runner.

"You are one of the so famous Runners!" said Eustacie, regarding him with rapt admiration. "You must be very brave and clever!"

The Runner coughed rather self-consciously, and murmured something inarticulate. He had not previously given the matter much thought, but now the lady came to mention it he realized that he was rather a brave man.

"What is your name?" inquired Eustacie. "And why have you come here?"

"Jeremiah Stubbs, miss," said the Runner. "I am here in the execution of my dooty."

Eustacie opened her eyes to their widest extent, and asked breathlessly whether he had come to make an arrest. "*How* I should like to see you make an arrest!" she said.

Mr. Stubbs was not impervious to flattery. He threw out his chest a little, and replied with an indulgent smile that he couldn't say for certain whether he was going to make an arrest or not.

"But who?" demanded Eustacie. "Not someone in this inn?"

"A desprit criminal, missy, that's the cove I'm after," said Mr. Stubbs.

Eustacie's straining ears caught the sound of an opening door upstairs and a light footfall. She said as loudly as she dared: "I suppose you, who are a *Bow Street Runner*, have to capture a great many desperate criminals?" As she spoke she moved towards the fire, so that to address her Mr. Stubbs had to turn slightly, presenting his profile, and no longer his full face to the staircase.

"Oh well, miss," he said carelessly, "we don't take much account of that!"

Eustacie caught a glimpse of Ludovic at the top of the stairs, and said quickly: "Bow Street Runners! It must be very exciting to be a Bow Street Runner, I think!" She glanced up as she spoke, and saw that Ludovic had vanished. Feeling almost sick with relief, she pressed her handkerchief to her lips, and said mechanically: "Who is this criminal, I wonder? A thief, perhaps?"

"Not a thief, miss," said Mr. Stubbs. "A murderer!"

The effect of this announcement was all he had hoped for. Eustacie gave a shriek and faltered: "Here! A m-murderer? Arrest him at once, if you please! But at once!"

"Ah!" said Mr. Stubbs, "if I could do that everything

would be easy, wouldn't it? But this here murdering cove has been evading of the law for two years and more."

"But how could he evade you, who must, I know, be a clever man, for two years?"

Mr. Stubbs began to think rather well of Eustacie, French though she might be. "That's it," he said. "You've put your finger on it, missy, as the saying is. If they'd had me on to him at the start p'raps he wouldn't have done no evading."

"No, I think not, indeed. You look very cold, which is not at all a thing to wonder at when one considers that there is a great *courant d'air* here. I will take you into the parlour, where it is altogether cosy, and procure for you a glass of cognac."

Mr. Stubbs's eye glistened a little, but he shook his head. "It's very kind of you, miss, but I've a fancy to stay right where I am, d'ye see? You don't happen to be staying in this here inn, do you?"

"But certainly I am staying here!" responded Eustacie. "I am staying with Sir Hugh Thane, who is a Justice of the Peace, and with Miss Thane."

"You are?" said Mr. Stubbs. "Well now, that's a very fortunate circumstance, that is. You don't happen to have seen anything of a young cove—a mighty flash young cove— Lurking?"

Eustacie looked rather bewildered, and said: *"Plaît-il?* Lurking?"

"Or skulking?" suggested Mr. Stubbs. He drew forth from his pocket a well-worn notebook, and, licking his thumb, began to turn over its pages.

"What is that?" asked Eustacie, eyeing the book with misgiving.

"This is my Occurrence Book, missy. There are plenty of coves would like to get their dabblers on it, I can tell you. There's things in this book as'll send a good few to the Nubbing Cheat one day," said Mr. Stubbs darkly.

"Oh," said Eustacie, wishing that Nye would come, and wondering how to lure Mr. Stubbs away from the stairs. If only Ludovic had not injured his shoulder he might have climbed out of a window, she thought, but with one arm in a sling that was out of the question.

Mr. Stubbs, finding his place in his Occurrence Book, said: "Here we are, now. Has there been a young cove here, missy, with blue eyes, light hair, features aquiline, height above five feet ten inches——"

Eustacie interrupted this recital. "But yes, you describe to me Sir Hugh Thane, only he is taller, I think, and me, I should say that he has grey eyes."

"The cove this here description fits is a cove by the name of Loodervic Lavenham," said Mr. Stubbs.

Eustacie at once executed a start. "But are you mad? Ludovic Lavenham is my cousin, *enfin!*"

Mr. Stubbs stared at her fixedly. "You say this Loodervic Lavenham's your cousin, miss?" he said, his voice pregnant with suspicion.

"Of course he is!" replied Eustacie. "He is a very wicked creature who has brought disgrace to us, and we do not speak of him even. Why have you come to look for him? He went away from England two years ago!"

Mr. Stubbs caressed his chin, still keeping eyes on Eustacie's face. "Oh!" he said slowly. "He wouldn't happen to be staying in this inn right now, I suppose?"

"Staying here?" gasped Eustacie. "In the same place with *me?* No! I tell you, he is in disgrace—quite cast-off!"

"Ah!" said Mr. Stubbs. "What would you say if I was to tell you that this very Loodervic Lavenham is lurking somewhere in these parts?"

"I do not think so," said Eustacie, with a shake of her head. "And I hope very much that it is not true, because there has been enough disgrace for us, and we do not desire that there should be any more." An idea occurred to her. She added: "I see now that you are a *very* brave man, and I will tell you that if my cousin is truly in Sussex you must be excessively careful."

Mr. Stubbs looked at her rather more fixedly than before. "Oh, I must, must I?" he said.

"You have not been warned then?" cried Eustacie, shocked.

"No," said Mr. Stubbs. "I ain't been warned particular."

"But it is infamous that they have not told you!" declared Eustacie. *"Je n'en reviendrai jamais!"*

"If it's all the same to you, miss, I'd just as soon you'd talk in a Christian language," said Mr. Stubbs. "What was it they had ought to have warned me about?"

Eustacie spread out her hands. "His pistols!" she said dramatically. "Do you not know that my cousin is the man who put out sixteen candles by shooting them, and did not miss one?"

Mr. Stubbs cast an involuntary glance behind him. "He put out sixteen candles?" he demanded.

"But yes, have I not said so?"

"And he didn't miss one of them?"

"He never misses," said Eustacie.

Mr. Stubbs drew in his breath. "They *had* ought to have warned me!" he said feelingly.

"Certainly they——" Eustacie broke off, startled by a crash in the room above their heads, and the muffled sound of a shriek. Who could possibly be upstairs save Ludovic, she could not imagine, but Ludovic would hardly shriek, even if he had knocked something over in one of the bedchambers.

Then, to her amazement, she heard a door open, and hurrying footsteps approach the head of the stairs. A high-pitched voice wailed: "Oh, oh, what shall I do? Oh, Mr. Nye, look what I've done!" And down the stairs came a gawky female in a large mob-cap and a stuff gown which Eustacie, transfixed by astonishment, instantly recognized as Miss Thane's. A shawl enveloped the apparition's shoulders, and she held one corner of it up to her eyes with her left hand. In her right she carried the fragments of a flagon that had once contained Miss Thane's French perfume. "Oh, Mr. Nye!" she whimpered. "Mistress will kill me if she finds out—*oh!*" The last word took the form of a scream as the new-comer caught sight of Eustacie. "Oh, miss, I beg pardon!" she gasped. "I thought you was gone out! I've—I've had an accident, miss! Oh, I'm that sorry, miss, I'm sure."

Eustacie made a strangled sound in her throat, and rose nobly to the occasion. Running forward, she seized the gawky female's right wrist, and cried in a quivering voice: "Wretched, wicked creature! You have broken my scent bottle! Ah, it is too much, *enfin!*"

The jagged framents of glass were relinquished into her keeping, and with them, slid into the palm of her hand, a great ruby ring.

Chapter IX

A TORRENT of impassioned French smote the Runner's bemused ears. He stared, quite aghast, at Eustacie, who had
changed in a flash from a pleasant-spoken young female into
a raging virago. She snatched the jagged fragments of glass
from the abigail's hand, broke into English for one moment
to implore Mr. Stubbs to look at what the wicked, clumsy
creature had done, threw the fragments into the grate, shook
the abigail, and in French said rapidly: "He means to search
the house. Have you taken your clothes out of your room?
Answer yes, or no!"

"Oh yes, miss, indeed I took them to Sir Hugh's room, like
you told me!"

Mr. Stubbs began to feel sorry for the hapless abigail,
whose sobs grew more and more shattering. This suddenly
terrible little Frenchwoman seemed to have what he would
call a real spiteful temper. Nothing appeased her: he was not
at all surprised to see the abigail so frightened; he wouldn't
put it beyond the young lady to box the poor girl's ears at
any moment.

In the middle of this spirited scene Nye came into the
coffee-room with Clem at his heels, and stopped upon the
threshold, transfixed by astonishment. For a moment he did
not connect Ludovic with the great gawky girl, noisily weeping into her shawl, but before he had time to speak, Eustacie
whirled round to face him, and poured forth a string of com-
plaints about her supposed abigail. She desired him to tell her
whether she had not sufficient cause to hand the girl over to
the Law, and indicated with a sweep of her hand the presence of a Bow Street Runner.

Nye, who had caught the glint of pale-gold hair peeping
from under the gawky female's mob-cap, now observed that
her left arm seemed in some odd fashion to be wound up in
the voluminous shawl. The puzzled look vanished from his
face; he came farther into the room, and joined with Eustacie

in reproaching "Lucy" for her carelessness. Mr. Stubbs, quite overwhelmed by so much loud and confused talk, withdrew to the other end of the room, and mopped his brow. He gazed at Eustacie in growing consternation, and took a hasty step backward, when she suddenly rounded on him and demanded why he stood there doing nothing, instead of instantly arresting "Lucy."

"Oh come, miss! Come, now!" said Nye soothingly. "It's not as bad as that! The wench meant no harm. I'll have Clem take up a pail of water and a scrubbing-brush, or we'll have the whole house reeking of scent."

"And in my room!" exclaimed Eustacie. "It is an outrage! It must be at once scrubbed, and I will tell you that it is Lucy herself who shall scrub it, for it is not at all Clem's fault. Up, you!"

The Runner, seeing "Lucy" driven towards the staircase, heaved a sigh of relief. Mistress and maid vanished from sight; Clem, at a nod from Nye, went away to draw a pail of water; and Nye turned to his unwelcome visitor, and said with a wry smile, and a jerk of his thumb over his shoulder: "Them Frenchies!"

"Unchristian, that's what I call 'em," responded Mr. Stubbs severely. "I fair compassionate that wench."

"She'll be turned off," said Nye with a resigned shrug. "That will make the third in as many weeks. Miss has the temper of a fiend, *as* I know. What can I do for you?"

Above, in Miss Thane's bedchamber, Eustacie, from whom stifled giggles had escaped all the way up the stairs, sank down upon the bed, and with her handkerchief pressed to her mouth, gave way to inextinguishable laughter. Ludovic twisting the shawl more securely round his arm, said: "Of all the spitfires! I wouldn't be a maid of yours for any money. Now what's the matter?"

"You l-look so rid-ridiculous!" gasped Eustacie, rocking herself to and fro.

Ludovic looked critically at his reflection in the mirror. "A fine, strapping girl," he said. "But what beats me is how you females ever contrive to dress at all. *I* couldn't do up the plaguey hooks and eyes on this gown. That's why I took the shawl. I don't care for Sarah's scent much, do you?"

Indeed, the room reeked of heavy scent. Eustacie raised her head to say unsteadily: "But of course not, a whole bottle on it! It is *affreux*! Open the window! Those Runners have come for you, Ludovic. What are we to do?"

He had thrust open one of the casements, and was leaning out to breathe the unscented air, but he turned his head at that. "How many of them are there?"

"Two. There is one on guard over the backstairs. I think it is Basil who must have told them to look for you here."

"I saw the one on the backstairs. If there are no more than two, and Nye can't fob them off, we'd better lock them up in the cellar, I think. Just until I've found my ring," he added reassuringly, seeing Eustacie's face of disapproval.

"But no, for if we lock them up we shall be put in prison for it!"

"There is that, of course," agreed Ludovic. "Still, if only I could clear myself of this murder charge I shouldn't mind taking the risk. Ten to one we'd get off with a fine."

They were still arguing the point when Clem appeared with a pail and a scrubbing-brush. They pounced upon him for news, and he was able to tell them that Nye had the situation well in hand, and had already gone far towards convincing the Runners that they had been sent to look for a mare's nest. At the moment he was regaling them with brandy, after which he had promised to conduct them personally all over the inn. Hearing this, Eustacie was at once struck by the notion of spreading a few pieces of female apparel about Ludovic's room. She went off to do this, leaving Ludovic with instructions to start scrubbing the floor the instant he heard the Runners ascending the stairs.

By the time Mr. Stubbs, fortified by brandy, did come up, Eustacie had returned to Miss Thane's room, and no sooner did Nye tap on the door, asking whether the officer might come in, than she broke forth again into indignant repinings. Both the Runner and Nye were adjured to come in and judge for themselves whether the smell of the perfume would ever be got rid of. When Nye asked permission for the Runner to search her room, she first stared at him with an expression of outrage on her face, and then flung open the door of the cupboard and said tragically that it needed only this, that a great rough man should pry into her wardrobe. She begged Mr. Stubbs not to consider her feelings in the least degree, but to pull all her dresses out, and throw them on the floor if he pleased. Mr. Stubbs, acutely uncomfortable, assured her that he had no desire to do anything of the kind. She said that she wished she were back in France, where ladies were treated with civility, and, covering her face with her handkerchief, burst into tears. Ludovic, inexpertly scrubbing the damp patch on the floor, sniffed dolefully over the pail of water, and the Runner, casting a perfunctory glance into the wardrobe and another under the bed, beat a somewhat hasty retreat.

It was not long before Nye returned, this time alone. He found Eustacie peeping out of the window at the receding forms of the two officers, and Ludovic, the mob-cap and shawl already discarded, trying to extricate himself from Miss Thane's gown. Characteristically, the first words he addressed to Ludovic were of decided reproof. "And who might those clothes belong to, my lord, if I may make so bold as to ask?"

"To Miss Thane, of course. Help me to come out of this curst dress!"

"And that's a nice thing!" said Nye. "Couldn't you find nothing else to break but a flask of scent that don't belong to you? For shame, Mr. Ludovic!"

Eustacie came away from the window. *"Enfin,* they are gone. Do they believe that my cousin is not here, Nye?"

"That's more than I can tell you, miss," replied Nye, picking up Miss Thane's dress from the floor. "Nor I don't think they've gone far. They would have put up here for the night if I hadn't shown them that I haven't a bed to spare. It's my belief they're off no farther than to the ale-house down the road."

"Do you mean to tell me those fellows are going to hang around this place?" said Ludovic, himself again in shirt and breeches. "Who set them on?"

Nye shook his head. "They wouldn't say. The fat one don't seem to me to set much store by the information. But for all that, I'll have the cellar made ready for you, sir."

"Make it ready for the Runners," said Ludovic briskly. "We'll have to kidnap them."

"There'll be no such foolishness in this house, Mr. Ludovic, and so I'll have you know!"

Some twenty minutes later Miss Thane, accompanied by her brother, came back to the Red Lion, and was at once met by Eustacie, who drew her upstairs to her room, her story tripping off her tongue.

"Runners in the house, and I not here to see them?" exclaimed Miss Thane, suitably impressed. "I declare I am the most ill-used creature alive! How I should have liked to have helped to hoodwink them!"

"Yes, it was very sad for you to be out, but you did help

us, Sarah, because Ludovic put on one of your dresses, and pretended to be my maid."

They had by this time reached Miss Thane's bedchamber. Eustacie opened the door and Miss Thane took one step into the room and recoiled.

"It's only the scent," said Eustacie kindly. "And indeed it is already much fainter than it was. Ludovic thought that it would be a good thing to break the bottle, pretending that it was mine. In that way, you understand, he was able to hide his face, because he made believe to cry, and to be frightened. And I scolded him—oh, *à faire croire!*"

"I'm glad," said Miss Thane. "I suppose it had to be my French perfume?"

Ludovic, hearing their voices, strolled across the passage from his own room, and said with a grin: "Sarah, are you savage with me for having spilled your scent? I will buy you some more one day."

"Thank you, Ludovic!" said Miss Thane with feeling. "And this is the gown you chose to wear, is it? Yes, I see. After all, I never cared for it above the ordinary."

"It got split a trifle across the shoulders," explained Ludovic.

"Yes, I noticed that," agreed Miss Thane. "But what is a mere gown compared with a man's life?"

Eustacie greeted this sentiment with great approval, and said that she knew Sarah would feel like that.

"Of course," said Miss Thane. "And I have been thinking, moreover, that we do not consider Ludovic enough. Look at this large, airy apartment of mine, for instance, and only consider the stuffy little back chamber he is obliged to sleep in! I will change with you, my dear Ludovic."

Ludovic declined this handsome offer without the least hesitation. "I don't like the smell of the scent," he said frankly.

Miss Thane, overcome by her emotions, tottered to a chair and covered her eyes with her hand. In a voice of considerable feeling she gave Ludovic to understand that since he had saturated the carpet in her room with scent, he and not she should sleep in that exotic atmosphere.

The rest of the day was enlivened by alarms and discussions. The Runners had, as Nye suspected, withdrawn merely to the ale-house a mile down the road, and both of them revisited the Red Lion at separate times, entering it in the most unobtrusive, not to say stealthy, manner possible, and explaining their presence in unexpected corners of the house by saying that they were looking for the landlord. The excuses they put forward for these visits, though not convincing, were accepted by Nye with obliging complaisance. Secure in the knowledge that Ludovic was hidden in his secret cellar, he gave the Runners all the facilities they could desire to prowl unaccompanied about the house. The only person to be dissatisfied with this arrangement was the quarry himself who, in spite of the amenities afforded by a brazier and a couple of candles, complained that the cellar was cold, dark, and devilish uncomfortable. His plan of remaining above-stairs in readiness to retreat to the cellar upon the arrival of a Runner was frustrated by the tiresome conduct of these gentlemen, who seemed to spend the entire afternoon prowling around the house. Twice Eustacie was startled by an inquiring face at the parlour-window, and three times did Clem report that one of the officers was round the back of the house by the stables, hobnobbing with the ostler and the post-boys. Even Sir Hugh became aware of an alien presence in the inn, and complained when he came down to dinner that a strange fellow had poked his head into his bedchamber while he was pulling off his boots.

"A demmed, rascally-looking fellow with a red nose," he said. "Nye ought to be more careful whom he lets into the place. Came creeping up the passage and peered into my room without so much as a 'by your leave.' "

"Did he say anything to you?" asked Miss Thane anxiously.

"No," replied Sir Hugh. He added fair-mindedly: "I don't say he wouldn't have, but I threw a boot at him."

"Threw a boot at him?" cried Eustacie, her eyes sparkling.

"Yes, why not? I don't like people prowling about, and I won't have them poking their red noses into my room," said Sir Hugh.

"Hugh, you will have to know, so that you may be on your guard," said Miss Thane. "That was a Bow Street Runner."

"Well, he's got no right to come prying into my room," replied Sir Hugh, helping himself from a dish of beans. "Where's young Lavenham?"

"In the cellar. He——"

Sir Hugh laid down his knife and fork. "What's he found there? Is he bringing it up?"

"No. He is in the cellar because the Runners are looking for him."

Sir Hugh frowned. "It seems to me," he remarked somewhat austerely, "that there's something queer going on in this place. I won't have anything to do with it."

"Very proper, my dear," approved his sister. "But do contrive to remember that you know nothing of Ludovic Lavenham! I fear that these Runners may try to get information from you."

"Oh, they may, may they?" said Sir Hugh, his eye kindling a little. "Well, if that red-nosed fellow is a Runner, which I doubt, I'll have some information to give him on the extent of his duty. They're getting mighty out of hand, those Runners. I shall speak to old Sampson Wright about 'em."

"Certainly, Hugh; I hope you will, but do, pray, promise me that you won't divulge Ludovic's presence here to them!"

"I'm a Justice of the Peace," said Sir Hugh, "and I won't have any hand in cheating the Law. If they were to ask me I should tell them the truth."

Eustacie, pale with alarm, gripped the edge of the table, and said: "But you must not! you shall not!"

Sir Hugh cast an indulgent glance towards her. "They won't ask me," he said simply.

It seemed improbable that the Runners' zeal would lead them to haunt the vicinity of the Red Lion after dark, so as soon as the windows were bolted and the blinds drawn, Ludovic emerged from his underground retreat and joined the rest of the party in the parlour. Some expectation was felt of receiving a visit from Sir Tristram, and at a little after eight o'clock he walked into the inn, having taken advantage of the moonlight to drive over from the Court.

He was met by demands to know whether he had met any men lurking outside the house. He had not, but the anxious question at once aroused his suspicions, and he asked what had been going forward during his absence. When he heard that information had been laid against Ludovic in Bow Street, he did not say anything at all for some moments, thus disappointing Eustacie, who had hoped to startle him into an expression at least of surprise. When he did speak, it was not in admiration of the stratagem which had hoodwinked the Runners, but in a serious voice, and with his eyes on his cousin. "If you won't go to Holland, will you at least leave Sussex, Ludovic?"

"Devil a bit! There's no danger. The Runners think they're on a wild-goose chase." He observed a tightening of Shield's lips, a certain considering look in the eyes which rested on himself, and sat up with a jerk. "Tristram, if you try to kidnap me, I swear I'll shoot you!"

Sir Tristram laughed at that, but shook his head. "I won't promise not to kidnap you, but I will promise to get your gun first."

"It never leaves me," grinned Ludovic.

"That's what I'm afraid of," retorted Shield. "If there's an attempt made on you, you'll shoot, and there'll be a charge of real murder to fight."

Eustacie said sharply: "An attempt on him? Do you mean on his life?"

"Yes, I do," replied Shield. "We may not be certain that the Beau killed Plunkett, but we can have no doubt that it is he who has brought the Runners down on Ludovic now. He would like the Law to remove Ludovic from his path, but if the Runners fail, I think he may make the attempt himself. Have you ever considered how easy of access this place is?"

Eustacie cast an involuntary glance over her shoulder. "N-no," she faltered. "Is—is it easy? Perhaps you had better go after all, Ludovic. I do not want you to be killed!"

"Ah, fiddlesticks," Ludovic said impatiently. "The Beau don't even know I'm here. He may suspect it, but there's not a soul has seen me outside ourselves, and Nye, and Clem."

"You are forgetting the Excise officer," interpolated his cousin.

"What odds? I'll admit it was he who put the notion into Basil's head, but it's no more than a notion, and when Basil hears the Runners found no trace of me, he'll think himself mistaken, after all. Nye's of the opinion they don't set much store by the information laid."

"It's plain they set very little store by it, since they didn't send their best men down to investigate it, but they are likely to take a more serious view of the matter when they discover that Eustacie has no abigail with her."

"Ludovic," said Miss Thane in a meditative voice, "thinks it would be a good thing to capture the Runners and bestow them in the cellar."

"A famous plan!" said Sir Tristram sardonically.

"Yes, but me, I do not agree," said Eustacie, frowning.

"You surprise me."

"Just a moment!" interposed Thane, who all this time had been sitting at a small table by the fire, casting his dice, right hand against left. "You can't imprison law officers in the cellar. For one thing, it's a criminal offence, and for another there's a deal of precious liquor in the cellar. I don't like that red-nosed fellow; I think he ought to be got rid of. What's more, I've had a score against Sampson Wright for a long time, and I don't mind putting a spoke in his wheel. But I won't have his Runners kidnapped."

"Well!" said his sister. "I think you are most unreasonable, Hugh, I must say. After all, it was you who threw a boot at the Runner."

"That's a very different thing," replied Thane. "There's nothing to be said against throwing a boot at a fellow who comes nosing into one's room. But kidnapping's another matter."

"Oh well!" said Ludovic airily. "Ten to one we shan't see any more of them. I dare say they will go back to London on to-morrow's coach."

Had Mr. Stubbs followed his own inclination, he would not have waited for the morrow's coach but would have boarded the night mail, deeming a night on the road preferable to one spent at the ale-house. But his companion, a grave person with a painstaking sense of duty and an earnest desire to prove himself worthy of his office, held to the opinion that their search had not been sufficiently thorough.

"What we've done is, we've Lulled them," he said, slowly nodding his head. "Properly Lulled them, that's what we've done. We didn't find no trace of any desperate criminal, and they know we didn't find no trace. So what happens?"

"Well, what does happen?" said Mr. Stubbs, lowering his tankard.

"They're Lulled, that's what happens."

"You said that before," remarked Mr. Stubbs, with slight asperity.

"Ah, but what do we do now we've got them Lulled?" demanded his companion. "We makes a Pounce, and takes this Ludovic Lavenham unawares."

Mr. Stubbs turned it over in his mind. "I won't say you're wrong, William," he pronounced cautiously. "Nor I've no objection, provided we *do* take him unawares. It's a queer thing, but I can't get out of my mind what that French hussy told me about this Loodervic being so handy with his pops. It makes things awkward. I won't say no more than that. Awkward."

"I've been thinking about that," said the zealous Mr. Peabody, "and the conclusion I've come to, Jerry, is that she made it up out of her head just for to scare you."

For a moment Mr. Stubbs pondered this. Then he said somewhat severely: "She should ha' known better." He took a pull at his ale, and wiping his mouth on the back of his hand, added: "Mind you, I've had my doubts about it all along. Sixteen candles is what she said. Now, I put it to you, William, is that a likely story?"

Mr. Peabody gave it as his opinion that it was a most unlikely story. They discussed the question for a little while, Mr. Stubbs contending that had Eustacie spoken of six candles, he might have believed her, and Mr. Peabody, a more practical man, distrusting the entire story on the grounds that there was no sense in firing at candles at all.

They had, by these divergent paths, arrived at the same comfortable conclusion when their privacy was disturbed by the arrival of a visitor, who turned to be none other than Gregg, Beau Lavenham's discreet valet. He came into the tap-room with a prim little bow and a tight-lipped smile, and ordered a brandy with hot water and lemon. Until this had been procured for him, he stayed by the bar, only glancing once out of the corners of his eyes at the two Runners snugly ensconced in the ingle-nook by the fire. When his glass had been handed to him, however, he walked over to the fireplace, drew up a chair close to the high-backed settle, and bade the Runners good evening.

They returned this civil greeting without showing any marked degree of cordiality. They were aware that he was the man to whom they were indebted for what information they had, but although they would be grateful for any further information that he might be able to give them, they had a prejudice against informers as a race, and saw no reason to make an exception in this one's favour. Accordingly, when Gregg leaned forward in his chair, and said in a keen but subdued voice: "Well?" it was in chilly accents that Mr. Stubbs replied: "It ain't well. We've been fetched down for nothing, that's what."

"So you didn't find him!" said Gregg, frowning.

"Nor him, nor any sign of him. Which I will say didn't surprise me."

"But he was there, for all that," said Gregg, tapping his front teeth with one finger-nail. "I am sure he was there. You looked everywhere?"

"There now!" said Mr. Stubbs, with scathing irony. "If you haven't put me in mind of it! Dang me, if I didn't forget to look inside of one of the coal-boxes!"

Gregg, perceiving that he had offended, smiled and made a deprecating movement with his hand. "It is an old house, and full of nooks and hidden cupboards. You are sure—I expect you are sure—that he had no opportunity to seek safety in the cellars?"

"Yes," replied Mr. Stubbs. "I am sure. By the time I was in by the front door, Mr. Peabody here was in by the back. And not so much of a sniff of any criminal did we get. What's more, we had very nice treatment from the landlord, very nice indeed we had. There are plenty as would have behaved different, but Mr. Nye, he made no bones at all. 'It's not what I like,' he says, 'but I don't blame you, nor I'm not one to stand in the way of an officer what is only executing his dooty.' "

The valet's light eyes flickered from one stolid face to the other. "He had him hidden. When I went he was not hidden. The tapster would not let me set foot outside the tap-room. They did not wish me to go anywhere inside the house. It was most marked."

"That don't surprise me," said Mr. Stubbs. He put his empty tankard down and regarded the valet narrowly. "What's your interest in this Loodervic Lavenham? What makes you so unaccountable anxious to have him laid by the heels?"

The valet folded his lips closely, but after a moment replied: "Well, you see, Mr. Stubbs, that is my business. I have my reasons."

The Runner eyed him with growing disfavour. "Lookee!" he pronounced. "When I go ferreting for news of a desprit criminal, that's dooty. When you does the same thing, Mr. Gregg, it looks to me uncommon like Spitefulness, and Spitefulness is what I don't hold with, and never shall."

"That's right," agreed Mr. Peabody.

The valet smiled again, but unpleasantly, and said in his silky way: "Why, you may say so if you choose, Mr. Stubbs. And I hope I may ask whom you saw at the Red Lion?"

"I didn't see no desprit criminal," answered Mr. Stubbs. "It's my belief there ain't no desprit criminal. Is it likely the place would house such with a Justice of the Peace putting up there?"

"You went into the little back bedchamber? They let you go there?"

"I went into two back bedchambers, one which is the landlord's and the other which the young French lady's maid has."

The valet's eyelids were quickly raised. "Her maid? Did you see her maid?"

"Ay, poor wench, I saw her right enough, and I heard Miss a-scolding of her all for breaking a bottle."

"What was she like?" demanded Gregg, leaning forward again.

Mr. Stubbs looked at him with a shade of uneasiness in his eyes. "Why, I didn't get much sight of her face, she being crying into her shawl fit to break her heart."

"Ah, so you didn't see her face!" said Gregg. "Perhaps she was a tall girl—a very tall girl?"

Mr. Stubbs had been engaged in filling a long clay pipe, but he laid it down, and said slowly: "Ay, she was a rare, strapping wench. She had yaller hair, by what I could see of it."

Gregg sat back in his chair and set his finger-tips together, and over them surveyed the Runners with a peculiar glint in his eyes. "So that was it!" he said. "Well, well!"

"What do you mean, 'that was it'?" said Mr. Stubbs.

"Only that you have seen Ludovic Lavenham; yes, and let him slip through your fingers too, I dare say."

Mr. Peabody, observing his colleague's evident discomfiture, came gallantly to the rescue. "That's where you're wrong," he said. "What we've done is, we've Lulled him—if so be it is him, which we ain't proved yet. What we have to do now is to make a Pounce, and that, Mr. Gregg, is what we decided to do without any help of yourn."

"You had better have made your pounce when you had him under your hand," said the valet dryly. "It is said in these parts that there are cellars below the ones you may see at the Red Lion; cellars which only Nye and Clem know the way into."

"If that's true, we shall find them," said Mr. Stubbs, with resolution.

"I hope you may," responded Gregg. "But take my advice, and go armed! The man you are after is indeed desperate, and I fancy he will not be without his pistols."

The Runners exchanged glances. "I did hear tell of him being handy with his pops," remarked Mr. Stubbs in a casual voice.

"They say he never misses," said Gregg, lowering his eyes

demurely. "If I were in your shoes, I should think it as well to shoot him before he could shoot me."

"Yes, I dare say," said Mr. Stubbs bitterly, "but we ain't allowed to go a-shooting of coves."

"But if you told—both of you—how he shot first, and would have escaped, it would surely be overlooked?" suggested Gregg gently.

It was left to Mr. Peabody to sum up the situation, but this he did not do until the valet had gone. Then he said to his troubled companion: "You know what this looks like to me, Jerry? It looks to me like as if there's someone unaccountable anxious to have this Ludovic Lavenham put away quick—ah, and quiet, too!"

Mr. Stubbs shook his head gloomily, and after a long silence, said: "We got to do our dooty, William."

Their duty took them up the road to the Red Lion very early next morning. Their plan of surprising the household was frustrated by Nye, who had taken the precaution of setting Clem on the watch. By the time the Runners had reached the inn Ludovic had been roused, and haled, protesting, to the cellar, and his room swept bare of all trace of him. The Runners were not gratified by the least sign of surprise in Nye, who greeted them with no more than the natural annoyance of a landlord knocked up at an unseasonable hour. In the tap-room Clem was prosaically engaged in scrubbing the floor; he turned a blank, inquiring face towards the Runners, and with the stolid air of one who has work to do, returned to his task.

"Well, and what might you be wanting at this hour of the morning?" asked Nye testily.

"What we want is a word with that abigail we saw yesterday," said Mr. Stubbs.

"Do you mean Mamzelle's Lucy?" said Nye.

"Ah, that's the one I mean," nodded Mr. Stubbs.

"Well, if you want a word with her, you'd best get on the Brighton stage. She ain't here any longer."

Mr. Stubbs gave him a very penetrating look, and said deeply: "You're quite sure of that, are you, Mr. Nye?"

"Of course I'm sure! I told you yesterday how it would be. Miss turned her off. What do you want with her? She was a rare silly wench, and not so well-favoured neither."

"You know what I want with her," said Mr. Stubbs. "You're harbouring a dangerous criminal, Mr. Nye, and that wench was him!"

This pronouncement, so far from striking terror into the landlord, seemed to afford him the maximum amount of amusement. After staring at the Runners in a bemused way for several minutes, he allowed a smile to spread slowly over his face. The smile led to a chuckle, the chuckle to a veritable paroxysm of laughter. The landlord, wiping his eyes with the corner of his apron, bade Clem share the joke, and as soon as it had been explained to him, Clem did share it. In fact, he continued to snigger behind his hand for much longer than the Runners thought necessary.

When Nye was able to stop laughing he begged Mr. Stubbs to tell him what had put such a notion into his head, and when Mr. Stubbs, hoping that this card at least might prove to be a trump, said that he had received information, he at first looked at him very hard, and then said: "Information, eh? Then I'll be bound I know who gave you that same information! It was a scrawny fellow with a white face and the nastiest pair of daylights you ever saw! A fellow of the name of Gregg: that's who it was!"

Mr. Stubbs was a trifle disconcerted, and said guardedly: "I don't say it was, and I don't say it wasn't."

"Lord love you, you needn't tell me!" said Nye, satisfied that his shot had gone home. "He's had a spite against me since I don't know when, while as for his master, if a stranger was to stop for half a day in this place, he'd go mad thinking it was Mr. Ludovic come home to stop him taking what don't belong to him. You've been properly roasted, that's what you've been."

"I don't know about that," replied Mr. Stubbs. "All I know is it's very highly suspicious that that abigail ain't here no more, and what I want to see, Mr. Nye, is those cellars of yourn."

"Well, I've got something better to do than to take you down to my cellars," said Nye. "If you want to see 'em, you go and see 'em. I don't mind."

An hour later, when Sir Hugh came down to breakfast, a pleasing idea dawned in Nye's brain, and as he set a dish of ham and eggs before his patron, he told him that the Runners were in the house again. Sir Hugh, more interested in his breakfast than in the processes of the Law, merely replied that as long as they kept from poking their noses into his room, he had no objection to their presence.

"Oh, they won't do that, sir!" said Nye, pouring him out a cup of coffee. "They're down in the cellar."

Sir Hugh was inspecting a red sirloin, and said in a preoccupied voice: "In the cellar, are they?" Suddenly he let his eyeglass fall, and swung round in his chair to look at the landlord. "What's that you say? In the cellar?"

"Yes, sir. They've been there the best part of an hour now —off and on."

Sir Hugh was a man not easily moved, but this piece of intelligence roused him most effectively from his habitual placidity. "Are you telling me you've let that red-nosed scoundrel loose in the cellars?" he demanded.

"Well, sir, seeing as he's an officer of the Law, and with a warrant, I didn't hardly like to gainsay him," said Nye apologetically.

"Warrant be damned!" said Sir Hugh. "There's a pipe of Chambertin down there which I bought from you! What the devil are you about, man?"

"I thought you wouldn't be pleased, sir, but there! what can I do? They've got it into their heads there's a secret cellar. They're hunting for it. Clem tells me it's something shocking the way they're pulling the kegs about."

"Pulling the——" Words failed Sir Hugh. He rose, flinging down his napkin, and strolled from the parlour towards the tap-room and the cellar stairs.

Fifteen minutes later Miss Thane, entering the room, was mildly surprised to find her brother's chair empty, and inquired of Nye what had become of him.

"It was on account of them Runners, ma'am," said Nye.

"What! are they here again?" exclaimed Miss Thane.

"Ay, they're here, ma'am, a-hunting for the way into my hidden cellar. Oh, Mr. Ludovic's safe enough! But on account of my mentioning to Sir Hugh how them Runners was disturbing the wine downstairs, he got up, leaving his breakfast like you see, and went off in a rare taking to see what was happening."

Miss Thane cast one glance at Nye's wooden countenance, and said: "You were certainly born to be hanged, Nye. What *was* happening?"

"Well, ma'am, by what I heard in the tap-room they had pulled my kegs about a thought roughly, and what with that and Sir Hugh getting it into his head they was wishful to tap the Nantes brandy, there was a trifle of a to-do. Clem tells me it was rare to hear Sir Hugh handle them. By what I understand, he's laid it on them not to move my kegs by so much as an inch, and what he told them about wilful damage frightened them fair silly—that and the high tone he took with them."

"They didn't ask him what he knew of Lord Lavenham, did they?" said Miss Thane anxiously.

"They didn't have no chance to ask him, ma'am. He told them they might look for all the criminals they chose, so long as they didn't tamper with the liquor, nor go nosing round his bedchamber."

"But, Nye, what if they find your hidden cellar?" said Miss Thane.

He smiled dourly. "They won't do that—not while they keep to the open cellars. In fact, while Sir Hugh was telling them what their duty was, and what it wasn't, I was able to take Mr. Ludovic his breakfast."

"Where is your secret cellar, Nye?"

He looked at her for a moment, and then replied: "You'll be the ruin of me yet, ma'am. It's under the floor of my store-room."

Sir Hugh came back into the room presently. He gave it as his opinion that the Runners were either drunk or half-witted, and said that he fancied they would have no more trouble with them. Upon his sister's inquiring hopefully whether he had contrived to get rid of them, he replied somewhat severely that he had made no such attempt. He had merely defined their duties to them and warned them of the consequences of overstepping the limits of the law.

Both Nye and Miss Thane were dissatisfied, but there was no doubt that the irruption of Sir Hugh into the cellars had done much to damp the Runners' ardour. His air of unquestionable authority, his knowledge of the law, and the fact of his being acquainted, apparently, with the magistrate in charge at Bow Street made them conscious of a great disinclination to fall foul of him again. Nor could they feel, when they had discussed the point between themselves, that a house which held so rigid a legal precisian was the place in which to look for a hardened criminal. They had failed on two occasions to find the least trace of Ludovic Lavenham; the landlord, who should be most nearly concerned, seemed to look upon their search with indifference; and had it not been for the suspicious circumstance of the abigail's disappearance, they would have been much inclined to have returned to London. The valet's words, however, had been explicit. They decided to prosecute a further search for a hidden cellar, and

to keep the inn under observation in the hope of surprising
Ludovic in an attempt to escape.

While this search, which entailed a patient tapping of the
walls and floor of the other cellars, was in progress, Nye
seized the opportunity to visit Ludovic. He returned presently
and reported that his lordship wouldn't stay patient for long;
in fact, was already threatening to come out of hiding and
deal with the Runners in his own fashion.

"Really, one cannot blame him," said Miss Thane judicially. "It is most tiresome of these people to continue to
haunt us. It quite puts an end to our adventures."

"Yes, it does," agreed Eustacie. "Besides, I am afraid that
Ludovic will catch cold in the cellar."

"Very true," said Miss Thane. "There is nothing for it:
since Hugh had been so useless in the matter, we must get rid
of the Runners ourselves."

"*You* have not seen them," said Eustacie bitterly. "They
are the kind of men who stay, and stay, and stay."

"Yes, they seem to be a dogged couple, I must say. I am
afraid it is your abigail who is at the root of their obstinacy."
She broke off, and suddenly stood up. "My love, I believe I
have hit upon a notion! Would you—now, would you say I
was a strapping wench?"

"Of a certainty I should not say anything of the kind!" replied Eustacie, indignant at the implication that she could be
capable of such discourtesy. "You are very tall, *bien entendu*,
but——"

"Say no more!" commanded Miss Thane. "I have a Plan!"

Chapter X

In pursuance of her plan, Miss Thane took care to remain out of sight of the two Runners for the rest of the day. She repaired to her own room, and sat there with an agreeable and blood-curdling romance, and from time to time Eustacie came up to report on the proceedings below-stairs.

Mr. Stubbs took an early opportunity of subjecting Eustacie to a searching cross-examination, but from this she emerged triumphant. Having established a reputation for excitability, it was easy for her when in difficulties to become incoherent, and consequently (since she at once took refuge in the French tongue) unintelligible. At the end of half an hour's questioning, Mr. Stubbs, and not his victim, felt quite battered.

He and his companion spent a wearing and an unsatisfactory day. The cellar, besides being extremely cold, revealed no secrets, and a locked cupboard which Mr. Peabody discovered in a dark corner of the passage leading to the kitchen was responsible for an unpleasant interlude with the landlord. As soon as Mr. Peabody discovered the cupboard, which was partly hidden behind a pile of empty cases and baskets, he demanded the key of Nye. When the landlord, after a prolonged search in which Clem joined, announced that he had lost it, the hopes of both Runners rose high, and Mr. Stubbs warned Nye that if he did not immediately produce the key, they would break in the door. Nye retorted that if damage were done to his property, he would lodge a complaint in Bow Street. He said so many times, and with such unwonted emphasis, that there was nothing in the cupboard but some spare crockery that both Runners became agog with suspicion, and resembled nothing so much as a couple of terriers at a rat-hole. They pulled all the empty cases away from the cupboard door, so that Miss Nye, coming out of the kitchen with a loaded tray fell over them, smashing three plates and scattering a dish of cheese-cakes all down the nar-

row passage. Miss Nye, too deaf to hear Mr. Peabody's profuse apologies, spoke bitterly and at length on the subject of
Men in general, and Bow Street Runners in particular, and
when Mr. Peabody, with an unlucky idea of repairing the
damage, collected all the dusty cheese-cakes together on the
larger portion of the broken dish and handed them to her,
she so far forgot herself as to box his ears.

The next thing to do, Miss Nye having retired, seething, to
the kitchen, was to break down the door of the cupboard.
Mr. Stubbs thought that Mr. Peabody should perform this office, and Mr. Peabody considered Mr. Stubbs, who was of
bulkier build, the man for the task. It was not until the argument had been settled that they discovered that the door
opened outwards. When Mr. Stubbs demanded of Nye why
he had not divulged this fact at the outset, Nye replied that
he did not wish them to break into that cupboard. He added
that they would regret it if they did, a hint that made Mr.
Stubbs draw an unwieldy pistol from his pocket, and warn
the supposed occupant of the cupboard that if he did not instantly give himself up, the lock would be blown out of the
door. No answer being forthcoming, Mr. Stubbs told his as-
sistant to stand ready to Pounce, and, setting the muzzle of
his pistol to the lock, pulled the trigger.

The noise made by the shot was quite deafening, and an
ominous sound of breaking glass was heard faintly through
its reverberations. Commanding Mr. Peabody to cover the
cupboard with his own pistol, Mr. Stubbs seized the handle
of the door and pulled it open, carefully keeping in the lee of
it as he did so.

Mr. Peabody lowered his gun. The cupboard was quite a
shallow one, and contained nothing but shelves bearing glass
and crockery. Such specimens as had come within the range
of the shot had fared badly, a circumstance which roused
Nye to immediate and loud-voiced wrath.

The explosion had been heard in other parts of the house,
and even a dim echo of it by Miss Nye. She erupted once
more from the kitchen, this time armed with the rolling-pin,
at precisely the same moment as Sir Hugh Thane, eyeglass
raised, loomed up at the other end of the passage.

"What the devil's toward?" demanded Sir Hugh, with all
the irritability of a man rudely awakened from his afternoon
sleep.

Mr. Stubbs tried to say that it was only a matter of his
duty, but as Miss Nye, who had the peculiarly resonant voice

of most deaf persons, chose at the same time to announce that if she were given her choice, she would sooner have a pair of wild bulls in the house than two Runners, his explanation was not heard. Before he could repeat it, Nye had given Sir Hugh a brief and faithful account of the affair, particularly stressing his own part in it. "Over and over again I told them there was only some spare crockery in the cupboard, sir, but they wouldn't listen to me. I hope I'm a patient man, but when it comes to them smashing four of my best glasses, not to mention spoiling a whole dish of cheese-cakes that was meant for your honour's dinner, it's more than what I can stand!"

"It's my belief," said Sir Hugh, looking fixedly at the unfortunate Runners, "that they're drunk. Both of them."

Mr. Stubbs, who had not been offered any liquid refreshment at all, protested almost tearfully.

"If you're not drunk," said Sir Hugh, with finality, "you're mad. I had my suspicions of it from the start."

After this painful affair the Runners withdrew to watch the inn from the outside. While one kept an eye on the back door from the post-boy's room, the other walked up and down in front of the inn. From time to time they met and exchanged places. They were occasionally rewarded by the sight either of Nye or of Clem peeping out of one or other of the doors as though to see whether the coast were clear. These signs of activity were sufficiently heartening to keep them at their posts. But it was miserable work for a raw February day, and had the house under observation been other than an inn, it was unlikely that a sense of duty would have triumphed. However, although Nye, according no more nice treatment to the Runners, might withhold all offers of brandy, he could not refuse to serve them as customers. The only pleasant moments they spent during the remainder of the afternoon were in the cosy tap-room, and even these were somewhat marred by the black looks cast at them by the landlord and the caustic comments he made on the drinking proclivities of law officers.

But when dusk fell they had their reward. It was Mr. Stubbs' turn to sit at the window of the stable-room, and it was consequently he who saw the back door open very gradually, and Eustacie look cautiously out into the yard. He knew it was she, because the candles had been lit inside the house, and she stood full in a beam of light.

Mr. Stubbs drew back from the window and watched from

behind the curtain. Behind him one post-boy sprawled in a chair by the fire, snoring rhythmically, and two others sat at the table playing cards.

Eustacie, having peered all round through the twilight, turned and beckoned to someone inside the house. Mr. Stubbs, breathing heavily, reached for his stout ash-plant, and grasped it in his right hand. With his eyes starting almost out of his head, he saw a tall female figure, muffled from head to foot in a dark cloak, slip out of the house and glide round it towards the front, keeping well in the shadow of the wall. Eustacie softly closed the door; but Mr. Stubbs did not wait to see this. In two bounds he had reached the yard, and was creeping after his quarry, taking care, however, to stay well behind until he could summon Mr. Peabody to his assistance.

The cloaked figure was moving swiftly, yet in a cautious fashion, pausing at the corner of the house to look up and down the road before venturing further. Mr. Stubbs stopped too, effacing himself in the shadows, and realized, when the quarry made a dart across the road, that Mr. Peabody must be enjoying a session in the tap-room, saw dimly that the unknown female (or male) was hurrying down the road under cover of the hedge, and bounced into the inn, loudly calling on Mr. Peabody for support.

Mr. Peabody, ever-zealous, hastened to his side, wiping his mouth on the back of his hand. When he heard the glorious news, he stayed only to pick up his cudgel, and ran out with Mr. Stubbs in pursuit of the fugitive.

"It were that self-same abigail, William," panted Mr. Stubbs. "All along I thought—too big for a female! There he goes!"

Hearing the sounds of heavy-footed pursuit, the figure ahead looked once over its shoulder, and then broke into a run. Mr. Stubbs had no more breath to spare for speech, but Mr. Peabody, a leaner man, managed to shout: "Halt!"

The figure ahead showed signs of flagging; the Runners, getting their second wind, began to gain upon it, and in a few moments had reached it, and grabbed at the enveloping cloak, gasping: "In the name of the Law!"

The figure spun round, and landed Mr. Stubbs a facer that made his nose bleed.

"Mind his pops, Jerry!" cried Mr. Peabody, grappling with the foe. "Lordy, what a wild cat! Ah, would you, then!"

Mr. Stubbs caught the figure's left arm in a crushing grip, and panted: "I arrest you in the name of the Law!"

The captive said in a low, breathless voice: "Let me go! Let me go at once!"

"You're coming along of us, that's what you're going to do," replied Mr. Stubbs.

The sound of a horse trotting towards them made the Runners drag their captive to the side of the road. The horse and rider came into sight, and the prisoner, recognizing the rider, cried: "Sir Tristram, help! Help!"

The horse seemed to bound forward as under a sudden spur. The prisoner, struggling madly, shrieked again for help, and the next instant Sir Tristram was abreast of the group, and had swung himself out of the saddle. Before the Runners could explain matters, he had taken the management of the affair into his own swift and capable hands. Mr. Stubbs, starting to proclaim his calling, encountered a smashing right and left which dropped him like a log, and Mr. Peabody, releasing his captive and aiming a blow at Sir Tristram with his cudgel, quite failed to find his mark, and the next moment was sprawling on the road, having been neatly thrown on Sir Tristram's hip.

Sir Tristram paid no further heed to either of them, but took a quick stride towards the cloaked figure, saying sharply: "Are you hurt? What in heaven's name is the meaning of this, Miss Thane?"

"Oh, I am bruised from head to foot!" shuddered Miss Thane. "These dreadful creatures set upon me with cudgels! I shall die of the shock!"

This dramatic announcement, instead of arousing Sir Tristram's chivalrous instincts anew, made him look penetratingly at her for one moment, and say in a voice torn between amusement and exasperation: "You must be out of your mind! How dared you do such a crazy thing?"

The Runners had by this time begun to pick themselves up. Mr. Stubbs, cherishing his nose, seemed a little dazed, but Mr. Peabody advanced heroically, and said: "I arrest you, Ludovic Lavenham, in the name of the Law, and it will go hard with them as seeks to interfere!"

Sir Tristram released Miss Thane's hands, which he had been holding in a sustaining manner, and replied: "You fool, this is not Ludovic Lavenham! This is a lady!"

Mr. Stubbs said thickly: "It's the abigail. It ain't no female."

"Oh, don't let them touch me!" implored Miss Thane, shrieking artistically towards Sir Tristram.

"I've no intention of letting them touch you, but don't get in my way," said Sir Tristram unromantically. "Now then, my man, perhaps you will tell me what the devil you mean by arresting this lady?"

"It ain't a lady!" said Mr. Peabody urgently. "He's a desperate criminal dressed up for an abigail! No lady couldn't fight like him!"

"I tell you she is Sir Hugh Thane's sister!" said Sir Tristram. "Look, is this a man's face?" He turned as he spoke, and put back the hood from Miss Thane's head.

The Runners peered at her doubtfully. "When my brother hears of this, you will be sorry!" said Miss Thane in a tearful voice.

A look of deep foreboding stole into Mr. Stubbs's watering eyes. "If we've made a mistake——" he began uncertainly.

"It's my belief it's a plot, and they're both in it!" declared Mr. Peabody.

"Take me to my brother!" begged Miss Thane, clinging to Sir Tristram's arm. "I fear I may be going to swoon!"

Mr. Stubbs looked at her over the handkerchief which he was holding to his nose. Also he looked at Sir Tristram, and rather unwisely accused him of having assaulted an officer of the Law.

"Oh, you're law officers, are you?" said Sir Tristram grimly. "Then you may come and explain yourselves to Sir Hugh Thane. Can you walk, ma'am, or shall I carry you?"

Miss Thane declined this offer, though in a failing voice, and accepted instead the support of his arm. The whole party began to walk slowly towards the Red Lion, Sir Tristram solicitously guiding Miss Thane's tottering steps, and Mr. Peabody leading Sir Tristram's horse.

They entered the inn by the door into the coffee-room, and here they were met by Eustacie, who, upon sight of Miss Thane, gave a dramatic start, and cried: *"Bon Dieu!* What has happened? Sarah, you are ill!"

Miss Thane said faintly: "I scarce know. . . . Two men attacked me. . . ."

"Ah, she is swooning!" exclaimed Eustacie. "What an outrage! What villainy!"

Miss Thane, having assured herself that Sir Tristram was close enough to catch her, closed her eyes, and sank gracefully back into his arms.

"Hartshorn! vinegar!" shrieked Eustacie. "Lay her on the settle, *mon cousin!"*

Nye, who had come in from the tap-room, said: "What! Miss Thane in a swoon? I'll call Sir Hugh this instant!" and strode away to the parlour.

Sir Tristram carried his fair burden to the settle, and laid her down upon it. A glance at her charming complexion was sufficient to allay any alarm he might otherwise have felt, and with his fingers over her steady pulse, he said: "I think we should throw water over her, my dear cousin. Cold water."

Miss Thane's lips parted a little. A very soft whisper reached Sir Tristram's ears. "You dare!" breathed Miss Thane.

"Wait! I will instantly fetch the hartshorn!" said Eustacie, and turning sharp on her heel, collided with Mr. Peabody, who was anxiously peeping over her shoulder at Miss Thane's inanimate form. "Brute! Bully! *Imbécile!*" she stormed.

Mr. Peabody stepped aside in a hurry. Having seen Miss Thane's shapely figure in the candlelight, he was now quite sure that a mistake had been made, and the look he cast at Mr. Stubbs, standing glumly by the door, was one of deep reproach.

Eustacie came running down the stairs again just as Sir Hugh walked into the coffee-room with the landlord at his heels.

"What's all this?" demanded Sir Hugh. "Here's Nye telling me some story about Sally fainting. She never faints!"

Sir Tristram, looking down at Miss Thane, saw a shade of annoyance in her face. His lips twitched slightly, but he answered in a grave voice: "I fear it is too true. You may see for yourself."

"Well, of all the odd things!" said Sir Hugh, surveying her through his eyeglass with vague surprise. "I've never known her to do that before."

"She has sustained a great shock to her nerves," said Shield solemnly. "We can only trust that she has received no serious injury."

"Ah, *la pauvre!*" exclaimed Eustacie, enjoying herself hugely. "I wonder she is not dead with fright!" She thrust her cousin out of the way as she spoke, and sank upon her knees by the settle, holding the hartshorn under Miss Thane's nose. "Behold, she is recovering! *C'est cela, ma chère! Doucement, alors, doucement!*" Over her shoulder she addressed Sir Hugh. "Those wicked men attacked her—with sticks!" she added, observing the Runners' cudgels.

It took a moment for Sir Hugh to assimilate this. He

turned and stared at the two Runners, incredulous wrath slowly gathering in his eyes. "What!" he said. "They attacked my sister? These gin-swilling, cross-eyed numskulls? This pair of brandy-faced, cork-brained——"

Miss Thane interrupted this swelling diatribe with a faint moan, and opened her eyes. "Where am I?" she said in a weak voice.

"*Dieu soit béni!*" said Eustacie devoutly. "She is better!"

Miss Thane sat up, her hand to her brow. "Two men with sticks," she said gropingly. "They ran after me and caught me. . . . Oh, am I safe indeed?"

"A little brandy, ma'am?" suggested Nye. "You are all shook up, and no wonder! It's a crying scandal, that's what it is! I never heard the like of it!"

"Sally," said Sir Hugh, "do you tell me that these blundering jackasses set upon you?"

She followed the direction of his pointing finger, and gave a small shriek, and clutched his arm. "Do not let them touch me!"

"Let them touch you?" said Sir Hugh, a martial light in his eye. "They had better try!"

"It was all a mistake, ma'am! No one don't want to touch you!" said Mr. Peabody. "I am sure we never meant no harm! It was the poor light, and us not knowing you."

"All a matter of Dooty," said Mr. Stubbs, still holding his handkerchief to his nose.

"You hold your tongue!" said Sir Hugh. "Sally, what happened?"

"I scarce know," replied his sister. "I went out for a breath of air, and before I had gone above a dozen steps I heard someone running behind me, and turning, saw these two men coming for me, and waving their sticks. I tried to escape, but they caught me, and handled me so roughly that I was near to swooning away on the spot. Then, by the mercy of Providence, who should come riding by but Sir Tristram! I screamed to him for help—indeed, I thought I was to be murdered or beaten into insensibility—and he flung himself from his horse and rescued me! He knocked the fat man down, and when the other one made for him with his cudgel threw him sprawling in the road!"

"Tristram did that?" exclaimed Eustacie. "*Voyons, mon cousin,* I begin to like you very much indeed!"

Sir Hugh, his wrath giving place momentarily to professional interest, said: "Threw him a cross-buttock, did you?"

"On my hip," said Shield. "You know the trick."

Sir Hugh put up his glass and surveyed Mr. Stubbs's afflicted nose. "Drew his cork, too," he observed, with satisfaction.

"No," replied Sir Tristram. "I fancy Miss Thane deserves the credit for that."

"I did hit him," admitted Sarah.

"Good girl!" approved her brother. "A nice, flush hit it must have been. But what were they chasing you for? That's what beats me."

"They said I was Ludovic Lavenham, and they arrested me," said Miss Thane.

Sir Hugh repeated blankly: "Said you were Ludovic Lavenham?" He looked at the Runners again. "They *are* mad," he said.

"Drunk more like, sir," put in the landlord unkindly. "They've spent the better part of the afternoon in my taproom, drinking Blue Ruin till you'd wonder they could walk straight."

A protesting sound came from behind Mr. Stubbs's handkerchief.

"So that's it, is it?" said Sir Hugh. "You're right: they reek of gin!"

"It ain't true, your Honour!" said Mr. Peabody, much agitated. "If we had a drop just to keep the cold out——"

"Drop!" ejaculated the landlord. "Why, you've pretty near had all there is in the house!"

Mr. Stubbs ventured to emerge from behind his handkerchief. "I take my solemn oath it ain't true," he said. "We suspicioned the lady was this Loodervic Lavenham—that's how it come about."

Sir Tristram looked him over critically. "That settles it: they must be badly foxed," he remarked.

"Of course they are," agreed Thane. "Thought my sister was a man? I never heard of anything to equal it! They're so foxed they can't see straight."

Mr. Peabody hastened to explain. "No, your Honour, no! It were all on account of that abigail we saw here, and which was turned off so sudden, and which we thought was the lady."

"You are making matters worse for yourselves," said Sir Tristram. "First you say you thought Miss Thane was Ludovic Lavenham, and now you say you thought she was my cousin's abigail. Pray, what were you about to chase an abigail?"

"It's as plain as a pikestaff what they were about," said Thane severely.

"I knew she was a low, vulgar wretch!" cried Eustacie, swift to improve on this point.

The maligned Runners could only gape at her in dismay.

"Well, Wright shall know how his precious Runners conduct themselves once they are out of his reach!" promised Sir Hugh.

"But, your Honour—but, sir—it weren't like that at all! It was the abigail we thought was Loodervic Lavenham, on account of her being such a great, strapping wench, and when Miss here came so cautious out of the back door, like as if she was scared someone might see her, it was natural we should be mistook in her. What would the lady go out walking for when it was almost dark?"

Sir Hugh turned to look at his sister, his judicial instincts roused. "I must say, it seems demmed odd to me," he conceded. "What were you doing, Sally?"

Miss Thane, prompted partly by a spirit of pure mischief, and partly by a desire to be revenged on Sir Tristram for his inhuman suggestion of throwing cold water over her, turned her face away and implored her brother not to ask her that question.

"That's all very well," objected Thane, "but did you go out by the back door?"

"Yes," said Miss Thane, covering her face with her hands.

"Why?" asked Sir Hugh, faintly puzzled.

"Oh," said Miss Thane, the very picture of maidenly confusion, "must I tell you, indeed? I went to meet Sir Tristram."

"Eh?" said Thane, taken aback.

Miss Thane found that she had underrated her opponent. Not a muscle quivered in Shield's face. He said immediately: "This news should have been broken to you at a more suitable time, Thane. Spare your sister's blushes, I beg of you!"

Miss Thane, for once put out of countenance, intervened in a hurry. "We cannot discuss such matters now! Do, pray, send those creatures away! I will believe they meant me no harm, but I vow and declare the very sight of them gives me a Spasm!"

This request was so much in accordance with the Runners'

own wishes that they both looked hopefully at Sir Hugh, and gave him to understand that if he cared to order them back to London, they would be very glad to obey him. The day's disasters had succeeded in convincing them that their errand was futile; and their main concern now was not to arrest a fugitive from the Law but to induce Sir Hugh to refrain from complaining of them to his friend, Sampson Wright. They were not drunk, and their motives had been of the purest, but against the testimony of Sir Hugh, and his sister, and Sir Tristram, and the landlord, they did not feel that they had any hope of being attended to in Bow Street.

Somewhat to their surprise, Miss Thane came to their support, saying magnanimously that for her part she was ready to let the matter rest.

"Wright ought to know of it," said Sir Hugh, shaking his head.

"Very true, but you forget that they have been punished already for their stupidity. Sir Tristram was very rough with them, you know."

Sir Hugh was slightly mollified by this reflection. After telling the Runners that he hoped it would be a lesson to them, and warning them that if he ever caught sight of their faces again, within the portals of the Red Lion it would be the worse for them, he waved them away. They assured him they would go back to London by the night mail, and with renewed apologies to Miss Thane, bowed themselves out of the inn as fast as they could.

"Well, now that they've taken themselves off," said Nye, "I'll go and let Mr. Ludovic out of the cellar."

Sir Hugh was not at the moment interested in Ludovic's release. He was regarding Shield in a puzzled way, and as soon as the landlord had left the room, accompanied by Eustacie, said: "I dare say Sally knows what she's about, but I don't think you should appoint her to meet you like that. It's not at all the thing. Besides, there's no sense in it. If you want to see her, you can do it here, can't you? *I've* no objection."

"I fear you can have no romantic leanings," said Shield, before Miss Thane could speak. "A star-lit sky, the balmy night breezes——"

"But this is February! The breeze isn't balmy at all—in fact, there's been a demmed north wind blowing all day," pointed out Sir Hugh.

"To persons deep in love," said Sir Tristram soulfully, "any breeze is balmy."

"Hateful wretch!" said Miss Thane, with deep feeling. "Pay no heed to him, Hugh! Of course, I did not go to meet him!"

Sir Tristram appeared to be overcome. "You play fast and loose with me," he said reproachfully. "You have dashed my hopes to the ground, shattered my self-esteem——"

"If you say another word, I'll box your ears!" threatened Miss Thane.

Sir Hugh shook his head at her in mild disapproval. "I see what it is: you've been flirting again," he said.

"Don't be so vulgar!" implored Miss Thane. "There's not a word of truth in it! I went out merely to trick the Runners. Sir Tristram's arrival was quite by chance."

"But you told me——"

"The truth is that you have stumbled upon a secret romance, Thane," said Sir Tristram, with a great air of candour.

Thane looked from Sir Tristram's imperturbable countenance to his sister's indignant one, and gave it up. "I suppose it's all a hum," he remarked. "Are you coming into the parlour? There's a devilish draught here."

"Presently," replied Sir Tristram, detaining Miss Thane by the simple expedient of stretching out his hand and grasping her wrist.

She submitted to this, and when her brother had gone back to the parlour, said: "I suppose I deserved that."

"Certainly you did," agreed Sir Tristram, releasing her. "You would have been well served had I really thrown cold water over you. Are you at all hurt?"

"Oh no, merely a bruise or two! Your intervention was most timely."

"And if I had not happened to have been there?"

"I should have allowed them to drag me back here, of course, and fainted in Hugh's arms instead of yours."

He smiled a little, but only said: "You shouldn't have done it."

"Oh, perhaps it was not, as Eustacie would say, quite *convenable*," she replied, "but you will admit that it has rid us of a grave danger."

"You might have been badly hurt," he answered.

"Well, I was not badly hurt, so we shall not consider that."

At this moment Ludovic strolled into the room, and slid his sound arm round Miss Thane's waist, and kissed her cheek. "Sally, I swear you're an angel!" he declared.

"Anything less angelic than her conduct during the past half-hour I have yet to see," observed Sir Tristram. "An accomplished liar would be nearer the mark."

"*Quant à ça,* you also told lies," said Eustacie. "You pretended to be in love with her: you know you did!"

"Did he?" said Ludovic. "Perhaps he is in love with her. I vow I am!"

"Cream-pot love, my child," interposed Miss Thane composedly. "You are pleased with me for having rid you of those Runners. And now that they have gone, when shall we break into the Dower House?"

"Rid your mind of the notion that you are to make one of that party," said Shield. "Neither you nor Eustacie will come with us—if we go at all."

"Hey, what's this?" demanded Ludovic. "Of course we shall go!"

Miss Thane looked at Shield with a humorous gleam in her eyes. "Now pray do not tell me that after all the trouble I have been put to to remove the bars of our adventure we are not to have any adventure!"

"I think you are likely to have all the adventure you could desire without going to the Dower House to look for it," replied Shield. "I fancy the Beau's suspicions will not be as easily allayed as the Runners' were."

"Well, if Basil comes spying after me himself, we shall see some sport," said Ludovic cheerfully. "I wish you will discover when he means to go to town, Tristram."

This was not a difficult task to accomplish, for the Beau, paying a friendly call upon his cousin that evening after dinner, volunteered the information quite unprompted. He wandered into the library at the Court, a vision of pearl-grey and salmon-pink, and smiled sweetly at Shield, lounging on the sofa by the fire.

Shield greeted him unemotionally, and nodded towards a chair. "Sit down, Basil: I'm glad to see you."

The Beau raised his brows rather quizzically. "My dear Tristram, how unexpected!"

"Yes," said Shield, "I've no doubt it is. I feel you should be told of an excessively odd circumstance. Are you aware that there have been a couple of Bow Street Runners in the neighbourhood, searching for Ludovic?"

For a moment the Beau made no reply. The smile still lingered on his lips, but an arrested expression stole into his eyes, as though he found such direct methods of warfare disconcerting. He drew up a chair to the fire and sat down in it, and said: "For Ludovic? Surely you must be mistaken? Ludovic is not in Sussex, is he?"

"Not that I am aware of," replied Sir Tristram coolly, "but from what I could make out from the Runners someone has started a rumour that Eustacie's smuggler was he."

The Beau opened his snuff-box. "Absurd!" he murmured. "If Ludovic were in Sussex, he must have sent me word."

"That is what I thought," agreed Shield. "You are quite sure he has not sent you word?"

The Beau was in the act of raising a pinch of snuff to his nostrils, but he paused and looked across at his cousin with a slight frown. "Certainly not," he answered.

"Oh, you need not be afraid to tell me if you have heard from him," said Sir Tristram. "I wish the boy no harm. But if the rumour *should* be true, after all, you would be wise to get him out of the country again."

The Beau did not say anything for several moments, nor did he inhale his snuff. His eyes remained fixed on Shield's face. He shut his snuff-box again, and at last replied: "Perhaps. Yes, perhaps. But I do not anticipate that I shall hear from him." He leaned back in his chair and crossed one leg over the other. "I am amazed that such a rumour should have arisen—quite amazed. It had not reached my ears. In fact, my errand to you had nothing to do with poor Ludovic, wherever he may be."

"I am happy to hear you say so. What is your errand to me?"

"Oh, quite a trifling one, my dear fellow! It is merely that I find myself obliged to go to London on a matter of stern necessity to-morrow—my new coat, you know: it sags across the shoulders: the most lamentable business!—and it occurred to me that you might wish to charge me with a commission."

"Why, that is very good of you, Basil, but I believe I need not trouble you. I expect to leave this place almost any day now."

"Oh?" The Beau regarded him thoughtfully. "I infer then that Eustacie is also leaving this place?"

Sir Tristram replied curtly: "I believe so. Shall you be in London for many days? Do you mean to return here?"

"Why, yes, I think so. I shall remain in town for a night

only, I trust. I have given the servants leave to absent themselves for no longer. Ah, and that reminds me, Tristram! I wish you will desire that fellow—now, what is the name of Sylvester's carpenter? Oh, Johnson!—yes, I wish you will desire him to call at the Dower House some time. My man tells me the bolt is off one of the library windows. He might attend to it, perhaps."

"Certainly," said Shield impassively. But when his cousin presently went away, he looked after him with a faint smile on his lips, and said: "How very clumsy, to be sure!"

Ludovic, however, when the encounter was described to him on the following morning, exclaimed, with characteristic impetuosity: "Then to-night is our opportunity! We have gammoned the Beau!"

"He seems to have been equally fortunate," said Shield dryly.

Ludovic cocked an intelligent eyebrow. "Now what might you mean by that?" he inquired.

"Not quite equally," said Miss Thane, with a smile.

"No," admitted Shield. "He did underrate me a trifle."

Ludovic perched on the edge of the table, swinging one leg. "Oh, so you think it's a trap, do you? Nonsense! Why should you? He can never have had more than a suspicion of my being here, and you may depend upon it we have convinced him that he was mistaken."

"I do not depend upon anything of the kind," replied Shield. "In fact, I am astonished at the crudity of this trap. Consider a moment, Ludovic! He has told me that he will be in London to-night, that he has given his servants leave of absence, and that the bolt is off one of the library windows. If you are fool enough to swallow that, at least give me credit for having more common sense!"

"Oh well!" said Ludovic airily. "One must take a risk now and again, after all. Basil daren't lay a trap for me in his own house. Damn it, man, he can't take me prisoner and hand me over to the Law! It wouldn't look well at all."

"Certainly not," answered Sir Tristram. "I have no fear of Basil himself coming into the open, but you are forgetting that he has a very able deputy in the shape of that valet of his. If his servants were to catch you in the Dower House, and hand you over to the Law as a common thief, you would be identified, and beyond any man's help while Basil was still discreetly in London. He would dispose of you without incurring the least censure from anyone."

"Well, they may try and take me prisoner if they like," said Ludovic. "It'll go hard with them if they do."

Miss Thane regarded him in some amusement. "Yes, Ludovic, but it will make everything very awkward if you are to leave a trail of corpses in your wake," she pointed out. "I cannot help feeling that Sir Tristram is right. He is one of those disagreeable people who nearly always are."

Ludovic thrust out his chin a little. "I'm going to take a look in that priest's hole if I die for it!" he said.

"If you go, you'll go alone, Ludovic," said Sir Tristram.

Ludovic's eyes flashed. "Ratting, eh? I'll get Clem in your stead."

"You may take it from me that Clem won't go with you on this venture," replied Sir Tristram.

"Oh, you've been working on him, have you? Damn you, Tristram, I must find the ring!"

"You won't do it that way. It's to run your head into a noose. You've a better hope than this slender chance of finding the ring in a priest's hole."

"What is it?" Ludovic said impatiently.

"Basil's valet," replied Shield. "He lodged the information against you. I judge him to be fairly deep in Basil's confidence. How deep I don't know, but I'm doing what I can to find out."

"I dare say he is, but what's the odds? Depend upon it, he's paid to keep the Beau's secrets. Slimy rogue," Ludovic added gloomily.

"No doubt," agreed Shield. "So I have set Kettering to work on him. If he knows anything, you may outbid Basil."

"Who is Kettering?" interrupted Miss Thane. "I must have everything made clear."

"Kettering is the head groom at the Court, and one of Ludovic's adherents. His son works for the Beau, and he is on good terms with the servants at the Dower House. If he can put it into Gregg's head that I am collecting evidence that will make things look ugly for Basil, we may find it quite an easy matter to induce the fellow to talk. Have patience, Ludovic!"

"Oh, you're as cautious as any old woman!" said Ludovic. "Only let me set foot in the Dower House——"

"You may believe that I am too much your friend to let you do anything of the kind," said Sir Tristram, with finality.

Chapter XI

Ludovic, knowing his cousin too well to attempt to argue with him once his mind was made up, said no more in support of his own plan, but left Miss Thane to entertain Shield while he went off to try his powers of persuasion upon the hapless Clem. Quite forgetting that he must not run the risk of being seen by any stranger, he walked into the tap-room, saying: "Clem, are you here? I want you!"

Clem was nowhere to be seen, but just as Ludovic was about to go away again, the door on to the road opened, and a thick-set man in a suit of fustian walked into the inn. Ludovic took one look at him, and ejaculated: "Abel!"

Mr. Bundy shut the door behind him, and nodded. "I had word you was here," he remarked.

Ludovic cast a quick glance towards the door leading to the kitchen quarters, where he judged Clem to be, and grasped Bundy by one wrist. "Does Nye know you're here?" he asked softly.

"No," replied Bundy. "Not yet he don't, but I'm wishful to have a word with him."

"You're going to have a word with me," said Ludovic. "I don't want Nye to know you're here. Come up to my bed-chamber!"

"Adone-do, sir!" expostulated Bundy, standing fast. "You know, surelye, what I've come for. I've a dunnamany kegs of brandy waiting to be delivered here so soon as Nye gives the word."

"He won't dare give it yet; the house is full. I've other work for you to do."

Bundy looked him over. "Are you joining Dickson on board the *Saucy Annie* again?" he inquired.

"No; my grandfather's dead," said Ludovic.

"He'll be a loss," remarked Mr. Bundy thoughtfully. "Howsever, if you're giving up the smuggling lay, I'm tedious glad. What might you be wanting me to do?"

"Come upstairs, and I'll tell you," said Ludovic.

As good luck would have it, there was no one in the coffee-room. Ludovic led Bundy through it and up the stairs to the front bedchamber which had once been Miss Thane's. It still smelled faintly exotic, a circumstance which did not escape Mr. Bundy. "I thought there was a wench in it," he observed.

Ludovic paid no heed to this sapient remark, but having locked the door, just in case Sir Tristram should take it into his head to come up to see him again before he left the inn, thrust Bundy towards a chair, and told him to sit down. "Abel, you know why I took to smuggling, don't you?" he asked abruptly.

Mr. Bundy laid his hat on the floor beside him, and nodded.

"Well, understand this!" said Ludovic. "I didn't commit that murder."

"Oh?" said Bundy, not particularly interested. He added after a moment's reflection: "Happen you'll have to prove that if you'm wishful to take the old lord's place."

"That's what I mean to do," replied Ludovic. "And you are going to help me."

"I'm agreeable," said Bundy. "They do tell me we shall have that cousin of yourn up at the Court, him they call the Beau. It would be unaccountable bad for the Trade if that come about. He'll give no aid to the Gentleman."

"You won't have the Beau at the Court if you help me to prove it was he committed the murder I was charged with," said Ludovic.

Mr. Bundy looked rather pleased. "That's a rare good notion," he approved. "Have him put away quiet same like he'd be glad to do to you. How will we set about it?"

"I believe him to have in his possession a ring which belongs to me," Ludovic answered. "I haven't time to explain it all to you now, but if I can find that ring, I can prove I was innocent of Plunkett's death. I want a man to help me break into my cousin's house to-night. You see how it is with me: that damned riding-officer winged me."

"Ay, I heard he had," said Bundy. "I told you you shouldn't ought to have come." He looked ruminatingly at Ludovic. "I don't know as I rightly understand what you'm about. Milling kens ain't my lay. Seems to me you'd have taken Clem along o' you—if he'd have gone."

"I might be able to make him, but I've a cousin here—a

cursed, cautious, interfering cousin, who don't mean me to make the attempt. He thinks it's too dangerous, and it's odds he's persuaded Clem into seeing eye to eye with him."

Mr. Bundy scratched his nose reflectively. "One way and another, you've been in a lamentable deal of danger since you growed up," he remarked.

Ludovic grinned. "I shall be in some more yet."

"Happen you will," agreed Bundy. "There's some as seem to be born to it, and others as takes uncommon care of their skins. It queers me how folks manage to keep out of trouble. I never did, but I know them as has."

"Devilish dull dogs, I'll be bound. There may be trouble at the Dower House to-night, and for all I know there's been a trap laid for me. Will you take the risk?"

"How I look at it is this way," said Bundy painstakingly. "It ain't no manner of use trying to keep out of trouble if so be you'm born to it. For why? Because if you don't look for trouble, trouble will come a-looking for you—ah, come sneaking up behind to take you unawares, what's more. Does Joe Nye know what's in the wind?"

"No. He's hand-in-glove with my cousin."

Mr. Bundy looked rather shocked. "What, with that dentical, fine gentleman?"

"Lord, no! Not with him! My cousin Shield—my cautious cousin."

Mr. Bundy stroked his chin. "I never knew Joe to be mistook in a man," he said. "I doubt I'm doing wrong to go against his judgment. However, if you've a fancy to go, I'd best come with you, for you'll go anyways, unless you've changed your nature, which don't seem to me likely. What's the orders?"

"I want a horse to be saddled and bridled ready for me at midnight," answered Ludovic promptly. "Everyone should be asleep here by then, and I can slip out. Have a couple of nags waiting down the Warninglid road, as close to this place as you can come without rousing anyone. I'll join you there. We'll ride to the Dower House—it's only a matter of five miles—and once inside the place, the rest should be easy. You may want your pistols, though I'd as soon not make it a shooting affair, and we shall certainly need a lantern."

"Well, that's easy enough," said Bundy. "There's only one thing as puts me into a bit of a quirk, and that's how to keep Joe from suspicioning what we'm going to do. Joe's not one

of them as has more hair than wit: there's a deal of sense in
his cockloft."

"He must not know you've been here to-day," said Ludovic. "You can get away without him seeing you if I make
sure all's clear."

"Oh ay, I can do that," agreed Bundy, "but it's odds they'll
tell him in the stables I've been around. I've left my nag
there."

"The devil you have! Well, you'd best see Joe if that's so,
but take care you don't let him guess you've had speech with
me. You might ask for me. He won't let you see me, and it'll
look well."

In accordance with this plan. Bundy, having been smuggled
out of the inn by the back way, ten minutes later entered
through the front door a second time. He found Clem in the
tap-room, and Clem no sooner laid eyes on him than he said
that upon no account must Mr. Ludovic know of his presence. He thrust him into Nye's stuffy little private room and
went off to summon the landlord. Mr. Bundy sat down by the
table and chewed a straw.

His interview with Nye did not take long, nor, since both
men were taciturn by nature, was there much conversation.
"Where's young master?" inquired Bundy over his tankard.

Nye jerked a thumb upward. "Safe enough."

"I reckoned you'd hide him up," nodded Bundy, dismissing
the subject.

"Ay." The landlord regarded him thoughtfully. "He's ripe
for mischief, I can tell you. Maybe you'd best keep out of his
way. You're as bad as Clem for letting him twist you round
his finger."

"Happen you'm right," conceded Bundy, retiring into his
tankard.

Sir Tristram did not wait for Ludovic to reappear, and for
obvious reasons Nye did not tell him of Bundy's presence in
the inn. He had a great value for Sir Tristram, but he preferred to keep his dealings with free-traders as secret as possible. So Sir Tristram, having extracted a promise from Clem
not to assist Ludovic to leave the inn that night, departed, secure in the conviction that without support this reckless young
cousin could achieve nothing in the way of housebreaking.

"I am afraid we shall have Ludovic like a bear with a sore
head," prophesied Miss Thane pessimistically.

But when Ludovic came downstairs to the parlour again,

he seemed to be in unimpaired spirits, a circumstance which at first relieved Miss Thane's mind, and presently filled it with misgiving. She fancied that the sparkle in Ludovic's angelic blue eyes was more pronounced than usual, and after enduring it for some little while, was impelled to comment upon it, though in an indirect fashion. She said that she feared that Sir Tristram's decision must be unwelcome to him. She was embroidering a length of silk at the time, but as she spoke she raised her eyes from her task and looked steadily at him.

"Oh well!" said Ludovic. "I've been thinking it over, and I dare say he may be in the right of it."

Voice and countenance were both quite grave, but Miss Thane was unable to rid herself of the suspicion that he was secretly amused. He met her searching look with the utmost limpidity, and after a moment smiled, and reminded her that it was uncivil to stare.

She was quite unable to resist his smile, which was indeed a very charming one, but she said in a serious tone: "It would be useless if you were to make the attempt alone, you know. You would not do anything so foolish, would you?"

"Oh, I'm not as mad as that!" he assured her.

She lowered her embroidery. "And you would not—no, of course you would not!—take Eustacie upon such a venture?"

"Good God, no! I'll swear it, if you wish."

She resumed her stitchery, and as her brother came into the room at that moment said no more. When, later, Ludovic discussed exhaustively the various means by which the Beau's valet might be induced to disclose what he knew, she concluded that her suspicions had been unfounded; and when, midway through the evening, he sat down to play piquet with Sir Hugh she felt herself able to retire to bed with a quiet mind. She had seen him play piquet before, and she knew that once a green baize cloth was before him, and a pack of cards in his hand, all other considerations were likely to be forgotten. Neither he nor Sir Hugh, she judged, would seek their beds until the small hours, by which time he would be too sleepy, and not sufficiently clear-headed (for it was safe to assume that a good deal of wine would flow during the course of the play) to attempt anything in the way of a solitary adventure. He bade her a preoccupied good night, and she went away without the least misgiving. She was not, however, privileged to see the swift, sidelong look he shot at her as she went through the doorway.

That was at half-past nine. At ten o'clock Ludovic under-
took to mix a bowl of rum punch for Sir Hugh's delectation.
He promised him something quite above the ordinary, and
Sir Hugh, after one sip of the hot, potent brew, admitted that
it certainly was above the ordinary. Ludovic drank one glass,
and thereafter sat in admiration of Sir Hugh's capacity.
When Sir Hugh commented upon his abstinence, he said
frankly that a very little of the mixture would suffice to put
him under the table. Sir Hugh, rather pleased, said that he
fancied he had a harder head than most men. During the
next half-hour he proceeded to demonstrate the justice of this
claim. The only effect Ludovic's punch had upon him was to
make him unusually sleepy, and when Ludovic, as the clock
struck eleven, yawned, and said that he was for bed, he was
able to rise from the table with scarcely a stagger, and to
pick up his candle without spilling any more wax on to the
floor than was perfectly seemly. Ludovic, relieved to discover
that at least the brew had made him feel ready for bed at an
unaccustomed hour, conducted him upstairs to his room and
saw him safely into it before tiptoeing along the corridor to
his own apartment.

Nye had locked up the inn and gone to bed some time before. Ludovic stirred the logs in his fireplace to a blaze, and
sat down to while away half an hour.

His preparations for the venture took him some time, since
his left arm was still almost useless, but he contrived, though
painfully, to pull on a pair of top-boots, and to struggle into
his great-coat. Having assured himself that his pistols were
properly primed, he stowed one into the top of his right boot,
and the other into the right-hand pocket of his coat, and putting on a tricorne of the fashion of three years before, stole
softly out on to the corridor, candle in hand.

The stairs creaked under his feet as he crept down them,
but it was not this noise which awoke Miss Thane. She was
aroused, ironically enough, by the rhythmic and resonant
snores proceeding from her brother's room across the passage. She lay for a few minutes between waking and sleeping,
listening to these repulsive sounds, and wondering whether it
would be worth while to get up and rouse Sir Hugh, or
whether the snoring would recommence the instant he fell
asleep again. Just as she had decided that the best thing to do
was to draw the bedclothes over her ears, and try to ignore
the snoring, a faint sound, as of a bolt being drawn downstairs, jerked her fully awake. She sat up in bed, thought that

she could hear the click of a latch, and the next instant was standing on the floor, groping for her dressing-gown.

An oil lamp burned low on the table by the bed. She turned up the wick, and picking up the lamp, went softly out on to the passage.

The house was in pitch darkness, and only Sir Hugh's snores broke the silence, but Miss Thane was convinced that there had been other and very stealthy sounds. Her first thought was that someone had entered the house, presumably in search of Ludovic, and she was about to steal along the passage to rouse Nye, when another explanation of the faint sounds occurred to her. She went quickly to Ludovic's room and scratched on the door-panel. There was no answer, and without the slightest hesitation she turned the handle and looked in.

One glance at the unruffled bed was enough to send her flying along the passage to wake Nye. This was easily done, and within two minutes of an urgent, low-voiced call to him through the keyhole, he was beside her on the passage, with a pair of breeches dragged on over his night-shirt, and his night-cap still on his head. When he heard that Ludovic was not in his room he stared at Miss Thane with a pucker between his brows, and said slowly: "He wouldn't do it—not alone!"

"Where's Clem?" demanded Miss Thane under her breath.

He shook his head. "No, no, Clem was of my own mind over this. You must have been mistook, ma'am. He wouldn't set out to walk that distance, and he can't saddle a horse with his arm in a sling." He broke off suddenly, and his eyes narrowed. "By God, you're right, ma'am!" he said. "He must have seen Abel! That accounts for him being so uncommon cheerful, drat the boy! Get you back to your room if you please, ma'am. I'll have Clem saddle me a horse while I get some clothes on, and be off after them."

Miss Thane had been thinking. "Wait, Nye, I've a better notion. Send Clem to inform Sir Tristram. You'll not catch that wretched boy in time to stop him entering the Dower House, and once he has stepped into whatever trap may have been set for him, Sir Tristram's perhaps the one person who might be able to get him out of it."

Nye paused. After a moment's reflection he said reluctantly: "Ay, that's true enough. And Clem's a smaller man than what I am, and will ride faster. It's you who have the head, ma'am."

While Clem was flinging on his clothes, and Nye was in the stable saddling a horse, and Miss Thane was sitting on the edge of her bed wondering whether there was anything more she could do to avert disaster from Ludovic, the object of all this confusion was striding down the lane leading to Warninglid, quite oblivious of the possibility of pursuit. The moon, hidden from time to time behind drifting clouds, gave enough light to enable him to see his way, and in a little while showed him two horses, drawn up in the lee of a hedge of hornbeam.

Abel greeted him with a grunt, and offered him a flask produced from the depths of his pocket. "Play off your dust afore we start," he recommended.

"No, I must keep a clear head," replied Ludovic. "So must you, what's more. I don't want you disguised."

"You've never seen me with the malt above the water—not to notice," said Mr. Bundy, refreshing himself with a nip.

"I've seen you as drunk as a wheelbarrow," retorted Ludovic, taking the flask away from him and putting it in his own pocket. "It makes you devilish quick on the pull, and taking the fat with the lean, I think we won't do any shooting unless we're forced. My cautious cousin's against it, and I admit there's a deal in what he says. I don't want to be saddled with many more corpses. Give me a leg-up, will you?"

Bundy complied with this request, and asked what he was to do if it came to a fight.

"Use your fists," answered Ludovic. "Mind you, I dare say there'll be no fighting."

"Just as well if there ain't," said Bundy, hoisting himself into the saddle. "A hem set-out it will be if you get yourself into a mill with only one arm! I doubt I done wrong to come with you."

This was said not in any complaining spirit but as a mere statement of fact. Ludovic, accustomed to Mr. Bundy's processes of thought, agreed, and said that there was a strong likelihood of them ending the night's adventure in the County Gaol.

They set off down the lane at an easy trot, and since Clem had chosen the shorter but rougher way to the Court that led through the Forest, they were not disturbed by any sound of pursuit. As they rode, Ludovic favoured his companion with a brief explanation of what they were to do at the Dower House. Bundy listened in silence, and at the end merely expressed his regret that he was not to be given an opportunity of darkening Beau Lavenham's daylights for him. His animosity towards the Beau seemed to be groundless but profound, his main grudge against him being that he stood a good chance of stepping into Sylvester's shoes. When he spoke of Sylvester he betrayed something as nearly approaching enthusiasm as it was possible for a man of his phlegmatic temperament to feel. "He was a rare one, the old lord," he said simply.

When they arrived within sight of the Dower House they reined in their horses and dismounted. The house stood a little way back from the lane, in a piece of ground cut like a wedge out of the park belonging to the Court. After a brief consultation they led their horses through a gap in the straggling hedge, and tethered them inside the park. Bundy set about the task of lighting the lantern he had brought while Ludovic went off to reconnoitre.

When he had circumnavigated the house he returned to Bundy's side to find that that worthy, having covered his lantern with a muffler, was seated placidly beside it on a tree-stump.

"There's no light showing in any window that I can see," reported Ludovic. "Now, the Beau told my cautious cousin that the bolt was off one of the library casements, and as that's the room I fancy I want, we'll risk a trap and try to get in by that window." He drew the pistol from his boot as he spoke, and said: "If there is a trap this is our best safeguard. In these parts they believe I can't miss, and it makes 'em wary of tackling me. If they mean to capture me they'll try to take me unawares."

"Well," said Bundy judicially, "I'm bound to say I disremember when I've seen you miss your target."

Ludovic gave a short laugh. "I missed an owl once, the fool that I was!"

Bundy looked at him with disapproval. "What would you want to go shooting owls for, anyways?"

"Drunk," said Ludovic briefly. "Now, get this into your head, Abel! If we walk into a trap it's one laid for me, not for you, and I'll save myself. Get yourself out of it, and don't trouble your head over me. All I want you to do is to help me to get into the house."

Mr. Bundy arose from the tree-stump and picked up the lantern, vouchsafing no reply.

"Understand?" said Ludovic, a ring of authority in his voice.

"Oh ay!" said Bundy. "But there! When I see trouble I'm tedious likely to get to in-fighting with it. If you take my advice, which I never known you do yet, you'll turn up that coat-collar of yourn, and pull your hat over your face. You don't want no one to reckernize you."

Ludovic followed this sage counsel, but remarked that he had little expectation of being known. "The valet would know me, if he's there, but the butler is since my time."

"Maybe," said Bundy. "But I'll tell you to your head what I've said a-many times behind your back, Master Ludovic, which is that you've got a bowsprit that's the spit and image of the old lord's."

"Damn this curst family nose!" said Ludovic. "It'll ruin me yet."

"That's what I'm thinking," agreed Bundy. "However, there's no sense in dwelling on what can't be helped. If you're ready to start milling this ken we'd best start without wasting any more time. And if you keep in mind that though maybe there ain't enough light for anyone to know you by, there's enough and to spare to make you a hem easy target for any cove as might be sitting inside the house with a gun, I dare say you'll come off safe yet."

"It's odds there's no one there at all," returned Ludovic. "But you needn't fear me: I'm taking no risks to-night."

This remark seemed to tickle Bundy's sense of humour. He went off without warning into a paroxysm of silent laughter, which made his eyes water and his whole frame shake like a jelly. Ludovic paid not the least heed to this seizure, but led the way to a wicket-gate at the back of the house, which gave on to the park from the shrubbery.

Traversing the shrubbery they made their way round to the front of the house, taking care not to tread upon the gravel path. Under the tall casement windows there were flower-erbeds, in which a few snowdrops thrust up their heads. Ludovic counted the windows, made up his mind which room must be the library, and indicated it to Bundy with a jerk of his head. Bundy stepped across the path on to the flowerbed, and laid his ear to the glass. He could detect no sound within the room, nor any light behind the drawn curtains, and after a few moments of intent listening he put down his muffled lantern and produced a serviceable knife from his pocket. While he worked on the window Ludovic stood beside him, on the look-out for a possible ambush in the garden. His hat cast a deep shadow over his face, but the moonlight caught the silver mountings on his pistol, and made them gleam. The garden was planted with too many trees and shrubs to make it possible for him to be sure that no one was in hiding there, but he could discover no movement in any of the shadows, and was more than ever inclined to discount his cousin Tristram's forebodings.

A click behind him made him turn his head. Bundy jerked his thumb expressively at one of the windows, and shut his knife. Having forced back the latch he gently prised the window open with his finger-nails. It swung outwards with a slight groan of its hinges. Bundy picked up his lantern in his left hand, unveiled it, and with his right grasped a fold of the velvet curtain, and drew it aside. The muzzle of Ludovic's gun almost rested on his shoulder, but there was no need for it. The lantern's golden beam, travelling round the room, revealed no lurking danger. The room was empty, its chairs primly arranged, its grate laid with sticks ready to be kindled when the master should return.

Bundy took a second look round, and then whispered: "Will you go in?"

Ludovic nodded, slid the pistol back into his boot and swung a leg over the window-sill.

"Easy now!" Bundy muttered, helping him to hoist himself into the room. "Wait till I'm with you!"

Ludovic, alighting in the room, said under his breath: "Stay where you are: I'm not sure whether it's this room I want, or another. Give me the lantern!"

Bundy handed it to him, and he directed its beam on to the wainscoting covering the west wall. Bundy waited in untroubled silence while the golden light travelled backwards and forwards over carved capitals, and fluted pilasters, and the rich intricacies of a frieze composed of cartouches and devices.

It came to rest on one section of the frieze, shifted to another, lingered a moment, and returned again to the first. Ludovic moved forward, counting the divisions between the pilasters. At the third from the window-end of the room he stopped, and held the lantern up close to the wall. He drew his left arm painfully from its sling, and raised it, wincing, to fumble with the carving on the frieze. His tongue clicked impatiently at his own helplessness; he returned his arm to the sling, and stepped back to the window. "You'll have to hold the lantern, Abel."

Bundy climbed into the room and took the lantern, directing its beam not on to the wainscoting but on to the lock of the door. He looked thoughtfully at it, and said: "No key."

Ludovic frowned a little, but replied: "It may be lost. Wait!" He trod softly over the carpet to the door, and stood listening with his ear to the crack. He could hear nothing, and moved away again. "If I don't find what I want in the priest's hole we'll open that door, and take a look round the rest of the house," he said. "Hold the light so that I may see the frieze. No, more to the right." He put up his hand, and grasped one of the carved devices. "I think—no, I'm wrong! It's not the fourth, but the third! Now watch!"

Bundy saw his long fingers twist the device, and simultaneously heard the scroop of a door sliding back. The sudden noise, slight though it was, sounded abnormally loud in the stillness. He swung the lantern round, and saw that between two of the pilasters on the lower tier the panelling had vanished, disclosing a dark cavity.

"The lantern, man, give me the lantern!" Ludovic said, and almost snatched it from him.

He reached the priest's hole in two strides, and as he bent peering into it, Bundy heard a faint sound, and wheeling about saw a thin line of light appear at one end of the room, gradually widening. Someone was stealthily opening the door.

"Out, sir! Save yourself!" he hissed, and pulling his pistol out of his pocket prepared to hold all comers at bay until Ludovic was through the window.

Ludovic heard the warning, and quick as a flash, thrust the lantern into the priest's hole, and swung round. He said clearly: "The window, man! Be off!" and bending till he was nearly double, slipped backwards into the priest's hole, and pulled the panel to upon himself.

Wavering candlelight illumined the room, a voice shouted: "Stand! Stand!" and Bundy, hidden behind the window-curtains, saw a thin man with a pistol in his hand rush into the room towards the priest's hole, and claw fruitlessly at the panel, saying: "He's here, he's here! I saw him!"

The butler, who was standing on the threshold with a branch of candles in his hand, stared at the wainscoting and said: "Where?"

"Here, behind the panel! I saw it close, I tell you! There's a priest's hole; we have him trapped!"

The butler looked a good deal astonished, and advancing

further into the room said: "Since you know so much about this house, Mr. Gregg, perhaps you know how to get into this priest's hole you talk of?"

The valet shook his head, biting his nails. "No, we were too late. Only the master knows the catch to it. We must keep it covered."

"It seems to me that there's someone else as knows," remarked the butler austerely. "I'm bound to say that I don't understand what it is you're playing at, Mr. Gregg, with all this mysterious talk about house-breakers, and setting everyone on to keep watch like you have. Who's behind the panel?"

Gregg answered evasively: "How should I know? But I saw a man disappear into the wall. We must get the Parish Constable up here to take him the instant the master gets back and opens the panel."

"I presoom you know what you're about, Mr. Gregg," said the butler in frigid tones. "If I were to pass an opinion I should say that it was more my place than yours to give orders here in the master's absence. These goings-on are not at all what I have been accustomed to."

"Never mind that!" said Gregg impatiently. "Send one of the stable-hands to fetch the Constable!"

"Stand where you be!" growled a voice from the window. "Drop that gun! I have you covered, and my pop's liable to go off unaccountable sudden-like."

The valet wheeled round, saw Mr. Bundy, and jerked up his pistol-hand. The two guns cracked almost as one, but in the uncertain light neither bullet found its mark. The butler gave a startled gasp, and nearly let the candles fall, and through the window scrambled a third man, who flung himself upon Bundy from the rear, panting: "Ah, *would* you, then!"

Abel Bundy was not, however, an easy man to overpower. He wrenched himself out of the groom's hold, and jabbed him scientifically in the face. The groom, a young and enthusiastic man, went staggering back, but recovered, and bored in again.

The butler, seeing that a mill was in progress, set down the branch of candles on the table, and hurried, portly but powerful, to join in the fray. Gregg called out: "That's not the man! The other's here, behind the panelling! This one makes no odds!"

"This one's good enough for me!" said the groom between his teeth.

It was at this moment that Sir Tristram, mounted on Clem's horse, reached the wicket-gate at the back of the garden. He had heard the pistol-shots as he rode across the park, and had spurred his horse to a gallop. He pulled it up, snorting and trembling, flung himself out of the saddle, and setting his hand on the wicket-gate, vaulted over, and went swiftly round the house to the library window.

An amazing sight met his eyes. Of Ludovic there was no sign, but three other men, apparently inextricably entangled, swayed and struggled over the floor, while Beau Lavenham's prim valet hovered about the group, saying: "Not that one! I want the other!"

Sir Tristram stood for a moment, considering. Then he drew a long-barrelled pistol from his pocket, and with deliberation cocked it and took careful aim. There was a flash, and a deafening report, and the branch of candles on the table crashed to the ground, plunging the room into darkness.

Sir Tristram, entering the library through the window, heard the valet shriek: "My God, he must have gone out! No one else could have fired that shot!"

"Oh, could they not?" murmured Sir Tristram, with a certain grim satisfaction.

Half in and half out of the window, his form was silhouetted for a moment against the moonlit sky. The valet gave a shout of warning, and Sir Tristram, coolly taking note of his position from the sound of his voice, strode forward. The valet met him bravely enough, launching himself upon the dimly-seen figure, but he was no match for Sir Tristram, who evaded his clutch, and threw in a body-hit which almost doubled him up. Before he could recover from it Sir Tristram found him again, and dropped him from a terrific right to the jaw. He crashed to the ground and lay still, and Sir Tristram, his eyes growing accustomed to the darkness, turned his attention to Bundy's captors. For a few seconds there was some wild fighting. The groom, leaving Bundy to the butler, tried to grapple with Shield, was thrown off, and rattled in again as game as a pebble. There was no room for science: hits went glaringly abroad, furniture was sent flying, and the confused bout ended in Shield throwing his opponent in a swinging fall.

Bundy, who had very soon accounted for the butler, turned

to assist his unknown supporter, but found it unnecessary. He was thrust towards the window, and scrambled through it just as the groom struggled to his feet again. Sir Tristram followed him fast, and two minutes later they confronted one another on the park side of the wicket-gate, both of them panting for breath, the knuckles of Shield's right hand bleeding slightly and Bundy's left eye rapidly turning from red to purple.

"Dang me if I know who you may be!" said Bundy, breathing heavily. "But I'm tedious glad to meet a cove so uncommon ready to sport his canvas, that I will say!"

"You may not know me," said Shield wrathfully, "but I know you, you muddling, addle-pated jackass! Where's Mr. Ludovic?"

Bundy, rather pleased than otherwise by this form of address, said mildly: "What might you be up in the bows for, master? I misdoubt I don't know what you'm talking about."

"You damned fool, I'm his cousin! Where is he?"

Bundy stared at him, a slow smile dawning on his swollen countenance. "His cautious cousin!" he said. "If he hadn't misled me I should have guessed it, surelye, for by the way you talk you might be the old lord himself! Lamentable cautious you be? Oh, l-a-amentable!"

"For two pins I'd give you into custody for a dangerous law-breaker!" said Shield savagely. "Will you answer me, or do I choke it out of you? Where's my cousin?"

"Now don't go wasting time having a set-to with me!" begged Mr. Bundy. "I don't say I wouldn't like a bout with you, but it ain't the time for it. Mr. Ludovic's got himself into that priest's hole he was so just about crazy to find."

"In the priest's hole? Then why the devil didn't he come out when I shot the candles over?"

"Happen it ain't so easy to get out as what it is to get in," suggested Bundy. "What's more, the cat's properly in the cream-pot now, for that screeching valet knows where he is, ay, and who he is! He means to watch till his precious master gets home."

"He'll do no watching yet awhile," said Sir Tristram. "I took very good care to put him to sleep. He's the only one we have to fear. The butler has never seen my cousin, and I doubt is not in his master's confidence."

"You'm right there," corroborated Bundy, "he ain't. But he knows there's a man in the priest's hole, because t'other cove told him so."

"I can handle him," said Shield briefly, and catching his horse's bridle, set his foot in the stirrup. "Stay here, and if I whistle come to the window. I may need you to show me where to find the catch that opens the panel." He swung himself into the saddle as he spoke, wheeled the horse, and cantered off towards the gap in the hedge through which Ludovic and Bundy had entered the park.

Mr. Bundy, tenderly feeling his contused eye, was shaken by inward mirth for the second time that evening. "Lamentable cautious!" he repeated. "Oh ay, l-a-amentable!"

Sir Tristram, breaking through on to the road, turned towards the Dower House, and rode up the neat drive at a canter. Dismounting, he not only pulled the iron bell violently, but also hammered an imperative summons with the knocker on the front door.

In a few minutes the door was cautiously opened on the chain, and the butler, looking pale and shaken, and with a black eye almost equal to Bundy's, peered out.

"What the devil's amiss?" demanded Sir Tristram. "Don't keep me standing here! Open the door!"

"Oh, it's you, sir!" gasped the butler, much relieved, and making haste to unfasten the chain.

"Of course it's I!" said Sir Tristram, pushing his way past him into the hall. "I was on my way home from Hand Cross when I heard unmistakable pistol-shots coming from here. What's the meaning of it? What are you doing up at this hour?"

"I'm—I'm very glad you've come, sir," said the butler, wiping his face. "Very glad indeed, sir. I'm so shook up I scarce know what I'm about. It was Gregg's doing, sir. No, not precisely that neither, but it was Gregg as had his suspicions there was a robbery planned for to-night. He was quite right, sir: we've had house-breakers in, and one of them's hidden in some priest's hole I never heard of till now. I've never been so used in all my life, sir, never!"

"Priest's hole! What priest's hole?" said Shield. "How many house-breakers were there? Have you caught any of them?"

"No, sir, and there's Gregg laying like one dead. There was a great many of them. We did what we could, but the candlestick was shot over, and in the dark they got away. It was the one in the panelling Gregg set such store by catching, so I've left one of the stable-lads there to keep watch. In the library, sir."

"It seems to me you have conducted yourselves like a set of idiots!" said Sir Tristram angrily, and walked into the library.

The candelabra had been picked up from the wreckage on the floor, and the candles, most of them broken off short by their fall, had been relit. The valet's inanimate form was stretched on a couch, and the young groom, looking bruised and dishevelled but still remarkably pugnacious, was standing in the middle of the room, his serious grey eyes fixed on the wainscoting. He touched his forelock to Sir Tristram, but did not move from his commanding position.

Shield went over to look at the valet, who was breathing stertorously. "Knocked out," he said. "You'd better carry him up to his bed. Where's this precious panel you talk of?"

"It's here, sir," answered the groom. "I'm a-watching of it. Only let the cove come out, that's all I ask!"

"I'll keep an eye on that," replied Sir Tristram. "You take this fellow's legs, and help Jenkyns carry him up to his room. Get water and vinegar, and see what you can do to bring him round. Gently, now!"

Under his authoritative instructions the groom and the butler lifted Gregg from the couch, and bore him tenderly from the room. No sooner had they started to mount the stairs than Sir Tristram closed the library door and called softly: "Ludovic! All's clear: come out!"

"Happen he's suffocated inside that hole," remarked Mr. Bundy's fatalistic voice from the window.

"Nonsense, there must be enough air! Where's the catch that opens the panel?"

Bundy, leaning his head and shoulders in at the window indicated the portion of the frieze where it might be found. Shield ran his hands over the carving, presently found the device Ludovic had twisted, and turned it. The panel slid back once more, and Shield, picking up the candelabra, went to it, saying sharply: "Ludovic! Are you hurt?"

There was no answer. Sir Tristram bent, so that the candles illumined the cavity, and looked in. It was quite empty.

Chapter XII

SIR TRISTRAM put the candelabra down, and once more twisted the device, closing the panel. "He's not there," he said.

Mr. Bundy betrayed no surprise. "Ah!" he remarked, preparing to climb into the room. "I'd a notion we shouldn't get out of this so hem easy. As good be nibbled to death by ducks as set out on one of Master Ludovic's ventures! Where's he got to, by your reckoning?"

"God knows? He must have slipped out after the candles were knocked over. Don't come in!"

Bundy obediently stayed where he was. "Just as you say, master. But it ain't like him to keep out of a fight."

"He'd be no use in a mill with one arm in a sling," replied Sir Tristram. "Go and see if he has gone back to where you left your horses. If he's not there he must be somewhere in the house."

"Well, I'll do it," said Bundy, "but I reckon it's no manner of use. 'Twouldn't be natural if young master were to start behaving sensible all on a sudden. You'd be surprised the number of cork-brained scrapes he's got himself into these two years and more."

"You're wrong; I shouldn't," retorted Sir Tristram.

"Ah well, he's a valiant lad, surelye!" said Bundy, indulgently, and withdrew.

Sir Tristram stayed where he was, and in a very few minutes Mr. Bundy once more appeared at the window and said simply: "He ain't there."

"Damn the boy!" said Sir Tristram. "Get away from that window! There's someone coming!"

Bundy promptly ducked beneath the level of the window-sill just as the door opened, and Gregg staggered in, supported by the butler.

His jaw was much swollen and two front teeth were broken. Sir Tristram put his grazed right hand into his pocket. It was evident that although his head might be swimming, the valet still had some of his wits about him, for no sooner did his bleared gaze fall upon Shield than he turned an even more sickly colour, and catching at a chair-back to steady himself, said in a thick voice: "It's like that, is it? But I'll watch. I have the keys of the doors. If he's there still he won't get away!"

The groom came into the room and said in his serious young voice: "I'd get him a drop of brandy if I were you, Mr. Jenkyns. Regular shook to pieces he is. Now, don't you fret, Mr. Gregg! No one can't get out while you've got them keys."

The butler, who thought that a drop of brandy would do him good also, said graciously that he believed the lad was right, and went away to fetch the decanter. The groom, coming up behind the valet, said solicitously: "You shouldn't ought to have come down, Mr. Gregg," and knocked him out with one nicely-delivered blow under the ear. The unfortunate valet collapsed on the floor, and the groom, looking down at him with a smouldering expression of wrath in his pleasant grey eyes, said grimly: "Maybe that'll be a lesson to you, you cribbage-faced tooth-drawer, you!"

Before Sir Tristram, considerably astonished by this unexpected turn events had taken, had time to speak, the butler, hearing the sound of Gregg's fall, came hurrying back into the room. The groom at once turned to meet him, saying: "Blessed if he ain't swooned off again, Mr. Jenkyns! Done to a cow's thumb, he is!"

"Carry the poor fellow up to his room again, and this time keep him there!" commanded Sir Tristram, recovering from his surprise.

"Just what I was a-going to do, sir," said the groom. "Now, Mr. Jenkyns, if you'll take his legs we'll soon have him in his bed!"

"Ah, I warned him not to get up!" said the butler, shaking his head.

The groom thrust a hand into Gregg's pocket and extracted the keys from it. "I'm thinking your Honour had best keep these," he said, and held them out to Sir Tristram.

The butler, puffing as he bent to raise Gregg, agreed that Sir Tristram was certainly the man to take charge of the keys. For a second time the valet was borne off upstairs. Mr. Bundy, reappearing at the window, like a jack-in-the-box, remarked phlegmatically: "It looks to me like young master's met a friend. Who's that young cove?"

"I fancy he must be Jim Kettering's boy," replied Sir Tristram.

"Well, he's caused us a peck of trouble this night," said Bundy, "but I'm bound to say he seems an unaccountable nice lad! Handy with his fives he is."

At this moment Ludovic strolled into the room. "Well, of all the shambles!" he remarked, glancing around. "I'd give a monkey to see the Beau's face when he comes home! What brought you here, Tristram?"

"Clem fetched me," replied Shield. "How did you get out of the priest's hole, and what the devil have you been doing all this while?"

"There's another way out of the hole," explained Ludovic. "I thought there might be. It leads up to Basil's bedchamber. It seemed to me I might as well hunt for the ring since you had the affair so well in hand down here. Then I heard Bob Kettering's voice, and gave him a whistle——"

"Gave him a whistle?" echoed Sir Tristram. "With the whole household looking for you, you *whistled?*"

"Yes, why not? I knew he'd recognize it. It's a signal we used when we were boys. Bob hadn't a notion he'd been set on to hunt for me. Lord, we used to go bird's-nesting together!"

"I thought you'd met a friend," nodded Bundy. "Did you happen to find that ring o' yourn?"

Ludovic's face clouded over. "No. Bob helped me to ransack Basil's room, but it's not there, and it wasn't in the priest's hole."

"Did young Kettering chance to remember that he is in Basil's service?" inquired Sir Tristram.

Ludovic looked at him. "Yes, but this was for *me,* my dear fellow!"

Sir Tristram smiled faintly. "I suppose he is as shameless as you are. Do you feel that you have done enough damage for one night, or is there anything else you'd care to set your hand to before you go?"

"Damage!" said Ludovic. "If that don't beat everything! Who smashed all this furniture, I should like to know? *I* didn't!"

The groom came back into the library as he spoke, and said urgently: "Mr. Ludo, you'd best go while you may. We'll have Jenkyns down again afore we know where we are!"

"Have you ever thought to go into the prize-ring, young fellow," interrupted Bundy, who was leaning in at the window with his arms folded on the sill, after the fashion of one who was prepared to remain there indefinitely. "You've a sizeable bunch of fives, and you display none so bad."

Kettering grinned rather deprecatingly, and said in an apologetic tone to Sir Tristram: "I didn't know it was Mr. Ludo, sir. Nor I didn't know it was you neither. I'm proud, surelye, to have had a turn-up with you, even if it were in the dark."

"Well, it's more than I'd care to do," remarked Ludovic. "To hell with you, Bob! Don't keep on pushing me to the window! I'll go all in good time, but I've mislaid that damn lantern."

Sir Tristram grasped him by his sound shoulder, and propelled him to the window. "Take him away, Bundy. Kettering can find the lantern when you've gone. If you don't go you'll find yourself in difficulties again, and I warn you I won't get you out of any more tight corners."

Ludovic, astride the window-sill, said: "You don't call this a tight corner, do you? I was as safe be damned!"

"Just about, you were," growled Bundy, trying to haul him through the window, "playing your silly rat-in-the-wall tricks, with a whole pack of gurt fools fighting who was to find you first! And you saying you wasn't going to take no risks! Now, come out of it, master!"

"I can't help it if you disobey my orders!" said Ludovic indignantly. "Didn't I tell you to save yourself? Instead of doing anything of the kind you blazed off your pistol (and a damned bad shot it must have been) and started a mill, so that my cousin had to make a wreck of the place to bring you off! What's more, that's not the sort of thing he likes. He's a cautious man—aren't you, Tristram?"

"I am," replied Sir Tristram, thrusting him through the window into Bundy's arms, "but my love of caution isn't going to stop me knocking you on the head and carrying you away if you don't go immediately. Wait for me by your horses. I shan't be many moments."

He saw Ludovic go off under Bundy's escort, and turned back to Kettering. His level gaze seemed to measure the younger man. He said: "I take it you can keep your mouth shut?"

The groom nodded. "Ay, sir, I can that. Me to help trap

Mr. Ludo! Begging your pardon, sir, but it do fair rile me to think of it!"

"Well, if you get turned off for this night's work come to me," said Sir Tristram. "Now where's that butler?" He went out into the hall, and called to Jenkyns, who presently came hurrying down the stairs. "Here are your keys," said Sir Tristram, holding them out to him. "Now let me out!"

The butler took the keys, but said in a blank voice: "Are —are you going now, sir?"

"Certainly, I am going," replied Shield, with one of his coldest glances. "Do you imagine that I propose to remain here all night to keep watch for a house-breaker who, if he ever entered the priest's hole (which I take leave to doubt), must have escaped half an hour ago?"

"No, sir. Oh no, sir!" said the butler very chap-fallen.

"You are, for once, quite right," said Shield.

Five minutes later he joined Ludovic in the park and dismounted from Clem's horse. Clem had by this time reached the scene of activity, having walked from the Court, and Ludovic was already in the saddle, looking rather haggard and spent. Sir Tristram gave his bridle into Clem's hand, and looked shrewdly up at his young cousin. "Yes, you are feeling your wound a trifle," he remarked. "I am not in the least surprised, and not particularly sorry. If you had your deserts for this night's folly you would be in gaol."

"Oh, my wound's well enough!" replied Ludovic. "Do you want me to say that you were in the right, and there was a trap? Well, then, you were damnably right, even to saying that I'd not find my ring. I haven't found it. What else?"

"Nothing else. Go back to Hand Cross, and for God's sake stay there!"

Ludovic let the reins go, and stretched down his hand. "Oh curse you, Tristram, I am sorry, and you're a devilish good fellow to embroil yourself in my crazy affairs! Thank you for coming to-night!"

Shield gripped his hand for a moment, and said in a softer voice: "Don't be a fool! We will find your ring, Ludovic. I'll see you to-morrow."

"I'll try and keep out of trouble till then," promised Ludovic. He gathered the reins up again, and the irrepressible twinkle crept back into his eyes. "By the way, my compliments: a nice shot!"

Shield laughed at that. "Was it not? Gregg thought you must have fired it."

"Extravagant praise, Tristram: you shouldn't listen to flattery," retorted Ludovic, grinning.

When the adventurers got back to the Red Lion they found both Nye and Miss Thane awaiting them by the coffee-room fire. Relief at seeing Ludovic safe and sound had its natural effect on Nye, and instead of greeting his graceless charge with solicitude he rated him with such severity that Bundy was moved to expostulate. "Adone-do, Joe!" he said. "There's no harm done, and we've had a nice little mill. Just you take a look at my eye."

"I am looking at it," replied Nye. "If I ever meet the man as gave it you I'll shake him by the hand! I wish he'd blacked t'other as well."

"You'd have kissed him if he had," remarked Ludovic. "It was Bob Kettering."

"Bob Kettering!" ejaculated the landlord. "Now, what have you been about, sir? If I ever met such a plaguey——where's Sir Tristram?"

"Gone home to bed," yawned Ludovic. "I dare say he'll be glad to get there; he's had a full evening, thanks to you, Sally."

Mr. Bundy nodded slowly at Nye. "It would do your heart good to see that cove in a turn-up, Joe. Displays to remarkable advantage, he does. Up to all the tricks."

"Many's the time I've sparred with Sir Tristram," replied Nye crushingly. "I don't doubt he'd be a match for the lot of you, but what I do say, and hold to, is that he hit the wrong man."

"I don't know when I've took such a fancy to a cove," said Bundy, disregarding this significant remark. "He gave the valet one in the bone-box, and a tedious wisty castor to the jaw. What he done to young Kettering I don't know, but from the sounds of it he threw him a rare cross-buttock."

At this point Miss Thane interrupted him, demanding to be told the full story of the night's adventure. It seemed to amuse her, and when Sir Tristram arrived at the Red Lion midway through the following morning, she met him with a pronounced twinkle in her eyes.

He saw it, and a rueful smile stole into his own eyes. He took the hand she held out to him, saying: "How do you do? This should be a day of triumph for you."

She put up her brows. "I believe you are quizzing me. Why should it be a day of triumph for me?"

"My dear ma'am, did you not guess that at last you have succeeded in making me feel grateful towards you?"

"Odious creature!" said Miss Thane, without heat. "I had a mind to go myself to rescue Ludovic."

"You would have been very much in the way, I assure you. How is the boy this morning?"

"I fancy he has taken no harm. He is a little in the dumps. Tell me, have you any real hope of finding his ring?"

"I have every hope of clearing his name," he replied. "His adventure last night will at least serve to convince the Beau that we mean to bring him to book. While no danger threatened, Basil was easily able to behave with calmness and good sense, but I do not think he is of the stuff to remain cool in the face of a very pressing danger."

"You think he may betray himself. But one must not forget that last night's affair must surely have betrayed *you*."

"All the better," said Shield. "The Beau is a little afraid of me."

"I imagine he might well be. But he cannot be so stupid that he will not realize what your true purpose in his house must have been."

"Certainly," he agreed, "but his situation is awkward. He will hardly admit to having laid a trap for the man whose heir he is. He will be obliged to pretend to accept my story. Where is Ludovic, by the way?"

"Eustacie has persuaded him to stay in bed this morning. Five miles to the Dower House, and five miles back again, with an adventure between, was a trifle too much for one little better than an invalid. Do you care to go up? You will find Hugh with him, I think."

He nodded, and waited for her by the door, and when she seemed not to be coming, said: "You do not mean to secede from our councils, I hope?"

She smiled. "You are not used to be so civil. Fighting must have a mellowing effect upon you, I think."

"Have I been uncivil?" he asked, looking at her with disconcerting seriousness.

"Well, perhaps not uncivil," she conceded. "Just disapproving."

He followed her out of the room, and as they mounted the stairs, said: "I wish you will rid yourself of this nonsensical notion that I disapprove of you."

"But do you not?" inquired Miss Thane, turning her head.

He stopped two stairs below her, and stood looking up at her, something not quite a smile at the back of his eyes. "Sometimes," he said.

They found Ludovic drinking Constantia wine, and arguing with Sir Hugh about the propriety of breaking into other people's houses to recover one's own property. Eustacie, seated by the window, upheld the justice of his views, but strongly condemned the insensibility of persons who allowed others to sleep while such adventures were in train. She was rash enough to appeal to her cousin Tristram for support, but as he only replied that he had not till now thought that he had anything to be thankful for with regard to last night's affair, he joined Miss Thane in her ill-graces.

Ludovic's immediate desire was to learn from his cousin by what means he now proposed to find the talisman ring, but they had not been discussing the matter for more than five minutes when a chaise was heard approaching at a smart pace down the road. It drew up outside the inn, and Eustacie, peeping over the blind, announced in a shocked voice that its occupant was none other than Beau Lavenham.

"What audacity!" exclaimed Miss Thane.

"Yes, and he is wearing a waistcoat with coquelicot stripes," said Eustacie.

"What!" ejaculated Ludovic. "Here, where's my dressing-gown? I must take a look at him!"

"Oh no, you must not!" said Sir Tristram, preventing his attempt to leap out of bed.

"It is too late: he has entered the house. What can he want?"

"Probably to convince us that he was really in London last night," said Shield. "We'll go down to him, Eustacie."

"Je le veux bien! What shall I say to him?"

"Whatever you please, as long as it does not concern Ludovic." He looked across the room at Miss Thane. "Do you think you can contrive to be as stupid and talkative as you were when he last saw you?"

"Oh, am I to be allowed to take part?" asked Miss Thane. "Certainly I can be as stupid. To what purpose?"

"Well, I think it is time we frightened Basil a little," said Sir Tristram. "Since he must now be very sure that Ludovic is in Sussex, we will further inform him that we suspect him of being Plunkett's real murderer."

"That's all very well," objected Ludovic, "but what do you expect him to do?"

"I haven't a notion," said Shield calmly, "but I am reasonably certain that he will do something."

"Tell me what you wish me to say!" begged Miss Thane.

Beau Lavenham was not kept waiting long in the parlour. In a very few minutes his cousins joined him there. He shot a quick searching look at them under his lashes, and advanced, all smiles and civility. "My dear Eustacie—Tristram, too! You behold me on my way home from a most tedious, disagreeable sojourn in town. I could not resist the opportunity of paying a morning call upon you. I trust I do not come at an awkward time?"

"But no!" said Eustacie, opening her eyes at him. "Why should it be?"

Sir Tristram came over to the fire in a leisurely fashion, and stirred it with his foot. "Oh, so you've not yet been home, Basil?" he inquired.

"No, not yet," replied the Beau. He put up his ornate quizzing-glass, and through it looked at Shield. "Why do you ask me so oddly, my dear fellow? Is anything amiss at the Dower House?"

"Something very much amiss, I am afraid," said Shield. He waited for a moment, saw the flash of eagerness in the Beau's eyes, and added: "One of your Jacobean chairs has been broken."

There was a moment's silence. The Beau let his glass fall, and replied in rather a mechanical voice: "A chair broken? Why, how is that?"

The door opened to admit Miss Thane. Until she had exclaimed at finding the Beau present, greeted him, inquired after his health, the condition of the roads and the state of the weather in London, there was no opportunity of reverting to the original subject of conversation. But as soon as she paused for breath the Beau turned back to Shield, and said: "You were telling me something about one of my chairs being broken. I fear I don't——"

"Oh!" exclaimed Miss Thane, "have you not heard, then? Has Sir Tristram not told you of the shocking attempt to rob you last night? I declare I shall not know how to go to bed this evening!"

"No," said the Beau slowly. "No. He has not told me. Is it possible that my house was broken into?"

"Exactly," nodded Sir Tristram. "If your servants are to be believed a band of desperate ruffians entered through the library window."

"Yes," chimed in Miss Thane, "and only fancy, Mr. Lavenham! Sir Tristram had been dining with us here, and was riding back to the Court when he heard shots coming from the Dower House. You may imagine his amazement! I am sure you should be grateful to him, for he instantly rode up to the house. You may depend upon it it was the noise of his arrival which frightened the wretches into running away."

The glance the Beau cast at his cousin was scarcely one of gratitude. He had turned rather pale, but he said in quite level tones: "I am indeed grateful. What a fortunate chance that you should have been passing the house just at that moment, Tristram! I suppose none of these rogues was apprehended?"

"I fear not," replied Shield. "By the time I entered the house there was no sign of them. There had been (as you will see for yourself presently) a prodigious struggle in the library—quite a mill, I understand. I am afraid your fellows were much knocked about. In fact, your butler," he pursued, stooping to put another log on the fire, "welcomed my advent with profound relief."

"No doubt!" said the Beau, breathing rather quickly. "I do not doubt it!"

"The poor butler!" said Miss Thane, with a tinkling laugh. "I am sure I do not wonder he should be alarmed! He must feel you to be his preserver, Sir Tristram. He will be doubly glad to exchange his masters!"

The Beau looked at her. "I beg your pardon, ma'am?"

Miss Thane said: "I only meant, since he was about to enter Sir Tristram's service——"

"You are mistaken, Miss Thane," Sir Tristram interrupted, frowning at her. "There is no question of my cousin's butler leaving his service that I know of."

"Oh, how stupid of me! Only you was saying to Eustacie that you had found Mr. Lavenham's butler, and she asked, do you not remember, whether his memory——"

Eustacie said in a hurry: "I hope so much that nothing has been stolen from your house, Basil. To have——"

"So do I hope it, my dear cousin. But pray let Miss Thane continue!"

Miss Thane, encountering a frown from Eustacie, stammered: "Oh, indeed it was nothing! I would not for the world —I mean, I was mistaken! I confused one thing with another. My brother tells me I am a sad shatterbrain."

Sir Tristram intervened, saying in his cool way: "I am

making no attempt to steal your butler from you, I assure you, Basil."

"Of course not! The stupidest mistake!" said Miss Thane, all eagerness to atone. "It is not your present butler, Mr. Lavenham, but one you was used to employ. I remember perfectly now!" She looked from Sir Tristram to Eustacie and faltered: "Have I said something I ought not? But you *did* tell Eustacie."

The Beau was gripping his snuff-box tightly. "Yes? A butler I once employed? Are you thinking of taking him into your service, Tristram?"

"Why, yes, I confess I had some such notion," admitted Shield. "You have no objection I trust?"

"Why should I?" said the Beau, with a singularly mirthless smile. "I doubt, though, whether you will find him so useful as you expect."

"Oh, I dare say I shall not engage him after all," replied Shield, and made haste to change the subject.

The Beau did not linger. Excusing himself on the score of being obliged to go home to ascertain what losses, if any, he had sustained, he very soon took his leave of the party, and drove away in the direction of Warninglid.

No sooner had he left the inn than Eustacie cast herself upon Miss Thane's bosom, announcing that she forgave her for her unfeeling conduct of the night before. "You did it so *very* well, Sarah! He was *bouleversé*, and I think frightened."

"He was certainly frightened," agreed Miss Thane. "He forgot to smile. What do you suppose he will do, Sir Tristram?"

"I hope he may make an attempt to find Cleghorn and buy his silence. If he does he will have delivered himself into our hands. But don't let Ludovic stir from the house! I'll warn Nye to be careful whom he lets into the inn."

"I can feel my flesh creeping already," said Miss Thane, with a shudder. "It has suddenly occurred to me that that very unpleasant person thinks Ludovic is occupying the back bedchamber."

Eustacie gave a gasp. "Oh, Sarah, you do not think he will come to murder Ludovic, do you?"

"I shouldn't be at all surprised," said Miss Thane. "And *I* am occupying the back bedchamber! I just mention it, you know."

"So you are!" Eustacie's face cleared. "But it is of all things the most fortunate! It could not be better, *enfin!*"

"That," said Miss Thane, with strong feeling, "is a matter of opinion. *I* can see where it could be much better."

"But no, Sarah! If Basil comes to murder Ludovic in the night he will find not Ludovic, but you!"

"Yes, that was what I was thinking," said Miss Thane.

"Well, but it would be a good thing, Sarah!"

"A good thing for whom?" demanded Miss Thane with asperity.

"For Ludovic, of course! You do not *mind* doing just that little thing to help him, do you? You said that you wanted to have an adventure!"

"I may have said that I wanted to have an adventure," replied Miss Thane, "but I never said that I wanted to be murdered in my bed!"

"But I find that you are absurd, Sarah! Of course he would not murder you!"

"Unless, of course, he regarded it as a good opportunity to rid the world of a chattering female," said Sir Tristram, with a gravity wholly belied by the twinkle in his eyes. "That is a risk, however, which we shall have to run."

Miss Thane looked at him. "You did say 'we,' didn't you?" she said in a failing voice.

He laughed. "Yes, I said it. But in all seriousness, Miss Thane, I do not think there will be any risk. If you are afraid, share Eustacie's bed."

"No," said Miss Thane, with the air of one going to the stake. "I prefer that my blood should be upon your heads."

She spoke in jest, and certainly did not give the matter another thought, but the exchange had made an impression on Eustacie's mind, and for the rest of the day she could scarcely bear to let Ludovic out of her sight. When Sir Tristram had gone, and Miss Thane proposed they should take their usual morning walk, she refused with such resolution that Miss Thane forbore to press the matter, but went out with her brother, leaving Eustacie keeping guard over Ludovic like a cat with one kitten.

As the day drew towards evening Eustacie's fears became more pronounced. When the candles were lit and the blinds drawn, she persisted in hearing footsteps, and fancying some stranger to have got into the inn. She confided in Miss Thane that she was sure there was someone in the house, hiding, and insisted, in spite of his protestations that no one could have entered without his knowledge, upon Nye's searching every nook and cranny. The house was an old and rambling

one, and the boards creaked a good deal. Miss Thane, when
Eustacie held up her finger for the fifth time, enjoining silence that she might listen for a fancied noise, said roundly:
"A little more, and I shall be quite unable to sleep a wink all
night. *Now* what's amiss?"

Eustacie, drawing the curtains more closely across the window, said: "There was just a crack. Someone might look in
and see Ludovic. I think it will be better if I pin the curtains
together."

Sir Hugh, who was engaged upon his nightly game of piquet with Ludovic, became aware of her restlessness, and
turned to look at her. "Ah!" he said. "So you don't like the
moonshine either! It's a queer thing, but if ever I have a bad
dream you may depend upon it the moon's up. There's another thing, too: if ever it gets into my room it wakes me.
I'm glad to meet someone else who feels the same."

No one thought it worth while to explain Eustacie's real
motive to him, so after recounting various incidents illustra-
tive of the baneful effect of the moon upon human beings, he
returned to his game, and speedily became oblivious of Eustacie's fidgets.

Since Eustacie could not bring herself to go up to bed leaving Ludovic, quite heedless of danger, below-stairs, the piquet
came to an early end, and the whole party went up to bed
soon after ten o'clock. Having assured herself that the windows in Ludovic's room were securely fastened and his pistols loaded and under his pillow, Eustacie at last consented,
though reluctantly, to seek her own couch. Ludovic took her
in his sound arm, and kissed her, and laughed at her fears.
She said seriously: "But I am afraid. I love you so much that
it seems to me very probable that you will be taken away
from me. Promise me that you will lock your door and draw
the bolts!"

He laid his cheek against her hair. "I'll promise anything,
sweetheart. Don't trouble your pretty head over me! I'm not
worth it."

"To me, you are."

"I wish I had two arms!" he sighed. "Do you know that
you are marrying a ne'er-do-weel?"

"Certainly I know it. It is just what I always wanted," she
replied.

Miss Thane came along the passage at this moment and
put an end to their *tête-à-tête*. She quite agreed with Eustacie
that Ludovic must lock his door. She had every intention, she

said, of locking her own. She bore Eustacie off to her room, stayed with her till she was safely tucked up in bed, turned the lamp down, made up the fire, and went away wondering whether there really might be something to fear, or whether they had allowed their fancy to run riot. This problem kept her awake for some time, but after a couple of hours spent in straining her ears to catch the sound of a footfall she did at last fall asleep, lulled by the monotonous rise and fall of her brother's snores, drifting to her ears from across the passage.

At one o'clock these ceased abruptly. The moon had reached a point in the heavens from which its rays were able to find out a chink between the blinds over Sir Hugh's window. A sliver of silver light stole across his face. Its baleful influence was instantly felt, Sir Hugh awoke.

He knew at once what had roused him, and with a muttered curse, got up out of bed and stalked over to the window. A tug at the blind failed to put matters right, and Sir Hugh, blinking with sleep, perceived that a fold of the chintz had been caught in the hinge when the casement was shut. "Damned carelessness!" he said severely, and opened the window to release the blind.

There was a smart wind blowing; a sudden gust tore the casement out of his slack hold, and flung it wide. He leaned out to pull it to again, and as he did so noticed that one of the windows in the coffee-room directly beneath his bed-chamber was also standing wide. It seemed to him unusual and undesirable that windows should be left open all night, and after regarding it for a moment or two with slightly somnolent disapproval, he drew in his head, turned up the wick of the lamp that stood by his bed, and lit a candle at its flame. Yawning, he groped his way into his dressing-gown, and then, picking up the candlestick and treading softly for fear of waking the rest of the household, sallied forth to rectify Nye's omission.

He went carefully down the steep stairs, shading the flame of the candle from the draught. As he reached the bend in the staircase, and rounded it, he caught the glow of a light, suddenly extinguished, and knew there was someone in the coffee-room.

Sir Hugh might be of a naturally indolent disposition, but he had a rooted objection to fellows nefariously creeping about the house. He reached the bottom of the stairs with most surprising celerity, and, holding up the candle, looked keenly round the room.

A figure loomed up for an instant out of the darkness; he had a glimpse of a man with a mask over his face, and a dagger in his hand, and the next moment the candle was struck from his hold.

Sir Hugh launched himself forward, grappling with the unknown marauder. His right hand encountered something that felt like a neckcloth, and grasped it, just as the hilt of the dagger crashed down upon his shoulder, missing his head by a hair's breadth. Before the unknown could strike again he had grabbed at the dagger-hand, and found it, twisting it unmercifully. The dagger fell; and Sir Hugh's grip slackened a little. The masked man, putting forth every ounce of strength, tore himself free, and made a dart for the window. Sir Hugh plunged after him, tripped over a stool, and came down on his hands and knees with a crash. The intruder was visible for a brief moment in the shaft of moonlight; before Sir Hugh could pick himself up he had vanished through the window.

Chapter XIII

Sir Hugh swore, and got up. The noise of his fall seemed to have penetrated to the rooms above, for a door was opened, footsteps were heard flying along the passage towards his bedchamber, and Eustacie's voice sounded, begging the landlord to wake up and come at once.

"It's only I!" called Sir Hugh, tenderly massaging his grazed shin-bone. "Don't start screeching, for the lord's sake! Bring me a light!"

Another door opened; Miss Thane's voice said: "What was that? I thought I heard a crash!"

"I dare say you did," returned her brother. "I fell over a demmed stool. Send that scroundrel Nye down here. I've a bone to pick with him."

"Good gracious, Hugh!" exclaimed Miss Thane venturing half-way down the stairs, and holding up a candle. "What in the world are you doing there? You do not know what a fright you put me into!"

"Never mind that," said Sir Hugh testily. "What I want is a light."

"My dear, you sound very cross," said Miss Thane, coming down the remainder of the stairs, and setting her candlestick on the table. "Why are you here?" She caught sight of the curtain half-drawn back from the windows, and the casement swinging wide, and said quickly: "Who opened that window?"

"Just what I want to ask Nye," replied Sir Hugh. "The moon woke me, and I chanced to look out of my own window and saw this one open. I came down, and I'd no sooner got to the bottom of the stairs than a demmed fellow in a loo-mask knocked the candle out of my hand and tried to hit me on the head. No, it's no use looking round for him: he's gone, thanks to Nye leaving stools strewn about all over the floor."

Eustacie, who had come downstairs with Nye, gave a sob

of fright, and stared at Miss Thane. "He did come!" she said. "Ludovic!" She turned on the word, and fled upstairs, calling: "Ludovic, Ludovic, are you safe?"

Sir Hugh looked after her in somewhat irritated surprise. "French!" he said. "All alike! What the devil does she want to fly into a pucker for?"

Nye had gone over to the window and was leaning out. He turned and said: "The shutter's been wrenched off its hinge, and a pane of glass cut out clean as a whistle. That's where he must have put his hand in to open the window. You didn't get a sight of his face, sir?"

"No, I didn't," replied Sir Hugh, stooping to pick up the dagger at his feet. "I keep telling you he wore a mask. A loo-mask! If there's one thing above others that I hate it's a lot of demmed theatrical nonsense! What was the fellow playing at? Highwaymen?"

"Perhaps," suggested Miss Thane tactfully, "he did not wish to run the risk of being recognized."

"I dare say he didn't, and it's my belief," said Sir Hugh, bending a severe frown upon her, "that you know who he was, Sally. It has seemed to me all along that there's a deal going on here which is devilish unusual."

"Yes, dear," said Miss Thane, with becoming meekness. "I think your masked man was Ludovic's wicked cousin come to murder him with that horrid-looking knife you have in your hand."

"There ain't a doubt of it!" growled Nye. "Look what's here, ma'am!" He went down on his knees as he spoke and picked from under the table a scrap of lace, such as might have been ripped from a cravat, and an ornate gold quizzing-glass on a length of torn ribbon. "Have you ever seen that before?"

Sir Hugh took the glass from him, and inspected it disparagingly. "No, I haven't," he said, "and what's more, I don't like it. It's too heavily chased."

Miss Thane nodded. "Of course I've seen it. But I was sure without that evidence. He must be feeling desperate indeed to have taken this risk!"

At this moment Eustacie came downstairs again, with Ludovic behind her. Ludovic, in a dressing-gown as exotic as Thane's, looked amused, and rather sleepy, and dangled a pistol in his right hand. His eyes alighted first on the dagger, which Thane had laid down on the table, and he put up his brows with a rueful expression of incredulity, and said:

"What was that pretty thing meant to be plunged into my heart? Well, well! What have you got there, Thane?"

"Do you recognize it?" said Miss Thane. "It is your cousin's quizzing-glass."

Ludovic glanced at it casually, but picked up the dagger. "Oh, is it? No, I can't say I recognize it, but I dare say you're right. To think of the Beau daring to come and tackle me with nothing better than this mediæval weapon! It's a damned impertinence, upon my soul it is!"

"Depend upon it, he hoped to murder you while you slept, and so make no noise about it," said Miss Thane. "And, do you know, for all I jested Sir Tristram over it, I never really thought that he would come!"

Sir Hugh looked at Ludovic and said: "I wish you would be serious. Do you tell me it was really your cousin here tonight?"

"Oh, devil a doubt!" answered Ludovic, testing the dagger's sharpness with one slender forefinger.

"A cousin of yours masquerading about in a loo-mask?"

"Was he?" said Ludovic, interested. "Lord yes, that's Basil all over! He'd run no risk of being recognized."

"And you think he came here to murder you in your bed?" demanded Sir Hugh.

For answer, Ludovic held up the dagger.

Sir Hugh looked at it in profound silence, and then said weightily, "I'll tell you what it is, Lavenham, he's a demmed scoundrel. I never heard of such a thing!"

Eustacie, who had sunk into a chair, raised a very white face from her hands, and said in a low, fierce voice: "Yes, and if he does not go to the scaffold I myself will kill him! I will make a sacred vow to kill him!"

"No, don't do that!" said Sir Hugh, regarding her with misgiving. "You can't go about England killing people, whatever you may do in your own country."

"Yes, I can, and I will," retorted Eustacie. "To fight a duel, that is one thing! Even to try to take what belongs to Ludovic I can pardon! But to try to stab Ludovic in the dark, while he sleeps, *voyons*, that is an infamy of the most vile!"

"There's a great deal in what you say," acknowledged Sir Hugh, "but to my mind what you need is a sip of brandy. You'll feel the better for it."

"I do not need a sip of brandy!" snapped Eustacie.

"Well, if you don't, I do," said Sir Hugh frankly. "I've

been getting steadily colder ever since I came down to this demmed draughty coffee-room."

Miss Thane, taking Eustacie's hand, patted it reaasuringly, and suggested that they should go back to bed. Eustacie, who felt that at any moment the Beau might return to make a second attempt, at first refused to listen to such a notion, but upon Nye's saying grimly that she need have no fears for Ludovic's safety, since he proposed to spend the rest of the night in the coffee-room, she consented to go upstairs with Miss Thane, having first adjured Nye and Sir Hugh on no account to let Ludovic out of their sight until they saw him securely bolted into his bedchamber.

Sir Hugh was quite ready to promise anything, but his rational mind had little expectation of further adventures that night, and as soon as the two women had disappeared round the bend in the staircase, he reached up a long arm, and placing the Beau's quizzing-glass on the mantelshelf above his head, said: "Well, now that they've gone, we can make ourselves comfortable. Go and get the brandy, Nye, and bring a glass for yourself."

There were no more alarms during the rest of the night, but next morning Nye, and Miss Thane, and Eustacie met in consultation, and agreed that, however distasteful to him it might be, Ludovic must at least during the day be confined to the cellar. Nye, uncomfortably aware that there were no less than three doors into the Red Lion which must of necessity be kept unlocked and any number of windows through which a man might enter unobserved, flatly refused the responsibility of housing Ludovic if he persisted in roaming at large about the inn. The boldness of the attempt made in the night convinced him that the Beau would not easily relinquish his purpose of disposing of Ludovic, and he could not but realize that for such a purpose no place could be more convenient than a public inn. The month being February, there were very few private chaises on the Brighton road, but from time to time one would pass, and very likely pull up at the Red Lion for its occupants to refresh themselves in the coffee-room. In addition to this genteel custom there was a fairly constant, if thin, flow of country people drifting in and out of the tap-room, so that it would be quite an easy matter for a stranger to step into the inn while the landlord and Clem were busy with their customers.

As might have been expected, Ludovic, when this decision

was made known to him, objected with the utmost violence to his proposed incarceration. Not all Nye's promises of every arrangement for his comfort being made could reconcile him to the scheme. Comfort, he said roundly, could not exist in a dark cellar, smelling of every kind of liquor and crowded with pipes, barrels, spiders, and very likely rats.

Sir Hugh, wandering into the parlour in the middle of this speech, and imperfectly understanding its significance, said that, for his part, he had no objection to the smell of good liquor; in fact, quite liked it, a remark which made Ludovic retort: "You may like the smell of liquor, but how would you like to be shut up in a wine-cellar the whole day long?"

"It depends on the wine," said Sir Hugh, after giving this question due consideration.

In the end the combined arguments and entreaties of the two ladies prevailed with Ludovic, and he consented to repair to his underground retreat, Eustacie offering to share his imprisonment, and Sir Hugh, appealed to by his sister, promising to visit him for a game of piquet during the afternoon. "Though why you should want to go and sit in the cellar if you don't like the smell of liquor I can't make out," he said.

This unfortunate remark, pounced on immediately by Ludovic to support his own view of the matter, called forth a severe rebuke from Miss Thane. She tried to explain the exigencies of Ludovic's situation to Sir Hugh, but after listening incredulously to her for a few minutes, he said with a resigned shake of his head that it all sounded like a lot of nonsense to him, and that if any more people came poking and prying into the inn they would have him to deal with.

"Very likely," said Miss Thane, displaying admirable patience, "but if you did not happen to see Beau Lavenham enter the house he might well kill Ludovic before you knew anything about it."

"If that fellow calls here to-day I want a word with him," said Sir Hugh, his brow darkening. "I've a strong notion I've caught another demned cold, thanks to him getting me up out of my bed in the small hours."

"I may have only one sound arm," interrupted Ludovic, "but if you think I can't defend myself, you much mistake the matter, Sally."

"I am quite sure you can defend yourself, my dear boy, but I want your cousin's corpse on my hands as little as I want yours."

Sir Hugh was never at his best in the early morning, nor

did a disturbed night, crowned by liberal potations, help to dispel a certain sleepy vagueness that clung to him, but these significant words roused him sufficiently to make him say with decision that he had borne with a great deal of irregularity at the Red Lion, what with Bow Street Runners bobbing in and out the house, people living in cellars, and scoundrels breaking in through the windows, but that his tolerance would on no account extend to corpses littering the premises.

"Mind, Sally!" he said. "The first corpse I find means that we go back to London, wine or no wine!"

"In that case," said Miss Thane, "Ludovic must certainly go down to the cellar. The man we want now, of course, is Sir Tristram. I wonder if he means to visit us to-day, or whether we should send for him?"

"Send for him?" repeated Sir Hugh. "Why, he practically lives here!"

Ludovic, descending into the cellar, announced that he proposed to spend the morning making up his loss of sleep, and taking Miss Thane aside, told her to take Eustacie upstairs, and, if possible, for a walk. "It's not fit for her down here," he said. "Don't let her worry about me! She's a trifle done up by all this romance."

She laughed, promised to do what she could to keep Eustacie from fretting, and departed to suggest to her that they should presently go for a walk in the direction of Warninglid, in the hopes of encountering Sir Tristram.

At about eleven o'clock the weather, which had been inclement, began to improve, and by midday a hint of sunshine behind the clouds tempted Eustacie to put on her hat and cloak and go with Sir Hugh and his sister upon their usual constitutional. While Ludovic was in the cellar she could feel her mind at rest, and since he would not permit her to join him there, even a staid walk down the lane was preferable to sitting in the inn parlour with nothing to do and no one to talk to.

The sun came through the clouds in good earnest shortly after they left the Red Lion and made walking pleasant. They stepped out briskly, the two ladies discussing the night's adventure and trying to decide what were best to be done next, and Sir Hugh interpolating remarks which were occasionally apt and were more often inappropriate. Half-way to Warninglid they were compelled to abandon their scheme of meeting Sir Tristram and to turn back to retrace their footsteps, but they had not gone very far when he overtook them, hacking a fine bay hunter which instantly attracted and held Sir Hugh's attention.

He dismounted as soon as he drew abreast of the walking party, and looked pleased at the encounter. Eustacie, barely allowing him to exchange greetings with the Thanes, poured into his ears the full history of the night's adventure, while Sir Hugh commented upon the hunter's points. The account of masked men, daggers, and broken shutters was punctuated by such irrelevant phrases as a sweet-goer, a beautiful-stepper, and Sir Tristram had to exert all his powers of concentration to prevent himself from becoming hopelessly confused. Miss Thane took no part in the recital, but derived considerable amusement from watching Shield's face while he tried to resolve two conversations into their component parts.

"——like his knee-action—came to murder Ludovic—had a thoroughbred hack like him once—he had a dagger—kept on throwing out a splint—tried to stun Sir Hugh—took his fences as well standing as flying—wore a mask—had a slight curve in his crest!" announced Eustacie and Thane in chorus.

Sir Tristram drew a deep breath, and desired Miss Thane to give him a plain account of the affair.

She did so; he listened in silence, and at the end observed that he had hardly expected so prompt or so desperate a response to his veiled challenge. "I am afraid you have had an alarming night of it," he said, "but I must confess I am delighted to hear that we succeeded so well in frightening the Beau. He must feel his position to be more dangerous than we suspect."

"It seems to me that it is Ludovic who is in a dangerous position," Eustacie pointed out.

"Not if you have had the sense to hide him in the cellar," replied Sir Tristram.

"We have done so, but he went under protest, and I think won't remain there long," said Miss Thane.

"He can take his choice of remaining there or being shipped out of the country," said Sir Tristram briefly. "That Basil went actually to the length of attempting to kill Ludovic with his own hand convinces me that that one-time butler of his knows something."

"You have not found him yet?"

"No. He seems quite to have disappeared. If Basil knows his whereabouts and seeks him out I shall hear of it, however. I have been at pains to see young Kettering and have instructed him to keep me posted in the Beau's movements. Depend upon it, if Basil sees that butler, so shall I."

They walked on up the lane, quickening their steps as the sky became once more overcast, with a threat of rain to come. Sir Hugh discovered that they had been out more than an hour, promised Shield a glass of very tolerable Madeira at the Red Lion, and, with another appraising look over the hunter's points, inquired whether he had any notion of selling the horse.

"None," replied Shield. "It is not in my power."

"How is that?" demanded Sir Hugh.

"He is not mine," said Shield. "He belonged to my great-uncle, and—provided we can reinstate the boy—is now Ludovic's property."

"Well, I've taken a strong liking to him," said Sir Hugh. "He looks to be well up to my weight. It seems to me that the sooner young Lavenham takes possession of his inheritance the better. I'll speak to him about it as soon as I get back to the inn."

Upon arrival at the Red Lion, however, Sir Hugh's first thought was to call to Nye to bring up a bottle of Madeira. Receiving no response he walked into the tap-room to look for him. There was no sign either of Clem or Nye, and a gentleman in a moleskin waistcoat, who was waiting patiently by the bar, volunteered the information that he himself had been hollering for the landlord till he was fair parched. He added that if the Red Lion wanted no customers there were other inns which did, and upon this bitter remark, stumped out to go in search of one.

Sir Hugh went back to the coffee-room, and had just begun to say that Nye seemed to have gone out when a cry from above made him break off and look inquiringly towards the staircase. Miss Thane, who had gone up to take off her hat and coat, came quickly down, looking perturbed and startled. "Sir Tristram, something has happened while we have been out! Someone has been here: my room has been ransacked, all our rooms! Where is Nye?"

"That," said Sir Tristram grimly, "is what we shall have to find out. A more pressing question is, where is Ludovic?"

Ludovic was found to be sleeping peacefully in his underground retreat. He had heard nothing, and when he learned that every room in the house had been turned upside down by unknown hands, he showed a marked inclination to laugh, and said that he supposed Basil had been searching for him again.

"Well, if he expected to find you amongst my clothing I can only say that he must have a very indelicate idea of me," said Miss Thane. "Sir Tristram, do you suppose him to have kidnapped Nye and Clem?"

"Hardly," Shield answered, shutting the cellar door upon Ludovic, and replacing the chest that stood upon the trap. He walked across the passage to the tap-room, noticed that the trap leading down to the main cellar was shut, and pulled it up, calling: "Nye! Are you there, man?"

No one answered him; Sir Hugh strolled in to report that he had found no trace of Nye, and observing that Shield had opened the trap-door said that the particular Madeira he had in mind was not in that cellar.

Shield had found a taper by this time, and kindled it at the fire. "What I want to find is Nye, not Madeira!" he said, and went down the stairs into the gloom of the cellar. A moment later his voice sounded, summoning Sir Hugh to his assistance. "Thane! Bring a lamp down here, I've found them!"

Sir Hugh selected a lamp from several standing on a shelf, and lit it in a leisurely fashion. Armed with this he descended into the cellar, where he found Shield calmly waiting for him, with the taper in his hand, and at his feet two neatly-trussed, gagged men. "Well, I'll be damned!" said Sir Hugh, blinking. "First it's one thing and then it's another! This is the queerest inn I've ever stayed at in my life."

Shield blew out his taper, directed Sir Hugh to put the lamp down and ungag Clem, and set to work to free the landlord. This was very soon done, and no sooner was Nye able to speak than he said: "Is Mr. Ludovic safe still?"

"He's safe enough," replied Shield. "What the devil happened? Who set upon you?"

"I never seen them before to my knowledge," Nye said, rubbing his cramped limbs. "Lord, to think of them taking me unawares! *Me!* They come in, as I thought, off the Brighton stage. There was no one in the tap-room but myself at the time, and I hadn't no more than turned my back to get a couple of mugs down from the shelf when something hit me on the head, and when I woke up, here I was like you saw with Clem beside me! I've got a lump on the back of my head like a hen's egg."

"Good God, Nye, the oldest trick in the world, and you must needs fall a victim to it!" said Sir Tristram scornfully.

"I know it, sir: there ain't no call for you to tell me. Fair bamboozled I was."

"This sort of thing," said Sir Hugh, cutting the cord that bound Clem's arms, "is past a jest! Were you knocked on the head too?"

Clem, however, had escaped this particular violence. He was a good deal shaken and bruised, but his assailants had overpowered him without being obliged to stun him. He recounted that he had heard someone calling for the drawer, and had gone at once to the tap-room. He had seen only one man, standing in quite an innocent-seeming fashion by the bar, but no sooner had he entered the room than a heavy coat had been thrown over his head by someone hidden behind the door, and before he could disentangle himself from its folds both men were upon him and he was speedily gagged and trussed up like the landlord.

Having released the captives Sir Tristram's next concern was to discover what the intruders had done in the inn. This was soon seen. They had visited every bedchamber, wrenched drawers out of the chests, and turned their contents on to the floor, ripped the clothes out of the wardrobes, burst open the locks of Sir Hugh's cloak-bags, and tossed out their contents higgledy-piggledy.

Sir Hugh, when he beheld the havoc amongst his possessions, was rendered quite speechless. His sister, staring about her said: "But it is mad! This can have been no search for Ludovic! One would imagine they must have been common house-breakers, but there is my trinket-box broken open and my trinkets in a heap on my dressing-table. Have you lost anything, Hugh? I think I have not."

"Have I——" Sir Hugh choked. "How the devil can I know whether I've lost anything in this confusion?"

Shield was looking frowningly round the disordered room. "No, they were not searching for Ludovic," he said. "But what were they searching for? What can you have that the Beau wants so desperately?"

Sir Hugh caught the name and said: "Do you mean to tell me that this outrage was committed by this cousin of Lavenham's who broke in last night?"

"I am afraid so," replied Shield, smiling a little at Sir Hugh's face of Jovean wrath.

"Then understand this, Sally!" said Sir Hugh. "Not a yard from this place do I stir until I have that fellow laid by the heels! It's bad enough when he comes creeping into the house to try to stick a knife into young Lavenham, but when he has the infernal impudence to turn my room into a pig-sty, then I say he's gone a step too far!"

"The knife!" exclaimed Eustacie. "He came for the knife, of course! Sir Hugh seized it last night, Tristram!"

"Where was it put?" asked Shield. "Has it been taken?"

Nye said: "We'll soon see that, sir. Sir Hugh left it on the coffee-room table, and thinking we might need to produce it as evidence I put it away this morning in my china-cupboard —the same them Runners blew the lock out of, sir."

"Go and see if it's there," commanded Sir Tristram. "It may have been that—I suppose it must have been that, yet somehow——" He broke off, obviously puzzled.

"But yes, Tristram, he does not wish to be known to have come here last night, *naturellement*, therefore he must re-cover his dagger for fear we might recognize it!"

"It seems to me a most unnecessary risk to run," said Sir Tristram. "As matters now stand we cannot bring him to book for breaking in here any more than he can bring us to book for breaking into the Dower House. He must know that! He's not a fool."

"I believe him to be too much alarmed to think calmly," said Miss Thane.

Nye came back into the room. "Well, they didn't think to look in the back premises, your Honour, that's certain. Here's the dagger."

Sir Tristram took it in his hand and looked at it, more puz-zled than ever. "I dare say it is his," he said, "but I for one could not swear to it. It is in no way remarkable."

Miss Thane said suddenly: "Oh, how stupid of us! Of course he did not come to look for that! He came for his quizzing-glass. There could be no mistaking *that!* It is quite an unusual one: I knew it immediately for his and so did Nye. Now what became of it? Hugh, you had it! Where did you put it?"

"Put what?" said Sir Hugh, who was wandering about the room, attempting in a singularly helpless fashion to restore order.

"The Beau's quizzing-glass, my dear. I am sure you had it in your hand when Eustacie and I went up to bed last night."

"I don't know where I put it," said Sir Hugh, stooping to pick up a crumpled cravat. "I laid it down somewhere."

"Where?" insisted Miss Thane.

"I forget. Sally, this is my new riding-coat, I'll have you know! Just look at it! It's ruined!"

"No, dear, Clem will iron out the creases for you. You must know where you put that quizzing-glass. Do think!"

"I've something more important to think about than a quizzing-glass that don't belong to me, and which I don't like. Ugly, cumbersome thing, it was. I dare say I left it on the table in the coffee-room."

Nye shook his head. "It wasn't there this morning, sir."

"Well, I may have brought it upstairs. I tell you I don't know, and I don't care."

"I suppose it doesn't signify," said Miss Thane reflectively. "Depend upon it, that was what the Beau wanted. I must say, I hope he found it, for the prospect of any more ransacking I find quite appalling."

Eustacie, helping Sir Hugh to smooth and fold several crumpled neckcloths, said carefully: "This is a very good adventure, and of course I am enjoying it—*cela va sans dire!*—but—but do you think that Basil will again try to come and kill Ludovic?"

"I should think it unlikely," answered Shield, "but I am going to ride back to the Court for my night-gear, and spend the night in Ludovic's room."

"Famous!" said Miss Thane. "I declare I never dreamed of such a romantic adventure as this turns out to be. In a little while we shall be barricading ourselves into the inn in a state of siege. Nothing would be more delightful!"

"I've no objection to Shield's putting up here, if he wants to," stated Sir Hugh, "but if I am to be roused out of my bed by fellows in loo-masks I won't be answerable for the consequences!"

Miss Thane, perceiving that his placidity was seriously impaired, set herself to coax him back into good humour. Nye promised to send Clem up immediately to put away all the scattered belongings, and he presently allowed himself to be escorted down to the parlour and installed in an easy chair by the fire, with a bottle of Madeira at his elbow. All he asked, he said, was a little peace and quiet, so his sister tactfully withdrew, leaving him to the mellowing influence of his wine.

Sir Tristram did not remain long at the Red Lion, but soon called for his horse, promising to return in time for dinner. No more startling events occurred during the course of the afternoon, and no suspicious strangers entered the tap-room.

Sir Tristram came back shortly after six o'clock, and Nye, bolting the door into the coffee-room, released Ludovic, who had reached the point of announcing with considerable acrimony that if coming into possession of his inheritance entailed many more days spent underground, he would prefer to return to his free-trading.

After dinner Miss Thane had the tact to suggest that they should sit down to a game of loo, and in this way the evening passed swiftly, Ludovic's problem being for the time forgotten, and the game proving so engrossing that it was not until after eleven o'clock that Miss Thane thought to look at the timepiece on the mantelshelf. The party then broke up, and the ladies had just picked up their candles when Nye's voice was suddenly heard somewhere above-stairs, raised in ferocious surprise.

Sir Tristram, signing to the others to remain where they were, went quickly out into the coffee-room, just as Nye came down the stairs, dragging by the collar a scared-looking stable-boy. When he saw Shield he said: "I've just found this young varmint in Sir Hugh's bedchamber, your Honour. Down you come, you! Now then, what were you doing up there?"

The stable-boy whimpered that he meant no harm, and tried to squirm out of the landlord's hold. Nye shook him, almost lifting him from the ground, and Sir Tristram said: "Is he one of your lads, Nye?"

"Ay, sir, he's one of my lads right enough, but he'll belong to the Parish Constable in the morning," said Nye with awful meaning. "A thief, that's what he is, and will likely be transported. That or hanged."

"I ain't a thief! I never meant no harm, Mr. Nye, I swear I didn't! I ain't took a thing that belongs to the big gentleman, nor wouldn't!"

"What were you doing in his bedchamber?" demanded Nye. "You've no business inside the house, and well you know it! Came creeping in through a window, that's what you did, and don't you dare to deny it! There's the ladder you used for anyone to see. Feeling in the pockets of Sir Hugh's coats he was, sir, the young vagabond! What's that you've got in your hand? Give it up this instant!"

The boy made a futile attempt to break away, but Nye seized his right arm and gave it a twist that made him cry out and relinquish the object he had been trying to conceal. It was a quizzing-glass belonging to Sir Hugh Thane.

Nye stared at it for a moment, his countenance slowly reddening with wrath. His grip tightened on the stable-boy's collar. "So that's it, is it?" he said. "You'll be sorry for this, Sam Barker!"

Sir Tristram, taking the glass from him, interposed in his quiet way: "Let him go, Nye. Now, my lad, if you speak the truth no harm shall come to you. Who told you to steal this?"

The boy cowered as far from Nye as he was able, and said: "It were Mr. Lavenham's gentleman, your Honour, and 'deed I didn't know there was any harm! He come asking me if I'd like to earn twenty guineas for myself, all for finding an eyeglass Mr. Lavenham mislaid here. It was the big gentleman as had got it, he said, and if I found it, and no one the wiser, there's be twenty golden guineas for me. It weren't like stealing, sir! I ain't a thief!"

"Oh, you ain't, eh?" said Nye. "And if Mr. Lavenham mislaid his glass what should stop him coming to ask for it open? Don't tell me you didn't think there was any harm in it!"

"It was Mr. Lavenham's eyeglass. Mr. Gregg said if I didn't ask no questions there'd be no trouble for anyone."

"There will be a great deal of trouble for you at least if you do not do precisely what I tell you now," said Sir Tristram sternly. "If you had your deserts you would be handed over to the Constable. But if you keep your mouth shut I will engage for it that Nye will overlook this fault. Understand me, I want no word of what has occurred to-night to come to Gregg's ears, or to Mr. Lavenham's. If you are questioned you will tell them that you have had no opportunity to search Sir Hugh's room. Is that clear?"

The stable-boy, thankful to have escaped the retribution he had thought inevitable, assured him that it was quite clear. He stammered out his gratitude, promised eternal good behaviour, and fled.

Nye drew a long breath. "Begging your pardon, sir, but I'd a deal rather be rid of the young good-for-nothing. My own lads bribed! What next will we have, I'd like to know?"

Sir Tristram was looking at the quizzing-glass in his hand. He said slowly: "So they didn't find it! I wonder . . ." He broke off, and strode suddenly towards the parlour. He was met by demands to know what had happened, and replied briefly: "One of Nye's stable-hands had been bribed to find the Beau's quizzing-glass. He found this instead."

"But that's mine!" said Sir Hugh, regarding it fixedly.

"I know it."

"Do you mean to tell me I've had my room ransacked again?" demanded Sir Hugh.

"No, I think you've merely had your pockets turned out. That's not important."

"Not important!" ejaculated Sir Hugh, considerably incensed. "And what if I've been robbed? I suppose that's not important either! Burn it, I never was in such a house in my life! It's for ever full of a set of rascals broken out of Newgate, and what with masked assassins, and Bow Street Runners, and young Lavenham here taking it into his head to live in the cellar. I don't know where I am from one minute to the next. What's more, you're as bad as the rest of them, Sally!"

"You haven't been robbed," said Sir Tristram. "What I want to discover is why it is so vital to Basil to regain possession of that glass. Thane, where did you put it? For God's sake try to remember! I suspect it may be of the utmost importance!"

"It is still in the inn, then!" Miss Thane said. "Hugh, think, I implore you!"

"Are you talking about the quizzing-glass you all said was Basil's?" inquired Ludovic.

Shield turned. "What do you mean, Ludovic? Did you not recognize it?"

"No, I can't say that I did," answered Ludovic. "Not that I'm disputing that it's his, mind you. I dare say he bought it since my time."

"That," said Sir Tristram, "is precisely what I think he did do. It must be found if we have to turn this whole place upside down to do it!"

"You needn't do that," said Ludovic calmly. "Thane put it on the mantelshelf in the coffee-room. I saw him do it."

Sir Tristram wheeled about, and went quickly back to the coffee-room, and stretching up his arm ran his hand along the high mantelpiece. The quizzing-glass was just where Sir Hugh had left it. Shield held it in his hand, looking at it so oddly that Nye, who was standing beside him, ventured to ask if anything were amiss.

Sir Tristram shook his head, and carried the prize back into the parlour.

"You have found it!" exclaimed Eustacie. "But why is it important?"

He put her aside, and sitting down at the table, subjected

the quizzing-glass to a minute inspection. The others gathered round him, even Sir Hugh betraying a mild interest.

"Myself I like 'em made slimmer," remarked Ludovic. "The shaft's too thick. Clumsy."

Sir Tristram said dryly: "I think there is a reason." He had picked up Sir Hugh's eyeglass, and through its magnifying lens was looking at the heavily-encrusted circlet at the end of the shaft, through which a ribbon was meant to pass. He put Sir Hugh's glass down and inserted his thumb-nail into a groove on the circlet.

There was a tiny click; the circle parted, and something fell out of it on to the table, rolled a little way, and lay still.

"The talisman ring!" said Sir Tristram.

Chapter XIV

A SOUND almost like a sob broke from Ludovic. His hand shot out across the table and snatched up the ring. "My ring!" he whispered. "My ring!"

"Well, upon my soul, that's a devilish cunning device!" said Sir Hugh, taking the quizzing-glass out of Shield's hand. "You see, Sally? The ring fitted into the circlet at the end of the shaft."

"Yes, dear," said Miss Thane. "I see it did. When I think how it has been lying where anyone might have found it I feel quite faint with horror."

Eustacie was looking critically at it. "Is that a talisman ring?" she enquired. "I thought it would be quite different! It is nothing but a gold ring with some figures on it!"

"Careful, Eustacie!" said Sir Tristram, with a slight smile. "You will find that Ludovic regards it as sacrosanct."

Ludovic raised his eyes from adoration of the ring. "By God, I do! There is nothing I can say to you, Tristram, except that I could kiss your feet for what you have done for me!"

"I beg you won't, however. I have done very little."

Miss Thane said: "It has been under our very noses. The audacity of it! How could he dare?"

"Why not?" said Sir Tristram. "Would any of us have suspected it had it not been lost, and then searched for in such a desperate fashion?"

An idea occurred to Miss Thane. She turned her eyes towards her brother, and said in moved tones: "So we owe it all to Hugh! My dear, this becomes too much for me. I shall not easily recover from the shock."

"And everything—but everything!—we did was quite useless!" said Eustacie, quite disgusted.

"I know," said Miss Thane, sadly shaking her head. "It does not bear thinking of."

"I do not know why you should complain," remarked Sir

Tristram. "You have had a great deal of adventure, which is what I understood you both to want."

"Yes, that is true," acknowledged Eustacie, "but some of it was not very comfortable. And I must say that I am not at all pleased that it is you who have found the ring, because you did not want to have an adventure, or to do anything romantic. It seems to me very unfair."

"So it is!" said Miss Thane, much struck by this point of view. "It is quite odious, my love, for who could have been more disagreeable, or more discouraging? Really, it would have been better in some ways had we insisted upon his remaining the villain."

Sir Tristram smiled a little at this, but in rather an abstracted way, and said: "It's very well, but we are not yet out of our difficulties. Let me have the ring, Ludovic. It is true that we have found it, but we did not find it in the Beau's possession. Oh, don't look so dubious, my dear boy! I shan't lose it."

"Ah!" said Miss Thane, nodding wisely. "One has to remember, after all, that you are a collector of such things. I don't blame him, I dare say it is all a Plot."

"Sarah, you're outrageous!" said Ludovic, handing the ring across the table to his cousin. "For God's sake be careful with it, won't you, Tristram? What do you mean to do?"

Sir Tristram fitted the ring back into its hiding-place, and closed the circlet with a snap. "For the present I'll keep this. I think our best course——" He stopped frowning.

They waited in anxious silence for him to continue, but before he spoke again Nye caught the sound of a coach pulling up in the yard and said apologetically: "Beg pardon, sir, but I'll have to go. That'll be the night-mail."

Sir Tristram's voice arrested him as he reached the door. "Do you mean it's the London mail, Joe?"

"Ay, that's the one, sir. I want a word with the guard, if you'll excuse me."

Sir Tristram's chair rasped on the oaken floor as he sprang up. "Then that's my best course!" he said. "I'll board it!"

Nye stared at him. "If that's what you mean to do, you'd best make haste, sir. It don't take them more than two minutes to change the horses, and they'll be off the moment that's done."

"Go and tell them to wait!" ordered Sir Tristram. "I have but to get my hat and coat."

"They won't wait, sir!" expostulated Nye. "They've got their time to keep, and you've no ticket!"

"Never mind that! Hurry, man!" said Sir Tristram, thrusting him before him out of the room.

"But what are you going to do?" cried Eustacie, running after them.

"I've no time to waste in explaining that now!" replied Sir Tristram, already halfway up the stairs.

Miss Thane, following in a more leisurely fashion with Ludovic, said darkly: "I said it was a Plot. It's my belief he is absconding." She discovered that her butt was already out of hearing, and added: "There! How provoking! That remark was quite wasted. Who would have supposed that the wretched creature would be taken with such a frenzy?"

Sir Tristram reappeared again at this moment, his coat over his arm, his hat in his hand. As he ran down the stairs, he said: "I hope to return to-morrow if all goes well. For God's sake take care of yourself, Ludovic!"

He was across the coffee-room and out of the door almost before they could fetch their breath. Miss Thane, blinking, said: "If only we had a horse ready saddled!"

"Why? Isn't the mail enough for him?" inquired Ludovic.

"If there had been a horse, I am persuaded we should have seen him ride off *ventre à terre!*" mourned Miss Thane.

"But where is he going?" stammered Eustacie. "He seems to me suddenly to have become entirely mad!"

"He's going to London," replied Ludovic. "Don't ask me why, for I haven't a notion!"

"Well!" Eustacie turned quite pink with indignation. "It is too bad! This is *our* adventure, and he has left us without a word, and, in fact, is trying to take it away from us!"

"Men!" said Miss Thane, with a strong shudder.

Sir Hugh came wandering into the coffee-room at this moment, and asked what had become of Shield. When he heard that he had departed suddenly for London, he looked vaguely surprised, and complained that he seemed to be another of these people who spent their time popping in and out of the inn like jack-in-the-boxes. "It's very unrestful," he said severely. "No sooner do we get comfortably settled than either someone breaks into the house or one of you flies off the Lord knows where! There's no peace at all. I shall go to bed."

Nye came back just then and announced with a reluctant

smile that Sir Tristram had succeeded in boarding the coach, in spite of all the guard's representations to him that such high-handed proceedings were quite out of order. When asked by Ludovic if he knew what Sir Tristram meant to do, he replied in his stolid way: "I do not, sir, but you may depend upon it he'll do what's best. All he said to me was, I was to see you safe into your room. Myself, I'm having a truckle-bed set up here, and it'll be a mighty queer thing if anyone gets into the house without I'll hear them. Not but what it don't seem to me likely that anyone will try that game to-night. They'll be waiting up at the Dower House till to-morrow in the hopes that Sam Barker will have found that plaguey ring of yours, sir."

Miss Thane sighed. "How abominably flat it will seem to have no one breaking in any more! Really, I do not know how I am to support life once all these exciting happenings are at an end."

Nye favoured her with a grim little smile. "By what I can make out, they ain't ended yet, ma'am. We'll do well to keep an eye lifted for trouble as soon as that Beau learns Barker ain't found his quizzing-glass. I'll be glad when I see Sir Tristram back, and that's a fact. Now, Mr. Ludovic, if you're ready, I'll help you get to bed. You'll have to go down to the cellar again to-morrow, and the orders are I'm to see you into it before I unbar the doors in the morning. And what's more, sir," he added, forestalling Ludovic's imminent expostulation, "I've orders to knock you out if you don't go willing."

This ferocious threat was not, however, put into execution. Ludovic descended into the cellar at an early hour on the following morning, and the rest of the party, with the exception of Sir Hugh, who was only interested in his breakfast, prepared themselves to meet whatever peril should lie in store for them. Eustacie, who thought that she had taken far too small a part in the adventure, was feeling somewhat aggrieved, Ludovic having refused without the least hesitation to lend her one of his pistols. "I never lend my pistols," he said. "Besides, what do you want it for?"

"But to fire, of course!" replied Eustacie impatiently.

"Good God! What at?"

"Why, at anybody who tries to come into the house!" she said, opening her eyes in surprise at his stupidity. "And if you would let Sarah have one too, she could help me. After all, we may find ourselves in great danger, you know."

"You won't find yourselves in half such danger as you would if I let you have my pistols," said Ludovic, with brutal candour.

This unfeeling response sent Eustacie off in a dudgeon to Miss Thane. Here at least she was sure of finding a sympathetic listener. Nor did Miss Thane disappoint her. She professed herself to be quite at a loss to understand the selfishness of men, and when she learned that Eustacie had planned for her also to fire upon possible desperadoes, she said that she could almost wish that she had not been told of the scheme, since it made her feel quite disheartened to think of it falling to the ground.

"Well, I do think we ought to be armed," said Eustacie wistfully. "It is true that I do not know much about guns, but one has only to point them and pull the trigger, after all."

"Exactly," agreed Miss Thane. "I dare say we should have accounted for any number of desperate ruffians. It is wretched indeed! We shall be forced to rely upon our wits."

But the morning passed quietly, the only excitement being provided by Gregg, who came to the inn with the ostensible object of inquiring whether Nye could let his master have a pipe of burgundy. He left his horse in the yard, and was thus able to exchange a word with Barker, who, with the fear of transportation before him, faithfully obeyed Sir Tristram's instructions, and said that he had no chance yet to search for the quizzing-glass.

In the afternoon Sir Hugh, following his usual custom, went upstairs to enjoy a peaceful sleep. Miss Thane and Eustacie watched the Brighton mail arrive, but since it did not set Sir Tristram down at the Red Lion, their interest in it swiftly waned. They had begun to question whether they were to experience any adventures whatsoever when, to their amazement, Beau Lavenham's chaise passed the parlour window, drew up outside the coffee-room door, and set down the Beau himself.

He alighted unhurriedly, took care to remove a speck of dust from his sleeve, and in the calmest way imaginable walked into the inn.

"Well," said Miss Thane, "I think this passes the bounds of reasonable effrontery! Do you suppose that he has come to pay us a ceremonious visit?"

Apparently this was his purpose, for in a few minutes Nye ushered him into the parlour. He came in with his usual smile, and bowed with all his usual flourish. "Such a happiness to find you still here!" he said. "Your very obedient, ma'am!"

"If you should be needing aught, ma'am, you have only to call," said Nye, with slow deliberation.

"Oh yes, indeed! Pray do not wait!" said Miss Thane, slipping into her rôle of empty-headed femininity. "I will certainly call you if I need anything. How delightful it is to see you, Mr. Lavenham! Here you find us yawning over our stitchery, quite enchanted to be receiving company. You must know that we have made all our plans for departure, and mean to set forward for London almost immediately. I am so glad to have the opportunity of taking leave of you! So very obliging you were in permitting me to visit your beautiful house! I am for ever talking of it!"

"My house was honoured, ma'am. Do I understand that your brother has at last recovered from his sad indisposition? It must have been an unconscionably bad cold to have kept him in this dull inn for so many days."

"Yes, indeed, quite the worst he has ever had," agreed Miss Thane. "But he has not found it dull, I assure you."

"No?" said the Beau gently.

"Indeed, no! You must understand that he is a great judge of wine. A well-stocked cellar will reconcile him to the hardest lot. It is quite absurd!"

"Ah, yes!" said the Beau. "Nye has a great deal in his cellars, I apprehend—more perhaps than he will admit."

"That is true," remarked Eustacie, with considerable relish. "*Granpère* was used to say that he would defy anyone to find what Nye preferred to keep hidden."

"I fear he must have been speaking with a little exaggeration," said the Beau. "I trust Nye will never find himself compelled to submit to a search being made for his secret cellar. Such things are very well while no one knows of their existence, but once the news of them gets about it becomes a simple matter to discover them."

Miss Thane, listening to this speech with an air of the most guileless interest, exclaimed: "How odd that you should say that! I must tell you that my brother said at the very outset that he was convinced Nye must possess some hidden store!"

"I felicitate you, ma'am, upon being blessed with a brother of such remarkable perspicacity," said the Beau in a mellifluous voice. He turned towards his cousin. "My dear Eustacie, I wonder if I may crave the indulgence of a few moments' private speech with you? Miss Thane will readily understand that between cousins——"

Miss Thane interrupted him at this point, with an affected little cry. "Oh, Mr. Lavenham, no, indeed! It is not to be thought of! You must know that I am this dear child's chaperon—is it not ridiculous?—and such a thing would not do at all!"

He looked at her with narrowed eyes, and after a moment, said: "I do not recollect, ma'am, that these scruples weighed with you so heavily when you visited my house not so long since."

Miss Thane looked distressed, and replied: "It is very true. Your reproach is just, sir. I'm such a sad shatterbrain that I forgot my duties in admiration of your library."

He raised his brows in polite scepticism. Eustacie said: "I do not have secrets from mademoiselle. Why do you wish to see me alone? *Je n'en vois pas la nécessité!*"

"Well," said the Beau, "if I may speak without reserve, my dear cousin, I desired to drop a word of warning in your ear."

She looked him over dispassionately. "Yes? I do not know why I must be warned, but if you wish to warn me, I am perfectly agreeable."

"Let us say," amended the Beau, "that I desire you to convey a warning to the person most nearly concerned. You must know that I am aware—have been aware from the outset—that you are concealing—a certain person in this house. I do not need to mention names, I am sure. Now, I wish this person no harm; in the past I think I may say that I have been very much his friend, but it will not be in my power to assist him if once his presence in this inn becomes known. And I fear—I very much fear—that it is known. You have already been a trifle discommoded, I collect, by two Runners from Bow Street. They seem, by all accounts, to have been a singularly stupid couple. But you must remember that all the Runners are not so easily—shall we say, duped?" He paused, but Eustacie, contenting herself with gazing at him blankly, said nothing. He smiled slightly, and continued: "You should consider, dear cousin, what would happen if someone who knows this person well were to go to Bow Street and say: 'I have proof that this man is even now lying in a hidden cellar at the Red Lion at Hand Cross.'"

"You recount to me a history of the most entertaining,"

said Eustacie, with painstaking civility. "I expect you would be very glad to know that Ludovic—I name names, me—had gone abroad."

"Very glad," replied the Beau sweetly. "I should be much distressed if he brought any more disgrace on the family by ending his career on the scaffold. And that, my dear Eustacie, is what he will do if ever he falls into the hands of the Law."

"But I find you inexplicable!" said Eustacie. "I thought you at least believed him to be innocent."

He shrugged. "Certainly, but his unfortunate flight, coupled with the disappearance of the talisman ring which was at the root of all the trouble, will always make it impossible for him to prove his innocence." He put the tips of his fingers together, and over them surveyed Eustacie. "It is very disagreeable to be a hunted man, you know. It would be much better to have it given out that one had died—abroad. I am anxious to be of what assistance I can. If I had proof that my cousin Ludovic was no more, I would gladly engage to provide—well, let us say a man who looked like my cousin Ludovic but bore another name—to provide this man, then, with an allowance I believe he would not consider ungenerous." He stopped and took a pinch of snuff.

"I ask myself," said Eustacie meditatively, "why you should wish to overwhelm Ludovic with your generosity. It is to me not at all easy to understand."

"Ah, that is not clever of you, dear cousin," he replied. "Surely you must perceive the disadvantages of my situation?"

"But yes, very clearly," said Eustacie, with disconcerting alacrity.

"Precisely," smiled the Beau. "Of course, were there but the slimmest chance of Ludovic's being able to prove his innocence, it would be another matter. But there is no such chance, Eustacie, and I should be a very odd sort of a creature if I did not look forward with misgiving to an indefinite number of years spent in waiting beside a vacant throne."

"A vacant throne?" suddenly said Miss Thane, raising her head from the book she had taken up. "Oh, are you speaking of the murder of the French King? I was never more shocked in my life than when I heard the news of it!"

The Beau paid no heed to her. His eyes still rested on Eustacie; he said pensively: "One may live very comfortably on the Continent, I believe. *You*, for instance, would like it excessively, I dare say."

"I? But we do not speak of me!"

"Do we not? Well, I shall not pretend that I am not glad to hear you say so," he said. He got up from his chair. "You will think over what I have said, will you not? You might even tell Ludovic."

Eustacie assumed an expression of doubt. "Yes, but perhaps if he did what you suggest you would not give him any money after all," she said.

"In that case," replied the Beau calmly, "he would only have to come to life again to deprive me of title, land, and wealth. One might almost say that he would hold me quite in his power."

"True, yes, that is very true," nodded Eustacie. "But I do not know—it is not possible for me to say——"

"My dear cousin, I do not wish you to say anything. No doubt you will discuss the matter with Ludovic and inform me later of your decision. I will take my leave of you now." He turned and bowed to Miss Thane. "Your servant, ma'am. Do not trouble to accompany me to the door, my dear cousin; I know my way. I have been here before, you know." He broke off and said: "Ah, that reminds me! I believe that upon the occasion of my last visit I lost my quizzing-glass here. I wonder if it has been found?"

"Your quizzing-glass?" repeated Eustacie. "How came you to lose that, pray?"

"The ribbon was a trifle worn," he explained. "The glass is of sentimental value to me. May I have it, if you please?"

She shook her head. "You are mistaken. It is certainly not here."

He sighed. "No? Tax your memory again, cousin. It would be wiser to remember, I think."

"It is impossible. I do not know where your glass may be," said Eustacie, with perfect truth.

Miss Thane, quite unable to resist the temptation of taking part in this scene, said: "A quizzing-glass? Oh yes, I know!"

"Indeed, ma'am?" The Beau turned rather quickly. "Enlighten me, I beg of you!"

Miss Thane nodded at Eustacie. "Do you not remember, my love, how Nye found one half hidden beneath a chair only yesterday? Oh no, I believe you were not by at the time! He laid it on the mantelshelf in the coffee-room. I will fetch it for you directly."

"Do not put yourself to the trouble, ma'am," said the

Beau, breathing a little faster. "I am quite in your debt, and will recover the glass upon my way out."

"Oh, but it is not the least trouble in the world!" declared Miss Thane, rising, and going to the door. "I can place my hand upon it in a trice!"

"You are too good." He bowed, and followed her to the coffee-room.

She checked for an instant on the threshold, for the room was not, as she had expected to find it, empty. A powerful-looking man in a blue coat and buckskins was seated on the settle beside the fire, warming his feet and refreshing himself from a mug of ale. He turned his head as Miss Thane came in, and although he did not look at her for more than a couple of seconds, she had an uncomfortable feeling that the look was not quite as casual as it seemed to be. She caught Eustacie's eye, and found it brimful of warning. Comforting herself with the reflection that even if the stranger were in Beau Lavenham's pay, there was no fear of either of them finding the quizzing-glass, she tripped forward to the fireplace. "I know just where he put it," she informed the Beau over her shoulder. "This end it was—no! Well, that is the oddest thing! I could have sworn—Do you reach up your arm, Mr. Lavenham: you are taller than I am."

The Beau, who did not need this encouragement, ran his hand the length of the mantelpiece. "You are mistaken, ma'am," he said, his voice suddenly harsh. "It is not here!"

"But it must be!" she said. "I am positive it was put there. Someone must have moved it!" An idea seemed to strike her. She said: "I wonder, did your valet take it? He was here this morning, you know, and stayed for quite some time. I could not imagine what he was about! Depend upon it, he must have discovered it, and you will find it awaiting you at the Dower House."

He had turned pale, and said with his eyes fixed on her face: "My valet? You say my valet was in this room to-day?"

"Yes, indeed he was," averred Miss Thane unblushingly. "Of course, I never dreamed the glass was what he was looking for, or I would have shown him at once where it was. All's well that ends well, however. You may be sure he has it safe."

Eustacie, lost in admiration of Miss Thane's tactics, watched the smile vanish completely from the Beau's face. An expression half of doubt, half of dismay took its place; it

was plain that while he suspected Miss Thane of prevaricat-
ing, he was unable to banish from his mind as impossible the
thought that his valet, guessing that the quizzing-glass held a
vital secret, might have come to search for it on his own account. She saw his hand open and close, and his lips
straighten to a thin, ugly line, and was observing these signs
of mental perturbation with critical interest when she became
aware of being addressed by the stranger on the settle.

"Very cold day, ma'am," he remarked, with the unmistakable air of one whose habit it was to enter into chat with anybody who crossed his path.

Eustacie glanced at him with a certain amount of misgiving. She supposed that the landlord of an inn could hardly refuse to allow a customer to drink his ale in the coffee-room if
he wished to, but she could not help feeling that Nye might
have contrived on this occasion at least to have lured him
into the tap-room and to have kept him there under his own
eye. On the other hand, it was, of course, possible that the
man was known to Nye. She replied civilly: "Yes, very cold."

"Bitter wind blowing outside," pursued the stranger. "Ah
well, it's seasonable, ain't it, ma'am? We hadn't ought to complain. Begging your pardon sir, if I might put another log o'
wood on the fire—Thank you, sir!"

The Beau, who was standing by the basket containing
wood, moved to allow the stranger to approach it.

"That's the worst of a wood fire," said the stranger, select-
ing a suitable log. "They fall away to nothing in less than no
time, don't they, sir? But we'll have a nice blaze in a minute,
you'll see." He bent to pick up another log, and said in a surprised tone: "Well! and what might this be, all amongst the
wood?" He straightened himself as he spoke, and Miss Thane
saw that he was holding the Beau's quizzing-glass in his hand.

For a moment it seemed to her that she could neither
speak nor think. While her eyes remained riveted to the glass,
her brain whirled. Had not Sir Tristram taken charge of the
glass? Could he have been guilty of the unpardonable carelessness of mislaying it? How did it come to be in the wood-
basket? And what in heaven's name was one to do?

She pulled herself together, met Eustacie's eyes across the
room, and saw them as startled as she felt sure her own must
be. She became aware of the stranger's voice, marvelling with
amiable fatuity at the queer places things would get to, to be
sure, and suddenly realized why Nye had left a stranger alone
in the coffee-room, and what his purpose must be. She shot a

warning frown at Eustacie, still standing at the foot of the stairs, and said: "Why, there it is! Well, of all the fortunate happenings!"

The Beau held out his hand. It was shaking a little. He said: "Thank you. That is mine."

The stranger looked rather doubtfully at him. "Yours, is it, sir? Well, if you say so, I'm sure it is so, but maybe I'd best give it to the landlord—not meaning any offence, your Honour, but seeing as it's a valuable kind of a trinket, and me having found it."

A fixed smile was on the Beau's lips. He said: "Quite unnecessary, I assure you. You will perceive that it is of unusual design. I could not mistake it."

The stranger turned it over in his hand. "Well, of course, sir, if you say so——" he began undecidedly.

"My good fellow," interrupted the Beau. "You must have seen me look for something upon the mantelshelf a minute ago. Your scruples are quite absurd, believe me. Anyone will tell you that that glass belongs to me. Be good enough to give it to me, if you please."

"Oh yes, certainly that is Mr. Lavenham's quizzing-glass!" said Miss Thane. "There can be no doubt!"

The stranger advanced, holding the glass out to the Beau. He grasped it, and in that instant a suspicion of the trap into which he had walked seemed to flash into his brain, and he sprang back, glaring at the man before him.

"Then, in the name of the Law I arrest you, Basil Lavenham, for the wilful murder of Matthew John Plunkett!" said the stranger.

Before he had finished speaking the Beau had whipped a pistol from his pocket and levelled it. The smile on his lips had become a ghastly grimace, but it still lingered. He said, quick and low: "Stand where you are. If you move you are a dead man!" and began to back towards the door.

The Bow Street Runner stood still perforce. Miss Thane, standing a little behind the Beau, perceived that the moment for a display of heroism had arrived, and in one swift movement got between the Beau and the door. In the same instant Eustacie shrieked: "Nye! *À moi!*"

The Beau, keeping his would-be captor covered, reached the door, and Miss Thane, behind him, caught his arm and bore it downwards with all her strength. He was taken unawares, gave a snarl of fury, and wrenching free from her clutch struck at her with his clenched fist. The blow landed on her temple, and Miss Thane subsided in an inanimate heap on the floor.

*   *   *   *   *   *

She became aware of a throbbing pain in her head, of the smell of Hungary Water, and of the feel of a wet cloth across her brow. "Oh dear!" she said faintly. "The quizzing-glass! Did he get away?"

"By no means," replied a calm voice. "There is nothing to worry you: we have him safely held."

Miss Thane ventured to open her eyes. Sir Tristram was sitting on the edge of the couch in the parlour on which she had been laid, bathing her forehead. "Oh, it's you!" said Miss Thane.

"Yes," said Sir Tristram.

"I knew you must have returned," murmured Miss Thane.

He replied in his cool way: "If you knew that, what in the world possessed you to try and stop the Beau? He had no hope of escaping. I was outside with a Runner to take him if he broke from Townsend."

"Well, pray how was I to know that?" demanded Miss Thane.

"I imagine you might have guessed it."

She closed her eyes again, saying with dignity: "I have the headache."

He sounded amused. "That is not very surprising, since you were hit on the head."

A rustle of skirts heralded Eustacie's approach. Miss Thane opened her eyes again and smiled, "Oh, you are better!" said Eustacie. *"Ma pauvre,* I thought he had killed you! And I must tell you that he wrenched open the door and stepped backwards right into Tristram's arms! It was of all things the most exciting! And, do you know, he tried to throw the quizzing-glass into the fire, which was entirely stupid, because that made it quite certain that he knew where the ring was hid. I do think that this has been the most delightful adventure!"

"So it has," agreed Miss Thane. "Positively *épatant!* What have you done with the Beau, and where is Ludovic?"

"Oh, the Runners took Basil away in a chaise, and as for Ludovic, Nye has gone to let him out of the cellar."

Miss Thane sighed. "Well, I suppose it is all for the best,

but you know I cannot help feeling disappointed. I had quite made up my mind to it that Sir Tristram had absconded with the talisman ring, and I had thought of several famous schemes for recovering it. I never knew anyone so provoking!"

"Yes," agreed Eustacie. "I must say, that is true. He is very provoking, but one must be just, *enfin,* and own that he has been very clever and useful."

Miss Thane turned her head to look up at Sir Tristram. "I wish you will tell me what you did," she said. "You were not on the Brighton mail, were you? Is it possible that you rode here *ventre à terre?*"

"No," replied Sir Tristram. "I came post."

Miss Thane seemed to abandon interest in his proceedings.

"Bringing with me," continued Sir Tristram, "a couple of Bow Street Runners. When we arrived here I learned from Nye that by some stroke of good fortune the Beau was actually in the house. I had been wondering how we were to prevail upon him to own the quizzing-glass, and the difficulties of luring him to this place without letting him get wind of a trap seemed to me to be quite considerable. When we heard that he was already here, it was easy to set our trap. The only thing I feared was that one or other of you might put him on his guard by showing surprise at seeing the quizzing-glass. You are to be congratulated on concealing your emotions so well."

"At first," confessed Eustacie, "I was entirely *bouleversée,* and quite unable to speak. Then Sarah frowned at me, and I thought it would be better to remain silent. *I* thought the Runner was one of Basil's men, did not you, Sarah?"

"Yes, I did at first," replied Miss Thane. "But when he picked up the glass I knew Sir Tristram must be at the back of it. Is Ludovic safe now? Will he be able to take his place in the world again?"

"Yes, there can be no doubt of that. Basil lost his head, and his attempt to dispose of the ring was a complete betrayal. How do you feel, Miss Thane?"

"Very uneasy," she replied. "I believe there is a lump on my forehead."

"It is already much less pronounced that it was," said Sir Tristram consolingly.

Miss Thane regarded him with misgiving. "Tell me at once, have I a black eye?" she said.

"No, not yet."

She gave a shriek. "Not *yet?* Do you mean that I shall have one?"

"I should think it highly probable," he said, a laugh in his voice.

"Bring me the hartshorn!" begged Miss Thane in failing accents, and once more closing her eyes.

"Certainly," said Sir Tristram. "Eustacie, fetch the hartshorn."

"She does not really want it, you know," explained Eustacie. "She is jesting."

"Nevertheless, fetch it," said Sir Tristram.

"Eh bien!" Eustacie shrugged, and went away to look for it.

Miss Thane opened her eyes again, and looked at Sir Tristram with even more misgiving than before.

"Sarah," said Sir Tristram, "I have a very important question to put to you. How many seasons have you spent at Almack's?"

Miss Thane gazed at him with an expression of outrage in her face, and said: "Tristram, are you daring—actually daring—to choose this out of all other moments to make me an offer?"

"Yes," replied Sir Tristram. "I am. Why not?"

Miss Thane sat up. "Have you *no* sense of romance?" she demanded. "I won't—no, I *won't* be proposed to with my hair falling down my back, a bandage round my head, and very likely a black eye as well! It is quite monstrous of you!"

He smiled. "Indeed, you will. You look delightfully. Will you marry me?"

"I have wronged you," said Miss Thane, much moved. "If you think I look delightfully at this present, you must be a great deal more romantic than I had supposed."

"It is a long time now since I have been able to look at you without thinking how very beautiful you are," said Sir Tristram simply.

"Oh!" said Miss Thane, blushing, "you forget yourself! Do, pray, recollect that you do not look for romance in marriage! Remember your previous disillusionment! This will never do!"

"I see that I shall not easily be allowed to forget that nonsense," said Sir Tristram, taking her in his arms. "Now be serious for one moment, Sarah! Will you marry me?"

"To be honest with you," said Miss Thane, with the utmost

ravity, "I have been meaning to marry you these ten days
nd more!"

A moment later Eustacie came into the room with Sir Hugh
t her heels. She checked on the threshold in round-eyed
mazement, but Sir Hugh merely said: "Oh, so you're back,
re you?"

"Yes," said Shield, releasing Miss Thane. "Have I your
ermission to pay my addresses to your sister?"

"Oh, certainly, my dear fellow, by all means! Not that it's
nything to do with me, you know. She's her own mistress
ow. What have you done to your head, Sally?"

"Ludovic's wicked cousin knocked me down," explained
Miss Thane. "I have had a very exciting afternoon, throwing
myself into the breach, and being stunned, and then having
an offer of marriage made to me."

"I thought there was a devilish amount of noise going on
downstairs," remarked Sir Hugh. "It's time we finished with
this cousin of Ludovic's. I'll bring an action against him for
assaulting you."

"An excellent notion, my dear, but the Crown is already
bringing an action against him for murdering Sir Matthew
Plunkett."

"Never heard of him," said Sir Hugh. "Not that I'm
against it, mind you. A fellow who creeps about in a demned
loo-mask——"

"Sir Matthew Plunkett," said Miss Thane patiently, "is the
man Ludovic was accused of murdering two years ago. You
must know that Ludovic will now be able to stop living in the
cellar, and take up his rightful position at Lavenham Court."

"Well, I must say I'm glad to hear that," said Sir Hugh. "It
never seemed to me healthy for him to be spending all his
time in the cellar. I think if it's true that he's going to come
into his inheritance, I'll go and speak to him about that horse
before it slips my memory."

He left the room as he spoke. Eustacie, finding her tongue,
blurted out: "But, Sarah, do you *want* to marry Tristram?"

Miss Thane's eyes twinkled. "My love, when a female
reaches my advanced years, she cannot be picking and choosing, you know. She must be content with the first respectable
offer she receives."

"Oh, now I know that you are laughing at me!" Eustacie
said. "But I do not understand it. I find it quite extraordi-
nary!"

"The truth is," said Miss Thane confidentially, "that I cannot any longer bear his odious way of calling me ma'am. There was no other means of putting an end to it."

"But, Sarah, consider! You are romantic, and he is not romantic at all!"

"I know," replied Miss Thane, "but I assure you I mean to come to an understanding with him before the knot is tied. . . . Either I have his solemn promise to ride *ventre à terre* to my death-bed or there will be no marriage!"

"It shall be included in the marriage vow," said Sir Tristram.

Eustacie, looking from one to the other, made a discovery. *"Mon Dieu,* it is not a *mariage de convenance* at all! You are in love, *enfin!*" she exclaimed.

#1 BESTSELLING NOVEL,
#1 BESTSELLING AUTHOR!

"As addictive as all of Patterson's books . . . You have no choice: You must read it."
— ***Denver Rocky Mountain News***

"Eerily believable . . . frightening . . . vintage Patterson, the latest in a series of thrillers featuring the eminently admirable and likable Detective Alex Cross . . . Keeps you guessing until the end . . . will keep Patterson readers in suspense until his next book. We can only hope it comes out soon."
— ***Providence Sunday Journal***

"As exciting as anything Patterson has written . . . The action reels around the country, from D.C. to California to Las Vegas to North Carolina, and readers will be swept away by it and by Patterson's expert mixing of Cross's professional and personal challenges. Is there a writer hotter than Patterson?"
— ***Publishers Weekly***

"Satisfyingly creepy."
— ***San Francisco Chronicle***

"Breathless . . . certain to please his multitude of fans . . . a lot of fun to read."
— ***Fort Worth Morning Star-Telegram***

more . . .

"If there really were human superheroes, Alex Cross would be at the head of the class . . . and, with each installment in the series, Patterson makes sure his superhero gets bigger and better while at the same time becoming more vulnerable."

—*New York Times*

"A sparkling addition to a popular series . . . Like Patterson's other Cross novels, this one can suck readers in and . . . keep them guessing. Plot twists are seamlessly woven into a tight story. Patterson has created a challenge for Cross that's a nightmare worth watching."

—*Knoxville News-Sentinel*

"Classic Patterson: Fast-paced, gripping . . . a sure winner. As the two story lines begin to merge, Patterson's crisp narrative builds toward a shocking end . . . For Patterson fans, another must-have installment."

—*Baton Rouge Magazine*

PRAISE FOR JAMES PATTERSON'S
OTHER ALEX CROSS THRILLERS

CROSS COUNTRY

"The most heart-stopping, speed-charged, electrifying Alex Cross thriller yet."

—*FantasticFiction.com*

"Intense, suspenseful, emotionally charged . . . One of patterson's best novels to date."
—BestsellersWorld.com

DOUBLE CROSS

"The suspense, chills, and thrills are there, and an ending I never saw coming. Another great outing from Patterson, and one that I simply loved. Highly recommended."
—NewMysteryReader.com

"Exhilarating and intense . . . Fans will be thrilled."
—NightsandWeekends.com

CROSS

"The story whips by with incredible speed."
—*Booklist*

"Another great one from James Patterson. Hold on to your seat!"
—ArmchairInterviews.com

MARY, MARY

"The thrills in Patterson's latest lead to a truly unexpected, electrifying climax."
—*Booklist*

more . . .

"*Mary, Mary* flows effortlessly and with mounting suspense to its final, shocking twist; a fascinating psycho will captivate the author's many fans."
—Library Journal

LONDON BRIDGES

"Exciting . . . a full package of suspense, emotion, and characterization . . . This thriller works so well . . . any thriller writer, wannabe or actual, would do well to study [it.]"
—Publishers weekly

"As with the best of Patterson's work, it is impossible to stop reading this book once started."
—BookReporter.com

THE BIG BAD WOLF

"The biggest, baddest Alex Cross novel in years."
—Library Journal

"Powerful . . . Your heart will race."
—Orlando Sentinel

FOUR BLIND MICE

"The pace is rapid . . . Action-packed."
　　　　　　—People

"Chilling."
　　　　　—New York Times

ROSES ARE RED

"Thrilling . . . swift . . . a page-turner."
　　　　　　—People

"There are no faster reads than Patterson's Alex Cross books. I can't wait for the next one."
　　—Denver Rocky Mountain News

CAT & MOUSE

"The prototype thriller for today."
　　　　—San Diego Union-Tribune

"A ride on a roller coaster whose brakes have gone out."
　　　　　—Chicago Tribune

more . . .

JACK & JILL

"Fortunately, Patterson has brought back homicide detective Alex Cross . . . He's the kind of multilayered character that makes any plot twist seem believable."
—*People*

"Cross is one of the best and most likable characters in the modern thriller genre."
—*San Francisco Examiner*

KISS THE GIRLS

"Tough to put down . . . Ticks like a time bomb, always full of threat and tension."
—*Los Angeles Times*

"As good as a thriller can get."
—*San Francisco Examiner*

ALONG CAME A SPIDER

"James Patterson does everything but stick our finger in a light socket to give us a buzz."
—*New York Times*

"When it comes to constructing a harrowing plot, author James Patterson can turn a screw all right . . . James Patterson is to suspense what Danielle Steel is to romance."
—*New York Daily News*